BRETHERTON

BRETHERTON

Khaki or Field-Grey?

by

W. F. Morris

CASEMATE
uk
Oxford & Philadelphia

Published in Great Britain and
the United States of America in 2016 by
CASEMATE PUBLISHERS
10 Hythe Bridge Street, Oxford OX1 2EW, UK
and
1950 Lawrence Road, Havertown, PA 19083, USA

Paperback Edition: ISBN 978-1-61200-376-4
Digital Edition: ISBN 978-1-61200-377-1

A CIP record for this book is available from the British Library

Printed in the Czech Republic by FINIDR.

For a complete list of Casemate titles, please contact:

CASEMATE PUBLISHERS (UK)
Telephone (01865) 241249
Fax (01865) 794449
Email: casemate-uk@casematepublishers.co.uk
www.casematepublishers.co.uk

CASEMATE PUBLISHERS (US)
Telephone (610) 853-9131
Fax (610) 853-9146
Email: casemate@casematepublishing.com
www.casematepublishing.com

PREFACE

A MONG the many strange events of the Great War, the case of Gerard Bretherton must, I think, be unique. I happened to know personally some of the men who were connected with those events; and although each man had only a limited, and therefore distorted, view of them, I was able to piece together the scraps of information I received and build up the whole story. I have decided, however, to sacrifice strict chronological order in favour of presenting these events where possible in the form and order in which I had them from the lips of eye-witnesses.

Part One therefore, which covers the Armistice and the few days preceding it, I have left as Captain Gurney wrote it. Part Two, which goes back to Christmas 1915, is taken from Captain Baron's diary. And Part Three, which begins in the middle of 1916 and ends at the Armistice, thus overlapping Parts One and Two, is a composite account compiled from information supplied by Bretherton himself, the American Doctor Harding, Helen Gurney, Colonel Liddel, and Lieutenant von Arnberg, whom I discovered driving a taxi-cab in post-war Vienna.

In strict chronological order, then, Part One really comes last, with the end of Part Three; and Part Two comes first, overlapping the beginning of Part Three. But I hope that the parts will be read in the order in which I have placed them.

H. E.

PART I

THE CHÂTEAU

CHAPTER I

I

M<small>Y</small> D<small>EAR</small> H<small>UGO</small>,
Here is the story at last; and I have neither added anything nor subtracted anything, though I must confess that since that day last December when we ran across each other in Piccadilly and sat far into the night talking of old times, I have had serious doubts of the wisdom of doing as you suggested. You know the cause of my reluctance. G. B. was my company officer in the old days, and a better soldier no man could wish to serve under. And there is my sister Helen to be considered. Therefore, now that the story is written, I must remind you of your promise to keep it to yourself, at any rate until a full explanation of it may be forthcoming.

A writer of popular thrillers, I suppose, would have called it "The Mystery of the Shelled Château," or by some such name, and having led the reader through three hundred pages in breathless suspense, have solved the mystery in one crisp, illuminating paragraph at the end. The whole series of mysterious events would run through the tale like a train of gunpowder to be ignited by the literary match on the last page. But the narration of actual events allows no scope for the display of imaginative genius; so that even if I had the skill to construct such an ending, I should be debarred from using it. Therefore there will be no final illuminating paragraph. The gunpowder is there, but I am unable to supply the match. I wish I could. But that is the provoking thing about real life: it always stops short at the interesting point.

Picture us then, two days before the signing of the Armistice, on the fringes of the wooded Ardennes, in the green, undevastated country beyond the Hindenburg Line; the enemy in full retreat, and the battalion concentrated with the cavalry to form the vanguard of the pursuit— open warfare at last. We had been held up for a day, and I had gone back to Corps Headquarters to get maps of the country ahead.

It was after midday when I left Headquarters and started back on my cycle through the silent, brick-littered streets of the little town. Above me the naked rafters of roofs that had shed their tiles on to the street below, gleamed in the sunlight like the whitened ribs of camels that border the desert tracks. On either side, houses, like dolls' houses with the fronts removed, exposed to the deserted street staircases, rooms, and attics; and open wardrobes, rumpled beds, and other furniture hung on the sagging floors and threatened an avalanche at each reverberating shell-clap.

I left this broken, cardboard town behind me and pedalled up the slope eastwards. On all sides lay signs of our advance and of the enemy's retreat. By the railway viaduct some sappers were digging into the high embankment in search of delay-action mines; and a field on the right was chock-a-block with captured German guns, bearing on their shields the units of the captors rudely scrawled in chalk.

I dismounted and walked the steepest bit of hill, and, as I neared the top, a car flashed over the crest towards me. I noticed that one of the occupants wore the red hat of the staff, but I was trudging along with my head down and did not notice them more particularly till I heard a voice calling my name. Then, when I turned back, I discovered that the staff fellow's companion was Gerard Bretherton.

I had not seen G. B. for more than a year, and we made the usual remarks and asked the usual questions. He was very interested to hear that the battalion was doing its proper job at last and he produced a map in order to see what ground we were covering. He wanted to know if it was anything like the training schemes we used to do on Salisbury Plain and in back areas. I told him it was exactly like a scheme, though vastly more entertaining.

"And you have got a company now, Gurney, I suppose," he said. "Which?" I told him it was 'A', his old company. "Gad, I wish I were with you!" he exclaimed, rather wistfully I thought. And then the staff fellow, who had been fidgeting and looking at his watch, butted in. We said "Cheerio," and the car glided on down the slope.

I pedalled on, thinking of old G. B. After the rough time he had on the Somme in '16 they gave him a soft job at

G.H.Q.; but he did not look as though it had agreed with him. We were all of us a little war-weary, I suppose; but in him the look was deeper than in most of us.

I rode through a deserted village on the fringes of a small wood in which there had been a little fracas a few days previously. Shutters hung lamely from the windows of the cottages, and several flattened bags of field-grey sprawled on the roadside. One figure had a rifle and rusty fixed bayonet still clasped in his wax-like hands, and beside him a civilian peasant lolled against the wall with his soiled trouser-legs stiff before him like a drunk on a doorstep. One of our own fellows lay stiffly on a mattress that had been dragged into the street for his comfort, though he would never worry again about a soft bed, poor chap. It was all rather theatrical out there in the November sunshine. Like a waxwork show.

At every cross-roads Fritz had left huge craters that one could have buried a lorry in. And he was still busy at the game; the dull boom of distant explosions sounded periodically ahead and on either hand. I met the skipper of an anti-aircraft battery sitting disconsolately on his lorry. He had been ordered to join our advance guard; but though he had covered, he declared, thousands of kilometres since morning and tried every road and track in northern France, sooner or later he had always come to one of those enormous holes. But the grateful civilians, newly delivered from the Hun, were working like galley-slaves to fill them in, carrying on far into the night with lanterns bobbing and women laughing and crying for joy.

It was dusk when I got back to the battalion. We were billeted in a château of sorts, standing a little distance from the road in a small park. It was a quiet place, a mile or two from any village, and we had chosen it on that account. We liked to get away from Generals, who are often a wet blanket on the proper enjoyment of a war. At nightfall, when the infantry took over the outposts, we retired to some comfy spot; for having cycles, we were able to choose a quiet billet out of range of the more persistent annoyances of war, and yet be ready on the mark for our vanguard at dawn.

We had a great time that night. The Comtesse something-or-other owned the place. It was practically untouched, having been until now well behind the fighting zone, and seemed a palace to us who had been sleeping in holes and ditches. Brother Bosche had behaved pretty decently there—he had even kept the Comtesse posted as to the position of her husband's unit of French seventy-fives—but she had taken the precaution of burying most of her linen and wine in the garden. She showed us where the wine was buried, and we soon had it up.

Patriotic and entente-cordialish sentiments were fired across the dinner table that night by Madame the Comtesse in her queer but prettily accented English, and were suitably responded to by us in our sledge-hammer French. After dinner we had the carpet up and the gramophone was put on. Our dancing partners consisted of the Comtesse, her maid, a gaunt old housekeeper, and a couple of tired-looking women from the cottages near by—hardly enough to go round; but it was a great success.

We sang the Marseillaise and God Save the King, the emotional Frenchwomen in high-pitched voices and with tears streaming down their faces, and Madame the Comtesse with her glass of Clicquot raised aloft and a Union Jack round her breast; whilst we stood to attention like graven images. And then early to bed; for at dawn we had to be out beyond the outpost line.

II

Dawn found us pushing eastward according to plan. On the last trip my company had been in reserve, and it was now our turn to lead the way. We advanced in our usual formation: point, advance section, and support. Cavalry patrols combed the country on either side, and to left and right among the folds and copses one caught glimpses of a trooper in full war-paint; steel helmet, drawn sword, spare bandolier round the horse's neck, and forage-net hanging from the saddle. Away on the left, C Company was moving in the same formation.

Thus we moved out that morning of the last full day of the Great War. For a short distance I rode just behind the point, and having had a good breakfast, I was in a contemplative mood. All around me sparrows were twittering in the quiet of the early morning; and I looked at the five steel-hatted figures ahead with the cold dawn-light gleaming on their bayonets, and reflected that this was the tapering spear-point of one of the British Armies in France thrusting forward to the Rhine. Unseen behind me came my support and the remainder of the vanguard, and farther back the mainguard would now be falling in; and many miles back behind the morning mist was the main body. With my mind's eye I could see them fall in and go swinging off along the many roads eastward, infantry, artillery, ammunition column, and baggage train—the batteries, battalions, brigades, divisions, and army corps that made up the hundred-and-fifty odd thousand men of the army behind us.

One of our planes droned overhead, the pilot sounding his klaxon horn to let us know that he had spotted us and was ready to start work; presently he would come droning back and drop us hastily scribbled stories of Hun machine-gun nests in unexpected places.

The sun was well above the tree-tops when we had our first serious hold-up. The machine-gun fire was particularly heavy, and there was a good deal of whiz-bang shelling, which seemed to indicate that we had run up against something bigger than usual. Away on the left C Company also were having trouble, and my supporting troop of cavalry had disappeared silently among the trees in an attempt to work round the enemy's flank.

The map showed a château in the woods, and near by two or three cottages marked 'La Péronnelle.' One of my platoons had worked its way up to the château grounds and was lining a ditch that commanded part of the garden. Dodd, the platoon commander, had his Lewis gun out on the right covering a track in rear of the house—to catch the blighters retreating, as he put it.

The C.O., Killick of the Lancers, Pagan, and myself had a brief pow-wow sitting on a fallen tree-trunk; and when a few minutes later I returned to my sector, I found things were much quieter. Dodd's Lewis gun had bagged some Bosches in rear of the house, and although a desultory fire still came from the woods on our right, the château itself was silent.

It was a gloomy building in nondescript style, with a number of blistered green wooden shutters spaced in rows on a dull brick façade. A balustraded terrace with steps at either end ran two-thirds of the length of the front, and four long French doors opened on to it. One of our shells had knocked a hole in the wall just below the second tier of windows, exposing the lathes and plaster of the ceiling within; and the shutter above hung outwards on one lower hinge, looking absurdly like a large ear cocked forward to catch what we were saying. Below the terrace was a wide stretch of grass that could hardly be crossed without the loss of several casualties, but away to the left a path leading off between high hedges promised cover from view right up to the château itself.

Bidding my servant follow, I moved along the path, and at the end of it, dodged across some flower-beds to a small courtyard that adjoined the château on that side. Our guns were lengthening range and were putting a few rounds into the woods behind the house; on my right Dodd's Lewis gun was stuttering away in short bursts, and one of our planes was droning about overhead. I was on the point of making a dash across the courtyard; but I drew back suddenly in astonishment.

Inside the château someone was playing a piano. The sound came out clearly; every note was distinct, played with a firm masculine touch, as though a man that loved music had sat down to amuse himself. And every moment I expected to hear a voice raised in song; but no voice came. My servant and I stood motionless, listening.

It really was rather startling, with the gunning still going on all around one, to be greeted by a tune on a piano when one had expected a sudden burst of machine-gun fire. The air was "Just a song at twilight," and in the middle of it I distinctly heard a round go off inside the château. The piano faltered but did not pause, and presently the tune changed to that ribald war-song, "Après la guerre finie."

We had been standing against a stable wall on the far side of the courtyard, my servant and I, he with his rifle and fixed bayonet handy, and I with my service revolver loose in the holster, both of us motionless; but at the sound of that old familiar tune I woke up. To this day I do not know why I did it, but I told my servant to stay where he was. It was wrong, of course; a company officer should never wander about alone under fire.

The tune changed to "Tipperary" as I dodged across the courtyard, and often as I have heard that hackneyed air, it seemed to sum up all that was best in the war as I heard it that sunny morning coming from a bombarded château with old Fritz sniping from the woods all around us. It occurred to me that one of my fellows had got into the house from the other side. Sergeant Pepper had the platoon over there, and this was just the absurd sort of thing he would do. Only two days previously, when a pair of Huns had come out of a wood on to the road a few yards from where he was standing and set off running at the sight of him, he had ejaculated "Gawd!" with fervour, taken off his tin hat, and thrown it after them in the manner of an urchin chasing butterflies.

I determined to give him a good cursing.

III

I got into the château by a broken window that faced the courtyard. A mattress propped against the sill and an empty belt-box showed that a German machine gun had occupied the window recently. Now, however, except for some muddy boot-marks on the carpet, the room was deserted. There was a door in the wall facing the window, and the muffled strains of "Farewell, Leicester Square" came from that direction.

I opened the door cautiously and found myself in one of those long, low, narrow passages that the builders of old French châteaux were so fond of making. Halfway along the passage I came upon the body of a German officer, a handsome young fellow with a messy wound in the shoulder. He had an automatic pistol in his right hand, and it looked to me as though he had shot himself; but he appeared to be dead, and I stepped over him and continued my exploration.

The sound of the piano had tailed off and ceased altogether by the time I reached the main entrance-hall into which the passage led. I was going carefully now with my service .45 in my hand; for I had not forgotten the round I had heard fired, although I thought that the fellow in the passage was the explanation of it. Several half-closed doors opened off to right and left, and the first two rooms I tried were unoccupied, although they had been used recently by a German staff, as the trestle tables, screwed-up balls of paper, and abandoned message-pads showed.

The hall was a large and gloomy place, and its silence depressed me. It was as though I had side-stepped from bustling life into the fourth dimension and was now a lonely looker-on. I have had the same feeling looking down the long dim nave of some Norman cathedral at the busy sunlit street framed in the west door, infinitely remote as though seen through the wrong end of a telescope. Involuntarily I crossed the paved hall on tiptoe and pushed open another door.

The first thing I saw was a man seated at a grand piano at the far end of a long room. I had made no noise in opening the door, and he neither turned nor moved. I crept cautiously across the threshold, but I had advanced no farther than a couple of paces across the thick carpet towards him before I stopped dead. The musician had his back to me, and was leaning forward in his chair over the piano; and I had seen at a glance that he was no sergeant of mine, but a German officer. It was not the sight of him, however, that had pulled me up with a jerk. I had my revolver in my hand, and apprehension was not the cause of my hesitation; the cause was sheer astonishment. Upon a sofa on my left lay a girl in evening dress, asleep

Very beautiful she looked lying there in her thin frock that left her white arms and shoulders bare, her pale form standing out sharply against the dark background of the sofa and the dull silk hangings of the walls; and for a moment or two I really thought she was a vision that would presently fade. Bursting thus suddenly from the noisy war into the calm presence of this sleeping girl made everything seem unreal, and how long I stood there gazing stupidly at her I do not know. But I dragged my eyes away at last and turned towards the German officer who, I realized, might prove dangerous.

I crossed the room very quietly towards him, and he made no movement of any kind; and when I drew near to him I saw by his attitude that he was either badly wounded or dead. His forehead rested upon the top of the piano, and his hands, which had slipped from the keyboard, hung limply at his sides. From his shoulder-straps I judged him to be of high rank, a colonel or a general—I am a little shaky on German rank marks. I propped him back in his chair and lifted his head—and then I had the greatest shock of my life.

The face of that German officer was the face of old G. B., whom I had seen only the day before on my way back from Headquarters. I was absolutely sure. G. B. and I had been together in the old battalion for nearly two years, and I knew his face as well as I knew that of my own father; and if confirmation were needed, there was the scar on his cheek that he had carried ever since that unlucky show on the Somme in '16.

He was dead. There was a little blood on his tight-fitting tunic in the centre of the chest, and a small neat slit such as is made by a bayonet. I stood looking down at the hunched figure and the lolling head whilst my brain whirled. A long official-looking envelope protruded from one of the side-pockets. I drew it out rather gingerly and read what was written on it. It was addressed to General von Wahnheim, Headquarters 91st Division.

I had forgotten the girl on the sofa till my eye caught the pale gleam of her dress. She was very beautiful, and her face had a look of high birth and breeding. She lay there sleeping as peacefully as though she were in her own boudoir a thousand miles from the war. I was feeling not a little jumpy, and I am afraid I shook her rather roughly by the arm; but her hand slid limply away from mine, and she did not stir. And then I realized that she too was dead.

There was no mark of any wound on her body that I could see, and she lay there calm and unruffled with closed eyes as though she had died in her sleep. But people do not die peacefully in their sleep in war, and this serene, beautiful girl scared me more than any of the most grue-some corpses I had seen. She did not look dead, and to my strained imagination she appeared to be watching me through her closed lids.

And old G. B. huddled over the piano with his back to me, he too seemed to be watching silently. The words he used the last time I had seen him, when I had told him what the battalion was doing, occurred to me: "By gad, I wish I were with you!"

I tried to think, but my mind was in a state of chaos. And then one or two loud explosions close outside warned me that Fritz was turning his guns upon the château. And I could hear the voices of my men laughing and calling to one another. I must do something.

I was still trying to think, though to no purpose. I stood foolishly in the middle of the room, while my eyes wandered over the furniture, the carpet, the large map pinned on the wall, and returned constantly to the huddled form at the piano and the serene figure in the sofa. A small table lay overturned at my feet, and automatically I righted it and picked up the objects that had fallen from it. My brain was numbed by the sight of the German General who looked like old G. B.—who *was* G. B., and yet could not be.

There came another shell-clap from the direction of the garden, louder than the others, and stones and dirt came flying through the windows. The next one landed on the house somewhere at the back. Things were getting lively. And then one brought down a chimney with a most unholy crash. Great chunks of ornamental plaster fell from the ceiling, and the room shook like a motor-bus; the dead General swayed, toppled from his chair, and collapsed with a heavy thud upon the floor.

At that I turned and bolted from the house.

IV

Young Stevenson and some of his men were moving across the lawn, and above the château a cloud of red dust bellied out as another shell landed with a vicious shriek and peppered the garden with fragments of tile. I shouted to Stevenson to keep his men clear of the château, and he answered me with a salute and passed on.

I then discovered that I was holding a photographic film in my hand. I must have picked it off the carpet with the other odds and ends when I righted the table. It was a small film, V.P.K. size, and I held it up to the light. And then I had another surprise. It was a film I knew well—or rather the positive, for I had not seen the negative before. It was a photograph of G. B. sitting outside a café in a French village. It had appeared on the picture-page of a newspaper early in '16, and its appearance had brought upon us a heavy strafe from divisional headquarters, cameras of course being forbidden. But we had never found out who took the photograph or who sent it to the paper.

"Getting a bit lively, sir," said a voice at my elbow; and I discovered my servant sitting behind a bank stolidly watching old Fritz knocking chunks off the château. Bits of it were flying all over the garden.

"Too damn lively!" I replied. "Let's get a move on."

CHAPTER II

I

WE got going again soon after that. The shelling ceased altogether, and the rifle and machine-gun fire dwindled. We pushed on again in vanguard formation. But I did my part of the business mechanically, for I was trying to put some reason into what I had seen in that château that was now only a heap of debris behind me. That room bristled with baffling questions. How could a dead German General be G. B.? ... Was G. B. at G.H.Q. or was he lying dead beneath the ruins of that château? ... Who had killed him? ... Who was that woman on the sofa? ... Why was she there, and in evening dress? ... How had she died? These and a dozen other questions clamoured for an answer; but I had no answer to give.

I wrenched my mind off the subject at last, for I had to attend to what was passing around me and conduct my little part of the war to the best of my ability. Crossroads were still gaily blowing up ahead, and many of the isolated farms had a pole flying a bed-sheet lashed to the chimney to show us that the place was unoccupied by the enemy.

I particularly remember a village street of some dozen houses on either side and a garish jerry-built mairie in the middle. When I rode into it, some of my advance section were still there. Dodd, very dirty, muddy, and sweaty, with his tin hat cocked over one eye and a garland of chrysanthemums hanging down over his gas-helmet, was politely listening to an emotional speech made by a little fat Frenchman on the steps of the mairie. The little man had the tricolour sash of his office round his waist, and at the end of his speech he stood on tiptoe and saluted Dodd on both cheeks, much to the delight of the grinning men. The other villagers followed the example of their mayor, and every man found himself in the arms of a Frenchman or Frenchwoman. I noticed that those who had the women were the last to break away.

When my flushed and breathless subaltern had extricated himself from the embrace of his ally, he saw me and saluted.

"What are you supposed to be?" I asked.

"Queen of the May, sir," he replied with a grin.

"Well, you look like a damn fool!" was my comment.

"I know," he answered; "but I'm afraid the local corporation would resent the removal of their decorations."

"If you go on like this, you will look like a hearse by the time we reach Berlin," I told him.

That was but one incident among many.

At dusk we ran into more opposition, heavy machine-gun fire and shelling—more than we could tackle alone. Our report to the General brought back orders for us to retire to Andigny-Deux-Eglises. We went back independently by platoons when relieved, and as I rode through the gathering gloom I had leisure to puzzle again over the mystery of what I had seen in the château. I put away the thoughts and questions that rushed at me from all sides, and tried to think the thing out logically. Putting aside for the moment many incomprehensible things, there were two alternatives, both obvious and both extremely unlikely: G. B. was either a British spy in the German Army or a German spy in the British Army.

The first alternative seemed plausible on the face of it, but it would not bear examination. The dead man in the château was a General—the C.O. had supplemented my shaky knowledge of German rank marks—and surely no intelligence officer of ours could have reached that rank in the German Army. Such a man would indeed be a super-spy; and even if such a remarkable man existed, It was certain that he would not be allowed to waste his time as a humble subaltern and captain in our army for the greater part of the war. From '14 to the latter part of '16 he had been with me in the battalion, and to my certain knowledge he had done no secret-service work during that period. He had been in hospital for the greater part of '17; Harding, our old Medical Officer, patched him up in his C.C.S. and my sister Helen had seen him in hospital at Le Touquet. Therefore his spy work—if spy he was—could not have begun before the end of '17; and this was the latter part of '18. A man does not rise to be a General in the German Army in a year. The idea was ridiculous.

The other alternative, namely, that G. B. was a German spy in the British Army, distasteful though it was, had to be considered. In ordinary circumstances I should not have entertained it for a moment, but the circumstances were not ordinary; and I was bound to confess that there were fewer objections to this alternative than to the other.

G. B. had lived in Germany before the war and spoke the language fluently. But he was absolutely English in his outlook and ways, and I felt that no Englishman—certainly no Englishman of G. B.'s type—could play such a dirty game. On the other hand, the difficulties of rank were not so great in this case, for supposing him to have been in the German Army before the war, and in their secret service, the position of General was not an impossible one for him to have attained. But old G. B. a spy! It was preposterous.

Both alternatives, then, seemed to be ruled out; and, even had either of them been satisfactory, the riddle would still have been far from being solved. How was one to explain the fact that on one day he had been seen in British uniform with a member of our staff, and on the next day had been found dead within the enemy's lines in a German uniform? And the girl on the sofa, who was she? Beautiful girls in evening frocks do not lie dead on sofas in shelled châteaux. How had she met her death? What was she to G. B., and he to her? And that photograph, that missing negative that had caused such a stir in the company in the old days on the Somme! To find it there with G. B. and the girl in those circumstances! What was one to make of it all? The more I tried to puzzle it out, the more inexplicable the mystery became.

II

Advance Guard Headquarters had allotted us billets close to the little railway-station. The cavalry squadron had been allotted a farmhouse standing by itself just beyond the station, and Killick, the squadron commander, decided to risk staying there because he had good standings for his horses.

Night had come, and there was no light in the village except the intermittent lightning-like flash of gunfire and the red lamp outside Headquarters that revealed the sentry at the door by the gleam on bayonet and steel helmet. I saw my men installed in their billets and in the dim candle-light taking bully-beef stew from their mess tins. Then I returned to our mess in the little front room of a cottage in the same street.

An old piano stood in a corner of the room, and Pagan was seated at it playing what he assured me was "Chu Chin Chow," though the air was almost unrecognizable since one note in every four was a dud. The billet had been occupied by the enemy not many hours previously, and he had left us two or three periodicals. I picked up one dated the 22nd of March. It was a dog-eared, illustrated paper, and although my knowledge of German was limited to *Verboten* and *Sturm-truppen*, the pictures were self-explanatory. There was one of the War Lord inspecting troops on the Western Front, another of a Berlin beauty dressed in hospital kit, and a third of a number of our Tommies in a prisoner-of-war camp.

I turned over the pages idly; for I was more interested in the question of how soon the mess corporal would have some grub ready than in the pictures. But suddenly I turned over a page and saw something that drove food, fatigue, and everything else out of my head. I am not superstitious; but at that moment I felt that I was caught up by some unseen agency. I found myself looking at the face of the beautiful girl I had left dead on the sofa in the Château Péronelle a few hours previously. The thing did not present itself to me in the light of a coincidence; it seemed to me that that paper had been placed there purposely. Some invisible but all-powerful influence was behind it all, arranging apparent trivialities and incidents according to a definite plan.

It was a full-page, head-and-shoulders portrait, and a very good one. In some respects the face seemed more beautiful than the original, though in others it fell far short of it. The portrait had vitality and animation, which had been lacking in the face I had seen only in death. But the wonderful colouring could not have been visualized from the photograph alone. Having seen both, however, I was able to combine the two and form some idea of what she must have looked like in the living flesh. It was a disturbing picture for a man's peace of mind that my brain conjured up.

Beneath the portrait was some letterpress. My ignorance of German, however, prevented me from reading the whole of it, but the name at least was clear: the Duchess of Wittelsberg-Strelitz, and from the word *Wien* which followed it I assumed that she was an Austrian.

Pagan was still thumping on the broken piano some tune which it was impossible to recognize, and I sat and stared and stared at that portrait…

Subconsciously I had been aware of one or two shells sailing over at intervals, but there came suddenly the most appalling crash I think I have ever heard. The two candles that were stuck to the table went out, as also did the acetylene lamp. Such glass as remained in the windows tinkled to the floor, plaster fell from the ceiling, and by the lightning-like glare which for a moment or two illuminated the room I saw that the door leading to the little hall was split from top to bottom.

The first great explosion was followed by a continuous rumble of smaller ones, and the sky outside was a kaleidoscope dancing between jet-black and brilliant light as though a dozen thunderstorms were in progress.

"Angels and ministers of grace defend us! Jerry is putting up an outsize in strafes," exclaimed the voice of Pagan. "Didn't think he had the guns up to do it."

I saw his face every half-second flickering like the very early movies.

Dodd struck a match and relighted the acetylene lamp, which was blown out again immediately by concussion.

"Big stuff anyway," he remarked.

There was a general movement towards the door leading to the street. Before I followed the others, however, I tore out the photograph and put it in my pocket.

Outside it was now nearly as light as day. A most infernal racket was going on in the direction of the little station, and the air was filled with buzzing noises in different keys, varying from the high-pitched hum of a mosquito to the deep vibrant note of a ship's shrouds singing in a gale. None of the individual sounds lasted more than a second or two, and all terminated in a sharp smack on the road or the walls round about.

"It's those ber-ludy trucks in the station!" cried Dodd. He drew in his head quickly, for each of those sharp smacks was made by a jagged piece of metal striking the ground.

"Oh ay, I don't want to die…" he sang.

"You won't—worse luck!" Pagan told him. "When beggars die, there are no comets seen. Meanwhile—try a light again."

We got the lamp going, although the candles still went out as fast as we lighted them.

Pagan unrolled his oilskin tobacco-pouch and began slowly to fill his pipe. "Reminds one of *Tannhäuser* at Covent Garden," he murmured with a reminiscent air. "*Tannhäuser* with storm effects."

"Poor ber-ludy Lancers!" exclaimed Dodd. "They were not more than a hundred yards from those trucks."

Pagan rolled up his tobacco-pouch and returned it to his pocket. "You may take it from me, they are a good deal more than that now," he grinned. "How about a fatigue party to sweep up the remains?"

We had another look outside, but it would have been madness to have attempted to approach the station, and we returned to the room.

A few moments later the door was pushed open, and Fanshawe, one of the squadron subalterns, came in.

"Dark and stormy night upon the Caucasus, darlings," he cried cheerfully. "Chunks of iron and what-not have been playing 'Home, sweet Home' on my battle-bowler all the way up your ruddy street. For God's sake give a fellow a drink."

He took off his tin hat, disclosing his fair, crumpled hair. As usual he looked immaculate, in spite of the mud on his polished riding-boots. He was one of those fellows who if he fell into a French midden would come out looking as though he had just had a hot bath. He dabbed his nose with a large silk handkerchief.

"Where is the squadron?" I asked.

"Watering down at the stream," he replied with a grin.

"The devil looks after his own," was Pagan's comment.

Fanshawe removed the handkerchief from his face and disclosed some blood on his nose. "Charles, sweetheart," he said to Pagan, "find me a nice dirty cobweb, will you? As I was passing up the local Bond Street a large obus blew out a window and dropped a lot of glass on my nose, and the damned thing won't stop bleeding."

We applied various blood-stopping devices to Fanshawe's nose till he yelled for mercy. "You beastly bicyclists!" he said reproachfully, as he tenderly fingered his damaged member. "Think you are mending a puncture?"

III

It was very cold that night. Our blankets were with the transport that would certainly not get past those exploding trucks, and with us we carried only our groundsheets. I found some straw in an old box, and wrapped it round my feet, but I awoke several times during the night stiff with cold, and lay awake for some time listening to the trucks which were still going up and thinking about G. B. and the dead Duchess.

Another thing puzzled me now. How had he met his death? There was old G. B. flopping dead over a piano and nothing to show for it except a little prick in the chest. How had he come by that wound? None of our men had been in the château, that I would swear to, for I questioned Dodd afterwards. And it could not have been a self-inflicted wound, for there was no weapon lying about.

And the girl on the sofa, the Duchess of Wittelsberg-Strelitz, how had she died? There was no wound nor mark upon her. Poison perhaps. But I was becoming melodramatic. Poison indeed! But this affair *was* melodramatic. I do not know much about poison, but I believe it makes a painful death—twisting of the limbs and all that. But that girl, however she may have died, lay calm and peaceful when I found her. It could not have been poison, then. It was a mystery; two people dead, one by the thrust of a mysterious bayonet, and the other—just dead. There must be some clue to it, some little thing perhaps that would make everything clear and logical; but I had not got it, and perhaps I never should have it. However, I was very cold but very tired, and there was not so much noise now. The dump had nearly blown itself out. I rearranged the straw around my legs and dozed off again.

CHAPTER III

I

WE turned out cramped and shivering in the dawn of the next morning. The dump had blown itself out, and with the exception of some machine-gunning from an aeroplane and a few shells sailing majestically over to detonate grumpily among the trees beyond the village, all was peaceful.

To us seated at breakfast in the drab little cottage parlour entered Bellamy, the Adjutant, waving a pink message-form.

"*Guerre finie!* War nah pool" he cried pithily.

"In the forest I met a fool!" proclaimed Pagan wearily. "Pass the canned cow-juice, Guerney. Merci! Your jokes are in bad taste this time o' day, Bellamy, and breakfast is a serious job, anyway."

"Read for yourselves, you guzzling Thomases," retorted Bellamy with dignity. And he threw the pink form on the table.

I picked it up and read that now famous message. We all read it, snatching it from one another to do so. Dodd absent-mindedly speared Wainright's ration of salt pork on to his own plate. "Grand Ecossais! Only three hours more of the giddy old war! What does one do now?" he demanded.

"Go up to the line and have a look-see," suggested Wainwright, deftly recovering the remains of his salt pork.

Pagan shook his head. "Not me," he said firmly. He produced the inevitable tobacco-pouch and pipe. "I'm going to find the deepest cellar in this carmine village and stay there till eleven ack emma. I'm not taking any chances in the last lap."

I must confess that I rather agreed with him. During those four years of war that had passed over my head I had grown accustomed to being in some danger, and except when the danger was imminent I succeeded in not thinking about it. It was so inevitable and the possibility of its cessation so remote that one became fatalistic about it. But now that I was suddenly confronted with the knowledge that in less than three hours the danger would cease altogether, my life seemed very precious. For a moment I felt almost afraid to go outside the room lest any one of the hundred-odd chances that normally one never thought about should rob me of that peace that was so near. It was the feeling that I have known just before going on leave; but now it was stronger.

The matter was settled by the Adjutant. "The General wants us to go up to-night to patrol the line," he announced. "And the C.O. says that no one is to go wandering about sight-seeing."

"Then a drink is clearly indicated," asserted Dodd.

Pagan, who with his head on one side was drawing at his pipe and over the top of it examining himself in the cracked mirror above the fireplace, threw away the match and remarked: "Quite so—if you think tea good enough. There is nothing else."

"Ye gods!" Dodd threw out his arms appealingly towards the ceiling, from which most of the plaster had fallen the night before. "The ruddy old war over at last and not a spot to celebrate it in! 'Nough to make a fellow start a new war on his own. I ask you."

Wainwright temporarily stopped munching ration biscuit and plum-and-apple jam to remark, "The civilians must have some wine buried in their gardens; and you bet they will dig it up today. I'm going out to reconnoitre presently."

Dodd, however, saved him that trouble.

II

The village presented a lively appearance that morning. The men off duty wandered about the streets or stood in groups talking. From some of the billets came the sound of lusty voices singing "I want to go home" and "Blighty." The C.O. paraded the battalion and read out the armistice message. It was received by the men in silence; they betrayed no signs either of joy or of sorrow. He explained to them that an armistice was merely a cessation of hostilities for the purpose of discussing terms of peace, that it did not necessarily mean the end of the war. If on the expiration of the armistice, peace terms had not been concluded, hostilities might recommence. But he thought it unlikely that this would happen.

The civilians were jubilant at the news. They chattered excitedly to one another, shook hands with one another and with every soldier they met, and shouted "Vivent les Anglais" on the slightest provocation. Also Wainwright proved to be a true prophet in the matter of wine; earthy cases were produced mysteriously from back gardens in the manner of rabbits from a conjurer's hat, broken open, and Tommies roped in from the highways and hedges to celebrate the occasion. Cries of "Voter santy, monsewer" came from every other house.

Dodd, who had reconnoitred the railway, reported that both the station and the trucks had disappeared and that the farm in which the Lancers had been billeted was as full of holes as a sieve. He had found one of the heavy iron wheels of a truck embedded in the ground over three hundred yards from the railway.

I think everyone looked at his watch rather often that morning. At half-past ten shells began sailing over again, though most of them fell in the fields beyond the railway. From the direction of the line the sounds of gunning increased. At a quarter to eleven a German plane came over and sprayed about with a machine gun, but my friend of the anti-aircraft battery had at last arrived, and the "archie" barrage he put up made the sky look like a blue wallpaper with a pattern of white powder-puffs. The Bosche plane retired.

The strafe roused itself for a final effort a few minutes before eleven. Judging by the continuous rattle of small arms, I should say that machine gunners were firing belt after belt, and every rifleman must have been putting up a creditable show upon this his last practice of rapid fire.

At eleven o'clock the racket diminished appreciably; by one minute past it had almost died away. A distant bugle sounded the "Cease Fire" and the "Stand Fast." The battalion bugler took up the call and made the village street ring with the notes. As he finished, another far-off bugle was faintly heard sounding an unfamiliar call. That I took to be a German one.

I had heard those few notes of the "Cease Fire" blown countless times at the end of schemes on Salisbury Plain and during field training in back areas, but I had never thought that I should hear them blown in earnest in the greatest war the world has yet seen. And I think it was this incident that brought home to me for the first time the real significance of that morning.

All sounds of firing had now ceased, and the silence was uncanny. Subconsciously my ear was strained in expectation that it would break out afresh, and I had to remind myself that in all probability I should never hear that familiar sound again.

For a few moments we stood and looked inquiringly at one another. What did one do now? The position was so strange and unreal. Also we felt a little flat; unconscious reaction, I suppose. And then the civilians and their womenfolk, whose supply of tears seemed to be inexhaustible, came among us, overwhelmed us with their congratulations, and carried us off to share in their joy.

III

The afternoon was an eventful one in many ways. First of all we had a funeral: two poor fellows who had been knocked out the night before. And though long usage had hardened me to these, I found this one strangely sad. It did seem hard luck to go through four years of more or less undiluted Hell, only to be knocked out when one's head and shoulders were above the brink. The civilians turned up in force and shed more tears, and when the clear notes of the "Last Post" rang out in that still unfamiliar silence, I almost wept myself.

As we entered the village on our return, we became aware of a noise. My repertoire of noises had become pretty extensive during the war, but this one was new to me. It resembled a large dogfight more than anything; but there was something human about it, despite the predominant animal note. We hurried round a corner to find what at first sight appeared to be a rugger scrum, but the pack was a very large one, composed entirely of women, and, judging by the cries they emitted, it was anything but a game.

The cause of the disturbance, we were told, was a Frenchwoman who owned a large house in the village and had been both lavish and indiscreet in her favours to German officers during the enemy's occupation. Her indignant fellow-townswomen were now venting four years of pent-up wrath upon her unfortunate body.

It took half a platoon of men to get her away from them. With streaming hair they fought like furies, biting and tearing with tooth and nail, and it was difficult to believe that the gory mess we eventually rescued from them had been a beautiful woman. They had torn her clothing to shreds and most of her hair from her head, and her face and body was just a dirty crimson mess.

We got her into an ambulance whilst the vengeful furies stood round with sullen faces and glowing eyes. I think Sergeant Pepper summed up the feelings of all of us when he said that if the next war was going to be anything like that, he would take care to be a conscientious objector. "I used to fancy I had a way with the ladies," he added. "But I might as well have made sheep's eyes at Sergeant-Major Craggs as at that beauty chorus."

It was very soon after this unpleasant incident that the first refugees began to come through. They were those civilians who had been trapped by the German advance of 1914, had been within the enemy's lines for four years, and recently been swept eastwards before the advancing tide of war. Now that the "Cease Fire" had sounded, the Germans were allowing them to pass through the lines, and they were returning to discover if any of their cottages had escaped the widespread destruction.

They were pitiful objects, long strings of men and women past middle age for the most part, though a few were young in years, but with faces prematurely aged. Some of them trundled wheelbarrows piled with a few pathetic domestic treasures. Most of them were ragged, and many of the women were in men's clothes. They trudged along slowly and stolidly, showing no signs of emotion; it would be time enough to rejoice when one found one's cottage still standing and the sister or daughter safe who had been left behind.

I was standing watching this dreary procession when I was suddenly startled to see among them a face I knew. Suddenly perhaps is not quite the right word, since although recognition was instantaneous, the certainty of it was a matter of several seconds; for the unshaven face, slovenly gait, and rough peasant clothes of the man before me caused a reasonable doubt to arise as to whether he could be the fairly spruce figure I had last seen decked out in red tabs and A.P.M. brassard.

He must have seen my bewilderment, for after a moment's hesitation he decided the question for me by saying with a nervous laugh, "Yes, it's Hubbard all right."

"Good Lord, man! What on earth are you doing!" I exclaimed.

He laughed again nervously, "It's a long story," he said. "But for God's sake give me a drink, and then I will tell it you."

I took him to our mess in the little cottage parlour and supplied him with a cigarette and a whisky from a bottle Pagan had cadged from Headquarters. Then I lighted my pipe and waited for him to begin. My curiosity to hear his story was natural. He had been in the divisional company in the old pre-battalion days, and in '16, when corps battalions were formed, had commanded B Company. At that time the Corps A.P.M. had employed some of our men on odd jobs—traffic control, prisoners' cages, and what not—and Hubbard had shown a preference for this unheroic but necessary kind of work. The A.P.M. had been only too pleased to have somebody to help him with his many jobs, and Hubbard had been attached to him for some months. Eventually Hubbard himself became an A.P.M., and the next we heard of him was from Italy, where he was A.P.M. of some town or other. I had come across him once in Boulogne when I was passing through on leave; and that was the last I had seen or heard of him till my eyes had fallen upon his unshaven face among the dreary procession of refugees.

And so I was curious to hear his story. But he seemed in no hurry to begin, and instead asked about the battalion. I gave him all the news and the history up to date, omitting of course the scene in the château. At last, after a second drink, he leaned back in his chair and told his story. I had never cared much for the man, but I felt sorry for him now; he must have had a trying time.

He had come back from Italy at the end of '17 to be A.P.M. of a division near Cambrai. On the morning of the great German drive of March '18 he had been looking after some of his traffic control posts at Adecourt, a couple of miles behind the line. He had left one of his men on duty at the cross-roads and was strolling down a side-street when he met a couple of hurrying Tommies, who shouted to him that Jerry was behind them. They were out of sight in the mist in a few seconds, He attached no importance to what they had said, but thinking that they might be stragglers, he turned back with the intention of questioning them.

He reached the cross-roads to find grey figures in coal-scuttle helmets moving through the mist around him. He got back into a side-street unseen and just avoided another party of the enemy by diving into a small house. In a few minutes the village was full of German troops, and it was not long before a battery of field guns came lumbering through the street. The fog had now lifted somewhat, and to have left the house would have meant capture.

Also it was certain that with the passing of the enemy's attacking waves the troops behind would occupy the village and search the houses.

Hubbard stripped off his uniform and put on an old suit of working clothes that he borrowed from the civilian occupant of the house. His uniform was burnt in the stove. He had hoped to get back through the lines after nightfall, but with the arrival of a General and his staff in the village, the civilians were lined up and evacuated. They were marched eastwards across our old front line and no-man's-land well back into the undevastated area behind the German lines.

Hubbard spoke French well, as I knew, and was therefore able to sustain the rôle of a French civilian, and for greater safety he posed as a half-wit. And so for nearly eight months he had played his part, living a wretched existence behind the enemy's lines, forced to work under German N.C.O.'s, and at the mercy of any civilian who liked to betray him.

Such was his story, and after he had reported to Advance Guard Headquarters I got him a lift back to Corps with the G.S.O.2, who was in the village.

IV

At tea-time the C.O. came into our little parlour mess in high good-humour. He had just come from Advance Guard Headquarters. The Corps Commander had been there and had expressed himself as very satisfied with the work of the battalion. He had asked how the men were, and the C.O. had told him that they were rather done up but still full of buck. "You want a rest in a quiet spot," the Corps Commander had replied. "Choose your place, and go there as soon as you like."

"And I have chosen Surcamps," said the C.O. "It is only a few kilometres from here; it is a quiet little one-horse village in the woods and has first-class billets. Pagan passed through it yesterday. We move off in half an hour. The R.S.M. is parading Orderly Sergeants now."

Our departure from Andigny-Deux-Eglises was rather like a triumphal progress; for the Lancers and ourselves had been the first British troops to enter the village and the inhabitants were determined to make a fuss of us. They cheered us in the funny jerky French manner and loaded us with presents. They had not much left to give, poor souls, but every villager found something. One of the men was presented with a large and very hideous clock. Nor would his benefactor be denied, and he had to tuck the atrocity under his arm; and some minutes later, as we were riding along a country road the whole battalion roared with laughter when the gift solemnly chimed five o'clock. We had to march out of the village; the enthusiasm of the inhabitants made riding impossible. Only when we were a couple of hundred yards from the last house were we able to mount.

Surcamps was an ideal place for a rest. The village, shut in on all sides by the woods, consisted of a number of quaint old cottages growing, as it seemed, round the four sides of a large green. The effect was rather that of the Great Court of Trinity dumped down in a forest and ruralized. Only one building encroached upon the green, and that was a large, comfortable-looking farmhouse with a wide expanse of weathered roof and numerous peaked gables. There we fixed the mess, and the C.O., the Adjutant, Pagan, and myself found billets there also. Fuel was plentiful in that wooded country, and we had a roaring fire halfway up the chimney of the large, low-ceilinged dining-room.

The mess broke up early that night, and I crossed the green with the others and made the complete circuit of the village, dropping members of the mess at their respective billets. Then the C.O., the Adjutant, Pagan, and I walked back across the grass. It was a brilliant moonlight night, and there was a touch of frost in the air. Before us was the farmhouse with the moonlight glinting on its roof, and beyond, the dark wall of trees that bounded the village on every side. Above them rose the little spire of the village church like a black finger against the moonlit sky. Far away in the distance a long, low rumble of sound broke the stillness.

"Fritz blowing up his dumps," commented the C.O.

We entered the cheery mess, had a last drink, and then taking our candles, mounted the broad, low-tredded stairs. I said good night to the C.O., the adjutant, and Pagan, and entered my room. It formed one corner of the house and had two heavily curtained windows at right angles to each other. Rarely have I seen such a picture of comfort. Private Twittey, my servant, had surpassed himself on Armistice night. A huge log fire blazed on the great hearth and sent cosy flickerings of light among the homely shadows of the big room. It turned one's thoughts to Christmas Eve and Dickens. I undressed and climbed into the huge old four-poster bed, and there I lay in the most delicious comfort, watching the firelight flickering on the low-beamed ceiling. The hiss and crackle of the logs on the hearth was the only sound that broke the country stillness.

This then, I thought, was the end of it all. This was the beginning of the long-hoped-for return to the life of simple comforts—a roof over one's head, decently cooked food, and a bed; and I snuggled farther down beneath the billowing eiderdown. So content was I that I ceased to worry about poor old G. B. If he were a spy, I told myself, then he had gained the reward of all traitors: he was dead. And no one would suffer pain on that account; for no one but myself knew it. And if he were not a spy, again no one but myself had any reason to doubt him. And that was as it should be. All, then, was for the best in this strange new world of peace.

I blinked drowsily at the firelight till I fell asleep.

PART II

THE OLD COMPANY

CHAPTER IV

I

THE year is 1915. It is three o'clock in the afternoon of Christmas Eve in the city of Amiens. The Rue des Trois Cailloux is thronged with people. Wizened Picardy farmers, rotund business men in pince-nez, harassed mothers with their broods, trim silken-legged workgirls with demure faces and laughing eyes, buxom countrywomen with baskets as bulging as their figures, struggle good-humouredly along the crowded pavements. Here and there is a fleck of horizon blue or the gold and scarlet kepi of a General of the Republic, and through the flowing throng runs a steady trickle of khaki like a clayey current in a dark river.

In a crowded *charcuterie* the harassed shopkeeper is listening with true Gallic politeness to the linguistic efforts of a perspiring subaltern who has forgotten the French for the commodity he wishes to purchase, whilst the other customers loudly debate its probable nature and make more or less helpful suggestions. The teashops are already full, and through the windows one may see red-tabbed staff-captains and debonair subalterns, plate in one hand and poised fork in the other, selecting fancy cakes from the mounds of confectionery on the counter.

Along the roadway moves an endless procession of staff cars, limbered waggons, farm buggies, motor-cycles, and mess-carts.

One mess-cart with a canvas tilt stands outside a poulterer's near the Place Gambetta. In the doorway of the shop a bustling Frenchwoman is assuring G. B. and myself that the turkeys we have ordered for the Company Christmas dinner will be ready in ten minutes.

"Right-oh, Madame!" I am saying. "*Dix minutes… bon!* That's a promise—*c'est un promis.* Come on, G. B.; while we are waiting we will call on Suzette and get the gramophone needles."

G. B. turned to the corporal standing by the mess-cart. "Stay here, Corporal, and see that nobody nips off with our birds; start loading up if they are ready before we get back. Come on, then, Baron; I want to fetch my camera from the shop by the cathedral."

We cruised off into the moving throng on the pavement and turned to the right into the gaily lighted arcade.

"Damnation!" I muttered as we reached the door of the music-shop. "Some blighter has clicked with Suzette."

A tall gunner captain was leaning over the counter in an attitude that brought his khaki cap nearer to the dark head of pretty Suzette than his occupation of examining a record rendered absolutely necessary. We walked into the shop.

"Sorry to butt in on your maiden romance and all that, Suzette," I said. "But business before pleasure, live and let live, and what-not." I addressed the tall officer leaning over the counter. "If you would lift your barrage for a minute, sir, just while Suzette gets me a box of needles."

The fellow grinned and murmured, "Carry on."

"*Bon jour, M'sieu* Bar-r-ron! *Bon jour, M'sieu* Geebee!" prattled Suzette in her pretty English.

"*Mal jour*, Suzette!" I retorted. "It's the plus maliest jour I've struck for many a day. My heart is broken—*cassé, démolie*. Give me my needles and let me take my hopeless passion to some lonely spot where I may die in peace."

"*Oh là, là! Farceur!*" she cried with a pretty French movement of her hands. "*Mais oui!* I 'ave a disc for you, M'sieu: that which you 'ave demande: 'They deedn't beeleeve me.'"

"Didn't they?" I said. "Showed their sense. Give it me, Suzette; I will wear it next my heart. Pay her, G. B., and take me away before I break down."

"What an ass you are, Baron!" laughed G. B. as we left the shop.

Old G. B. himself was a bit of a misogynist, I fancy. But it was not for lack of attractiveness, for as we marched along I noticed a lot of demure little glances being thrown at his solemn old face, and I returned them on his behalf. It seemed a pity that they should waste their sweetness on the desert air, so to speak.

We collected his camera from the *pharmacien* and returned to the poulterer's to find the corporal just beginning to load up.

"You get the papers, Baron," suggested G. B. "And I will go on ahead. I have to see the A.S.C. at La Houssoye about that football match. I will wait for you there."

I crossed the road to the paper-shop and secured my copies of *La Vie Parisienne* after a fierce struggle with the other troops; then I fetched my motor-cycle. I was trickling slowly through the traffic round the lamps in the middle of the Place Gambetta when the machine beneath me seemed to give, and I found myself on the ground. The front forks had collapsed. I picked myself up and stood there cursing inwardly, for in my mind's eye I saw that long road ahead and myself trudging along it. There was a chance, however, that the mess-cart had not yet gone. I called to a Tommy to look after my motor-cycle, dived through the crowd towards the Rue des Trois Cailloux, and overtook the mess-cart a few yards down the street.

We removed the turkeys and piled them on the island beneath the lamps, much to the amusement of the crowd. Then we heaved the motor-cycle into the cart, covered it with a blanket, and replaced the turkeys. But the cart was now so full that the wooden seat would not fit across it, and we had to make ourselves as comfortable as we could on top of the birds. Enthroned thus we drove off down the street of the three pebbles amid some laughter and cheers.

We were soon clear of the city and jogging contentedly along the straight Albert road. I sucked at my pipe and chuckled over *La Vie*, whilst the corporal and the mess cook sustained an argument respecting the charms of an artiste they had seen at the Chiswick Empire in 1914. We had not gone far before a moving black dot on the straight white road ahead resolved itself into G. B. careering towards us. He drew into the side of the road and sat astride his motor-cycle with his hands resting on his hips.

"Where is your bus?" he asked.

I pointed beneath the turkeys on which I was perched. "*Cassé!*" I grinned.

"Glad you had enough sense to put it underneath," he remarked.

"I have some rudiments," I replied dryly. "Get along, G. B. and tell 'em I'm coming."

"Right-oh!" He paddled his Douglas round and with a wave of his hand purred up the road and out of sight.

Dusk was falling as we passed through Pont Noyelles. I put away my papers and relighted my pipe. A ride through the gloaming on a slow-moving vehicle is a restful proceeding and good for one's soul. We passed a few trudging peasants who gave us "*Bon soir*" and "*Bon Noël*," and occasionally we met a long-maned farm-horse klippity-klopping homewards. A homing aeroplane droned over our heads and glided down to roost in a hollow on our left. The horse's feet clicked noisily through the little street of La Houssoye, where the sound of a gramophone came from a lighted window and one could distinguish the dark shapes of A.S.C. lorries parked on the roadside. Occasionally on the right we saw a huddle of lights where some village lay in the Ancre Valley below us in the darkness.

Just before we reached the lane leading to the village in which the company was billeted, we passed a dark shape in the shadow of the trees.

"What's that?" I asked the corporal.

"French lorry, sir," he answered. "They are making some earthworks over there and have brought up a load of pit-props."

"Pit-props!" I echoed. "Let's have a look."

We pulled up, and I clambered down to the road.

"How would they do for yule logs, Corporal?" I asked, as we stood peering into the back of the lorry, which was full of good-sized pit-props.

"Fine, sir!" he answered with a grin.

I glanced up and down the road; it was deserted.

"Come on, then—lend a hand."

We managed to get three of the props into the mess-cart, though it was rather a tight fit, and the turkeys suffered somewhat. Then we climbed back to our precarious seats.

"Bringing home the yule log—what!" I laughed.

Wants a bit o' music, sir," said the mess cook. He produced a mouth-organ, and to the strains of "Good King Wenceslas" we turned from the main road into the steep track that led down to the village.

II

We pulled up before the cook-house in the playground of the village school. I collected the papers and my various purchases, and made my way to the mess.

Approaching the mess in the dark was a hazardous undertaking, for one had to steer through a small arch-way between two barns and cross a farm courtyard by a narrow path bordered by a very large and juicy midden.

One false step and one was in the slough of despond. A lighted window in the house acted as a beacon, however, and I passed the danger-zone in safety.

The mess was in an inner room approached through the kitchen in which the family lived. With the exception of Monsieur, who was with his regiment, the family was in residence. Petit Jean was warming his small hands at the big coffin-shaped stove on which stood the inevitable coffee-pot, and Madame, with little Elise on her knee, was seated near by. I presented the two children with the gift of sweets we always brought them from Amiens, and then turned the handle of the door leading to the mess.

The upper part of this door was glazed and covered with a short curtain which did in some degree muffle the babel of sound in the mess-room beyond; but the moment I turned the handle, a blast of noise rushed out and smote my ears as though I had opened the door on a gale. The gramophone was grinding out "Watch Your Step." and to its accompaniment Pagan and Fanshawe of the Lancers were dancing with such gusto that every now and then the needle jumped and skipped several bars. G. B., seated at the sorry-looking piano in a corner of the room, was playing Bach's Preludes as though he were alone on a mountain-top. Killick, O.C. Lancers, and Melford, our own C.O., were carrying on a conversation in the raised tones which the barrage of other sounds made necessary; and Groucher, the Second-in-Command, with a pile of coppers before him, was playing nap with Adams of the Motor-machine Guns and Hubbard, and quarrelling noisily over some point in the game. And seated by the fire and looking rather bewildered by all this racket was an officer in tartan trews whom I did not know.

"Hullo, Baron, you've got back, then!" cried G. B., playing softly to himself.

Then each demanded the purchases he had commissioned me to make for him, and I acquitted myself very creditably, I think, having forgotten not more than half a dozen; and when I had distributed copies of *La Vie Parisienne* as peace-offerings to the aggrieved, I peeled off my British-warm and turned to the examination of my mail. There were letters from home and parcels of socks, mufflers, Balaclava helmets, and other munitions of war from patriotic aunts; but what pleased me most was a large iced cake with "Cheerio, Dicky" on it in pistachio nuts, a present from Helen, David Gurney's sister. I placed it triumphantly on the table.

"Ah ha!" cried Pagan, breaking off his dance with Fanshawe to admire my cake. "The King—Baron, I mean— doth wake tonight and take his rouse, keeps wassail, and the swaggering up-spring reels! Fetch the pioneer sergeant and his axe, and let the wassailling begin."

Pagan had a passion for quoting Shakespeare, but apart from this disgusting habit he was rather an amusing fellow. In civilian life he was the junior partner of a large firm of woollen manufacturers, and though one of the smartest and most efficient subalterns in the Company, he delighted in making remarks calculated to shock the orthodox regular soldier. On one occasion when he and

I were dining at Divisional Headquarters, Charteris, the A.D.C., a conceited young pup, asked in his supercilious manner what he did in civilian life. Pagan looked up innocently and replied without turning a hair, "I make woollen 'combs.'" The glittering assembly of khaki, red, and gold gasped, but the General was delighted and laughed till the tears came into his eyes. At last he managed to say, still laughing at the sight of Charteris's bewildered face, "Splendid, Pagan—splendid! Charteris doesn't know what they are. His friends don't wear 'em. They go in for georgette and chills on the liver."

Fanshawe of the Lancers was Pagan's great friend. He was a tall, fair-haired, fresh-faced youth who looked as though he took a bath every half-hour. He wore the most highly polished riding-boots and the most glittering spurs, and he carried his revolver holster strapped cavalry fashion across the thigh of his perfectly cut fawn riding-breeches. He joined Pagan in admiring my cake and helped himself to a couple of pistachio nuts. And then, to my relief, a diversion was caused by the entrance of Harding, the medical officer, followed by a mess waiter with half a dozen magnums of champagne.

At the sight of the champagne, Hubbard—called inevitably Mother Hubbard or simply Mother—left his noisy game of nap, and, seizing Harding by the waist, whirled him round, singing "Yankee Doodle" at the top of his voice. Harding was an American citizen who had been spending a holiday in England in '14, and had joined up in the R.A.M.C.

"Here's to Clicquot, the merriest of widows," cried Hubbard. "And to Uncle Sam, the best M.O. that ever pushed number nines down the throats of poor damn soldier-men."

I asked who was the fellow in tartan trews by the fire.

"Dodd," replied G. B. "Reinforcement in Evrington's place."

I made myself agreeable to the newcomer, and then escaped to my room to change into slacks for mess.

III

We had scarcely finished the meal before some of the Motor-machine-gun people arrived to take us to the Divisional Follies, and we all crowded into a box-body, with the exception of Mother Hubbard, who was orderly dog and had to stay behind to look after the shop. Adams, O.C. Motor-machine-gun Battery, drove. He was a lean-faced man who, among other things, had been a trooper in the North-west Mounted. To his intimates he was known as Fanny Adams, or Sweet Fanny Adams. To him a motor-car had only one speed: the highest it was possible to get out of it. We shot like a rocket along the two odd miles of dark, tree-shaded road beside the stream, turned right-handed over the bridge and past the château gates, where the red and green light and pacing sentry proclaimed Divisional Headquarters, into the village street.

The theatre was a *brasserie* decorated with flags and brightly lighted with electric light by the A.S.C. A stage had been rigged up at one end, and there was accommodation for two or three hundred people. It was really an extraordinarily good show—a pantomime, "Cinderella." The scenery was highly ingenious, if a little crude. The songs went with a swing, and the repartee was sparkling and highly topical. Cinderella herself was a dainty, pathetic little figure whose occasional bursts of impudence were unorthodox perhaps, but most diverting. Certainly no one would have guessed that her piquant little face with its crown of golden curls was in reality that of a martial bombardier.

After the show G. B. and I decided to walk back; there was really too much of a squash in the box-body. We were soon clear of the village and swinging along throughout the open country. It was a moonlight night and very quiet. But before we had covered half the distance a sudden continuous rumbling as though a number of lorries with square wheels were driving over a hollow stage broke forth, punctuated every now and then by a sound like that of a giant tea-tray being banged; and there were a lot of firework-like flashes, Verey light displays, and coloured rockets visible ahead in the direction of the line.

"Sounds like a raid," remarked G. B. "They are putting stuff into Méaulte," he added, as another tea-tray was dropped somewhere, in the valley ahead.

"It's like old Fritz to start a strafe on Christmas Eve," I growled. "He has as much imagination as a cow—the dirty dog!"

"I don't think one can blame him for this," replied G. B. seriously. "After all, he is perfectly right. The more uncomfortable you can make your enemy, the sooner he is likely to throw in his hand. War isn't a parlour game in which you all sit down to tea and carry on again afterwards. He knows more about it than we do, and he knows damn well one cannot win a war by knocking off on Sundays and Bank Holidays."

"I suppose you are right," I sighed. "But all the same, I don't love brother Bosche."

"Neither do I, but give him his due," insisted G. B.

"Anyway, I hope Number Six Platoon isn't getting in for this fracas," I said. "Gurney had bad luck in clicking for the line at Christmas. I suppose his mail has gone up?"

"Went up with the rations to-night," answered G. B.

"I'll send him a bit of Christmas cake to-morrow," I said. "His sister made it; so he ought to have a slice."

G. B. grunted approvingly. "I will take it up if you like," he suggested. "I thought of going up some time to-morrow just to say Happy Christmas and all that."

"Damned good of you, G. B.," I remarked.

And so it was. Not every man with the luck to spend Christmas in billets would go floundering up to the line just to be friendly.

CHAPTER V

I

A FEW mornings later we were assembled in the little brick-floored cottage-room that did duty for the company office. With the exception of Gurney, who was still in the line, and G. B., who was drawing the company's pay from the field cashier, we were all present—Melford, Groucher, Pagan, Hubbard, Dodd, and myself. Melford sat at the blanket-covered table, his cap cocked slightly over one eye, wearing his uniform in that to-the-manner-born fashion that we civilian soldiers of the New Armies had never quite acquired. Above the left breast pocket was the white and purple ribbon of the Military Cross which he had won at Ypres. He was a regular soldier and keen on his job, one of those unimaginative, good-humoured sportsmen that come by the dozen from the mould of Sandhurst. To him a civilian was only half a man, and many were the friendly arguments he had with Pagan respecting the merits and demerits of the Regular and New Army officer. And though Pagan's nimbler wit was usually victorious in these verbal encounters, the victory always left old Melford undisturbed and absolutely unchanged in his opinion.

Groucher, the Second-in-Command, was a ranker, a big red-faced fellow with a heavy moustache and the two South African ribbons on his chest. He wore yellow, bilious-looking collars till Melford ticked him off about it, and field-boots of a curious pattern that reached only half-way up his fat calves. He had the old army N.C.O.'s vice of drink, and consumed more whisky than any man I have ever met; though it is only fair to say that I never saw him drunk. Also he had a disgusting habit, when there were no early parades, of not shaving till after breakfast. He had all the old soldier's proficiency in eye-wash and was a master of the art of dodging any job that he regarded as a "fatigue." In the Melford and Pagan discussions he always supported the C.O., but whereas Melford, when verbally defeated, was always good-humoured though unconvinced, Groucher became loud-voiced and aggressive and dropped back into the coarse personal invective of the barrack-room.

Melford was talking about maps. In our rôle of a Divisional Cyclist Company we were expected to know the divisional front and area perfectly, and to have in addition a good knowledge of the two areas adjoining. Each officer had an ordnance map on which the topographical features were marked, and we had a few trench maps showing the German trench system, but not our own. Since, however, we were expected to know the location of all units in our area, Divisional Headquarters had given Melford a map on which were marked our own trench system, the area and names of all units, and the position of dumps, refilling points, headquarters, and batteries.

Melford was showing us this map and explaining to Dodd, the reinforcement, the elaborate system by which some thirty-odd thousand men, horses, and guns were supplied with food and ammunition.

"If ever it comes to open warfare again—about which I have my doubts," Melford was saying—"to be of any use as a cyclist you must know, in addition to your presumed knowledge of Infantry and Cavalry Training and Field Service Regs., the commanding officer of every unit in the division. You must make yourself personally acquainted with every member of the Divisional Staff and the Brigadiers and their staffs; and you must get to know the sappers and the gunners and the way in which they do their jobs. You will never be able to give a man the particular brand of information he wants unless you know his methods and have had a chat with him beforehand."

Dodd was rather staggered by the amount of knowledge he was expected to acquire and was visibly thankful for the interruption caused by the entrance of G. B., who unslung his haversack and handed it to the orderly-room corporal. Corporal Catchside took out the wads of notes that had been drawn from the field cashier and placed them on the table at Melford's elbow.

"And if you don't speak French," continued Melford to the unfortunate Dodd, "you must learn it at once. That will do for to-day. We will have another look at this map tomorrow."

I had been conscious of the intermittent hum of aeroplanes during Melford's lecture, and now Corporal Catchside, who was leaving the cottage, turned in the doorway and said: "There are a lot of Fritzes coming over, sir."

We all went to the door and looked up. Four little white planes, glittering like dragon-flies against the blue sky, snored far overhead. Groucher went back into the orderly-room and returned with his glasses, and through them he could make out the black cross of Germany upon the underwings.

A number of the men were standing in the village street staring upwards, and Melford bellowed to them to get under cover. "They could see your ugly upturned faces ten miles away," he cried. He turned to the orderly-room corporal. "Tell the sergeant-major to keep the men inside till they have gone." Corporal Catchside saluted and doubled down the street.

Then we heard a sharp, distant, whistling sound, followed a second later by a long whu... ump! whu... ump! whu... ump! And the cottage windows rattled noisily in their frames.

"That's in Sericourt," said Melford, "They are after the R.E. dump and the railway. Headquarters will want to know about this." He turned suddenly to G. B. and myself. "Quick! Get on a motor-bike and cut along into Sericourt and report."

Sericourt was a village less than a mile away on the opposite side of the stream; and several more explosions sounded in rapid succession as G. B. and I shot down the long avenue to the river, bumped over the narrow, high-pitched bridge, and turned into the street of the village. There were a number of bricks lying in the roadway, and on the left we passed a barn with a bulging wall and collapsed roof. Nearly all the glass in the village was broken, and the civilians with frightened faces stood huddled in their doorways. Near the church we met two casualties being carried away on stretchers.

The four planes had turned away southwards, and the hum of their high-powered engines was now no more than a distant murmur; but the throbbing drone of an engine still sounded overhead, and glancing upwards, I saw far above me a fifth plane like a silver moth forging swiftly across the wide expanse of sky.

G. B. and I were riding slowly across the little square, on the far side of which some women and a couple of Tommies were standing under the stone-arched entrance of a *brasserie*, when suddenly I heard again that sharp whistling sound, automatically I closed the throttle and rammed on the brakes, and the sudden stopping of the engine threw me forward on to the handle-bars.

A few yards ahead there came a blinding flash, followed by an ear-shattering roar, and I heard the deep-toned hum of flying metal passing over me. A hole yawned in the roadway ahead, and under the arch the women were huddled against the wall, supporting an ashen-faced girl who for a second I really thought was wrapped in a dark red cloak. One of the Tommies was bending over the other who was stretched on the ground.

"Fritz 'as got 'im, sir," said the man, rising from his knees. "An' he was goin' on leaf on Friday... an' 'er too—cut off 'er breast clean as a whistle, it 'as." He pointed with his foot at a flat, jagged fragment of one of the fins of the bomb that lay on the ground.

"Bloody swine!" I exclaimed hotly to G. B. "Bombing civilians. This isn't civilized warfare."

"I don't know," said G. B. in that detached, matter-of-fact way of his. "They are quite logical. War isn't a civilized operation, so why try to make it one? They are simply doing their damnedest and—well, that's war, isn't it?"

I was about to retort when I noticed some blood on the sleeve of his tunic.

"Hullo! Stopped a bit?" I cried.

"Yes—only a scratch, though," he answered. "I didn't notice it till this moment."

"Better have some anti-tetanus juice pumped into you," I said. "You cut along to the C.C.S., and I will get back and report."

I turned the motor-cycle, and as I shot back along the avenue out of the village, I heard the distant drone of engines, and there like wild duck against the pale sky were the four planes and the fifth some distance behind heading back towards the line.

II

I wrote my report and gave it to Melford, whom I found searching through a pile of papers in the orderly-room. He glanced at it abstractedly and passed it to Corporal Catchside, saying, "Just type this out and send it by motor-cyclist to Headquarters." He tilted his cap forward over his eyes and looked at me with a frown on his face. "You didn't pick up that map by any chance, did you?" he asked.

"Which map?" I inquired.

"The one of the area I was showing you this morning."

"No," I said. "You laid it on top of the pay when we went out to look at those planes."

"Yes, that's what I thought I did," he growled "But I can't find the damned thing anywhere now. It was not there when I put the pay in the dispatch-box, and I have looked since to see if it had got mixed up with the notes." He rubbed his jaw irritably. "Perhaps G. B. picked it up."

I told him what had happened to G. B.

"Well, he will be along presently, I suppose. I hope to goodness he has it; it's a damned nuisance anyway."

Just as I was leaving the company office, the post corporal came in with the mail and emptied the bags upon the floor as was his custom, and began sorting the letters into piles according to platoons. I stayed to see if I was mentioned in dispatches, as we used to call it.

This was before the days of ration-cards and meat-queues, and civilians in England still delighted to send parcels of food to their friends at the front. The arrival of the mail, therefore, was always something of an event. Pagan had come in, and now stood beside me watching the post corporal on his knees sorting letters.

"Private Christmas of Number Three seems to be a popular person, sir," said the corporal, as he tossed a letter on to one of the piles. "There are more than a dozen for him already; he had more than that yesterday, and nearly a bag of parcels to himself."

"Must be a ladies' man," I suggested.

"No accounting for tastes, sir," was the corporal's comment.

As the minutes passed, Private Christmas's pile of correspondence grew in size till it must have contained over thirty letters, and two of the four bags of parcels proved to be his.

"He must be a popular movie star in disguise," murmured Pagan.

"I don't know about that, sir, but the A.S.C. complained about the size of our mail this morning," replied the post corporal as he tied the letters for the mess into a neat little packet.

"What's that?" asked Melford, looking up from his table.

"The A.S.C. have been complaining about the size of our mail sir," said Pagan. "Most of it seems to be for Private Christmas of Number Three."

Melford left his seat at the table and came to look at the pile of letters and parcels addressed to Private Christmas. He pulled the lobe of his ear thoughtfully and then turned suddenly to Hubbard, who at that moment was clicking his heels in the doorway.

"What sort of man is Private Christmas of your platoon, Hubbard?" he asked.

"Not bad, sir. But not one of my best men by any means. Bit of a grouser."

"He's that weedy little pale-faced chap, isn't he? I know him. Sergeant-Major, send Private Christmas of Number Three here."

A few moments later Private Christmas entered the office, left-turned, halted, and saluted. Melford pointed to the pile of letters and parcels. "All that is your mail, Christmas. What about it?"

The only reply from Private Christmas was the flush that spread slowly over his ferrety little face.

"What does it all mean, man?" continued Melford. "What have you been up to? Where do they come from?"

Private Christmas stammered something about having a lot of brothers, sisters, uncles, aunts, and friends.

"Yes, there are a lot of Christmases about, no doubt," said Melford dryly. "Open one of those letters and hand it to me."

Private Christmas hesitated, glanced at Melford, caught his eye, and then quickly took a letter from the pile and tore it open. Melford just glanced at the heading and the signature, and then put the letter on the table before him.

"D. M. Brandon," he said. "Who is he and where does he live?"

"Friend of mine," stammered the unfortunate Christmas.

"Where does he live?" demanded the remorseless Melford.

Private Christmas looked helplessly to right and left. "London." he murmured at a venture.

"You are a liar, man," snapped Melford. "He lives at Reading, and it isn't a he, it's a she." He took up the letter. "With your permission, Private Christmas, I am going to read this letter aloud." He looked hard at the now quaking Christmas, cleared his throat, and began to read. "Dear Mr. Christmas,—This is in answer to your advertisement in the *Morning Bulletin*. I am so glad that I saw it, for it is so comforting to know that there is something, however small, that we can do for you brave fellows who are fighting for us in Flanders. It seems so sad to think of you over there with shells flying all round you every minute...'—Shut the door, Baron; some of them may get in!" interpolated Melford dryly—"'... and no mother and father, and no friends even to write to you. I shall be delighted to write to you as often as you like, and I am sending you a parcel containing a cake that I made myself and also some warm socks and mittens. As you have no home to go to, perhaps you would care to come and see me when you get leave. I must close now. Tell me if you liked my cake. Yours very sincerely, Dorothy M. Brandon.'"

During this recital Private Christmas's face had undergone a change in colour like that of a piece of photographic printing-paper exposed to daylight, and he shifted uneasily on his feet, an offence for which he was sharply reproved by the Sergeant-Major.

"So you have been advertising in the papers, have you, Christmas?" said Melford, putting the letter down. "Lonely soldier, orphan with no friends, would like to correspond with sympathetic soul! Well?"

"It was a joke, sir," murmured the unhappy Christmas at last.

"Joke!" echoed Melford. "Do you think the A.S.C. have nothing better to do than to bring up bags of letters and parcels for you? If every man in the division got as much as that, the rest of the army would have to stop fighting and turn postman. Do you call it a joke to impose upon the patriotic feelings of the people at home with your lying tales? Orphan indeed! God's teeth, is this a company of soldiers or a mob of whining, lying beggars?

"You will answer all those letters—every one of them. You will tell the truth and apologize for what you have done. You, Mr. Hubbard, will see that he does so—that's the penalty for having a damned fool in your platoon. And the contents of those parcels will be divided among the rest of the company."

Hubbard saluted with a comic look of resignation on his face and Private Christmas fled.

"Old Mother Hubbard has clicked for a good job," grinned Pagan as we left the orderly-room; "but I wish Melford had put that swine Groucher on the job."

III

Later that afternoon Pagan and I were in the mess making out the billeting return when Groucher came in. He helped himself to a whisky and turned, glass in hand, to G. B., who was playing cards by himself in a corner.

"How much did you draw from the field cashier this morning?" he asked.

G. B. looked up from his game of patience. "Two thousand five hundred," he said.

"You may have thought you did," growled Groucher, wiping his heavy moustache with the back of his hand;

"but you didn't. It's eighty-five francs short. Pretty hopeless even in this rag-time army when an officer can't draw a few francs without making a mistake!"

Groucher had a flair for putting one's back up, and he was always particularly offensive to G. B., possibly because G. B. gave him fewer opportunities for complaint than did most of us.

"Melford signed the imprest for two thousand five hundred," answered G. B. with obvious restraint. "And I drew two thousand five hundred—fifteen twenties, forty-five tens, and three hundred and fifty fives. It is down on the paper."

"Well, eighty-five in fives is missing now, anyway. Did you count them?"

"Oh no," replied G. B. sarcastically. "I just took a handful of notes when the field cashier wasn't looking and cleared off."

"You are damned funny, aren't you?" snarled Groucher. "But if you think you can chance your arm with me and waste my time and the men's, you are wrong—bloody wrong!" He thumped the table with his leg-of-mutton fist.

G. B. resumed his game of patience.

"You say you drew the right amount—well, it didn't arrive. You must have lost it; nobody handled it but you."

"I gave my haversack to the orderly-room corporal, and he took out the notes," said G. B.

"You suggest, then, that Corporal Catchside stole eighty-five francs! That's a nice gentlemanly statement to make," bawled Groucher.

"I don't suggest anything of the kind," said G. B. quietly. "You said that nobody except myself touched them: I am merely pointing out that you are inaccurate—as usual."

"And Melford put them in the dispatch-box," I added.

"How do you know?" Groucher turned on me like a bull

"Told me so himself," I said.

"And you must have handled them yourself, Groucher, or you wouldn't know they were short," chimed in Pagan.

"You suggest, then, that Melford or myself may have stolen them?" flashed Groucher with a scarlet face.

"Quite possibly," agreed Pagan cheerfully. "Or Corporal Catchside or G. B. You are all rather of the criminal type. I arrest you all in the name of King George—and may the Lord have mercy on your miserable souls."

"On the other hand," I put in, "there are eighty-five francs missing, but that does not necessarily mean that they have been stolen."

"On the other foot, Bold Baron—since you've used both hands," said Pagan—"it looks extraordinarily like it. G. B. says he brought two thousand five hundred francs to the orderly-room, and in spite of his admittedly revolting exterior I am inclined to believe him. By the way, has Melford found his map?"

"No," said Groucher, turning sharply.

"Then we may assume that the philanthropist who took the map took the francs also."

Groucher laughed contemptuously. "I can understand a man winning eighty-five francs, but not a map," he said.

"It was a very nice map," murmured Pagan. "Lots of pretty little battery positions marked on it—cute little headquarters and names of sweet little units. I am sure Brother Bosche would appreciate it."

"But good lord, Pagan," I exclaimed, "that would mean a spy!"

"Well, I have heard of such oddities in war-time," he said sweetly.

Groucher said "Bosh!" and left the mess. G. B. put out an ace and glanced up from his game. "The only thing is," he said, "wouldn't it be an error in tactics for a spy to steal a map when he might copy it?"

"O wise G. B.! O excellent young man! How I do honour thee! Yes—and let us hope that he will put it back when he has finished copying it. Meanwhile, I am going to see if there is any tinned crab in the canteen." Pagan kissed his fingers to us and went out.

Later that evening when I went into the company office I found Private Christmas with a mound of letters on either side of him carrying out his sentence of the morning. Hubbard was sitting on a table swinging his legs and cursing softly to himself. But he got some amusement out of it eventually, for one of the letters, which he judged by the handwriting and style to be from a young and sporting female, he answered himself. And he carried on a correspondence with her for some time, I believe, and went to see her when he was on leave.

CHAPTER VI

I

ON the following morning the whole company paraded in fighting order, and together with the other mounted troops rode out of the village to take part in one of our periodical tactical schemes. These were always enjoyable, for the men were keen and the friendly rivalry between platoons and units added zest to what was really a very interesting field game. Melford, Killick, and Adams often acted as umpires and left the control of the two opposing forces in the hands of two subalterns; and so one sometimes had the additional interest of handling a mixed force of cavalry, cyclists, and machine guns and putting into practice one's pet theories of the co-operation of mounted troops.

On this occasion Groucher commanded the "enemy" and G. B. led our rearguard. Groucher's tactics were fairly sound and strictly orthodox; but G. B. was an exhilarating man to serve under, for often he brought off really brilliant strokes and he could always be counted upon to do the unexpected.

He began operations with a dashing attack on the opposing vanguard which caused them to deploy their main forces, and then he took us well back to a position on the narrow ridge between the Ancre and the Somme, leaving Groucher methodically developing an orthodox attack upon an evacuated position. Altogether it was a neat little action, broken off at the right moment, and the retirement had gone like clockwork.

We arranged the men in the new position, pushed out patrols, and waited. Below us on the left meandered the little stream of the Ancre; on the right lay the broad, steep-cliffed valley of the Somme with its glittering lakes and the tree-bordered river zigzagging through it; and behind and below were the clustered roots of Corbie surrounding the grey towers of the old abbey church.

"Oh that this too, too solid flesh would melt!" yawned Pagan, when he had sat admiring the view for nearly an hour and there was still no sign of the "enemy." He rolled over on to his back, blew out an imaginary candle, and closed his eyes. "How irksome is this slothful ease to a man of action such as I!" he murmured.

G. B. came up at that moment and said, "Melford has ordered the limber to wait in Corbie, and he wants you, Baron, to go in when this scheme is over and bring back a barrel of beer for the canteen. That battalion that came in last night polished off the lot."

At the word "beer" Pagan sat up with theatrical sudden-ness. "Methought I heard a voice say, 'Sleep no more,'" he cried and scrambled to his feet. "Is this a barrel that I see before me?"

"*After* the scheme, Charles," I crooned soothingly. "*After* the scheme, Melford said."

He gripped my arm. "Comrade, this suspense unmans me. Who's for a game of hop-scotch?"

He produced some sous from his pocket, made some marks in the dust on the road, and showed us how to play. And thus it came about that three officers of the

British armies in France, like Drake on Plymouth Hoe, were engrossed in the homely game of hop-scotch when a car with a little red flag fluttering above the radiator crested the slope and bore down upon them.

"Good Lord, the General!" exclaimed Pagan.

We stood to attention and saluted as the car stopped and the Divisional Commander got out. G. B. had managed to efface most of the marks on the road with his foot as he sprang to attention, and Pagan and I stood with our feet covering the sous. I thought that if only we were not required to move, all would be well.

G. B., as senior officer, acted as spokesman, and in response to the General's inquiries explained the scheme, pointed out where the men were posted, the position of the machine guns and his headquarters, and lastly, and very wisely, for it was a thing that the General loved, showed some messages he had received from the patrols. In the course of the explanation we had to move round to face various points of the compass, and although I tried to shuffle the sous round with me, I failed, for presently Poole, the A.D.C., stooped and picked up a coin.

"Somebody has been throwing their wealth about," he remarked. And Pagan took possession of the coin with a surreptitious wink at me.

Then the General queried whether one of my men who was posted in a hedge for communication purposes could see the section he was keeping in touch with. I was thrown off my guard by this aspersion on the efficiency of my platoon, and I took the General over to see for himself, thereby revealing three sous lying on the spot on which I had been standing. The ever-courteous A.D.C. picked them up and handed them to me.

"You must have a hole in your pocket, Baron," suggested Pagan, with a face like wood.

"The fellow is raining sous," commented the A.D.C.

"He saves 'em up for slot machines," grinned Pagan.

Fortunately Groucher's force chose this moment to make their long-delayed appearance, and the General hurried off to watch the coming engagement.

II

As soon as the "Stand Fast" was blown, I handed my platoon over to G. B., and Pagan and I set off for Corbie.

We found the limber by the bandstand in the little square. Pagan went off to buy some papers, and I went to the *brasserie* and superintended the loading of our barrel of beer. Then Harding turned up, and when Pagan rejoined me we all three went into a café to have a drink.

"Groucher and G. B. were having one of their periodical differences when I left them," remarked Harding, as he dropped on to the red plush seat.

I unhooked my map-case and sat down beside him. "Groucher is a loathsome creature," I said. "Drinks his bath-water."

"God made him; therefore let him pass a man," quoted Pagan.

"True," drawled Harding; "but I guess it must have been on one of the Almighty's off-days."

"What was the fracas about?" I asked, when the waiter had finished swabbing the table and brought our order.

"I can guess," said Pagan. "Groucher didn't like the drubbing G. B. gave him on the scheme this morning."

"Top of the class, my son," drawled Harding. "Yes, Groucher said that G. B. did not know the first principles of tactics."

"Oh ho, that was rather good!" I exclaimed.

"And what did G. B. say to that?" asked Pagan.

"He said that the only use of first principles was that they enabled one to defeat an unimaginative enemy by disregarding them."

"That was one up for G. B.," grinned Pagan. "Good lad."

"Only Groucher would talk such tripe," I said. "G. B. has forgotten more about tactics than Groucher ever knew."

"Yes, G. B. may be an unsociable old cuss, but he does know something about tactics," agreed Pagan.

"Is that so!" Harding was puffing at one of those fat cigars we often chaffed him about.

"He is a wonder on a scheme," I said. "If ever we get through the trench line and get going on the other side, you will hear of G. B., mark my words. When we were on the Plain the General gave him three days' special leave for his part in a big four-days' scheme. He tied a brigade up in knots—and him only a second-lieut. And do you remember that time, Charles, when he made a night dash with his platoon and captured old Gor Blimy's operation orders?"

"Rather!" cried Pagan.

"Oh yes, G. B. was a rum cove," I continued. "Everybody in the division knew him. He joined at Colchester soon after I did and was given the worst platoon in the company. We were all pretty bad in those days, and he got a most undisciplined lot of toughs. But look at them now! The best platoon in the company, I don't mind admitting it, and I'm sure you will too, Charles; know their job from A to Z and first-class discipline. If ever we get a stiff job to do, Melford will send G. B. and his push to tackle it. It is always those tough, difficult chaps that turn out the best soldiers if they get somebody who can handle them—and they would follow G. B. anywhere."

"I expect Groucher will make him stump up that missing eighty-five francs, anyway," said Pagan.

"By the way, Charles," I said, "Melford hasn't found that map yet either."

"Of course not," answered Pagan serenely. "He never will."

"You have read too many penny shockers," I told him.

Harding cocked one large interrogative eye at me; the other was closed by reason of the smoke-screen from his cigar.

"Pagan's got spy fever," I explained.

"Well, I have a lot of nice maps," retorted Pagan, holding his *vin blanc* up to the light. "I leave 'em about my billet; I drop 'em in the mess; but I never lose 'em for more than an hour or two. I couldn't if I tried. They always turn up again. But Melford's hasn't. The only difference between my map and his is that his has more or less secret information on it and mine has not."

Harding was impressed. "That's real interesting," he opined.

"That's all very well," I said, "but how could anyone have taken it? You were there yourself, Charles, and you know that it would have been impossible."

"Suppose you two Solomons tell me something about it," put in Harding. "Remember I wasn't there. And I'm some sleuth when I strike a scent. Now, some bills and a map are missing, and Pagan assumes that they have been stolen. When was the map first missed?"

"Almost immediately after we went back into the office after gaping at those planes that bombed Sericourt," replied Pagan.

"And when was it last seen?" Harding chewed his cigar with an air of judicial solemnity.

"Melford laid it on top of the pay when we all went out," I answered.

"And when were the notes discovered to be missing?"

"When Groucher paid out in the afternoon," I said.

"And when were they last known to be complete?"

"G. B. drew them correctly from the field cashier and brought them straight to the office," answered Pagan. "So unless he stole them on the way we may assume…"

Harding raised a judicial hand. "The point is that since the map was seen after the notes arrived, and we are assuming that the same person stole both, we may also assume that he stole them both at the same time. Therefore no notes were missing when they arrived at the office."

"Marvellous how this hundred-per-cent American grey matter works," murmured Pagan.

"To pursue that point a little further," went on Harding imperturbably, "the loss of the notes was discovered after the loss of the map. But we are assuming that they were both stolen at the same time, so we have narrowed down the time of the theft to the period between Melford's placing of the map upon the notes and his discovery that it was missing when he returned to the office. Everybody happy?"

"Quite," I agreed.

Harding shook his head to Pagan's attempt to refill his glass. "Now then, what happened? You saw Melford place the map on the notes?"

I nodded.

"And so did I," said Pagan.

"And then?"

"Corporal Catchside went out of the office, but came back to say that there were German planes overhead."

"And then we all went out to have a look," said Pagan.

"All of you?" asked Harding.

"All."

"Sure?"

"Certain—don't you agree, Baron?"

"Wouldn't swear to it," I said. "But we were all outside at one time, I know."

"Who were there?"

"Melford, Groucher, G. B., Hubbard, Pagan, Corporal Catchside, and myself."

"Who came out last?"

"Couldn't say, could you, Charles?"

"No; but Corporal Catchside went out first," said Pagan. "He just looked in to say that the planes were overhead, and then went out again."

"Was that before Melford put the map down?"

"Yep."

"While you were outside, did anyone go back into the office?"

"Groucher did," I cried. "To get his field-glasses."

"By Jove, yes; so he did," cried Pagan. "He's the chap. Gory old Groucher. We'll have him shot at dawn, and I will command the firing party. Ten rounds rapid and F.P. Number One for any man that misses."

Harding grinned. "Sure, we will give you the job if it comes to that; but let us get on with our investigations. Did anyone besides Groucher go back into the office?"

"Couldn't say, could you, Charles?"

Pagan shook his head. "Possibly, but I don't think so. Corporal Catchside didn't, for Melford sent him off to get the men under cover."

"Then we may wash him out," said Harding.

"And I did not," I said. "Melford sent G. B. and myself to see what was happening in Sericourt."

"Then it was unlikely that G. B. went back?"

"Very, I should think; we went off to Sericourt almost at once."

"What happened then?"

"Oh, we watched the planes for a few minutes and then went back into the office—with the exception of Hubbard; he went off to the mess," said Pagan.

"Who went back into the office first?"

"I did," said Pagan.

"Was the map there then?"

"Don't know; didn't notice."

"And then?"

"Groucher went off to the Mayor with the billeting-book, and Melford locked up the notes in the dispatch-box."

"And the map was gone then?"

"I suppose so; for Melford would have had to take it off the notes had it been there. It was about five minutes later that he looked up and asked if I had seen it. We hunted all over the place, and then he unlocked the dispatch-box to see whether it had got mixed up with the notes."

"H'm!" growled Harding. "The map was there when you left the office but was gone when you returned. You didn't go far away from the door?"

"No; some of us were on the doorstep."

"There is only one entrance to the office, so no one could have got in without being seen."

"Quite."

"But there is an inner room," continued Harding, nodding his head.

"Where the Sergeant-Major sleeps," agreed Pagan.

"And somebody may have been in there," I exclaimed.

"I don't think so," objected Pagan. "Sergeant-Major Craggs went through the office whilst I was there, and he left his door open. If there had been anyone in his room I must have seen him. It is a tiny place, and there is only the stretcher that the S.M. sleeps on."

"And to get out, our thief would have had to pass through the office, in which case you must have seen him," said Harding.

"But there is a window in the S.M.'s room," I cried.

Harding nodded his head solemnly. "To sum up," he said: "whilst you were gazing at the clouds either one of you went back into the office and took the map…"

"Gory Groucher," put in Pagan.

"…or someone was in the Sergeant-Major's room and took advantage of your sky-gazing to slip into the office, take the map, and escape through the window in the back room."

"The only person who could possibly have been in the Sergeant-Major's room is his batman," I said.

"We have circumstantial evidence then—such as it is— against the Sergeant-Major's batman and Groucher," said Harding.

"I plump for Gory Groucher," cried Pagan, tossing off his drink at a gulp. "Now, infidel, I have thee on the hip! His kit ought to be searched."

"And the batman's," said Harding.

"And all of us who were there," I added.

"Right-oh! I will volunteer mine for search," agreed Pagan cheerfully.

"The only thing is," I put in, "it is a little late to start searching now. If someone has really stolen the map, he would not be such a carmine fool as to keep it in his kit."

"True, O King," agreed Pagan.

"Of course, if the map has been stolen, you won't see it again," said Harding.

"It's a sticky business," I commented.

"Yep. There's something rotten in the state of Denmark," murmured Pagan.

"But seriously," I said, "what will Melford do if it doesn't turn up? Headquarters will make an unholy stink about it."

"I don't think so," said Pagan calmly.

"I'm damned sure of it," I asserted.

Pagan shook his head. "Oh, pardon me, thou bleeding piece of earth, but Melford won't let Headquarters know anything about it. He will borrow the Lancers' map and make a copy of it."

"Which won't prevent Brother Bosche making use of the missing one—supposing he has got it, which I doubt."

"No; but it will prevent Melford getting his hair pulled, which is far more important to him—and us; and if Brother Bosche does put a few high-velocity obus into Divisional Headquarters, I don't suppose many of us will sob about it."

CHAPTER VII

I

G. B. and his platoon went up to relieve Gurney in the line, and back in billets the uneventful, boring life went on. Groucher, Hubbard, Dodd, and Adams of the M.M.G. spent every spare moment in the mess dealing cards and passing piles of coppers to one another; but since Melford believed that the Devil finds work for idle hands, the number of their spare moments was limited. Every morning we had parades and tactical schemes, every afternoon football or more parades and schemes, and every night we sent up a fatigue party of two officers and a hundred other ranks to dig cable trenches across a hillside near Fricourt; and this duty, which for us officers came every other night and exempted one from duty on the following morning, I welcomed as a break in the endless parades and schemes.

It was usually very quiet on that open hillside where we laboured all night beneath the stars. Below us the Verey lights from the front line rose and fell in solemn ghostly majesty; here and there among the dim bent figures of the men a spark showed where a descending shovel had struck a flint; at our feet the white tape line glimmered faintly. Occasionally a random round whimpered by us in the darkness, or there came a flicker of lightning, followed by the sudden pom... pom... pom... pom of a field battery night firing. The mist crept up the valleys, and the chill breeze wafted to our ears the distant nimble of German transport bringing up rations.

Sometimes the harsh clack-clack-clack-clack of a traversing machine gun ripped the silence, and the vicious smack of bullets in the turf sent us crouching in the shallow trench. Then the front would doze again till some sleepy German gunners left their warm dug-out to fire a round or two. Then without warning the lash of a giant's whip whistled viciously through the night, cracked deafeningly, and the door of a furnace was opened and closed swiftly on the bare hillside near one. Then silence. And then again out of the night that vicious lash, ear-splitting crack, and brief bright glow. And then silence again except for the crunch of shovels biting into chalk and the murmur of voices near the ground.

Digging there hour after hour one seemed to become part of the night. The hill-slope on which we toiled was the grand circle of a theatre; the lights were turned down; the play was ready to begin. Below us the Verey lights rose and fell, the footlights on a league-long stage. At any moment the orchestra of guns might strike up and the curtain rise on a bloody melodrama.

And then back in the dim dawn-light through the clean morning air we would come, blear-eyed and drunken with sleep, to our snug billets and a hot breakfast.

II

The missing map had not been found; but the matter did not reach the ears of Divisional Headquarters. Melford, no doubt, borrowed the Lancers' map and made a copy.

One more arrow of outrageous fortune, as Pagan would have said. It was he who handed me a copy of a daily paper one morning when I came into the mess late after an all-night digging fatigue. He pointed to the back page. On it were some half-dozen pictures, and among them was that of an officer seated at a table outside a French café. I read the legend beneath: "After the line, a glass of wine."

"And after the trenches, a couple of wenches," murmured Pagan. "But the photo—well?"

"G. B.!" I exclaimed.

"Full marks!" said Pagan promptly. "And it is the café at Ruilly."

I nodded. "And who's the fool that sent it to the paper?" I asked.

He shrugged his shoulders. "Ay, there's the rub!"

"There will be some hair-pulling over this," I remarked.

Pagan nodded. "Sure. It's G. B. plain enough; and if we can recognize him, so can Headquarters."

"That will please him immensely," I said grimly. "Anyway, he will know who the fool was."

"But that's just it; he doesn't. Melford sent Groucher up to ask him unofficially, and he says he knows nothing about it—who took it or who sent it to the paper."

"But, hang it all, he must know who took it," I protested.

Pagan shrugged his shoulders. "Says he doesn't. Probably Groucher rubbed him up the wrong way and he wouldn't tell him. But somebody took it, and three or four of us have cameras."

Later on Groucher came in. He spoke as he held his glass to the siphon. "Look here, you chaps, about this cursed photo. The C.O. knows nothing about it officially, of course; but he gave me a hint that in case Headquarters ask any questions it would be as well if he could say that none of his officers has a camera—savvy?"

"Bury the darned things in the back garden, eh?" said Harding.

"Or chuck 'em in the river—yes, that's the idea," said Groucher. He poked his cap back on his head and held his glass to his lips.

"That may pacify H.Q. if they are not out for blood, but supposing they are?" objected Pagan.

"Well then, the square-pushing fool that sent the photo to the papers will have to own up." Groucher mopped his heavy moustache with the back of his great hand. "And there can't be much doubt who he is," he added in a stage-whisper with his red face thrust forward and his bushy eyebrows raised. Then he smiled on us benignly, picked up the absurd knobbed ash walking-stick he had bought on his last leave, and went.

On the following day Melford received a chit from Divisional Headquarters drawing his attention to the photograph in the paper and requesting an explanation.

He had us all up in the company office, read the chit to us, and asked if any of us had sent the photograph to the paper. We denied having done so. He then asked if any of us had a camera. We had acted upon Groucher's hint and were able to say truthfully that we had not. Then Melford concocted a reply to Headquarters in which he stated that none of his officers knew anything about the photograph and that he was able to assert from personal knowledge that none of them was in possession of a camera. He also tactfully suggested that although the photograph in question was remarkably like G. B., there were several thousands of officers in France and it was not unlikely that some of them had doubles.

We awaited the result with interest. It all depended upon whether H.Q. were out for blood or not. If the A.A. and Q.M.G. had sent the chit just to justify his existence, he would accept Melford's reply as satisfactory, and there the matter would end; but, on the other hand, if this was to be made a point of discipline, further questions would follow. There would be a court of inquiry and possibly a court-martial.

The matter did not rest there. Melford was called up to Divisional Headquarters. The A.A. and Q.M.G. was polite but firm.

"Look here, Melford," he said, "you know as well as I do that the fellow in that photograph is your subaltern, Bretherton. I daresay this is not the first time that photographs have been taken out here contrary to army orders, and this is quite a harmless one as it happens; but orders are orders, and when a man is fool enough to send a photograph to the papers for everybody to see and recognize, he is asking for trouble—and he is going to get it. We have to tolerate a number of fools in the army nowadays, but we won't tolerate damned fools. So you have got to find out who it is.

The photograph was taken outside the officers' café here at Ruilly. Bretherton must know who took it, even if he does not know who sent it up, and he will have to say. You will send in a full report."

Melford broke the news to us that evening at mess as soon as the waiters had retired. G. B. had been recalled temporarily from the line to be present.

"Headquarters are out for blood," Melford announced. "I have tried 'em with the soft answer that turneth away wrath, but it won't work; and now the only thing is for the fellow that sent the photograph to own up. We don't want a court of inquiry and all that business. Whoever did it is an unspeakable fool, but I will do my best for him at Headquarters. We are in their good books fortunately, and if I speak up for him it will probably mean a reprimand only." He fingered his close-cropped moustache. "Who was it, now?"

There was a dead silence. Melford's face grew red, and there was an ominous tightening of his jaw. This affair coming on top of the missing map had upset his usual good-humour.

"We are all here," he continued. "One of you must know something about it. Nobody has been on leave lately, so that photograph must have gone through the post; therefore none of the men could have sent it without your knowledge—that is if you do your censoring of letters properly."

Still there was silence. We looked at one another and especially at G. B.

"G. B.," said Melford at last, "you must know who took that photograph."

G. B., at the end of the long trestle-table, his solemn face lit up by the candle stuck in a bottle before him, shook his head. "No, sir, I don't."

"We appreciate that you don't like giving another fellow away and all that," went on Melford, "but you cannot shield him now. We shall find out who he is, and if he hasn't the guts to own up, it is your duty to speak up for the good of the company."

G. B. crumbled his bread in silence for a moment. "I know neither who took it nor who sent it to the paper," he repeated without looking up.

Melford shrugged his shoulders. "Well, we will drop the subject now. I shall hold an inquiry to-morrow."

We sat in silence, and then Pagan wound up the gramophone and put on a rag-time tune.

III

Melford held an inquiry, but made no progress towards clearing up the mystery. G. B. stuck to his assertion that he knew nothing about the matter, and neither by threats nor by appeals for the good of the company could he be prevailed upon to add to what he had said.

"I'm fed-up with you, G. B.," said Melford afterwards. "I used to regard you as the best officer in the company, and here you are wrecking the company's good name and our high standing at Headquarters. Good lord, man, you must have known the photograph was being taken. You're not a fool!"

"He's a knave," murmured Groucher injudiciously. And Melford, whose patience was quite exhausted, turned on him swiftly. "Which is more than you have the wit to be," he growled. Whereat we all purred happily.

G. B. returned to the line, and Melford sent in his report to Headquarters.

The general opinion was that G. B. must know something about it, but that for some obscure reason he was holding his peace. It did not seem possible that the photograph could have been taken without his knowledge; and even if it had been, surely no one would have played such a low-down trick as to send it to the papers without his consent.

"G. B. is a stand-offish old buster," said Hubbard. "And he may be doing it out of pique; he may even have sent the photo himself. You never know."

"He is a queer cuss, but he isn't a carmine fool," was Harding's comment on this.

Pagan thought it was rotten of G. B. to let the company down in that way, and he had no right to do it—not even to shield his own grandmother. Dodd said that he had not been with us long enough to give an opinion, but on the face of it G. B. did not seem to be playing the game. Groucher was not in the least surprised; it was just the sort of thing G. B. would do—exemplified his lack of *esprit de corps* and general unsoldierliness. To this Pagan retorted hotly: "Oh yes, we know you are an old soldier, Groucher, a very old soldier—got the Crécy ribbon up, and all that; but you don't know everything—blast you!" Gurney thought that G. B. was either a practical joker in bad taste or was himself the victim of one. For my part I gave it up.

The reply which came back from Divisional Headquarters was brief and to the point. It directed that when Lieutenant Bretherton returned from the line he was to be placed under arrest.

Groucher was unashamedly jubilant at this turn of events. Harding, who was the only one of us of whom G. B. had made a real friend, remarked curtly, "If you lose this war it will serve you right." And Melford, to relieve his feelings, had us all out on parade and put us through two gruelling hours of company drill.

IV

It was my turn for the line, and I rode out of the village at the head of my platoon just before dusk. We climbed the long hill to the Bray-Corbie road where the trees stood fretted against the pearly sky, and the low hills around us, swathed in the rising mists of the Somme, loomed like dark islands on a grey sea. Then we dropped down into Bray and parked our cycles in a barn by the huge, buttressed old church. Night had come when we marched out of the village and up the slope eastward.

Here and there the aiming light of a battery twinkled in the darkness, and the hummocks of the gun-pits showed dimly against the sky. The smack of a gun smote our ears, and instantly the road, the bare hill-slope, the rank grass, the gun itself beneath its canopy of netting sprinkled with leaves, leapt out of the dark, vivid in every detail, and was gone again. A long-range shell rose out of the distance, waddled lazily across the night sky, and died away. And then a dull, distant crunch told that it had landed far back behind our lines. Faintly from some hidden burrow came the screech of a gramophone.

We halted below the crest, clear of the batteries, in that lonely belt of country that lies between where cultivation ends and the communicating trenches begin. The men lay upon the rank grass and weeds that flourished over all that desert area, and I sat with my back to a ragged tree that jutted stark against the sky. The night was very dark, but every now and then the hill-crest was outlined darkly against the bluey-greenish glow of a Verey light, and occasionally a light itself rose above the crest like a new and splendid planet, sank slowly, and expired.

Presently the night breeze brought intermittently to our ears strains of music and the sound of men's voices singing; and the next Verey light silhouetted for a moment a dark, crawling mass on the hill-crest. The tramp of feet reached our ears, and the tune became recognizable: it was "Tipperary," played on a couple of mouth-organs, and some of the men were singing. And then they passed, a short, dark, slowly jogging column on the opposite side of the road; and heads and shoulders showed dimly against the sky, the long peaked cap of the officer in front and then the men with slung rifles jutting vertically behind their heads, like figures on a frieze.

"That's Mr. Bretherton's platoon coming out," said my sergeant.

"Cheerio, G. B.!" I called.

And a voice came back from the darkness: "Hullo, Baron! I have left a guide at Piccadilly Redoubt. All serene and wind sou-sou-west."

And cries of "What cheer, Number Five!" "Poor old Number Three, you're for it!" were exchanged between the two parties.

Then they were gone, and we heard only the receding tramp of feet and the distant wail of mouth-organs. And I lay thinking of poor old G. B. under arrest and that platoon of his that would follow him to Hades; till a whizz-bang descended screaming out of the night, bloomed like a red flower in the darkness, and spattered us with earth.

My little column fell in again on the road, and whistling "Who's your lady friend?" moved off over the crest.

V

One night there came up with the rations a note from Pagan giving me the news. Headquarters had been unable to prove any charges against G. B. He had been summoned before the General, suitably cursed, and released from arrest; but the heavy cloud of the General's displeasure still hung over both him and the company. Also there was a note from Melford to say that a second platoon was coming into the line; that it was Hubbard's turn, but he was sick, and G. B., having volunteered to take his place, would join me with Hubbard's platoon the following night.

On the following night, therefore, G. B. arrived with Hubbard's platoon. I could well understand his desire to get away from the Mess, where Groucher would be openly offensive to him and the other members, no doubt, considered him responsible for their eclipse in favour at Headquarters. I congratulated him on his release from arrest, but he was so obviously disinclined to talk about it that I dropped the subject and never reopened it.

Our little party of two platoons was too small to hold a complete sector of the line, and we were in consequence attached to an infantry battalion. When this battalion became due for relief, G. B. reported at the orderly-room dug-out for orders. They had none for us, they said, but presumed that we were staying in, and they asked us if we would finish a job of wiring that they had been unable to do themselves through press of other work.

G. B. agreed to do this, though personally I disliked the prospect of being out in no-man's-land during the relief, for the incoming battalion, new to the sector, might, I thought, mistake us for an enemy patrol. Furthermore, in the sector on our left a mine was to be blown at eleven forty-five, and a party of bombers, bayonet men, and a machine gun were to rush into the crater and fortify the far side. Adams of the M.M.G. was providing the machine gun and gunners. We should of course get our wiring party back into the trench before the mine was due to blow; but, if the Bosche had got wind of what was intended, he was sure to plaster us heavily all the evening.

We climbed over the parapet soon after dark. I went first with my covering party, whose duty was to lie out beyond the wire and intercept any enemy patrols that might be prowling in the neighbourhood. Behind us came G. B. and his wiring party loaded with iron screw pickets, reels of barbed wire, wire cutters and wiring gloves. We reached our position and began our long vigil, whilst behind us G. B.'s party spread out and began work.

The night was very quiet and dark except for the soundless gun-flashes in the French area far south and the lazy rise and fall of Verey lights. These moving lights cast running shadows on the ground, and anyone lying out in no-man's-land at night and having imagination will see more than is actually there. But although they give a fairly brilliant light, it is very difficult to pick out an object unless it moves. In spite of my knowledge of this fact, however, a light soaring up near me always made me feel as though I were lying naked in Piccadilly Circus.

After ten o'clock I glanced rather often at my luminous wrist-watch; for although the mine was not timed to blow till eleven forty-five, the hour of these shows was sometimes advanced at the last moment, and I had no wish to witness the spectacle from the middle of no-man's-land, since the first big crash was sure to be the signal for bedlam to break loose. At last I heard the signal warning me that the wiring party had returned to the trench and, with a sigh of thankfulness, I passed the order to move back.

Just outside our own wire I was going on all-fours and had raised an elbow to crawl over what I took to be a low ridge of earth, when a bursting light showed me that the supposed ridge was a dead Bosche. But my weight was already too far over for me to draw back, and my forearm came down on the faded grey cloth. Down it went, but not against resistance; it clove through a damp sticky substance like rotten pears to the earth beneath, and I snatched it away covered with green frothy slime, having raised a stench that is indescribable.

The relief was just complete when we got back to the trench, and we had time to drink a mug of hot tea before standing-to for the mine. At the moment the activity was if anything a little below normal: an occasional shell bursting flower-like in the darkness, the mournful whimper of a stray round passing down the valley, and the periodical stutter of a machine gun; and I could plainly hear the rumble of transport behind the German trenches.

Then suddenly the night lifted as though a curtain had been tom down. The earth shook. The clouds overhead glowed blood red; and away on the left a vast sheet of flame shot up to the apex of the sky. Then came a crashing roar that stunned the senses and gradually subsided in lesser rumblings encircling the horizon. Immediately countless lightning-like flashes outlined the dark irregular line of the slope behind us as with a sound like the beating of side-drums our field guns opened fire; and the passage of their shells through the night was like a covey of partridges passing over.

The alarmed Germans signalled to their gunners. Tiny points of fire traced vertical patterns against the night,

Then suddenly the night lifted as though a curtain had been torn down.

burst with a faint pop, and glittering balls of red, green, and white floated downwards; Verey lights soared up like sparks from a furnace. A sudden crackle of rifle fire broke out, followed a few minutes later by the steady tat-tat-tat-tat of a machine gun that I recognized as one of our own. That was Fanny Adams in action on the far lip of the crater. Then the German gunners got to work and made our neat and nicely revetted trench look like a ditch that had been trampled by elephants.

VI

It was about half past one when I turned in, and at about half past two G. B., who was still on duty, came and roused me. "Turn out, Baron," he said. "I want you to take over for a few minutes. The Colonel wants me at Battalion H.Q. Sorry, old bird, and all that."

When G. B. returned some fifteen minutes later he said, "Somebody has made a mess of it again. We should have gone out with the K.L.I. This battalion has no orders about us, and so they rung up Brigade to ask. We are to go out at once; and the K.L.I. will give us billets in Morlancourt."

"Bit rough on the men just as they are getting a spot of rest," I grumbled. "However…"

We paraded the men and filed back along the communicating trench. We trailed slowly through the narrow trench, over the hill, and down into the dark valley where the Verey lights were obscured by the slope behind us. Those who have not taken a column of tired men through a long communicating trench at night cannot appreciate the exasperation of the task, but those who have done so will understand and sympathize. At length we filed out on to the pale ribbon of road in the little dark valley and formed up.

"It's a hell of a march through Bray to Morlancourt," I said to G. B.

"I know," he said. "But I'm going to cut across country."

"Pretty risky in the dark without a compass, isn't it?" I asked.

"A little," he admitted. "But it's worth it. I know this country pretty well. We go straight up over the hill till we strike the Bray-Albert road; there are three trees together almost in a straight line from here, and from them we leave the road at right-angles and go straight down into Morlancourt."

"If we are lucky," I said doubtfully. "It's a good seven miles, and plenty of latitude to go astray in."

We had one cycle with us that had been left at the end of the communicating trench. G. B. called up his servant and gave him the cycle.

"Take off your equipment," he said. "I'll carry that. Ride into Morlancourt; find the Quartermaster of the K.L.I. and tell him I want billets for sixty men. And try to get something hot to drink, if possible."

The man saluted and rode off into the darkness. G. B. looked about him once or twice to get his bearings, and then led the way off the road towards the dark hill-slope.

"You keep a look-out ahead for shell-holes," he said. "I will do the navigating."

The men were inclined to grumble. They were dog-tired and had been deprived of their overdue rest by a careless mistake, and Hubbard's platoon was not as well disciplined as my own. I staggered along half asleep through the darkness and found the shell-holes only by falling into them. G. B., who had had no rest whatever, must have been even more tired than I was, but presently he began to whistle. He whistled the chorus of "You Beautiful Doll" three times without result, but as he began the fourth repetition, shame triumphed over fatigue, and I pulled myself together and joined in. By the end of the sixth repetition my sergeant and two of the men had joined in, and at last someone produced a mouth-organ. Presently we could feel the party pull together and get into something of a swing behind us. G. B. stopped whistling with a sigh and turned his whole attention to guiding us.

After tramping for what seemed to be ages in a dream with the fitful wail of the mouth-organ in my ears, I spied three tall trees standing up dark against the sky less than twenty yards to my right. G. B. gave a grunt of satisfaction.

"Pretty good without a compass, G. B.," I said admiringly.

"Not bad," he admitted.

We crossed the road by the trees, and the men's feet rang out sharply and suddenly as they left the soggy ground for the few paces of hard surface. Then we tramped on and on through an interminable darkness towards a dim, ever-receding skyline. Hours later, it seemed, we were descending a hill into darkness.

"Scout out to the right and see if you can find a track, will you?" said G. B.

Thirty yards away I came upon a narrow rutted track converging upon our line of march. I shouted to G. B., and he led our little column towards it. Presently a barn loomed upon the right, and then another upon the left, and then we were in a dark narrow tunnel between cottages.

"Morlancourt," said G. B.

In the silent cross-roads a dark figure rose up and saluted G. B. It was his servant.

"The billets are in a barn, sir, over there," he said. "I had a little difficulty in getting them. The Quarter-master was in bed and did not want to be disturbed. He said we might use the cookhouse. I found the remains of a fire and made it up. I also made love to the cooks and borrowed some tea. A couple of dixies will be ready in a few minutes."

"Good man," said G. B. "Lead the way to the barn."

Whilst G. B. had been talking to his servant, I had been speaking to my sergeant, and I spoke loudly so that the men, and especially Hubbard's platoon, might hear. "Mr. Bretherton has saved us three or four miles by bringing us across country," I said. "A very difficult thing to do on a cloudy night without a compass."

G. B. halted the party outside the barn and, in spite of their fatigue, pulled them to attention with his sharp word of command as though on C.O's parade.

"When you dismiss and go to your billets," he cautioned them, "don't make a row. Troops are asleep in this village. There will be two dixies of tea ready in a minute or two.

Two men from each platoon will go with my servant to fetch it. Fall out, Mr. Baron."

I saluted and fell out. G. B. continued: "Party—'shun. Dis—miss!" The men turned to the right, smacked their butts, and stumbled into the barn. G. B. and I found a comparatively undraughty corner, and I was asleep even before G. B.'s admirable servant had brought his master a jug of hot tea.

CHAPTER VIII

I

ONE afternoon Melford, Groucher, Harding, and I were returning up a communicating trench near Vaux Wood which spills over the flank of a steep hill fringing a great loop of the Somme. Perched up there, one looked down upon the tree-bordered river zigzagging among a criss-cross pattern of dykes and lakes of shining water. The opposite hill-slopes were scarred with German trenches. This loop of the river-valley was no-man's-land and impassable to troops except by the narrow road from Vaux and one or two precarious footpaths threading the swamp.

We had been spying out the lie of the land, for it was to be our duty each night to patrol these paths. After the reconnaissance we had stayed a few minutes to watch a shoot by our gunners on the German trenches across the valley, and had then turned back up a trench on the forward slope of the hill. We had just passed a turn where three stark, ragged trees stood like sentinels in the bordering mound of excavated chalk and entered a longish straight stretch of trench, when without warning a heavy strafe opened on us.

At the first hurtling whistle I dropped flat. The air was rent with repetitions of that demoniacal shriek a shell makes a second before it lands; the ground shook at each ear-splitting detonation. The continuous patter and smack of bits of iron striking the ground sounded like a moderate performer on a typewriter; smoke drifted across the top of the trench in clouds, inky black, dirty grey, and vivid green; and at each explosion earth showered in upon me. The acrid smoke rocked with concussion and made my head ache abominably.

How long I lay there I do not know, possibly only a few minutes, but it seemed hours; and then came an explosion louder than the rest, and a great weight of earth descended on top of me, blotting out the daylight and the acrid smell of high explosive. My immediate dread of being buried alive was greater than that of being dismembered by chunks of flying metal, and I heaved upwards wildly with my shoulders. To my great relief, my head rose above the mound of loose earth, and at the same moment I saw Harding's head emerge less than a yard away. He shook the earth out of his eyes and hair like a dog and bawled, "Some guy has given them our ad-dress!" I grinned in reply, and then hastily buried my nose in the earth again as resounding smacks smote the sides of the trench and fresh showers of earth came over me.

Then followed a lull, which Groucher, who was in front of me, took advantage of to run the fifteen odd yards out of that dangerous straight bit of trench. I was about to follow him, when the tornado began again, and for the next nine or ten minutes I dared not raise my nose from the ground. Then it stopped as suddenly as it had begun, like the ceasing of an April shower when the sun comes out.

Harding and I stood up, grinned rather foolishly at each other, and brushed the dirt from our uniforms. The trench was in a filthy mess. Great mounds of earth blocked it in front and behind, and the sides had been knocked in and gaped widely all along.

"That's that," said Melford. "Better get back now it's fine."

We moved on in single file up the straight bit of trench, and just round the bend I nearly fell over Groucher, who was still lying prone by a great heap of debris.

"Get a move on, Groucher," I cried. "It's all over for this performance."

And then I saw that his tunic was ripped across one shoulder and that the frayed edges of the cloth were stained a dark brown.

"Look out!" I cried, pulling up short. "Groucher's been hit."

We turned him over gently, and he cursed us faintly for our clumsiness. Harding knelt down beside him and slit open the tunic with a pocket-knife. "You've got a Blighty one all right this time," he announced. "Give me a shell dressing, somebody; and one of you cut along for a stretcher."

II

Groucher was evacuated that night; and I do not think that anyone in the mess sorrowed over his going. His departure left vacant the position of Second-in-Command, which in the ordinary course of events G. B., as next in seniority, would have stepped into, but the affair of the photograph prejudiced Headquarters against him. Melford sent in his name, but Headquarters struck it out and substituted that of Hubbard, the next on the list; and in due course our Mother Hubbard added a stripe and a star to his tunic cuff.

If Groucher had erred on the side of officiousness and bully-ragging, Hubbard went to the other extreme. He was pathetic in his anxiety to avoid Groucher's faults, and he never gave us an order off parade without prefacing it by some such remark as "Awfully sorry to trouble you, old buster; would do it myself, but I have to pay out the men." And he was absurdly afraid that he might incur the enmity of G. B. "I'm awfully sorry, old buster," he said. "You ought to be Second-in-Command unquestionably; but it really isn't my fault. I didn't want the job; Headquarters put me in it, you know, and—well, I couldn't help it."

"You needn't worry," G. B. told him contemptuously. "I shall not refuse to obey orders. Pip collecting has never been one of my hobbies. I'm quite satisfied with the platoon."

And his platoon was quite satisfied with G. B. They were indignant that their officer had been passed over in favour of Hubbard, of whose military abilities they had no great opinion; but as the platoon sergeant was heard to remark, "We should have lost G. B., and we might have got Mother as platoon officer—Gawd help us!"

III

Meanwhile we lay under the baffled displeasure of Divisional Headquarters, which was manifested in the prompt raps over the knuckles that were delivered whenever Melford gave them an opening, which, to do him credit, was seldom. The subject of the photograph was never reopened in the mess; officially G. B. was exonerated from blame, but the mystery was still unexplained, and there remained a constant reminder of the fact in our strained relations with the staff. Therefore, any manifestation of official displeasure, which usually filters from the Commanding Officer down through the chain of command to the lowly private, with us found its billet in G. B.

But one of his exploits when patrolling the Somme swamp went far towards restoring him and the company to favour. He returned to the trenches one night with a German officer and two men as prisoners. When near the middle of the swamp he had told his patrol to wait and had himself gone on alone. He had run into an enemy patrol and replied to its challenge in his fluent German, and his deception had passed muster in the darkness. He had persuaded the officer and two of the men to follow him and had led them into his own patrol. I learned afterwards that it was G. B.'s custom to leave his patrol for a time and wander on alone.

Thus our name was re-entered in the good books of Headquarters; and shortly afterwards the General himself came to inspect us and our billets. Melford was well versed in the foibles of Generals and of this one in particular. Our billets were equipped with all the gadgets dear to the hearts of inspecting Generals: wire-netting beds, canteen, spick-and-span cook-house with white-garbed cooks and daily diet sheet, grease traps, latrines with fly-proof lids, and other eye-wash. And on our inspection we had the good fortune to stand next to a unit whose dirtiness and slovenly appearance acted as a foil to our spit and polish.

The General expressed himself as being very pleased with what he had seen, though whether this was really due to our turnout or was merely the effect of a good luncheon I will not venture to decide. He said that he expected a high standard of efficiency from us because we should be called upon to perform difficult and specialized work. "You have never yet seen a great battle," he concluded darkly, "but you will before very long."

Indeed, the signs and portents of this approaching battle were gathering thick about us. Guns of every size, queer deformed monsters many of them, rumbled through the village at night and were secreted among the hills before dawn; new roads were being made and old ones widened; field-gun ammunition was being taken far forward and buried; and last but not least significant, the infantry back in billets were assiduously practising bayonet fighting.

Headquarters began to take an unhealthy interest in our tactical schemes. Brass-hats appeared mysteriously from the hillsides to watch my point at work, and twice when I had halted on a main bound, the G.S.O.I. rode up, and after inspecting the position, offered friendly and helpful advice.

And there were rumours of a coming change in the organization of cyclist companies: we were to be corps instead of divisional troops, it was whispered, and companies were to be amalgamated to form battalions.

IV

Leave had been running fairly regularly in the company, and I was fortunate to get it sooner than I had anticipated. Headquarters unexpectedly allotted us another vacancy, and I was told one afternoon that I might go on leave that evening. It was my turn for patrol duty, but since the train did not leave railhead till four o'clock in the morning, I thought I could just manage it.

I was in a beatific mood that night as I trod the dark, labyrinthine solitudes of the Somme marshes. Above the dark hill-crests on either hand shone the same stars that I should soon be gazing upon from Piccadilly Circus; away to the northward, where the flicker of distant gunfire lit the sky, I should soon be seeing the coasts of England lift above the sea.

On my return to the trenches from the first patrol I found G. B. in the Infantry Company Headquarters dug-out.

"Hullo, Baron!" he said as I pulled aside the gas-curtain and stumbled down the steps. "You cut off on leave now; I'm taking over. You would have to go hell for leather all the way to railhead if you did the other patrols."

I was very grateful. By the guttering candle-light we had a tot of whisky together out of an enamel mug, and then I said good-bye.

"Cheerio!" said G. B. "Give my love to George Robey, Messrs. Cox & Co., and the other seven wonders of the war."

I left the dug-out and its aroma of damp clothes, whisky, and stale tobacco, and made my way up the dark, silent communication trench. At the top of the hill I climbed out and cut across country. I reached my billet a little after midnight, told my servant to wake me at half-past two, and then turned in for a couple of hours.

A few minutes later, it seemed, the sound of soft foot-steps awakened me, and I lay blinking sleepily at the narrow band of yellow light beneath the door; from outside came the soft soothing buzz of my little primus stove. Then in a flash came remembrance, and I was wide awake. I was going on leave.

In the passage I could hear my servant polishing my buttons and belt, and presently the door opened softly, and he tiptoed across the room. He hung my tunic on the back of a chair and lighted a candle. "Just half past two, sir," he said.

I shaved and dressed, put my washing kit, pyjamas, and a pair of slacks into a haversack, donned my trench coat, and set out. It was a cold morning, and metallic stars glittered above the poplars as I rode happily towards railhead. The village street was dark, silent, and deserted at that early hour, but the station, a very small one in which stood a very long train, though dark was neither silent nor deserted. Dim figures moved upon the platform, and against the sky one caught the sharp outline of a peaked cap and the up-jutting barrel of a rifle. The murmur of many voices came from the darkness, and every now and then a match flared up in the interior of the shadowy train and revealed for a second a little group of faces. All this subdued movement and murmur in the darkness of early morning had an air of expectancy of big things that set the pulses galloping. I wedged myself into a compartment, put my haversack between my feet, and watched the glow of cigarettes in the darkness.

We started. Dawn came, revealing the Picardy country-side moving slowly past the windows. It was after seven when we crawled through Amiens, and I was already stiff from sitting wedged with five people on a seat that was intended to hold only four. The train stopped with a jerk, and it was then that a bundle of blankets on the rack above the opposite seat stirred and the tousled head of a French soldier emerged; he lit a cigarette and grinned down upon us from his unconventional retreat.

Hour after hour we meandered through the green valleys of Normandy, and late in the afternoon puffed into the little station of Buissy. Here was a halt of half an hour, and I knew what to do. Before the train had ceased to move, I dropped from the footboard and sprinted towards the solitary little café by the railway bridge. Around me surged a horde of khaki, but I arrived breathless among the first half-dozen. Coffee and omelette was the prize of victory, coffee and omelette whilst the indignant vanquished gnawed their ration biscuits and filled their water-bottles at the pump. Then back once more to the crowded compartment thick with tobacco smoke.

Dusk fell and then night; conversation tailed off and ceased, and only the little red glow of pipes in the darkness showed that the compartment was occupied. Presently we were descending a steep incline; a breath of keen salt air blew in through the broken windows, and a semicircle of lights appeared below in the distance. "Harfleur," said somebody, and added, "Thank Gawd!"

Now the train was passing slowly through streets; lamp-light fell upon brick walls and large open sheds piled with bales and cases. We moved slowly past trucks loaded with G.S. waggons, gun-limbers, and eighteen-pounder shells. Ragged urchins ran beside the train and begged in their shrill voices for "biscuit" and "bullee bœuf." Then with many jerks the train came to a halt.

A tall red-capped Military Police corporal stood beside the Railway Transport officer in the deserted yard. The train vomited khaki. The Police corporal shouted, "This way," and turned on his heel. We streamed after him—through a large go-down, along a cobbled street open on one side to darkness and a strong salt wind, round the angle of another shed; and two rakish masts stabbed the night sky, and two black funnels belching smoke loomed above us, the leave-boat ready to sail.

I was aboard; the gangway was up and a widening lane of inky water lay between the ship and the quay. The M.L.O. and his sergeant slid slowly astern. We were off. We glided swiftly on through the night, and then a sudden curtsy of the ship and a smother of salt spray upon my face told me that we were at sea. A tremor shook the ship and she began to throb like a thing alive. Submarines were in the Channel and we had no escort; it was all lights out and "hell for leather" through the darkness for Blighty.

It was a dirty night and Tommy is notoriously a bad sailor. Down below there was not room to move; men were sitting back to back with their knees up. I preferred the slippery decks and the drenching spray to the stench below. I wedged myself into a corner in the lee of the weather-screens under the bridge and dozed, but all night long I was aware of the movement of the ship, the drumming of the wind, the crash of seas over the bows followed by the rattle of spray on the deck, and the racing of the screws as the stem lifted clear of the water.

Night was waning when I opened my eyes after a long stretch of dozing. Dawn had not broken, but the heavy pall of darkness had thinned, and one could distinguish water from sky and the great white-capped seas foaming up out of obscurity. I staggered to the bows and saw a dark line of coast on either beam. A light winked in the gloom ahead; the throb of the engines slackened, and we drove on more slowly towards the dark enfolding lines of coast. Behind us dawn was streaking the eastern sky; ahead a chess-board-painted fort parted the racing seas; on either beam the reeling coast was fast shedding the wrappers of night and stood revealed—Blighty.

Dishevelled, pale-faced troops appeared on deck as we steamed up Southampton Water and berthed by a shining rain-washed quay on which tall arc standards still burned. We trooped happily down the gangways through a large lighted go-down to the train.

We stopped only once—at Basingstoke. The platform was deserted at that early hour except for two girls with trays of chocolates and biscuits. A Gunner captain and I put our heads out of the window and called to them; it was not that we really needed the chocolates we bought, but we wanted to hear an English girl speaking English.

We glided into Waterloo, and even at that hour a little group of people was there to watch the leave-train disgorge its cargo of goat and sheepskin coats, British-warms and trench-coats.

From the pavement outside the station I surveyed the world and found it very good. I sniffed the smoky, petrol, tar-block smell with dilated nostrils; I read the old familiar advertisements of pills and mustard; I took deep draughts of the good old London air.

V

I will not attempt to describe that leave. A mere catalogue of dinners, dances, theatres, and jollifications would be boring. Contrast is the spice of life; and leave is a super-illustration of that truth.

I rang up Helen Gurney on the telephone the first morning and met her at the Piccadilly tube that afternoon. It is useless to attempt to describe Helen. The war was a time of brilliant high lights and inky shadows, and with certain few exceptions those war-time English girls were wonderful—and Helen was the most wonderful of all. I saw a good deal of her during that leave, and I can see her now as we sat in some cosily lighted restaurant, her calm healthy face and thoughtful grey eyes, and her hair like spun gold in the light of the table-lamp; or as we traversed the streets of London in a taxi, the lights flashing through the windows and giving me glimpses of her face, absurdly like her brother, young Gurney. London … leave… Helen…

One night—I have forgotten how it came about—we emerged from the tube at Finsbury Park to find that we had missed the last train. The streets were deserted, and taxis seemed non-existent; the only course open was to walk. We tramped on through endless, dull streets of villas and lost our way. Then we sat down, and I shall always remember Helen in her evening frock and cloak and myself in my blue patrol-jacket side by side on a doorstep. Then a sympathetic policeman put us on the right path.

Helen was growing tired, and I felt her arm link gently in mine. It was my last night of leave, and just before we reached the house, I blurted out, "Helen, old girl, I'm absolutely crazy about you."

She was silent for a moment or two and then pressed my arm slightly. "Are you?" she said in a low voice.

"Absolutely," I repeated inanely.

"I know," she said, and then was silent again.

"You do like me, Helen, don't you?" I pleaded. "Just a little bit?"

She laughed softly. "Of course. You are a great dear, Dicky boy. I like you… awfully…"

"Well, then," I broke in jubilantly.

"Let me finish, Dicky," she said. "Love is such a great big thing; it should sweep everything away and transform heaven and earth."

"It does," I agreed.

"I do like you, Dicky boy—awfully," she went on; "but not quite like that yet. It may grow to be like that, and if it does, it will be too… too…"

"Wonderful," I put in.

"Wonderful," she agreed in a low voice. "But until it does, don't let us spoil it all. Love is too big a thing to take risks with; it would be too horrible if we made a mistake. Let us go on as we are now… till I am sure… good pals and… and a little more perhaps."

"I'll promise anything on earth so long as I have a hope," I answered fervently.

She squeezed my arm and then suddenly threw her arms round my neck. "That's because you are going back to the front tomorrow, my poor old Dicky," she whispered.

CHAPTER IX

I

AT dusk on the following day we steamed down Southampton Water. The boat was less crowded than on the previous journey, and I managed to find a space in which I could lie full-length. It was a quiet night, and when I awoke we were already inside the breakwater at Havre. I reported at the R.T.O.'s office and found a note from G. B. awaiting me. "Get off at Corbie," it ran. "Great doings.—G. B."

It was half past four in the afternoon when we crawled into Corbie. I heaved my cramped limbs out of the compartment and was on my way to the R.T.O.'s office to inquire the whereabouts of the company when I noticed a couple of men with Army Cyclist Corps badges standing by a mess-cart outside the station. I went across to them, and one of the men, a lance-corporal, saluted and said, "Lieutenant Baron, sir? We have been sent to meet you."

I thought I knew every man in the company by sight, but both these faces were new to me, and the mess-cart was not ours. The lance-corporal saw that I was mystified, and as I got into the cart, said, "The battalion is at Ligny, sir."

"Battalion!" I echoed.

"Yes, sir. Corps troops now."

Then he told me all about it. Three days after I had gone on leave the changes of which we had heard rumours had been made. Two of the old divisional companies had been amalgamated to form a battalion. Melford had gone to be Second-in-Command of an infantry battalion, and a new man, Major Twist, had come to command us. There were three companies: A, B, and C. C Company was composed of officers and men from the other divisional company amalgamated with us and were all new to me; Hubbard commanded B and had Pagan as one of his subalterns; and G. B. had got his captaincy at last and was in command of A, with Gurney, Dodd, and myself as platoon officers. Harding was still with us as Medical Officer.

I found my battalion, as I must now call it, in a delightful little village on the banks of the Somme a few miles from Corbie. The village school had been turned into the mess, and G. B., Gurney, and I were billeted together in a clean little cottage on the river-bank. Fresh cream, butter, and eggs were obtainable in this undevastated country, and we were a very jolly party in the mess, quickly making friends with our new comrades and settling down into a well-knit battalion. We had found a piano in one of the rooms, and every night after dinner G. B. sat at the keyboard with his glass on top of the piano, and we bawled the profane old choruses:

> *Mademoiselle from Armentières, parley-vous,*
> *Mademoiselle from Armentières, parley-vous,*
> *Mademoiselle from Armentières,*
> *Never been kissed for forty years,*
> *Inky pinky parley-vous!*

But we were not allowed to enjoy this arcadian retreat for long. C Company was the first to go; they were attached to the Corps Provost-Marshal and moved off to various destinations up and down the corps area. And then Hubbard's company, B, was ordered to provide snipers for the corps front and to man the corps observation posts. This last job was given to Pagan and his platoon, and Gurney and I chipped him mercilessly with having to leave our peaceful village.

"Get thee to a nunnery: go!" he retorted. "Must B Company win the whole bloomin' war for you?"

"He that bridleth his tongue is greater than he that taketh a city," I quoted sententiously from where I sat on the pole of a farm-waggon.

"Ye gods!" cried Pagan with a grin as he rode off. "The bold, bad Baron lapses into Paganism!"

And then it was our turn. A Company was ordered up to dig pits for the trench-mortars that were to cut the wire for the now rapidly approaching big push; and we set about getting the company into light mobile trim.

G. B. had his valise spread out on the red-tiled floor of his billet and was on his knees beside it sorting the less necessary articles from the indispensable.

"We ought to cut our kit down to the minimum," he said. "Once this push gets started, we shall be pretty much on the move, and it will be less trouble to get rid of the stuff now than to have to dump and lose it later on."

I had strolled in from my room across the passage and was idly turning over some paper-backed novels and old photographs he had thrown on the bed.

"Hullo!" I exclaimed. "Is this you, G. B., dressed up?" I had picked up a photograph of an officer in the smart, tight-waisted German greatcoat and rakish peaked cap.

G. B. screwed his head round to look at it.

"What?" he asked. "Oh, that: no, that's a fellow I shared rooms with in Berlin."

I looked at the photograph with interest. "You certainly are alike," I told him. "He is a bit fatter perhaps, and of course the uniform makes a difference; otherwise it might be your ugly mug. Looks a bit of a swine," I added with a grin.

G. B. took the photograph from me and pushed it into the stove. "He was rather a good fellow really," he retorted.

"Oh ho, G. B., you've been making pals with the unspeakable Hun!" I ragged, wagging a finger at him.

He shrugged his shoulders and glanced at himself in the little polished steel field-mirror he had picked out of his kit. "They are quite a good lot individually when you really know them."

"Yes, they need a lot of knowing," I answered sceptically. "I knew a Bosche barber once, but I expect I didn't know him well enough."

He slipped the thin plate of steel back into its case and threw it on to the valise. "You are bigoted, Baron. You can't damn a whole nation like that."

"What about Louvain?" I retorted.

He shrugged his shoulders. "I'm not defending that. But there are good and bad in every crowd."

"Well, I've met the bad, and you seem to have met all the good," I retorted.

"Well," he answered patiently, "I have met hundreds. Till I was eight I lived in Germany—spoke German better than English at one time. And then I had three years at Heidelberg. I met some rotters, of course, but I met a lot of damn good fellows too."

"And supposing you meet this chap in the photograph— out in no-man's-land! What will you do? Kiss each other on both cheeks?"

"That's a French custom," he snapped. "And we shall not meet anyway, so why talk tripe?" He got up from his knees and took a cigarette-case from the breast pocket of his tunic. "Have a gasper, and don't be an ass," he said with a grin.

II

On the following morning we rode out. It was the first time that A Company had moved off in full kit as an independent unit under the command of its captain, and we were all in high spirits. As soon as G. B. gave "March at ease," the men began to sing, to the tune of "The Church's one Foundation":

> *We are Fred Karno's army:*
> *What blinking good are we?*
> *We cannot shoot; we cannot ride*
> *No bloomin' good are we.*
> *But when we get to Berlin*
> *The Kaiser he will roar:*
> *Ach, ach! mein Gott! what a bloody fine lot*
> *Are the Umteenth Cyclist Corps!*

We rode along the shady tow-path by the river and turned north through Bray to one of the little valleys among the slopes beyond the village. Here in the side of a hill a long line of elaborately designed dug-outs had been constructed for the use of Corps Headquarters when the advance should necessitate their moving forward. On the opposite slope a kind of large cattle-pen of barbed wire ten feet high was in course of erection for the accommodation of prisoners; in the blue sky above hung an observation balloon, yellow and glistening, like a bloated caterpillar on the hook of some heavenly fisherman; and the valley itself was filled with horse lines and transport; shelters of every kind, tents, tarpaulins, bivouacs, Stevenson huts, Nissen huts, huts of ammunition boxes and of galvanized iron cumbering every foot of ground.

Here we left our cycles, transport, and the C.Q.M.S., whose job it would be to send up rations and form a link with Battalion Headquarters. Then we marched out up the slope, on through the long communicating trench to a row of little tin-pot shelters in Carnoy, where we had a foretaste of the plastering we were to have on our nightly job of digging trench-mortar pits in rear of the fire trench. The men had just been detailed to their dug-outs, and the orderlies were coming up the trench with the dixies of tea when the hurtling roar of a "crump" descended out of the blue. The orderlies dropped the dixies and lay flat. The earth shook; twenty yards away a great black cloud bellied out above the trench and a gigantic sack of coals, it seemed, was tipped down a chute.

Gurney took his pipe from his mouth, and made a grimace. "Five-nine," he remarked.

The orderlies had risen unscathed and were picking lumps of earth out of the tea. From the dug-out next door rose the ironical chorus of the men:

> *I want to go home. I want to go home.*
> *Whizz-bangs and sausages make such a noise,*
> *I want to go home and be one of the bhoys.*
> *Take me over the sea*
> *Where the Alleman can't get at me.*
> *Oh my, I don't want to die; I want to go home.*

G. B. grinned and threw his tin hat on to his valise. "They will have more to say when they taste that tea," he remarked.

III

All this time, preparations for the great advance were being pushed forward. Villages behind the lines were crowded with troops. Over all the Somme uplands campa were springing up, and the cheerful sound of drum and fife or the skirl of pipes was heard as battalion after battalion came marching in. Farther back, the villagers were awakened from sleep by the clank of caterpillar tractors, and drew aside their curtains to see the great steel mountings and villainous squat barrels of nine-point-twos passing through. At night the roads to the trenches were blocked with transport; for, in addition to the usual ration parties, vast quantities of field-gun ammunition were going forward, to be buried till the guns should overtake it. By night, the little valley of Carnoy was like a beehive: men digging gun-pits, long chains of men passing shells from hand to hand, endless files of men staggering under the weight of toffee-apples—those bars of steel tipped with great iron balls that were the projectiles of the heavy trench-mortars—men half-naked, heaving and hauling and sweating in the darkness.

New batteries were springing up everywhere like mushrooms in a night, and every few yards along the front of the once-peaceful Billon Wood, the lean barrels of eighteen-pounders crouched among the undergrowth. Just off the road, a long-range gun had been installed, and periodically its great full-throated bang was heard and the shuffling hum of the shell on its ten-mile journey to Péronne. The French also were there in their horizon blue to relieve the monotony of the drab khaki, and the staccato bark of the famous soixante-quinze was added to the more dignified roll of our eighteen-pounders.

And night by night the quiet intervals became fewer and of shorter duration. Suddenly the hollows of the hills would be lit by the flash of guns as the great orchestra tuned up. And then up would soar the signal rockets, red, blue, green, white, and all hell break loose; across the devastated valleys sounded the dreary drumming of gas gongs, and men struggled into their respirators, and sentries peered anxiously over the parapets.

And through it all the ant-like activity went on: endless streams of men coming and going; staggering under heavy loads; half-naked and sweating, man-handling guns into pits; digging marching, falling into shell-holes, cursing, laughing, singing softly to the orchestra of the guns.

Six days before the hour of the attack, our bombardment opened. Day and night it went on ceaselessly, day and night that continuous rumble punctuated by the deep individual bur-r-rump of the heavies as a separate shout is heard above the roar of a mob. For six days and nights the earth trembled as when a division of cavalry gallops by. One was in a factory filled day and night with the thud and vibration of machinery Far back behind the line, it sounded like the roar of a distant furnace; and farther back, out of earshot, the steady rattling of the window-frames told that it was still going on. The pulsation and vibration of that bombardment worked into one's body and brain, but one grew accustomed to it as one grows accustomed to the engines of a ship. It was as if the machinery that spun the earth upon its axis had become audible.

IV

The attack was timed for seven-thirty, and the sun rose in splendour that fateful morning, dispersing the thin mist and flooding the torn and pounded Picardy hills with its cheerful light. With the passing of dawn the bombardment relaxed, as if to whisper to the anxious German staff, "It is not to-day"; but, as the hand of the clock moved slowly through the arc between seven and half past, it worked up again and rose to a pitch of fury.

The German trenches were hidden behind a wall of spouting earth and flame, like a heavy sea breaking on a rocky coast. And then, as an orchestra is silenced by the wave of the conductor's baton, it ceased, whilst the gunners lengthened range for the first lift, to break out again a moment later in undiminished fury. By the jagged scars in the earth that marked our trenches, the figure of a man appeared and stood for a second, the only living thing visible in all that flayed and pounded country; then other figures were beside him, and a long, irregular line rose out of the earth and moved slowly across the battered ribbon of no-man's-land. Behind them another line had risen from the earth—the second wave. Two mines went up with a sky-shattering roar and mountainous uprearing of earth and flame; the orchestra of the guns rose in crescendo, and the machine guns began their insane stuttering. In England, people were sitting down to coffee and bacon, and here, above the Somme, the biggest battle the world had yet seen had begun.

V

Our rôle for the moment was standing by, to go through when the enemy's line was broken. But the hoped-for break did not come. Day after day fresh battalions with rattle of drums or skirl of pipes swung up to the line; and day after day their battered remnants marched back for a brief respite. And the thunder of the guns went on.

Our turn came at last; our objective the crest of a low hill that gave an extended view over the country beyond.

"We are for it, young fellow my lad," said G. B., as he brought in the orders. "We're in the next attack—sandwiched between two battalions of the old division. Headquarters want information, and we are to supply it. From our objective, we ought to be able to see something of what is going on; though if old Fritz doesn't blow us off the top of it, it won't be his fault."

That night, in our quarters in the German old front line, we had a final look over the map and repetition of orders.

"All clear?" asked G. B. at the end of it.

"Quite," we all agreed.

"Right-oh, then," said G. B. And he folded up the map and put it in his case.

Gurney and Dodd took up their tin hats and went out to their platoons, which were falling in outside. G. B. lighted a last pipe and looked at me across the top of it as he flung away the match.

"Wind up, Dicky?" he asked.

"A little," I confessed. "Have you?"

"Not personally. It's more like waiting for the gun in the Mays at Cambridge: you know—ten, nine, eight, seven, six…"

I nodded.

"Just a wee bit afraid of catching a crab," he added.

"You!" I exclaimed. "Stroke is all right; he won't catch any crabs."

"Thanks," he said. "But, you see, this is the first big show the battalion has been in."

"Well, it is up to A Company," I said.

He nodded and took up his unfinished mug of whisky. "Well, it's over the bags and the best of luck," he answered.

VI

Some hours later, we stood in what had been a German reserve-line trench. The air rocked and trembled with concussion; the earth shook beneath our feet; hard, high-pitched detonations smote our aching ear-drums; the acrid smell of high explosive poisoned our nostrils. From horizon to horizon, across the front, great spouts of orange-coloured flame and flying earth leapt cease-lessly towards the drifting smoke—snow-white, green, and venomous-looking, black, woolly, and impenetrable.

My sergeant made a trumpet of his hands and bellowed, "That's the stuff to give 'em, sir!"

I nodded and glanced along the trench at the crouching steel-hatted figures. Every other second came detonations, ear-splitting, brain-numbing, close at hand. Earth stung the face, penetrated the nose and ears; helmets rang to blows of stones and twisted metal; figures sagged foolishly and collapsed.

G. B. had his eyes fixed upon his wrist-watch. I saw him raise the whistle to his lips and scramble out of the trench. The tornado of sound continued; figures scrambled up ladders and stood on the parapet, silhouetted against the dawn. A voice cried, "All aboard for Dixie!" and with a flicker of cold light on steel points, we went over.

Overhead was the drone of a million birds in flight. The hillside ahead erupted flame. Noise, noise, noise; the world was full of noise. The air was filled with droning, whining sounds; the earth resounded to patter, patter, smack; and incessantly there came the staccato tap-tap-tapping of machine guns.

Brown figures lay huddled on the bare chalky ground and among the black tangled wire that stretched like a foul cobweb across the rank grass.

Suddenly, at our feet yawned a shallow ditch scratched in the chalk, shapeless, unrecognizable as a trench; a litter of burst sandbags, scraps of equipment and humanity pounded into the chalky ooze by the belching guns, but revealing dark, half-blocked holes in the earth from which issued grey, dirt-stained figures with earth-matted hair, grimy, bloodless faces, and glaring, crazed eyes. Then came a flicker of bayonets, the gasping breathing of panting, striving men; grunts, groans, sobs, screams, and the crack of bursting bombs: and the wave passed on, leaving behind the foul, soggy, unspeakable ditch and the silly, lolling, grotesque, grinning figures.

Noise, noise everywhere: thudding, crashing in the earth; screaming, whirring, whistling in the air—noise that maddened the brain; and incessantly the insane tap-tap-tapping of machine guns. A fury of noise; a madness of sound. Men mad, shouting, cursing, praying; men with bloodshot eyes and ted-tipped bayonets tripping over wire, splashing through foul water, and stumbling into holes.

Then we halted on the far side of a low rise, and I realized that we had reached our objective. A battered half-filled trench ran diagonally across our front, and behind us a fragment of the angle of a wall, some ten feet high, was all that remained of the Sucrerie that had once stood there. Away to the left, a heavy barrage was beating upon the crest of a hill, but, except for an occasional shell that screamed over our heads and detonated in the ruined Sucrerie behind us, we ourselves received no attention. That, I realized, would come later when the Bosche gunners understood the situation.

Meanwhile, G. B. made us work like slaves, deepening the old trench and throwing up new protection. We had got into touch with the troops on our left, and Signals had laid a telephone wire up behind us.

The barrage was still pounding away on our left, and presently we understood the meaning of it, for grey figures could be seen moving across the flayed and broken ground, and the rattle of musketry and the crack of bursting bombs came from that direction. We poured in an enfilade fire, but the storm-centre moved steadily rearwards, and it became evident that this counter-attack had driven a deep wedge in on our left.

And then our turn came. The old Sucrerie began to spout flame and earth and brick-dust. We crouched in our shallow trench whilst the earth shook and broke around us and the results of our hard digging were destroyed in a few minutes. The hot sun beat down pitilessly upon our steel helmets. Our losses became heavier and heavier; and the pounding still went on. Twice in twenty minutes our telephone line was cut, and we lost men repairing it.

My senses became numbed by the concussion; I lay on my face, expecting every second to be blown to atoms, but I was too dazed to be afraid. In this inferno it was courting death to raise oneself, yet G. B. moved up and down his line and was ever on the watch.

Time passed on leaden feet; the air rocked with concussion and sang with flying fragments of iron. Suddenly I realized that it had stopped. G. B. shouted "Here they come!" and I saw him stand upright and his right arm whirl above his head as he flung a bomb.

The events of the next few minutes have left no clear impression upon my mind. I heard the sudden crack of rifles around me, the click of bolts working furiously, the crack of bombs. Men were growling and muttering on either side of me, and I myself was shouting. Grey figures in goblin-like helmets were streaming toward us. One of them lurched across the sights of my rifle, and I saw the wings of the foresight silhouetted against the faded grey cloth. I felt the kick of the butt against my shoulder without knowing that I had squeezed the trigger, and then the sights ran unimpeded to the opposite hill-slope.

How long it all lasted I do not know, but quite suddenly, it seemed, the battered ground was bare of movement again. We wiped the sweat from our faces and took a long breath. Then great concussions shook the air again, and great fountains of earth reared themselves among us. We crouched back into our shallow holes.

Thrice was this performance repeated; and during the long periods that we cowered under that titanic hammering

I saw... his right arm whirl above his head.

I grew to long for the time when the grey figures would stream upon us and rid us of this paralysing pounding. I told myself that we could not stand it much longer; no human beings could. G. B. must give the order to retire. Flesh and blood could not stand it. But no such order came from G. B., and we hung on.

The telephone wire had been cut in a dozen places, and we had given up attempting to mend it. Runners had been sent back, but none of them had returned, and it was not difficult to guess what had become of them. Way behind us, against the skyline I could see the line of trees upon the road that ran behind our old front line, and it seemed incredible that there a man could stand upright and walk upon his feet.

Darkness descended upon us, darkness lit by the flash of guns and the sudden glow of shell-bursts. The pitiless shelling slackened, and we stirred like a squad stood at ease. G. B. seized the opportunity to get the wounded back and to send runners to Headquarters. All night long we toiled at repairing our battered defences. A little before midnight, the rain came down in torrents and turned our shallow trench into a running brook, but it lessened the probability of a night attack.

VII

With the first glimpse of dawn, the Bosche came over again and without any preliminary shelling. I awoke from my first short snatch of sleep to find my platoon firing rapid into the grey dawn. But the attacking waves melted away and ceased, and then for an hour or more we were left in peace and hardly a shell came near us.

Some ammunition and rations had come up to us during the night, and our runner had returned with a basket of pigeons from the corps pigeon-loft to replace our cut telephone wire. With him came Harding, our cheery medical officer. He surveyed us now in the early morning light as we sat in a muddy hole, munching bully beef and ration biscuit.

"It is a good thing you are not a lady's man, G. B.," he said.

G. B. asked why.

"Well, you will not be worrying about your appearance," grinned Harding.

In truth, G. B., with his sodden and mud-stained tunic, stubbly chin, and haggard, grimy face, with runnels of dried sweat, was anything but a Beau Brummel, and the long gash across his cheek made by a flying stone, gave him a terrifying appearance.

"We should all of us be the better for a wash and brush-up," answered G. B. "To tell you the truth, Harding, we haven't had much time for titivating."

"This is the first chance I have had to think sanely since we went over yesterday morning," I said.

"Yes, you have arrived in the first real lull we have had," said G. B. "And if you take my advice, you will get back while it lasts."

"Not me," replied Harding. "I am staying right here. I am the Battalion M.O., and I cannot be with all three companies when they are detached, but, judging by the indentations on the ground that are spread so profusely about us, and presooming that there are more where they came from, A Company seems likely to need the services of the M.O. I strolled into the mess last night and found your runner looking pretty done up, being dosed with whisky, and I asked the Major what was the news of A Company. 'They're being pounded to Hell and counter-attacked every half-hour,' he answered. 'But they're hanging on, and G. B. is fighting like fourteen devils.' That's the place for me, I thought. And up I came, and here I stay. I've found an old Bosche shelter back of the Sucrerie there, and I'm going to use it as an aid-post."

"It's too far forward," said G. B. "However, if America wants to stay..." And he grinned.

We were not left long in peace. A big detonation in the Sucrerie ruins sent up a fountain of brick-dust, and then another shell pitched in front of us and covered us with mud.

I was absolutely done up; the sound of that first shell was like a knell in my ears. I had been dreading a renewal of the shelling. I felt that I could not stand it. The thought of the day that stretched ahead appalled me. As the shelling increased in volume, I lay in my funk-hole and quaked. It was only the knowledge that I was an officer and that the men looked to me for leadership that prevented me from turning and running—that and G. B.'s gaunt face. I was in the grip of two fears: a loathsome physical fear and the fear that G. B. should know it.

I have heard intellectuals sneer at physical courage as a brutal and often senseless quality, but that day, when

I myself lacked it, I knew it for a magnificent thing, and I saw its wonderful power over other men. I have heard it said that one brave man may inspire a whole army with courage, and that day I knew it to be true.

The shelling was very heavy, heavier than anything we had yet experienced, Harding had his hands full attending to the casualties. G. B. crawled up beside me with a serious face. "This cannot go on, Baron," he said. "We are losing too many men. Take a man with you and go back to Harding and see if there are any more of those old Bosche funk-holes in the dip behind the Sucrerie."

I called my servant and we crawled back through the spouting rubble-heap of the Sucrerie and down into the little dip beyond. Here we found some old German shelters dug into the far bank. They faced the wrong way, but they offered some protection. I returned to G. B. and reported.

"You and Gurney take your platoons back," he said, "and get them under cover. I will leave a man to keep touch, and you must watch the shelling carefully. At the first sign of its slackening you must bring up your men hell for leather."

Gurney and I got our men back into the shelters, though it was warm work getting there. We did not trust a man to watch; Gurney and I took it in turns to do so, for there was G. B. up there with only one depleted platoon.

At the first sign of slackening in the shelling, we gave the alarm and dashed out; and as we stumbled through the hummocks of the Sucrerie we heard a burst of rapid fire in front and a minute later saw the now familiar line of grey figures advancing. We flung ourselves down and let them have it.

I have no very clear idea of what followed. I saw grey figures behind me; I saw some of our men going back; I could not see G. B. And then we were back on the far side of the dip behind the Sucrerie firing mechanically, and I remember thinking that it was all over, that we could do no more, that they were through us. And then I realized that the grey figures were no longer advancing and that the opposite slope was bare of movement. And I saw G. B. again.

But this was only a respite: they would come on again and we could hold them no longer.

G. B. was at my side, saying, "This won't do, Baron. We can't see a damned thing from here. We must push them back again."

I stared at him in amazement. We were done to the wide; we could hardly stand upon our feet. Their next drive must swamp us. It was obvious. And here was G. B. talking of attacking I thought he must be joking, but his face was serious.

"Get the men together," he said.

"We have no artillery support," I stammered.

"We shall not want it," he answered. "We have fought them to a standstill, but they will have another try in a minute or two. They are getting ready for it now. We will give them ten rounds rapid and then go in with the bayonet. They will run like hares; you'll see."

I told the men that we were going to counter-attack. I saw amazement on their faces; their thoughts were the same as mine had been. "Captain Bretherton says that we shall go through them like sheep," I said.

They cheered up at that. They were saying to themselves that if G. B. said it was all right, it was all right.

The Bosche came on again in a minute or two as G. B. had foretold. We met them with a terrific burst of rapid fire. The attacking line wavered, struggled on half-heartedly, and stopped; and then G. B. let out a great yell, and we rose to our feet and went at them with the bayonet. I was yelling myself, and my voice sounded hoarse and cracked.

And then we were back in our old position in front of the Sucrerie. I lay there panting on the ground, and I realized that Harding was beside me.

"A Company is some company," he shouted in my ear.

I nodded. I cared for nothing now. I knew that I should go on like an automaton. If G. B. said get up, I should get up; and if he had told me to stand on my head, I believe I should have done so.

VIII

Time passed slowly, and I found myself dreading the coming of night. They would pound us hard, I felt, and then attack. For thirty hours we had been pounded and had repulsed attacks; we had had no rest and no sleep, and the casualty list was mounting up and up. Would we never be relieved? Were we to stay here till the last man fell and the grey tide swept over us?

Just before dusk, a plane droned overhead, flying low and attracting a fusillade of rifle and machine-gun fire from the enemy. It sounded our call on its klaxon horn and an object like a truncheon, tied to a handkerchief dropped from it and landed somewhere in the Sucrerie.

The message was brought to G. B. where he lay close beside me. He read it and turned to me. "We are to go back," he said with some bitterness. "No relief. They are abandoning this bit; just like them after we have done our damnedest to hold it."

"We are well out of this," said Gurney to me when he heard the news. "And to think that the poor old infantry do this sort thing every day. I take my hat off to them every time."

"Every time," I agreed heartily.

Gurney's and Dodd's platoons went first. Then it was my turn. My sergeant led the way, and I prepared to bring up the rear. I reported to G. B. when every man had gone, and he answered, "Right-oh. Get along."

I knew it was useless to argue with him, and I followed my men; but I waited on the fringe of the Sucrerie ruins, and I was very glad when he joined me.

It was now quite dark, and we were able to get to our feet and flounder through the mud. At the end of some twenty minutes, we found ourselves in a moderately good trench where men with cigarettes behind their ears and ground-sheets over their shoulders sat at the entrance to dug-outs and played housy-housy; and these famil-iar sights of trench life now seemed to us as civilized as a Mayfair drawing-room. And then we came out upon a road and fell into column of route. Ahead, a line of tall, shivered trees stood outlined against the night sky, and every now and then we were blinded by the flash of some unseen gun, and our ears were smitten by its reverberating bang. Behind us, the Verey lights rose and fell, the rockets curved against the sky, and the steady drum-fire went on.

We were a battered, ragged, depleted little body of scare-crows that trudged painfully along that road. Our destination was our old transport lines in that snug little valley where now was built the corps prisoner-of-war cage, presided over by Hubbard and some of B Company. It was a long, long trail for us, done up as we were, and the moon had risen long before we shuffled over the crest of the hill that led to our little valley. My invaluable Corporal Pepper, however, was game to the end; he produced a mouth-organ and played us— rather shakily, it is true—selections from the latest London revues. I marched—shuffled perhaps is the word—at the rear of the column, and I can see it now: the dark, slowly moving mass of men with the rifles standing up an inch of two above their heads and the moonlight glinting on their steel hats.

The Company Quartermaster-Sergeant knew of our coming and was at the entrance of the little valley to meet us, and so were Hubbard and a good number of B Company. When he saw them, G. B. turned his head and cried, "Pull yourselves together, A Company."

Stout young Pepper struck up "Keep the home fires burning," the drooping backs straightened, the nodding heads stiffened, the shuffling feet straightened out and began to beat in rhythm on the road, and to the melancholy wail of the mouth-organ we marched into camp, I declare, with something very nearly approaching a swagger.

CHAPTER X

I

THE Major came in as we sat at breakfast in our Stevenson hut.

"Well played, A Company," he said, "Well done, G. B. The Corps Commander is very pleased with your effort, and, between ourselves, he is putting you in for the M.C."

I expected that G. B. would be as pleased to hear this as I was, but he answered rather discourteously, I thought.

"Headquarters give decorations as lightly as they give up bits of the line that have cost lives to take."

The Major popped a lump of sugar into his mouth and shrugged his shoulders. "Well, you have done your job, G. B.; yours not to reason why."

G. B.'s leave was long overdue, but with the Somme battle dragging on there was little or no leave going. The Major rang up one morning, however, to say that H.Q. had a vacancy and that G. B. could go that day. He packed up then and there and went, and I was left temporarily in command of the company.

We were enjoying our rest in the little valley. I shared a tent with G. B., and now that he was away I had it to myself. It was perched on the slope above the valley, and from it I looked across the rolling Somme country to the scarred hillsides whereon the battle still raged; and at night the horizon, framed in the pyramid tent flaps, often resembled a Crystal Palace firework display. The valley itself was full of movement, troops coming and going, and an occasional high-velocity shell to liven things up. Below me was the corps prisoner-of-war cage presided over by Hubbard and some of B Company, and periodically a long grey column of prisoners wound its way out of the valley, shepherded by our friends the Lancers looking very warlike with their steel helmets and drawn swords and spare bandolier round their horses' glossy necks.

I wrote a long letter to Helen describing as much of it as I could, for the censorship was more stringent in those eventful days. When I had finished the letter I found that I had no envelope, and I rummaged in G. B.'s kit on the chance that he might have some. I found a whole packet and a few odd ones already stamped with the battalion censor stamp. I was rather amused at this. It was strictly against orders, of course, to stamp an envelope with the censor stamp before the letter was written, but we had sometimes done so in Melford's day to avoid the nuisance of taking the letter to the orderly-room. I put Helen's letter in one of the stamped envelopes, scrawled my name across the corner, and sent it off to the divisional post office at the far end of the valley.

On the following day I met Pagan standing by the Zoo, as we called the corps cage.

"Hast heard the news?" he asked.

"Yes," I replied promptly. "The old squire lies foully murdered!"

"And out in the snow with no roof to his mouth," grinned Pagan. "But seriously, have you heard the news?"

"Rather," I answered lightly. "The Esquimos have joined the Allies, and President Wilson has written another note to Germany."

"Funny ass!" he said. "B.F. cubed. But there are alarums and excursions going on at Battalion Headquarters."

"What about?" I asked, becoming interested at last.

"Headquarters are re-censoring a lot of letters now, you know."

"Well?"

"They have opened one containing a map of this front—positions and what not marked on it."

"Someone's a B.F. then, and for it. Who was it?"

"They don't know. There was no letter; only the map."

"But what has that got to do with us? Why is the Major perturbed about it?"

"Because," he said and paused oratorically, "because it has our censor stamp on it."

I whistled. "The battalion censor stamp?"

He nodded.

"Well, it can't be anyone in A or B Companies," I said, and then stopped short.

"No, because we get our letters stamped by the nearest unit and don't use the battalion stamp," he finished for me.

"Therefore it must be one of C Company," I put in hurriedly.

"But pardon me, thou bleeding piece of earth," he quoted smilingly. "Battalion Headquarters and C Company send their letters through the Corps post-office, and this particular letter happens to have been opened at the divisional office here."

"By Jove!" I exclaimed. "The one we send ours to."

"And ours also," added Pagan. "But there is more to come, as the story-books say; this mysterious missive—rather good that—contained a map, and that map happens to be the one Melford lost from the old Company."

"Sacred pigs!" I exclaimed; and then was silent for a moment. "You say that there was no letter with it?"

"No; therefore the charge lies against a person or persons unknown, as the lawyers say."

"But how about the officer who censored it? His name should have been in the corner of the envelope."

"It was 'A. Nemo'! Commands Z Company, perhaps!"

"Um! Sort of nom-de-plume, eh!"

"Nom-de-crayon—it was written in pencil. Evidently the fellow is a profound Latin scholar and not untouched by a sense of humour."

"How about the handwriting?" I suggested.

"Written with an entrenching tool and with the left hand, I should say," he replied.

"And the address?"

"Miss Smith, care of some little post-office at Hammersmith."

"Um! I shouldn't wonder if there were two or three Miss Smiths in Hammersmith," I commented.

"Exactly. He has covered up his tracks pretty well."

"But why on earth all this heavy plot stuff?" I exclaimed. "That wretched map is worthless now; every unit in France has been moved since it was made."

"Ah! that's the question, as laddie Hamlet said. My own theory is that we are harbouring a lunatic in our gentle bosoms— that or some bright lad who has been to the movies and found the excitement too much for him."

"That's rot, of course," I said. "But I'm dashed if I can see any other explanation. Some idiot steals a map—a secret map—keeps it till it is no good, and then risks cashiering by sending it to Miss Smith of Hammersmith! And the same perfect idiot sent that photograph to the papers, I suppose."

"Oh, somebody is potty all right," agreed Pagan. "You know, Baron, I always had a sneaking belief that it was Groucher that did this map and photograph business; but this proves it can't have been him."

"It's a good thing we are under corps and not under the old division, anyway," I growled. "If this had cropped up with them after the other business, there would have been hell to pay—and may be still as far as I know."

Pagan shook his head. "They won't stop the war for it," he said. "It's only a question of discipline; the map is worthless—and they have got their hands pretty full with this little battle. They will pull the Major's hair, and he will strafe the battalion, and that is all. We shall have him up here presently asking questions; you'll see. And now, having given you all the latest latrine rumours, for which I generously make no charge, I must get on with the war. B Company calleth."

II

On the following day G. B. returned from leave; and the C.O. came up to see us, as Pagan had prophesied. The officers of A and B Companies assembled under the tarpaulin that served B Company as a mess, and the Major began his strafe.

He told us that a divisional headquarters had opened a letter stamped with the battalion censor stamp and containing a map. He made no reference to the previous history of that map, for he knew nothing of it, and none of us felt called upon to enlighten him. He pointed out that a breach of the censorship regulations was a grave offence; that the lives of thousands of men might be involved; and that by failing in his duties as censor, an officer was as disloyal to his country as if he had deserted to the enemy. The sending of a map of that nature through the post was a flagrant crime, and the sender, whoever he might be, by signing a false name upon the envelope, showed that he realized the seriousness of what he was doing.

"Now, I am not suggesting that any of you sent that map," continued the C.O. "No one with a spark of patriotism or decency could do a thing like that. We all bear the King's commission—officers and gentlemen, as the phrase goes. The man who sent that map is certainly not a gentleman, and I do not believe that he was an officer—not one of mine at any rate.

"I prefer to think that one of the men—one of the new drafts—sent it. Not in the usual way of course; otherwise the letter would have gone to his platoon officer or company commander for censorship. I believe that the letter went direct from the sender to the post-office and arrived there already stamped with the censor stamp and signed with that false name.

"But the question then arises as to how the letter became stamped with the battalion censor stamp. The men have not access to it. I suggest that some man got hold of an empty envelope already stamped, scrawled that name in the corner, and so avoided the usual censorship. Therefore, what I want to ask you is this: Have any of you ever put the battalion censor stamp on a blank envelope or kept such envelopes in your kit? For if you have, you see it would be quite possible for someone else to get hold of one. Now I am going to put that question to each of you separately."

While the question was being put, I had my eyes on G. B.'s face, and when it came to his turn and he answered "No," our eyes met. It was only for a moment that they met, but something in my glance must have told him that I knew of those envelopes in his kit for I was instantly aware that he knew that I knew.

It was some time later, when we were alone together in our tent, that he looked up from the returns he was signing and said, "So you knew about those envelopes in my kit!"

"Yes," I replied. "I wanted one when you were on leave, and I looked to see if you had any."

He made no comment, and continued his checking of returns by the light of a candle stuck in a cigarette-tin.

"Why did you lie about it, G. B.?" I asked at last.

He went on with his work for a moment or two and then looked up. "Well," he said, "if I had admitted it, there would have been a row and it might have got to Headquarters; an that would have been very unhealthy for me after that photograph business."

"Might have lost you your M.C.," I suggested cuttingly, for I was angry with him.

He looked up sharply at that and seemed about to make some quick retort, but the look of annoyance passed, and he laughed and shrugged his shoulders. "Oh, I'm not worrying about that," he said.

III

The Somme battle dragged on, but the hoped-for breakthrough and return to open warfare did not come. We had one or two false alarms, and the battalion created some records in rapid concentration; but the gap through which we were to have pushed did not appear, and as the possibility of its appearance grew more and more remote, Corps Headquarters became less insistent on keeping us together. At first companies only had been detached, but now platoons and even sections were sent off on various duties. B Company was scattered over the whole Corps area on various jobs for the A.P.M., whose hand Hubbard licked with dog-like fidelity; and A Company also was split up. Gurney's platoon was away east of Montauban, Dodd and his platoon had taken over Pagan's job of manning the Corps observation posts, and my own platoon alone was with Company Headquarters doing odd jobs, chiefly burial fatigues.

Before long, however, orders of a different sort came from Crops. A biggish attack was coming off, and Corps wanted a platoon for a job of observation from a point in the first day's objective. G. B. was away when the orders arrived, and my own platoon being the only one available, I made the necessary preparations at once. But to my surprise, when he returned he said that he himself would take up my platoon and that I was to remain behind with the C.Q.M.S., sanitary men, and other odds and ends.

I was much annoyed at this order. Not that I was a fire-eater: Heaven forbid! The job was likely to prove as unpleasant as the last, and, like most men who have wandered about in a modern battle, I was not pining for repetition. But it was my own platoon that was going up, and it was my job to lead it. It would be employed on a job calling for special knowledge such as we were supposed to possess and which I believed I possessed, and my professional pride was hurt by this possible imputation that I was not up to the job.

G. B. reassured me on this point, but he would give no satisfactory reason for his action; and I was driven to the conclusion, rightly or wrongly, that in this stunt, which if successful would earn for us the praise of Corps Headquarters, he intended to take all the kudos for himself.

The platoon marched out at dusk, and when it had disappeared in the gathering gloom, I returned to my tent in a very touchy mood.

It returned next evening, or rather what was left of it returned, in charge of my sergeant; and it was from him that I learned what had happened. They had reached their objective—an exposed position—to be pounded heavily and counter-attacked. During the afternoon, when things were a little quieter, G. B. had taken two men and crawled out to a broken building that lay in front of their position. He returned after an absence of about half an hour to report some movement of the enemy, and then crawled back again with his servant to the two men he had left on watch. One of these came in with further information about twenty minutes later, and then an hour went by without any communication or sign from them.

At the end of an hour and a half the sergeant became anxious, and taking a man with him, crawled out to reconnoitre. On reaching the stunted, jagged walls of the broken building the first object that met their eyes was G. B.'s servant dead with a bullet through his forehead. Farther on they came upon the body of one of the other two men with one side of his face blown away. Cautiously continuing their exploration, they came upon the second man lying upon his back on a heap of brick rubble with a bayonet wound in his throat, but there was no sign of G. B. At considerable risk to themselves they crawled right round the building without finding any trace of him, and only when a minenwerfer began pitching flying pigs into the ruins and a bullet through his water-bottle warned the sergeant that a sniper had spotted them did he abandon the search.

They were rather heavily attacked soon after he rejoined the platoon, and I gathered that there was an unpleasant mix-up of bomb and bayonet; but he managed to hold his ground, though when things had quietened down again my poor old platoon had been reduced to something less than half its strength, Eventually a unit came up to relieve them, and he had thereupon got his men out safely and come straight back to me to report. That was his story.

I questioned him very closely about G. B., but both he and the man who had been with him were positive that G. B. could not have been in the ruined building or its immediate neighbourhood. They declared that had he been lying wounded they could not have failed to have found him. They had found his servant and the other two men at once and had spent nearly twenty minutes searching for G. B. The three men were dead, and the sergeant was positive that the third man had been killed by a bayonet jab.

"Jerry must have crept up and rushed 'em, sir," said my sergeant. "There was a lot of heavy stuff coming over all the afternoon, and we wouldn't have heard a little row like that. I told the Captain that it was very risky, but he would go; and now Jerry has got 'im, sir."

We still half hoped that G. B. might yet turn up, but the days went by, and it became evident that my sergeant's view of the situation was the true one.

G. B. was posted as missing.

IV

The Battle of the Somme dragged on into the Battle of the Ancre, and it was not till December that the Corps came out for a rest and we found ourselves in billets in a little village not far from Doullens. Hubbard's tireless cultivation of the Provost-Marshal bore fruit, for he left us to become an A.P.M. himself, and Pagan was given the command of B Company, an event of which he informed me in his usual fashion by an apt quotation from *Henry V.* Harding, our American M.O., also left us to become one of the big guns, I believe, in a base hospital. I went on my long overdue leave and found that Helen, though as comradely as ever, could not be induced to become Mrs. Baron even by the glamour of my three pips and the mention in dispatches which I had collected. Indeed the prospect of that event now seemed remote. I was rather badly hipped and in consequence, childishly perhaps, refused to write to her. But I will pass over these purely personal matters.

In the early spring the Canadians began that offensive which resulted in the capture of Vimy Ridge, and when they came out for a well-earned rest, our corps took over from them, and we moved up to the bleak hillsides just north of Arras. The ensuing attacks took us well over the ridge and on to the plain beyond, and there we stuck. The battle had reached that stage which we had now learned to regard as inevitable, the stage in which the enemy, having been driven back out of reach of our concentration of guns, had had time to mass his own guns and bring up reserves— the stage at which fresh operations on a large scale are necessary for any further advance. But G.H.Q. had learnt by experience the costly futility of hammering away at an enemy well prepared and forewarned; and they transferred the attack to another sector, leaving our line very thinly held.

Meanwhile the battalion had been equipped with Lewis guns, and we had one to each platoon. Six of our guns were always in the line, which, to tell the truth, was shockingly undermanned. One night the enemy put down a box barrage on us. In a box barrage, it must be explained, the shells pitch not only on the fire trench but on a line some distance behind it and to the right and left as well, thus cutting one off on all sides from reinforcements and placing one in a "box." The object of this device is to allow a raiding party to come over and to ensure that they will not be disturbed whilst dealing with the unfortunate troops in the box.

It was unpleasant while it lasted. Our parapet was blown up in several places, and one of my two guns was put out of action in the first few minutes. I spent an anxious time dodging along the empty fire-bays between the two guns. My one remaining gun was twice blown off the parapet, but my stout Number One got it back again into position and fired drum after drum into no-man's-land as fast as Number Two could ram them on the magazine post. He must have done a lot of execution, for when the raiding party loomed up on the heels of the barrage, there were very few of them.

The other gun team were working the bolts of their rifles like fields, and I believe that only two of the enemy got into the trench. One of them jumped on top of one of my men and then went down under a smashing blow from a steel helmet, delivered sideways. The other, an officer, with an automatic pistol in his hand, shot two of my men as he stood on the parapet. Then he jumped, and I let drive at him with my service revolver. He came down sideways and lay motionless in the bottom of the trench.

My other team got their gun firing again, but no more Germans appeared. One of the two men shot by the Bosche officer was dead with a bullet through the eye; the other had a flesh wound in the neck. I put a field-dressing on him and turned to have a look at the officer. I pulled the cumbersome German-pattern steel helmet off his head and switched on my torch.

It was then that for the first time in my life I doubted my sanity. My shaking thumb caused the torch-light to flicker, and in the wavering light the pale face appeared to be grimacing at me. Was this a preliminary sympton of a faint? I asked myself. I leaned back against the solid wall of the trench and was grateful for the support. The strain of those last few minutes must have been too much for me, I suppose, and I was "seeing things"; for the bloodless face of the German officer with closed eyes and head resting on a couple of empty Lewis-gun magazines seemed to me to be the face of G. B. I could even see the scar across his cheek that he had carried ever since that desperate stand of his on the Somme.

I knelt there staring at the man and trying to pull myself together, telling myself that this was not G. B. With my own eyes I had seen this German officer shoot two of my men, one of whom was an old A Company man and had served under G. B. in the old days. And then I remember a sudden dazzling light, a feeling of warmth, and a sensation of falling, falling… and no more.

V

When I opened my eyes I perceived a long brown level plain stretching from me and a broad low black arch silhouetted against the distant sky. Gradually my muddled brain began to function, and on reopening my eyes I slowly realized that the brown plain was an army blanket and the black arch the iron foot of a bed. I perceived with vague surprise that I was in a long hut and that there were other beds placed against the opposite wall with military regularity; and an army nursing sister was bending over one of them.

I closed my eyes and wandered again: I saw the German officer lying in the bottom of the trench and the face that was the face of G. B. A cold sweat broke out upon my forehead. I must pull myself together, I thought: I was losing grip—seeing things. A sign of nerves at the breaking-point. I must stick it; if the Bosche came over again… And then I opened my eyes and remembered where I was. I had done with all that for a time. A hospital now… Blighty perhaps…

But I was too tired to feel thrilled, and I dozed off into oblivion again.

PART III

"G. B."

CHAPTER XI

I

FRANCE, September 1916. The hot sun beat down on a shallow valley north of Bray-sur-Somme. A few months ago it had been a pleasant green, secluded valley, but now it was a dusty, noisy town. The level stretch of parched earth between the slopes was bare of grass and scored with wheel-ruts; and where it broadened out into an amphitheatre, rows of posts and been driven into the earth, and, tethered to the ropes between them, two hundred horses shook their heads and twitched their glossy hides in ceaseless efforts to dislodge the persecuting flies.

In one of the flanking slopes a line of dug-outs had been constructed, and their tunnelled entrances, flanked with flattened sandbags of the shape and colour of stone blocks, resembled the mortarless passages of an Aztec temple. On the slopes themselves a motley town had sprung up. Belltents, Stevenson huts, canvas-screened latrines, shacks of empty ammunition boxes, bivouacs and tarpaulins spilled from the crests to the dry, rutted track between. A thick barbed-wire fence ten feet high enclosed a large rectangle on a roughly level platform half-way up the southern slope. A similar but smaller enclosure stood near by. A hundred or more prisoners, all with the same close-cropped pale hair, faded grey uniforms, and dirty, calf-high boots, slept, sat, smoked, or stood sullenly within the larger enclosure; some half-dozen officers wearing rakish caps and long grey tight-waisted overcoats with gay-coloured facings occupied the smaller. A couple of bored British Tommies in steel helmets and with bayoneted rifles slung over one shoulder were on guard, and a number of loiterers in shirt-sleeves were watching through the wire a newly arrived prisoner with arms raised above his head being searched by a sergeant.

Men came and went in the mushroom town. A man in shirtsleeves sitting on an upturned bucket peeled potatoes into a large iron dixie and whistled a slow, lugubrious tune. Two men in shirt-sleeves and steel helmets were fusing a box of Mills grenades. A kilted piper marched to and fro like an automaton playing some skirling pibroch of the Highlands; and near his beat sat a sunburnt man, naked to the waist, plying needle and thread on a grey army shirt and proclaiming in song that the lady of his affection had an eye of glass but a heart of gold.

High overhead flew a German plane, a white fleecy-looking object against the hazy blue sky, and an invisible anti-aircraft battery behind the hill was "archying" it. Bang-bang, bangbang went the guns; and then pop-pop, pop-pop sounded far overhead. The tiny plane glided out from four white puffs of cotton-wool, banked steeply, and shot swiftly back eastwards.

Outside a long brown tarpaulin shack an officer in shirt-sleeves and light khaki drill shorts lounged in a canvas chair. A copy of *La Vie Parisienne* rested upon his bare sunburnt knees. Another officer, clothed also in shorts but with the three stars of a captain upon his tunic-cuff, came from under the tarpaulin and halted by the chair.

"My leave has come through, Baron," he said, stroking his close-clipped moustache with the stem of his pipe.

The officer in the chair looked up and tilted forward his cap to shade his eyes from the sun.

"Good for you, G. B.," he said. "But I thought there was no leave going."

Bang-bang, bang-bang went the guns again, and pop-pop, pop-pop came the answering shell bursts high up in the sky.

The other took off his khaki cap and stroked his short crisp hair. "Well, there isn't really," he answered. "Except for the gilded staff. Corps H.Q. got a twinge of conscience apparently and bunged along this vacancy to us; and the C.O. sent it to me. But for some damn silly reason or another I have to report at Domart before six pip emma, and some antediluvian vehicle takes us to Abbeville. It means lorry-jumping from here to Domart, I suppose."

"Domart! That's t'other side of Amiens, isn't it? A bit north though. There's a lorry route from Albert to Acheux, I know," said Baron. "And there's another from there to Candas. I believe. That's not far from Domart."

"Anyway, I shan't have too much time," answered Bretherton. "Brewster! Brewster!"

A private soldier in grey shirt-sleeves came running at the call.

"Brewster, I'm off on leave toute suite. Clean the buttons on my best tunic and give my belt a rub, will you?"

The man took the belt and disappeared beneath the tarpaulin.

"You are in charge of the shop, Baron. All the bumph is in the company office, but you have seen most of it; there's nothing needs explaining."

Bretherton strode off and entered his tent a few yards away. He washed in a canvas bucket and changed his shorts for riding-breeches and field-boots. Then he packed into a leather-seamed haversack pyjamas, khaki collars and socks, shaving and washing kit, a pair of khaki slacks, and a pair of brown shoes. Before the packing was finished, Brewster, the soldier-servant, came in with the belt and tunic over his arm. Bretherton put on the tunic with its glittering buttons and buckled the glossy belt round his waist. He slung the haversack over his shoulder, put the yellow leave warrant into a breast pocket, and picked up a trench-coat.

"Cheerio, Brewster," he said. "Mr. Baron will let you know when I'm coming back. If we move meantime, hand my kit in to the Q.M.S."

Outside the tent an officer with a very fresh boyish face was talking to Baron.

"Hear you are off to Blighty, G. B.," he said as Bretherton emerged. "Lucky dog! I have a little souvenir for the mater. I wonder if you would deliver it for me—or post it if it's too much of a bore. But my people would be jolly glad to see you—and put you up if you care to. Half an hour or thereabouts from Piccadilly. I have put the address on it."

Bretherton put the parcel into the pocket of his trench-coat.

"Right-oh, Gurney," he said. "Be very glad to look them up—and tell them all about their little David—what! Cheerio, you fellows. Don't finish the war before I get back."

"Give my love to dear old Piccadilly," said Baron.

"Marble Arch, Bond Street, Oxford Circus—change for Piccadilly," chanted Gurney, and added wistfully: "Lucky devil!"

Bretherton hurried off between the motley collection of huts down to the dusty valley-track and climbed the opposite slope. A short distance farther on, he reached the Albert road; and presently saw the town itself below him, a medley of roofs and chimneys buttressing the devastated square where broken houses gaped roofless to the sky and the Hanging Virgin of Albert upon the lofty battered brick church tower hung golden in the sunlight. He passed through the narrow streets of the town and crossed the shell-pocked, brick-littered square to the Doullens road.

Three hours later he climbed stiffly from a lorry at the crossroads in Candas. He beat the white dust from his uniform and set off to walk the few remaining miles. He was glad to breathe air untainted by petrol fumes and the smell of warm oil. It was real country here: not the kind of country just behind the line, where every village was filled with troops and every plot of uncultivated ground exuded huts, horse-lines, canteens, or latrines. There was not a hut in sight; only peaceful fields and green woods dozing in the afternoon sunlight. A car gave him a lift, and he was carried swiftly along the sunny country road and down the steep hill into the clean, broad, quiet street of Domart, where white-washed cottages snuggled against the hills and the flag of a reserve Army Corps hung above the door of the Hôtel de Ville.

II

At dusk a lorry loaded up in the village street. Bretherton sat in front with the driver and a sergeant; the dozen men in the body of the lorry with their packs and steel helmets piled in a corner were happy and sang their mournful, sentimental songs. They rolled out of the village and on through the quiet country roads. Darkness settled upon the fields, and from the front seat nothing was visible except the illuminated, uneven surface of the road ahead and the white wall of a cottage or barn as it sprang up suddenly in the glare of the headlights. From behind came fitfully the chorus of song timed to the rumble of the lorry.

Bretherton found the darkness, the cool air, the singing, and the rumble of the wheels soothing, and he dozed throughout the journey. Presently they were bumping over cobbles, and he opened his eyes to find that they were passing through the narrow streets of Abbeville. Outside the station the lorry stopped; the men clumped down to the road, passed out packs, rifles, and steel helmets, and trooped into the station.

It was past midnight when he reached Boulogne. He went to the Officers' Club for a bed, but all were taken. He tried the Meurice, the Folkestone, and several other hotels without success. A military police-sergeant he met in the deserted Rue Thiers suggested a small hotel on the other side of the harbour. He tramped back to the dark open space and chill wind that was the harbour, found the hotel, and was told that there was no room free, but that he could share one if he cared to do so. He closed with this offer, and was shown up a narrow flight of stairs to a small room at the top of the house. By the dim light of one candle he perceived a sam-brown belt and tunic with one star on the cuff hanging over the back of a chair; a pair of field-boots and riding-breeches lay on the floor. In one of the two beds a fresh-faced boy with tousled fair hair lay asleep in his khaki shirt. Bretherton undressed quietly, blew out the candle, and crept into the other bed.

III

Bretherton strode happily along the quay in the morning sunlight. The leave-boat lay moored between two cargo-boats. She was painted black from stem to stern, and a few white whisps of salt encrusted on her funnels told of a recent dirty crossing. He handed half of his yellow leave-warrant to the sergeant-major at the gangway and went aboard. A tip to a deck-hand secured a chair on the boat deck. He put his lifebelt underneath the chair, and filled in his embarkation card with indelible pencil. Two boats moved slowly out of the harbour, and then the gangways were drawn in, and the leave-boat slid into the fairway. It slipped swiftly between the piers at the harbour mouth and began to rise and fall to the motion of the sea.

A mile or more from the shore two destroyers steamed restlessly to and fro, and then took position on either beam of the little convoy of three ships. Lifebelts were put on, and half a dozen men with rifles were posted along the decks to fire at prowling periscopes.

The long, low destroyers buried themselves in the green seas, rose again, and shook themselves free from water like dogs. Cape Gris-Nez fell slowly astern. The two cargo-ships ahead wallowed drunkenly in the seas and trailed two long black plumes of smoke across the sky. Far away to port an observation balloon, towed by a destroyer, was hunting for submarines or mines. A blimp hove out of the distance and circled above the convoy; and an airman in leather coat and crash helmet waved his hand from the cockpit.

Bretherton went below in search of the Pullman man. The saloon was full of officers drinking and smoking and talking in high spirits; nearly everybody had met some acquaintance and was swopping experiences or discussing what shows one ought to see in London.

England was in sight when he returned to the deck; the white cliffs showed faintly across the heaving waste of grey-flecked water. Smudges of smoke showed where the ships of the coastwise traffic passed at the regulation number per hour. Three miles from Folkestone the two destroyers circled the convoy and went bucking back towards the French coast. The blimp had gone to roost somewhere on the cliffs above the harbour. One of the two cargo-boats steamed off up the coast in the direction of Dover; the other passed behind the breakwater. The leave-boat followed her in and berthed beside the train that stood waiting on the quay. The troops shouldered pack or haversack and streamed down the gangways.

Bretherton found his seat in the Pullman and studied the menu with leisurely enjoyment. The train moved slowly from the harbour through the streets of the town. Children climbed upon the gates of level-crossings and shouted shrilly as it went by; carters waved their whips and shouted unintelligible witticisms; women leaned from open windows and waved handkerchiefs. The leave-train from the front was passing by.

CHAPTER XII

I

BEHIND the barriers of Victoria Station the same eager throng of mothers, wives, and lovers awaited the arrival of the leave-train as had waited there every day for the past two years. Among them were others, neither relations nor friends, but kindly people who liked to share at second hand the fierce joy of those reunions, and grateful citizens past fighting age who came to murmur a word of thanks to the fighting men or to press a present upon a grinning Tommy. Predatory women were there too in search of prey, and idle sightseers who ran excitedly to another platform, as to a rival show, when a long hospital train slid slowly in.

But Bretherton had neither friends nor relatives awaiting him, and he threaded his way through the throng on the platform to join the crowd that waited on the pavement outside the station. Every minute a taxi with an urchin hanging out from the footboard descended the slope with a pleasant crackling sound of wheels on tarred wood blocks, loaded up, and whirred off. But the supply was unequal to the demand, and ten minutes elapsed before Bretherton secured a car.

He had been warned that he would find London crowded, but he had not expected to spend two hours in a fruitless search for hotel accommodation. The taxi driver insisted on dropping him at the end of twenty minutes, and he had to continue the search on foot.

After tea he found himself again in the neighbourhood of Victoria, and his attention was attracted by a party of half a dozen men who were moving parallel with him on the side of the road. They were in full marching order—enamel mugs dangling from haversacks, steel helmets under pack-straps, and slung rifles with khaki breech-covers. But it was the way in which they were marching that arrested his attention.

They were on the right side of the road, and that in itself was enough to show that they had come recently from France. The traffic streamed past them on one side, and on the other the throng of pedestrians moved along the pavement or loitered by the shop windows; but the busy life of London passed unheeded by these men. With heads thrust forward, expressionless faces, and hands clutching the web braces of their equipment, they trudged along with the slow, fatalistic, beast-of-burden step that was so familiar on the tracks leading to the trenches. And at their head walked a guide; not a man in fatigue dress and gas-helmet nor an old-young subaltern, but a girl in the neat blue uniform of a V.A.D., with head erect and elastic step. Presently she led off the road across the pavement, and the six trudging figures followed her like sheep up the steps of a large building which had been turned into a soldier's home.

Bretherton walked on, thinking of Joan of Arc at the head of the dejected veterans of the English wars, till a short distance beyond the building he saw an empty taxi coming towards him. He signalled to the driver, and as he stood waiting for it to come up he saw the little V.A.D. run back down the steps of the soldiers' home and walk quickly towards him. Then suddenly she glanced at the watch on her wrist and broke into a run.

He acted upon impulse. He had opened the door of the taxi, but he left it, and as she drew level with him he saluted and said, "I'm afraid you have made yourself late by showing those fellows the soldiers' home. Won't you take my taxi?"

She looked up at him quickly, and there was a glint of suspicion in her grey eyes; but his face reassured her apparently, for she smiled frankly and said, "That's awfully good of you. I am so late. But taxis are scarce; couldn't we share it?" Her voice was low, clear, and unhurried.

"By all means, if you don't mind," he said.

She gave the address of one of the many improvised hospitals, and he followed her into the cab.

"It was very good of you to guide those poor fellows," he said conversationally.

She turned a face full of distress towards him. "Oh, weren't they too tragic!" she cried. "I found them outside Victoria Station—standing like dumb animals in a market. They are going north, and there is no train till the early morning. The soldiers' home is full, but they will be looked after."

Bretherton nodded. "They will get a hot drink and something to eat, anyway. They have had a rough time by the look of them." There was silence for a moment, and then he said, "London is very full. I haven't found even a soldiers' home yet."

She turned from the window. "Can't you get in any-where:" she inquired.

"I've tried dozens of places, and so far I've had no luck."

"But that's serious at this time of the day. Would you like me to ask at the hospital? They may know of some place."

"That's very good of you, but please don't bother. A sub-altern of mine lives at Woodside Park, and I'm sure his people would put me up, if necessary. But you might be able to tell me the best way of getting there."

She laughed. "Rather! I live at Woodside Park. You want the Piccadilly Tube."

"Then you may know his people; Gurney is the name."

Her eyebrows went up in two little arches of surprise. "Know them! Yes, I know them. Why, David Gurney is my brother. I am his sister, Helen."

"Good Lord!" exclaimed Bretherton, sitting up in surprise.

"And of course you are G. B.—sorry! I mean Captain Bretherton." She regarded him with engaging friendliness. "I feel I know you awfully well, though we've never met before. I feel I know you all—Melford, Dicky Baron, Pagan, Dodd, Hubbard, that nice American doctor, and that awful man Groucher." She clasped her hands round one knee. "And to think that you are the great G. B.!" She examined him with her small head on one side like a bird's.

"And to think that you are young Gurney's sister!" he retorted smiling. "You are very much alike."

"We are twins," she said with twinkling eyes. "Of course we will put you up. We will kill the fatted calf for you.

You are rather a hero, you know. We have heard all about you from Davy. Davy's friends are my friends; and as for Mummy and Daddy—well, you know what parents are in these warlike days! They will probably weep over you."

"You are very kind," he said.

Her little face became very earnest. "You have been kind to Davy," she answered simply.

She was on duty till nine o'clock, and Bretherton suggested calling for her at that hour so that they could travel to Woodside Park together. She agreed, and he left her on the steps of a large house that had been turned into a hospital by the generosity of its owner.

II

Bretherton was welcomed very warmly by Gurney's people. In those trying days parents were greedy of first-hand news of their soldier-sons, and their sons' comrades-in-arms were treated as honoured members of the family. He was pressed to stay, and willingly consented. He played tennis with Helen in her limited spare time, and an evening which she had free from the hospital duty they spent at the theatre. And he passed quiet half-hours in the study discussing the military situation with Mr. Gurney senior, an alert, white-haired man who was an enthusiastic member of the Royal Defence Corps, known as the Gorgeous Wrecks from the letters G.R. on their armlets.

On Sunday afternoon, which Helen had free, they walked across the fields towards Totteridge, but a sudden rain-squall drove them to take shelter in an inn. A piano stood in one corner of the parlour, and she insisted on his playing.

"Do not pretend that you cannot," she said severely, "for I know that you can."

Obediently he played, passing from one air to another—grand opera, Gilbert and Sullivan, ballads, and selections from the latest revues—while the rain beat against the window-panes and the little low-ceilinged parlour was in semi-darkness, Helen sat in an old horsehair armchair near the piano, occasionly singing the words of a song and suggesting an air when he was at a loss.

"Play 'Tipperary,'" she cried as he hesitated with his fingers caressing the keys.

Obediently he played the music-hall air that had become the marching-song of the first Expeditionary Force. Helen had risen from her chair and stood beside him singing the words.

"I wish I were a man," she said suddenly, when he had ended.

He turned on the stool to look at her. "Why?" he demanded.

"A woman is so useless in a time like this." There was a faraway look in her eyes. He was strumming the air again very softly with one hand.

"I think it's splendid the way men back one another up in times of danger. I wish I were a man."

"And what would you do if you were one?" he asked, amused at her earnestness.

She turned to the window and stood watching the rain running down the panes. "I should be a private in A Company," she said at last.

"Splendid! And why A Company?" he asked.

"Because I feel that it is mine. I feel I know its officers, its men, its spirit. I am my brother's twin. It is the best company in the battalion, and its company commander…"

"Well, what about him?" asked Bretherton, swinging round to face her.

She turned from the window, and her intense, serious look gave way to a mischievous smile.

"Davy says he is a woman-hater," she ended.

He made a grimace. "I shall run Davy in for 'conduct to the prejudice of good order and military discipline,' " he grinned. "Now you play."

She moved to the piano and began to play softly. And presently she began to sing in her clear little voice: "Just a song at twilight."

Bretherton listened enchanted, and turning from the window saw her at the piano, flooded in the sunlight which had at last broken through the rain-clouds—a picture framed in the old parlour with its low-beamed ceiling and antimacassared chairs.

He crossed the room and stood beside her. "That makes me think of what is going on out there—in the line," he said. "Contrast, I suppose. Out there we get a song of hate at twilight—and dawn."

She looked up at his serious face with its contracted brows.

"Don't wish to be a man," he said suddenly. "Remain a woman; and comfort some poor broken devil who comes back."

Her grey eyes followed him as he turned abruptly away and slowly unrolled his tobacco-pouch. She struck a note two or three times with her finger. "Sometimes I think war is almost worth all the bloodshed and filth," she said irrelevantly.

III

On the last night of his leave he fetched her from the hospital in a taxi, and they sped through the dim streets, to which the blue-shaded lamps gave a ghostly air.

"It is funny to think that to-morrow you will be with my brother," she said.

"You are awfully alike," he answered thoughtfully; "both in looks and ways."

"We are twins, you know," she reminded him. "I believe that when you are with me you feel that you are with him, and so you don't hate too much being with a woman."

"I say!" he protested. "I suppose I have to thank Master David for this reputation."

She nodded. "Do you know how he described you in one of his letters? He said, 'G. B. is a thundering good soldier and a topping fellow, but he's a woman-hater!'"

"That's not true," he protested. "The truth is I have always been busy getting on with my job and I've had no time for philandering. It's true I'm not one of those fellows who fall in love with the first pretty face they meet and ten minutes later fall in love with another one. But it does not follow that I haven't the capacity for appreciating one."

"I was only ragging you," she said seriously. "And I only hope that when *the* girl does come along she will appreciate you as you deserve."

He gazed out of the window at the passing blue-shaded lamps for a moment or two. And then he said briefly, "She has come along."

"Oh! I had no idea," she said gently. "And—have you asked her?"

Again he was silent for a moment or two, and then he replied slowly and gently, "No; I'm asking her now."

She shot a sudden, startled look at him. "You mean … me?"

He nodded. She saw his face fitfully in the passing lights, solemn and serious.

"But—but you've known me only a week."

He laughed unsteadily. "Is it really only a week? It might be years… all my life. Does it matter how long?"

She was silent.

"I… I'm in deadly earnest… Helen, speak to me."

"What can I say—what can I say?" she answered in a stifled voice. "I hardly know you."

"Of course not," he answered gently. "Of course not. I don't expect you to be like me. I'm a clumsy great lout; I'm not used to women. But I'm going back to-morrow, and I had to tell you. Poor little girl! But you like me a little…?"

"Yes." She was holding her lower lip between her teeth and staring out of the window.

"Well then, perhaps…"

"I like you; yes," she interrupted gently. "But…"

"But what? Is there anyone else?"

She was silent for a moment, and then turned her head and looked at him. "In a way—yes."

"Ah!" He made a little gesture with his hands. "I'm sorry. You must forgive me. I didn't know."

She sat gazing with contracted brows at the swiftly passing lights. "Listen," she said suddenly. "It is only fair that I should tell you. Dicky Baron when he was home on leave— he asked me the same question. I told him that I didn't know… and I don't know now. I like him immensely, but…" She gave a little helpless shrug. "And we left it at that."

He took her hand and kissed it. "I understand," he said. "But I'm afraid I have spoilt your evening, little girl."

He took a cigarette from his case and squared his shoulders with an unconscious gesture.

She glanced at him quickly. "For God's sake, Gerard, don't say that!" There was a catch in her voice. "I shall cry in a moment."

He turned a puzzled face towards her. "You must not do that. Why should you?"

She beat her knees with her little clenched fists. "Why?" she exclaimed. "Why! Oh, for myself, for you, for the war, for life… for everything."

And then she tilted her chin and laughed a trifle unsteadily. "That is the girl-twin speaking. I must be the soldier-twin. Swear for me Gerard. Swear!" she cried fiercely. "Good round Flanders oaths. Let us damn fortune together."

IV

Helen saw him off at Victoria on the following day. Here and there upon the crowded platform a white-faced girl stood in silent misery gazing at her bronzed, khaki-clad companion with eyes that spoke the unspeakable; and he fidgeted on his feet and cursed softly beneath his breath. But there were no scenes. The men's train was the first to leave, and a half-stifled cheer went up as it moved slowly out. And then the whistle blew for the officers' train. Bretherton got into his compartment.

"Look after my young brother," said Helen as the train began to move.

"I will," he assured her. "And Dicky Baron too," he added.

She thanked him with a look. "Take care of yourself, Gerard," were her last words. He smiled and waved his hand, and withdrew his head from the window only when the train rounded a curve and the diminutive figure with the fluttering handkerchief was hidden from view.

CHAPTER XIII

I

IT was late in the afternoon on the following day when Bretherton trudged over the slope of the hill past a working party parading in clean fatigue and gas-helmets, and saw the prisoners-of-war cage and its grey cargo in the crowded valley below him. An aeroplane droned overhead, and he heard again the familiar rumble of the guns; and not till then did the depression that had accompanied him throughout the journey from Victoria lift.

This was the life he knew and understood. Crude and elementary perhaps, but straightforward. A man's job. He was unfitted for boudoirs and drawing-rooms, he told himself. He had no understanding of the subtleties of love-making or of the tortuous paths to a woman's heart. To him love was a passion as elementary as a bayonet charge. Leave was a mistake; an unsettling interruption of the normal routine of war. And he wished devoutly that he could erase the memory of this last one from the tablets of his mind.

But this was the life he understood; and he would throw himself the more whole-heartedly into it now that he was so much an alien in those unreal realms of peace. And therefore he was almost happy when he opened the door of the mess-hut and was greeted with shouts of: "Hullo, G. B.! Had a good leave?" "How's old Piccadilly?" and "Have they heard there's a war on yet?"

Here nothing was changed. There were the same old jokes about quartermasters and the staff, the same old

worries about ridiculous returns and impossible operation orders, and the same old smell of whisky, tobacco, and
chloride of lime. It was the same old war.

He waded through the chits that had come into the company office during his absence, picked up the thread of
company and battalion events, and quickly dropped back into
the worries and responsibilities of a company commander.

The Somme battle thundered on its staggering course.
Rattling tanks heaved their monstrous shapes slowly over
the mud. Day after day the guns sustained their hound-like
baying, and furiously and without respite men sweated to
answer the never-ending call for ammunition. Day after
day the rain poured down upon the lunar-like landscape;
and day after day the casualties mounted up. Day after
day the waves of steel-hatted figures floundered across the
quivering, glutinous ground; and day after day a hundred
yards or more of gory, stinking, pulverized hillside was
wrested from the enemy.

A Company was dismembered: Baron's platoon alone
remained intact. The other two platoons were scattered up
and down the corps area; and Bretherton spent his days
visiting detachments, motor-cycling over pot-holed roads,
trudging over shell-pocked hillsides, or floundering along
waterlogged trenches.

II

He returned to his headquarters one afternoon to find
that corps had ordered a platoon into the line. An attack
was to be made the next morning to straighten a dangerous

salient, and a platoon was to go up to the support line and, as soon as the attacking troops reached their objective, was to move to a position indicated by Corps Headquarters and establish an observation post there.

Baron, in his company commander's absence, had given the necessary orders and had taken it for granted that he would accompany his platoon, which was the only one available. But Bretherton decreed otherwise. There were no bonds to hold him to the peace-time life, to which in the nature of things all could not hope to return. But Baron must return; his life was entangled with the happiness of others in that post-war, peace-time England.

Thus Bretherton reasoned. As company commander his detailing of subalterns for particular duties might be a matter of life and death to them; and no conscientious commander would, without grave reason, substitute one officer for another. In the dangerous game of war each must take his chance in fair rotation. But it was permissible surely to make himself the substitute.

He himself would take up the platoon, and Baron should remain behind with the details.

Baron did not take kindly to the arrangement. He came into the hut of ammunition boxes that served as the company office, where Bretherton in his muddy field-boots was conning the orders from Corps Headquarters.

"The Sergeant-Major tells me that you are taking up my platoon," he began.

"Um!" Bretherton nodded without looking up.

"And I am to remain here with the details?"

"That's the idea."

Baron picked up a map and put it down again. "Is there any need to leave an officer? The Q.M.S. is here."

"Quite. But there's no need to send two officers with the platoon."

"But it's my platoon, G. B."

"Quite." Bretherton turned over a sheet.

"What is the idea, then?"

Bretherton shrugged his shoulders and threw the sheaf of orders on to the little table.

"You've been out all day, G. B. The men are parading in an hour, and you've had nothing to eat yet."

Bretherton glanced at his wrist-watch. "Well, then, run along to the mess like a good chap and tell them to have something ready for me in ten minutes."

Baron did not move; he stood playing with the half-dozen rounds of revolver ammunition that lay on the table. "Do you think I'm not up to my job? Is that the reason?"

"My dear fellow, of course not. Don't talk such rot."

Baron was frowning at the revolver round he was turning over and over in his hand. Suddenly he threw it decisively on the table and looked straight at Bretherton. "Look here, G. B., this isn't fair on me. It looks uncommonly as though you wanted to take all the kudos for yourself. You've got your M.C. What are you after now—a D.S.O.? You might give someone else a chance. It's my platoon and…"

"Mr. Baron," broke in Bretherton in his orderly-room voice, "I should be glad if you would refrain from criticizing my orders. I want you to inspect the platoon's gas-helmets when they fall in; and just let the mess know I'm back, will you?"

Baron allowed himself a tiny grimace of anger. He clicked his heels and saluted. "Very good, sir," he said, and left the hut abruptly.

Bretherton's eyes remained fixed thoughtfully on the doorway for some seconds after Baron had disappeared through it; and then with a little shrug of his shoulders he turned again to the map and orders.

III

The platoon marched out at dusk. It was a moonless night and very quiet, except that every five minutes to the second a gigantic sack of coals was tipped down a chute in a hollow away to the right: Fritz shelling some target in his usual methodical manner. The cool night-breeze had a faint, sweet aroma of pear-drops. Occasionally by some copse or hollow a lightning-like flash illuminated the track, and was followed by the sudden bang of an invisible gun and the retreating shuffle of the shell. Then all was quiet till the next sack of coals was tipped into the distant hollow. Sometimes the quiet intervals were broken by the stutter of a machine gun, and one heard the rat-tat-tat-tat-tat-tat-tat grow loud and faint alternately as the gun traversed, and then it ceased as abruptly as it had begun, leaving the night the quieter for the sudden interruption. And occasionally a distant heavy shell detonated with the lone, muffled solemnity of a passing bell.

The party halted in a shallow, sombre valley where the ground was pitted with shell-holes and littered with the debris of battle. Bretherton checked his position by a wood on his right—a number of ragged, leafless stumps like roughly trimmed clothes-props that showed against the sky—and gave the order to fall out. In a few shallow little burrows that had been scratched in the hillside the men made themselves as comfortable as possible and snatched a few hours' sleep.

They were up and on the move at dawn. Little files of steel-hatted figures were dribbling to and fro across the desolate valley that lay with all its scars and disfigurements revealed in the cold light of dawn. The guns were playing one of their favourite pieces, forte and allegro. Above the splintered poles of the leafless wood, tiny stars winked and little cotton-wool-like balls of white smoke appeared, grew rapidly in size, and drifted away on the breeze. Two or three contact planes flew low over the flayed hill-slopes.

Number One Platoon reached its allotted position with the loss of only five casualties. The sector consisted of a number of deep shell-holes on a pulverized slope, connected by hastily scratched trenches, barely deep enough to allow a prone man to pass unseen. Fifty yards to the front were the ruins of a building of some kind. A few mounds of bricks with a ragged gable projecting from one of them and here and there a jagged wall a few feet above the ground was all that remained. The officer from whom Bretherton took over said that he had a post of three men there. "We found it too unhealthy for more," he explained. "Fritz keeps pitching stuff into it all the time. And besides, you have a better field of fire here, and some wire."

Bretherton posted two men in the ruins, and when he had organized his little sector, went out to them himself. He spent the greater part of the afternoon with them, crawling back from time to time to his main position. The Germans had a trench-mortar close by, which every now and then threw flying pigs among the brick-heaps; and he determined to reconnoitre its position with a view to putting it out of action when night fell.

Followed by his servant, he crawled out from his main position towards the ruined building. On the far side of the first heap of bricks he came upon one of his men with the side of his face blown away. He crawled on through the rubble and debris to find the other man. Suddenly he saw an arm swing up from behind a stump of wall, and the next moment a German egg-bomb struck him on the forehead without exploding, and he dropped senseless. At the same moment his servant, who was crawling some yards away to the right, collapsed silently with a bullet through his head.

IV

When Bretherton recovered his senses he was lying on the far side of the ruined building. Two German soldiers in coal-scuttle steel helmets, dazzle-painted in red, green, and yellow, were lying behind a heap of bricks ten or twelve yards away. Their backs were towards him, and the nail-studded soles of their clumsy shin-high boots were the most conspicuous things about them. For a moment or two in his half-dazed condition he found himself counting the number of nails in each sole. Then with fully recovered consciousness he turned his head and found himself looking into the face of a man lying close beside him.

It was rather a pleasant face, that of a young man, tanned and with a little fair moustache upon the upper lip. The peak of a coal-scuttle steel helmet shaded his eyes, and the stiff collar of his grey tunic fastened closely about his neck. He grinned not unpleasantly as his eyes met Bretherton's, and moved forward his right hand. Bretherton saw that it held an automatic pistol. "*Prisonnier*," said the German officer in French. Bretherton grinned feebly in reply and nodded.

Presently the officer signalled to his men to retire, and the whole diamond formation turned about and, with the officer, his orderly, and Bretherton in the centre, crawled away from the ruins.

Thirty yards from the brick and rubble heaps they came upon a German post of four men roughly dug into a slight depression in the ground. They halted here for a few minutes, and then as they moved out on the far side, a British machine gun opened fire from a flank, and Bretherton had the unpleasant experience of lying with his body pressed close to the ground and hearing British bullets hissing and whipping a foot above his head. The gun ceased firing after a few seconds, and they crawled on and reached a trench in which they were able to rise to their feet. It had been made as a communicating trench of a reserve system, but now German soldiers in steel helmets and shirt-sleeves were digging furiously to convert it into a fire trench. They were hollow-eyed and hollow-cheeked, and many of them had that dazed look which is seen on the faces of men who have been subjected to long periods of heavy shell fire. It was evident that the strain of repeated attacks and bombardments was beginning to tell upon them.

Bretherton was taken down half a dozen steps into a small dug-out, and was allowed to sit upon a wooden bench while the young officer reported to a plump little German in glasses. He was glad of the opportunity to rest; his head ached abominably, and a small cut on his thigh, though neither deep nor dangerous, made walking painful. His message-pad, glasses, and prismatic compass were taken from him, but his personal belongings were returned to him. He had got rid of his map whilst passing through a muddy shell-hole. He was asked his name, rank, and regiment in French; and he replied in that language, thinking it advisable to conceal his knowledge of German.

After this preliminary examination he was marched off under the escort of a soldier with rifle and fixed bayonet and the young officer who had been responsible for his capture. This young man treated his prisoner very courteously. They were both fighting men, his attitude seemed to say, both initiates of the ancient order of mud, blood, and lice, though members of different lodges; this was a predicament in which any gentleman might find himself, and the positions might have been reversed. Bretherton was to discover later that hostility and hate increased in direct ratio to one's distance from the firing-line.

They passed slowly and, as far as Bretherton was concerned, painfully up a long zigzagging trench and out into a narrow, curved, sunken road where a long row of wounded were lying outside a dressing-station. Farther up the road, between high banks, a German fatigue party was parading with picks and shovels, and beyond them two British Tommies, prisoners, were seated on the ground with their backs against the bank. The face of one of them was swathed in bandages, but the inevitable cigarette protruded from the midst of them; the other, bare-headed and with a shock of tousled red hair, was playing "Mademoiselle from Armentières" on a mouth-organ. Bretherton gave them a cheery word as he passed, and the red-headed one took his instrument from his mouth, and with an obvious wink asked whether Bretherton 'ad 'eard that 'Aig was 'alf-way to Berlin!

"He is probably there by now," answered Bretherton, laughing.

"There y'are, Jerry! Y'ear what the orficer says!" cried the Tommy, looking up at his escort, a big, raw-boned Saxon. "That's what I've been a-tellin' 'em square-'eads, sir," he continued to Bretherton. "But they're a nignorant lot o' bastards—beggin' your pardon, sir." And he fell to with his instrument again and the strange classic adventures of the lady from Armentières.

In the deepest part of the cutting Bretherton was led into a dug-out cut into the bank. A number of orderlies loitered about the door or sat upon the ground outside, and from this and other signs he concluded that it was a regimental headquarters. The dug-out was a large one, running parallel with the road under the bank, and was divided into compartments by wooden partitions. In one of these a typewriter was clicking, and in another he caught a glimpse of the Brigadier or Regimental Commander with a telephone held to his ear, bending over a map. He was left alone in one of these compartments for a minute or two, and then an intelligence officer who spoke fluent English came to question him.

He was asked the number of our tanks, the names of the units in the line, about the reserves, the aircraft, and a number of other questions, all of which he refused to answer. A prisoner of war is bound to give his name and regiment, but nothing more. The intelligence officer, who was a hectoring, unhealthy-looking, middle-aged German, tried threats. To have carried out the threats would have been a grave breach of international law, but Bretherton did not feel altogether secure on that account. Nevertheless, he refused to answer all questions, protested that he was tired and hungry—which was an understatement—and suggested that the officer should cease to waste any more time. He was left alone for some minutes then, and the officer returned to say that since he would not answer the questions he must go to another headquarters.

They set off at once with an escort of two men. Dusk was falling, and it was dark before they had gone far. Everywhere around them in the darkness men were digging and putting up wire.

"Got the wind up badly!" said Bretherton maliciously to the intelligence officer.

The officer took no notice of the remark. He had changed his tactics. He chatted pleasantly about England, in which country he had lived for some years, and about the war in general. Bretherton guessed that his object was to draw him, and, refusing to be drawn, he took refuge in silence. He was too tired to carry on a conversation had he wished to do so. His leg pained him not a little, and he was sick and faint from hunger and fatigue.

They arrived at last at a large château surrounded by trees; but after nearly an hour had passed in fruitless efforts to get information from the prisoner, he was marched off to another headquarters. He began to suspect that this was a deliberate attempt to tire him into submission; a suspicion which was confirmed when he was made to wait two or three hours and was roughly awakened by his escort each time that he fell asleep.

V

Through the long night-hours he was marched from one headquarters to another, till he could scarcely drag his stumbling legs over the rough ground, and he became light-headed with fatigue and lack of sleep. And each time that his head nodded he was rudely awakened by one of his captors. One short respite he had, however, and one gleam of satisfaction. During the course of that endless night-march he picked up again as officer in charge of escort the middle-aged lieutenant whom he so much disliked; and whilst trudging along a narrow road bordered by a ditch, the party was heavily shelled by British guns. Escort and prisoner took refuge in the ditch, and there they lay for half an hour, till the shelling ceased. The escort and the little intelligence officer crouched shivering in the muddy, evil-smelling ditch, whilst Bretherton slept undisturbed.

At midday on the following day they gave up the attempt to tire him into submission. He was locked into a room in a headquarters château, and a sentry was placed outside the window. The sentry was superfluous; Bretherton could not have run ten yards had his life depended upon it. He lay down upon the floor and slept like a log.

At dusk he was put into a lorry and taken to a large town, which his escort said was Cambrai. He was handed over to the governor of the civil prison and locked in a cell furnished with a bed and blankets, table and chair. He was given a meal of thin soup and bread, and then he wrapped himself in his blankets and fell asleep.

Five days later, together with a hundred other prisoners both English and French, he entrained for Germany. The men were in cattle-trucks, and the officers, seven in number, travelled in a second-class coach. On the second night Bretherton awoke from sleep and saw below him the stars reflected in water. Shadowy, uprearing girders slid past the window in endless succession, and the rumble of the train had a hollow ring. A full minute passed, but still the giant girders patterned the night sky; and when at last they ended, and black-wooded hills closed in round the train, he knew that he had crossed the Rhine.

The party of seven officers detrained the following day at the little station of Ebenthal among wooded hills, and marched out to the prisoners-of-war camp that lay two miles beyond the village.

CHAPTER XIV

I

THERE were some two hundred prisoners in the officers' camp at Ebenthal. More than half that number were Russians, and the remainder were Belgian, French and British. The camp covered about fourteen acres, was rectangular in shape, and was enclosed by two separate fences of barbed wire. The prisoners, five to a room, were lodged in a large L-shaped building. The Russians were all together in one wing, and the British, French and Belgians occupied the other.

On that first evening when Bretherton left the kommandantur or orderly-room, in which all new arrivals were searched and had their particulars taken, he found the British prisoners and many of the French waiting in the passage to greet him. Among them was a tall, fair-haired officer who, though dressed in a shabby khaki pull-over and an old pair of grey flannel trousers, had the unmistakable carriage and smartness of the Regular Army that no clothes, however old, can disguise. He wrung Bretherton's hand and grinned.

"So Brother Bosche has bagged you, G. B.," he said in his familiar lazy drawl. "He got me up at Arras not a fortnight after I left the old company. How are the old bog-wheels going?"

"Comme ci, comme ca," answered Bretherton. "I expect Baron has got my company now; they nabbed me on the Somme."

Melford took him by the arm. "Bad luck! Come on; I'll show you round the cantonment."

The camp bore a good reputation on the whole. The food, though inadequate, was better than in many German camps, and since every prisoner had parcels sent from home, no hardships were suffered except on the rare occasions when the post was interrupted. Every afternoon football, hockey, or tennis was played on the exercise-ground behind the house, and the evenings were spent in ways varying with one's tastes. Several officers were learning Russian or French under native tutors; some played cards, others read books. Fancy-dress dances were organized periodically, and much ingenuity was expended upon designing and making costumes. And very jolly affairs they were.

A pianoforte had been hired from the village, and Bretherton's services were frequently in demand. Often he might have been seen surrounded by half a dozen officers bawling the old war-worn songs: "There's a long, long trail," "*Après la guerre finie*," "Old soldiers never die"; and when alone he sometimes sang the little song that Helen had sung: "Just a song at twilight."

But the chief diversion of a certain section of the camp was the concoction of plans of escape. Several officers had already made unsuccessful attempts, and two of them had got within a hundred yards of the Dutch frontier before being recaptured. Their valuable knowledge and experience was at the disposal of all who asked for it; and preparations for escaping were being made simultaneously by several officers. After the eight-thirty p.m. *appel*, when the prisoners were locked in the house and were left to themselves for the night, there were strange comings and goings in the passages; and in many rooms articles of escaping kit were being manufactured out of the most unlikely materials.

Ebenthal was not an easy camp from which to escape. The main impediment was the double barbed-wire fence surrounding it. The two fences were about twelve feet apart, and sentries patrolled the narrow strip of ground between them. The wire itself was not an impenetrable obstacle, for there were several pairs of home-made wire-cutters in the camp; but since a prisoner had cut his way out a month or two previously, the sentries had orders to fire at anyone loitering near the wire. And even if one succeeded in getting through the first fence, there remained the second fence, twelve feet beyond it, to be negotiated under the eyes of the sentry.

Therefore the prison-breaker's thoughts had turned to other methods of escape. One man had hidden in a large linen-basket and had been carried out of camp by the French and British orderlies; but the escort had noticed the unusual heaviness of the basket and had investigated the cause of it. Another man had hidden under the rubbish in the rubbish-box, and had been tipped on to the refuse-heap outside the camp. Unfortunately, the sole of one of his boots had become uncovered, and a thrifty member of the escort had tried to pick it off the heap. Two men who spoke German had bluffed their way out of the main gate disguised as German officers. The

Russian greatcoat with certain alterations is not unlike the German article. These two men had spent weeks in manufacturing German military caps and other articles of uniform; and then by great presence of mind and superb audacity they had persuaded the sentry to open the main gate for them, had marched right past the guard-house, and got away. They had been recaptured five days later by German Sunday sportsmen whose dogs had discovered their hiding place in a wood.

Popular taste had now turned in favour of tunnels. The L-shaped building stood towards one corner of the compound, and one wing of it was within twenty yards of the wire fence. A syndicate of six, including Melford, was actually engaged in such a tunnel; and when one of the number dropped out, Bretherton was invited to join.

Work could be carried on only at night when no Germans were within the building. A small section of the flooring of a room facing the fence had been cut out and replaced so neatly that the join was invisible from a distance of even a few inches, and below this a hole had been dug through the concrete to a depth of eight feet. The shaft had been sunk deeper than the tunnel in order to carry off any water that might filter in. The tunnel itself led off at right-angles at a depth of about five feet, and it had been necessary to cut through the thick foundation wall of the house before reaching the softer material beyond. When Bretherton joined the syndicate, it was calculated that the tunnel extended underground to about half-way between the house and the inner fence.

The six members worked in shifts; one in the tunnel scooping out the earth with an old table-knife, one filling the excavated earth into little bags made for the purpose, two carrying away the bags and hiding the earth under the flooring of the rooms, and the remaining two resting. It had been found that a quarter of an hour was as long as a man could stay in the tunnel. It was only just large enough to allow a man to worm his way along it, and working in these cramped conditions was very tiring. Also the air was very foul, so that the worker was in considerable danger of suffocation; and as the tunnel increased in length, it became necessary to rig a pumping apparatus to supply air to the sapper.

II

Meanwhile escaping kit was being collected and manufactured. The six members of the syndicate had agreed to separate outside the camp and to make their way to the frontier in pairs. Each pair was to collect its own escaping kit, plan its own route to the frontier, and, apart from the common work upon the tunnel, conduct its operations independently. Bretherton and Melford were paired together, and all their spare time was employed in completing their kit.

Clothes were the first consideration. A large number of British officers in the camp wore grey flannel trousers, and the camp authorities had been persuaded that these were part of the British uniform. This particular garment, therefore, presented no difficulties. Melford's military tunic had become unserviceable, and he had been permitted to purchase a German coat. The garment was brown in colour and rather like a Norfolk jacket in pattern. The Germans had sewed braid upon the shoulders, but this could easily be removed. Bretherton bought an old tunic from another officer and set about converting it into a civilian garment. He removed the four large, flap-covered, outside pockets and sewed on two side-pockets of civilian pattern; he exchanged the regimental buttons for bone ones; and finally he dipped the garment into a dye composed of ink and boot-polish dissolved in water. The result was a shabby coat of nondescript colour; but it would have needed a very keen eye to have recognized it as a British service frock.

Soft collars had been made from a flannel shirt, and there remained only hats to be found. The German civilian usually wore one of the Homburg variety, but this shape proved to be most difficult to make. Bretherton was compelled to abandon the attempt after much time had been wasted, and he made a passable cap out of some cloth from an old British-warm. Melford stole a shabby trilby from a civilian workman who was doing some repairs in the camp. The Germans raised a great fuss over its disappearance and searched the camp, but Melford had taken care to hide it where it could not be found.

Food was being collected: packets of chocolate, meat tablets, malted milk tablets, tinned food of various kinds, and solidified alcohol for cooking purposes. And they had collected a supply of pepper which, the veteran escapers said, would be very useful for putting dogs off the scent.

But the most important items of the kit were compass and maps. A French flying officer had a genius for manufacturing compasses, and both Bretherton and Melford obtained one from him. Maps were more difficult to get. There were several in the camp, but they were only rough copies of other maps, and even the originals had been taken from railway time-tables and were of no great value for a long march across country.

Melford undertook to get some from home. He had arranged a code with his people, and so was able to tell them both what he wanted and how the articles were to be concealed. The prisoners' parcels were put in the parcel-room when they arrived. A prisoner was informed that there was a parcel for him, and he went to the parcel-room to see it opened by the German N.C.O. detailed for that duty. Tinned food was opened and turned out on a plate, and things like cakes and puddings were probed with a skewer. Watching a parcel being opened was always an exciting and sometimes a nerve-racking experience.

Melford's maps arrived wrapped round a series of home-made cakes. The maps had been baked with the cake, so that the back of the paper was brown like that round an ordinary cake. The German N.C.O. probed the cakes with his skewer and allowed Melford to take them away.

It was then discovered that every German civilian was in possession of a pass. The syndicate discussed the question at some length and came to the conclusion that although a pass was not absolutely necessary, the risk of recapture was very much greater without one than with one. They were confident, however, that they could forge a pass if they had one to copy, but none of them had ever seen one. Finally, it was decided to try to steal one from the next civilian that came into the camp and return it after it had been photographed. Cameras were of course forbidden, but two had been smuggled into the camp, and arrangements were made with the owners for the loan of one of them.

Their chance came when a civilian carpenter was mending a cupboard in one of the rooms. The man had hung his coat on a nail in the wall; but a sentry had been placed at the door, and only the regular occupants of the room were allowed in. The syndicate held a hurried meeting and concocted a plan. Willing helpers were to be had on all sides. A number of these started a row at the end of the passage and lured the sentry from his post. Immediately Bretherton and Melford slipped into the room and searched the workman's coat, which was cleverly blanketed from view of the man himself by the regular occupants of the room. One of the syndicate kept guard at the door.

The pass was found in an inner pocket, and was quickly taken into the next room, where the camera experts were awaiting it. Three photographs were taken while all six members of the syndicate waited with their shoulders to the door to keep it closed should a German chance to try to enter the room; for the discovery of the cameras would have been a serious loss to the camp, apart from the failure of the attempt and the disciplinary action that would follow. No German appeared, however; the noise, which had now increased to an uproar, was monopolizing their attention. Bretherton slipped back and replaced the pass; then he sauntered down the passage towards the uproar. His appearance had a magical effect. The noise ceased as suddenly as it had begun, and in a few seconds the passage was empty except for the sentry and a *feld-webel* and two guards who had been rushed to the scene of strife. The whole affair had taken less than five minutes.

The pass proved to be easier to forge than had been anticipated. It was a small typewritten document containing the workman's name in ink, his photograph stamped with a rubber stamp, and the signature of the officer issuing the pass. That night the skeleton-key expert of the camp opened the door of the kommandantur, and the typewriter was borrowed. Before morning a dozen blank passes had been typed. The name chosen by each of the syndicate was then filled in in ink and the signature forged. Each member was photographed in his escaping clothes, and his photograph affixed to his pass. Finally, the passes were stamped with a home-made stamp cut out of cork by a clever Belgian officer.

III

Preparations for escaping were now complete. The tunnel was estimated to reach a foot or two beyond the outer fence and only needed to be extended to the copse. The building of the tunnel, however, was a great strain. It took more than five minutes to reach the place of working, and more than a quarter of an hour to get out again; there was no room to turn, and after working in this cramped position it was very tiring having to worm one's way out backwards. The whole syndicate loathed the work, and only their nearness to success kept them going. But the strain was beginning to tell upon them physically, and it was decided to rest for a week and go into strict training, as absolute physical fitness would be necessary for their long march to the frontier.

It was now almost on the eve of success that disaster occurred. There had been heavy rains for some days, and the ground was very soft, and, as luck would have it, a lorry drove round that side of the camp on which the tunnel had been dug. Such a thing had never happened before, and the possibility of its occurrence had not been considered. Part of the tunnel collapsed under the weight, leaving a shallow trench about six feet long. The Germans' suspicions were aroused. A party was set to dig, and the tunnel was discovered.

The disappointment of the syndicate was great. But Bretherton, who was the first to recover, pointed out that there were redeeming features. Nobody was in the tunnel at the time of the disaster; the Germans had no idea who was responsible for the attempt and therefore no disciplinary action could be taken, although the vigilance of the camp guards was increased; and finally, their laboriously collected escaping kit was intact and ready for another attempt. He suggested that they should continue their physical training, and in the meantime look out for fresh methods of escape.

But a plan was not easy to concoct. Cutting one's way through the wire was impossible; bluffing one's way out of the camp had been tried and was not at all likely to be successful a second time; being carried out in a linen-basket or refuse-box was out of the question since the last unsuccessful attempts; and now the tunnel had failed them.

It was Bretherton who thought of a plan. He was prowling around the camp one afternoon when he noticed a rubbish-box standing within three or four feet of the inner fence. This was a box that usually stood in one of the passages. Periodically the British and French orderlies under escort emptied it outside the camp, usually during the morning. Sometimes, however, when the box was filled up during the afternoon, it was stood out in the yard and emptied the next morning.

Bretherton meditated upon the germ of his idea for a couple of days and then consulted Melford; and together they discussed and enlarged the idea. One of them would hide inside the box; the box would be placed close to the wire fence, and through a hole cut for the purpose the man inside would cut the wire. That was the plan in outline. There were other difficulties to be overcome, principally the sentries and the second fence. The details would need to be worked out very carefully, but they were both agreed that there was meat in the idea and that by carefully thinking around the subject the difficulties could be surmounted.

For a week or more they discussed nothing else. A large number of fresh suggestions were made, most of which were discarded, though a few were retained. They worked on the system that if Melford made a suggestion, Bretherton put the case against it as strongly as possible; and Melford did the same to Bretherton's suggestions. Each acted as Devil's Advocate to the suggestions of the other, and ideas were adopted only after they had been mercilessly criticized. Step by step the whole plan was worked out and the details arranged to their satisfaction. But some knowledge of the topography of the camp is necessary for its understanding.

IV

One must imagine a large rectangular enclosure, near one corner of which is the L-shaped building surrounded by a small garden. The remainder of the enclosure formed the exercise-ground, and was bordered on three sides by the wire fence, and upon the fourth by the L building and an inner fence that separated the orderlies' quarters from the remainder of the camp. A line of trees, some ten paces apart, ran the length of the exercise-ground parallel with the wire fence and about thirty feet from it. At one end of the ground, and some twenty feet from the fence on that side, were the day latrines. There were two gates to the camp. The main gate faced a wing of the L building, and consisted two heavy wooden gates, one in each of the two fences. A sentry was always on duty here, and the guardroom was close to the gate just beyond the outer fence. The other entrance led out from the exercise-ground and was about half-way along the wire fence which bordered it. Like the main entrance, it consisted of two gates, but here

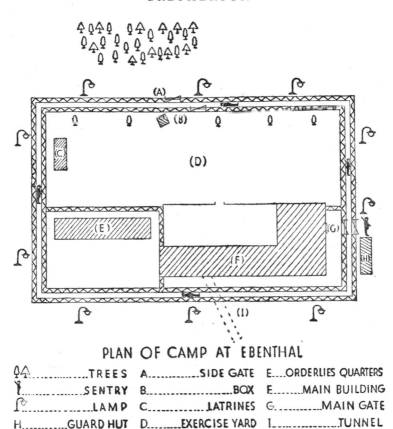

PLAN OF CAMP AT EBENTHAL

......TREES	A........SIDE GATE	E....ORDERLIES QUARTERS
......SENTRY	B..............BOX	F........MAIN BUILDING
......LAMP	C........LATRINES	G..........MAIN GATE
H........GUARD HUT	D......EXERCISE YARD	I..............TUNNEL

they were not opposite to each other. On passing the gate in the inner fence one had to walk a yard or two between the fences before reaching the outer gate. This was the gate which was used by the orderlies and their escort when carrying rubbish out of the camp. There was no permanent sentry here, but the sentry patrolling this side of the camp had the keys of the two gates.

The two fences were twelve feet apart, and the sentries patrolled between them. By day one sentry patrolled each of the four sides of the camp, but after dark an extra sentry was posted on each of the two longer sides. And finally, each of the two shorter sides of the enclosing fence was lighted by two electric standards, and each of the two longer sides by three standards.

Bretherton and Melford had considered these facts in detail, and their plan of escape was founded upon them. At night they had been hard at work upon the rubbish-box and had constructed a removable false bottom on which the rubbish could rest while a man lay concealed beneath. A panel large enough for a man to crawl through had been cut in one side of the box, and at one end a hole had been made, through which an arm could be thrust. Both these holes had been neatly filled in again and could be opened and closed from inside.

The scheme was to be put into execution at dusk just before the extra sentries came on duty. The electric standards would be lighted, but that could not be avoided. Melford, as senior, had chosen to be in the box. A party of trusty French and British orderlies would carry it out late in the afternoon across the exercise-ground and place it close to the wire, opposite the gate in the outer fence. Melford would put his arm through the hole and cut the wire. He would have only one sentry to watch, as the sentry patrolling the side at right-angles was masked, except at the very end of his beat, by the latrines. Bretherton was to watch from the latrines, and by whistling prearranged tunes, warn him of the sentry's approach. Bretherton had nicknamed the latrines the "conning-tower," for it was from here that he would control the subsequent operations.

On a given signal from him, a number of officers were to approach the wire in one corner and create a disturbance. It was hoped that the sentry would be induced to remain for a short time at the end of his beat where the disturbance was taking place. A second disturbance was to be staged in another corner for the benefit of the sentry on that side. Bretherton was then to flit across the thirty yards that separated the box from the conning-tower, slip through the hole in the first fence, and cross to the outer gate, which they had good reason to believe would be unlocked. Once through this gate there remained only ten or twelve yards of open lighted ground to be crossed before reaching the woods which grew close up to the camp on that side. Meanwhile, Melford would have crawled out of the box and be close behind.

The kommandantur closed at a quarter to seven each evening, and the staff passed out of the camp by this side gate; and Bretherton had noticed that although the sentry always locked the inner gate after them, he often left the outer gate unlocked for his relief and the extra sentry who came on duty at seven. However, in case the gate should prove to be locked, Bretherton was to carry a small crowbar with which to wrench off the padlock and staple. This outer gate was not the solid affair that the inner one was. They had examined the staple through glasses from the latrines, and one of the orderlies had assured them that it could easily be wrenched off.

Such was the scheme, but its success depended upon the accuracy with which the details were carried out. The box would have to be placed in exactly the right position and angle for cutting the wire, and much depended upon the choice of the actual moment of escape, which, in order to take full advantage of the dusk, would have to be left till after the kommandantur staff had passed out and just before the extra sentries were posted. Upon Bretherton rested the responsibility of deciding this moment.

CHAPTER XV

I

A t last their preparations were complete. The alterations in the box had been made, the band of orderlies chosen, and the two diversion parties—the song-and-dance items, as they called themselves—detailed.

The night before the eventful day, Bretherton and Melford emptied the box and fitted in the false bottom. The upper part of the box was refilled with rubbish, and the surplus carefully hidden. Then they made a final overhaul of their kit—clothing, food, matches, compasses and maps—to make quite sure that nothing had been forgotten. The food, maps, and compasses were distributed between the pockets of the civilian clothes and the haversack that each was to carry. They went over their plan of operations for the hundredth time and rehearsed the signals that Bretherton was to give from the conning-tower; and then, satisfied that each knew his part and that the scheme was as perfect as was possible in the circumstances, they went to bed.

The following day seemed to Bretherton the longest he had ever spent. The scheme now seemed madness and foredoomed to failure. A dozen exigencies might arise and ruin it. Too much depended upon a favourable coincidence of circumstances over which they had no control. Such were his thoughts as he prowled restlessly about the camp, thoughts bred by excitement, suspense, and inaction. He would be steady enough, he knew, when the time came for action.

He had marked with four stones the exact position in which the box was to be placed—a task that had taken him more than an hour, since loitering near the wire was both dangerous and likely to arouse suspicion. But it was essential that the box should be placed aright. The reach of a man's arm through a hole has very definite limits. Melford had got into the box at night, and they had ascertained the angle that would give the maximum of cover from the sentry and the greatest ease in cutting the wire. It had been impossible to rehearse the orderlies in their part, but a French officer had volunteered to disguise himself as an orderly and to superintend the placing of the box.

The kommandantur staff had a meal at midday, and advantage was taken of their absence to get Melford into the box. As soon as the scouts reported that the Germans had left the building, Melford put on his civilian clothes and haversack; the manhole in the box was opened, and he crawled inside. He would have seven hours to wait in his cramped quarters, but since the box stood in a long passage that led to the kommandantur it was thought to be too risky an undertaking to attempt to enter it when any Germans were in the building.

Melford was now safely in the box; and Bretherton resigned himself to wait until the next event, which was the carrying out of the box, was put into execution at four-thirty.

An orderly's clothes had been smuggled into the French officer's room, and at a quarter to four he made the necessary changes in his clothing and appearance. Bretherton, prowling restlessly about the exercise-yard, saw the three chosen orderlies pass one by one and by separate doors into the building. Presently Deane, the officer who was to pass the signal that the coast was clear, appeared at one of the doors and lounged negligently against the door-post. Bretherton covertly surveyed the enclosure. With the exception of the sentries patrolling between the wire, no Germans were about. He gave the signal by whistling a few bars of "The Tarpaulin Jacket"—"And six stalwart lancers shall carry me, carry me."

Deane slightly turned his head and tapped out his pipe against the door-post; and a few seconds later four orderlies carrying a large box of rubbish emerged from the doorway. They passed quite close to Bretherton as he sauntered about the yard, and the disguised French officer gave him a wink as he went by. To Bretherton's anxious eyes they seemed to stagger more than should be necessary with a box of that size; but they passed safely across the exercise-ground and approached the wire. The sentry stopped when he saw them coming, and walked slowly along his beat towards them.

Bretherton watched him anxiously. But the French officer did his part to perfection. He edged his party round so that they came up to the wire at the correct angle, and he dumped the box with apparent carelessness; but it rested on the exact place marked out by Bretherton. Then the four turned and marched back across the yard. The sentry stood looking at the box for a minute or two, and then, to Bretherton's relief, resumed his beat.

One more step in the scheme had been taken successfully; and once more he resigned himself to inactivity and an intolerable wait of two and a half hours before it would be time for him to take up his position in the conning-tower. After half an hour had elapsed, he smuggled his haversack over to the latrines and hid it there. Another hour went by, and he smuggled his civilian coat and cap to the same place. Three-quarters of an hour dragged by with incredible slowness, and then he walked over to the conning-tower.

Again he became a prey to anxiety. It was the kommandantur staff that worried him now. If they delayed the time of their departure even by a few minutes, Melford might not have time to cut the wire; for it had been decided not to cut the wire till after they had passed. It would take him less than five minutes, he had said, but the time for the whole operation of escaping had been cut very fine. The kommandantur staff did not leave till a quarter to seven, and the new guard and extra sentries came on duty at seven. Allowing five minutes for cutting the wire, only ten minutes remained for the actual escape. A slight hold-up might be disastrous.

Bretherton had synchronized his watch with the camp clock, and as the time approached a quarter to seven, he kept his eyes fixed on the door through which the kommandantur staff would appear. They never were late—they were going off duty; but this night of all nights they must not be late. If for any reason Bretherton thought that the wire should be cut earlier, he was to whistle "Coming thro' the Rye." In any case he was to give the signal as soon as the kommandantur staff was clear of the camp.

The hands of his watch pointed to a quarter to seven, and then to fourteen minutes to seven; but the kommandantur staff did not appear. He decided to give them one minute more. And then at last they appeared in the doorway just as his lips shaped themselves for the signal. At the same moment the lights around the camp were turned on. The Germans seemed to crawl across the exercise-ground. They reached the gate and stood within a yard or two of the box while the sentry fumbled with the lock. The gate swung open, and they passed through. The sentry closed and locked it behind them. They reached the outer gate; the sentry unlocked it; they passed through, but halted outside and stood talking to the sentry. It was now eleven minutes to seven.

At last the kommandantur staff walked away, but the sentry stood at the gate looking after them. Seconds passed and then he turned, closed the gate, and—locked it.

Bretherton muttered a curse beneath his breath. He would have to use the crowbar after all. He was cool enough now. His time for action had come. The moment the sentry moved off on his beat between the fences he whistled "Coming thro' the Rye" flung off his military tunic, and hurried into the civilian coat and haversack. He looked at his watch; eight minutes to seven. The light was failing rapidly. In another ten minutes it would be quite dark.

He made a rapid calculation. The new guard and extra sentries paraded outside the guard-hut at seven. They first relieved the sentry at the main gate, and then the sentry on that side of the camp. Then they marched round outside the wire to the side gate through which he must escape. All this took time. Nearly ten minutes must elapse from the time the guard paraded to the moment when they turned the corner of the camp and came into view of the side gate. The minutes of gathering darkness were precious; he would need all the concealment he could get during the time that he must stand up and wrench off the padlock. He determined to wait till seven when the guard paraded. He would be able to hear the sergeant's voice calling out the guard should they parade a minute or two earlier.

In the distance he could see the dim figure of the officer who for greater certainty was to pass on his signal to the song-and-dance party. It was now five minutes to seven, and if all had gone well, Melford had cut the wire. The minutes dragged slowly by. Daylight was almost gone.

At one minute to seven he heard the sergeant's voice from the guard-house on the other side of the camp. He took a long breath and whistled "Onward, Christian Soldiers." Across the exercise-ground someone began whistling, the same tune, and a moment later an uproar broke out in a far corner. The sentry, who was marching towards the side gate, paused at the noise, and after a momentary hesitation, turned and walked slowly towards it. Faint sounds of a distant argument came from the other direction.

It was now or never. Bretherton sped swiftly and silently from the latrines to the nearest tree, and from the tree to the box. He crouched behind it and rapped sharply upon the side. The manhole opened.

"The wire's cut, but you will have to part the strands," whispered Melford.

"The gate is locked," Bretherton told him. "Wait till I've opened it. No need for both to be shot at."

He threw one glance at the retreating back of the sentry, parted the strands of wire, and crawled through. A loose end caught in his haversack, but Melford released him. Bent double, he crossed the space between the two fences, stood boldly upright, inserted the crowbar in the staple, and heaved. The staple creaked but did not give. He was nearly midway between two light standards, and he was startlingly visible standing upright against the gate. Each moment he expected to hear the crack of a rifle and feel the brutal kick of a bullet in his body.

He pushed the crowbar farther through the staple and flung all his weight upon the lever. It moved. The staple flew from the post; the crowbar clanked to the ground. He glanced behind and saw that Melford was already through the wire. Then he pushed open the gate and ran for the shelter of the trees. He saw his elongated shadow dancing and sprawling ahead of him, the trees green and sharp-cut like theatrical scenery in the glare of the arcs. And then he lay panting among the undergrowth with Melford beside him.

"First lap," murmured Melford. They rose and ran without speaking deeper and deeper into the woods.

Bent double, he crossed the space between.

II

There were no sounds of pursuit behind them, and when they had gone four or five hundred yards, they took a compass bearing and marched north-north-west. A mile farther on they turned due west, thus passing round to the north of the camp and village. At the end of an hour they came to the edge of the woods. They halted within the shelter of the trees and held a council of war. Below them was the road which they had intended to follow. The veteran escapers had advised them to follow roads. After ten o'clock at night few or no walkers abroad would be met, and the slight additional risk one incurred in this way was more than compensated for by the increased pace and comfort of marching and immunity from having to make long detours to avoid impassable ground.

Their original plan had been to halt on the edge of the woods and continue the march along the roads after ten o'clock. Had the outer gate been unlocked, the Germans would not have discovered their escape till the morning *appel*, since arrangements had been made to fake the eight-thirty *appel*. This would not have been difficult, as a great deal of ragging always went on, and the Germans often had to count the prisoners three or four times, usually with a different total each time. But now that the padlock was wrenched off the gate, the new guard could hardly fail to draw the obvious conclusion, even though Melford had closed the box before leaving and had had the presence of mind to remove the tell-tale crowbar. Surrounding villages would be warned, and cyclists would be sent out to look for them. The road, therefore, was unsafe. Nor could they halt on the edge of the woods as they had originally intended.

On the hillside beyond the road the woods began again and extended for some miles beside it. They decided to cross to the woods opposite and move through them parallel with the road until they deemed it safe to venture on to the road itself.

It was a moonless night, but the sky was studded with stars. They crouched in the ditch beside the road while three men walked by, and then ran across it, ascended the opposite slope, and gained the shelter of the woods in safety. It was difficult going in the woods. The undergrowth was thick, and they made slow progress; but several times they heard voices below them, and were consoled by the thought that though their progress was slower and more laborious than it would have been on the road, it was sure.

About midnight they reached the end of the woods. The moon had now risen, and they saw a village lying below them in a little valley and the road running through it. Hop-gardens surrounded the village and appeared to extend for some distance on both sides of the road. These would be difficult to move through, and Melford was for going straight down to the road. Bretherton, however, thought that they were still too close to Ebenthal to make road tramping safe, and since another of the old escapers' maxims had been "of two counsels always choose the more cautious," his advice was followed. They sat down under a bush, and with a coat over his head, Bretherton struck a match and examined the map. Beyond the village the road curved steadily for several miles, swinging round gradually almost to south-west, so that by marching west-south-west across country, one should reach the road again and shorten the march by two or three miles. This they decided to do.

They took a compass bearing and then marched by the stars. Almost immediately they became entangled in hop-gardens. Every ten minutes or so they came to a house which entailed a detour, and when, as happened on two or three occasions, they came upon one suddenly dogs began to bark and kept up their clamour long after the wayfarers had passed. Fortunately all the dogs were tied up, and in only one place was a window opened and a head thrust out. But this part of the march was very nerve-racking, and Melford swore mighty oaths against the whole canine tribe.

They reached the road at last, though their short cut had proved expensive in the matter both of speed and of fatigue. Now, however, they were able to step out. They made a detour of the first village, but this led them through a muddy swamp and took so long that they determined to march boldly through the next one. This they did and met no one, though lights were burning in one or two cottages and the dogs kept up a chorus of barking long after they had passed. They met only two parties on the road: an old man who called "Good night" and to whom Bretherton replied, and three youths who passed without speaking.

Just before dawn they found a suitable place to lie up in, a wood upon the side of a hill with a stream below.

The undergrowth was thick, there was water close at hand, and there were no neighbouring villages from which lovers or sportsmen might wander and discover them. They sat on the margin of the wood and ate their ration of meat tablets and chocolate; and then Melford slept for an hour whilst Bretherton kept watch. At eight o'clock when the sun was up they returned to their hiding-place among the undergrowth, and Bretherton slept whilst Melford kept guard. The day passed uneventfully. They slept by turns all the morning and some of the afternoon. Occasionally they went to the edge of the wood and sunned themselves, for they found it tiring lying hour after hour among the undergrowth, and it was with difficulty that they restrained themselves from wandering about. But no one came near them. For some hours a shepherd sat upon the opposite hillside watching his sheep grazing upon the slopes; and once a girl driving a cow passed along the side of the wood.

They made another meal soon after dusk, and at ten o'clock the march was resumed. Their objective was the Rhine, where, they had been told, Dutch bargees could be found who, for a consideration, would smuggle one across the frontier.

On the fifth night they reached the little River Sieg, which flows into the Rhine near Bonn. They were now less than fifty miles from the great river, in hilly, thickly wooded country, and had but to follow the road and stream which meandered side by side between the hills. For two nights it had rained hard, and although drenched to the skin, they had no alternative during the day except to lie up in the dripping woods in their sodden clothes. On the fourth day the rain stopped, and they were fortunate in finding an open glade among the woods. There by turns they risked taking off their clothes and drying them in the sun.

They had grown accustomed to the dogs, and now they marched boldly through the villages to a chorus of barking. The night marches had become second nature to them. As they tramped hour after hour through the darkness, they seemed to have become part of the night like the trees and the unseen creatures that made bustling little noises in the darkness near them. Their feet fell rhythmically upon the pale ribbon of road that led between dark, forest-clothed slopes, through sleeping villages, across streams and rivers, among fields, and over windy open spaces. On they tramped like men condemned to march through darkness to the end of time; and often as they marched they sang German songs that Bretherton knew and even English airs, for there was little risk of anyone hearing them.

Food was running short, and they had cut down their already inadequate ration. They had hoped to find food as they went along, turnips or potatoes, and they had found a few; but a diet of raw potatoes is neither very appetising nor very sustaining to men with healthy appetites, leading a strenuous life in the open air and subjected to all the rigours of cold, wet, and fatigue.

III

Sunday morning found them in the neighbourhood of Eitorf; and soon after dawn they halted among the woods which extend for many miles around the village. They ate a portion of their now almost exhausted rations and some raw potatoes they had dug up in the course of the night's march, and then they slept by turns.

During the afternoon they heard the sound of guns in the woods and the barking of dogs; and remembering that many escapers had been recaptured through falling in with Sunday sportsmen, they were a little uneasy. But they could only lie still and trust that the shooting parties would not wander in their direction; to attempt to change their position might attract the attention of the dogs. The afternoon dragged away slowly, and now that they were approaching the end of their journey on foot, they were very impatient of this enforced inactivity. They were less than fifteen miles from the Rhine, which they hoped to reach in the course of that night's march.

Late in the afternoon they heard the sound of a gun close at hand; whereupon they hurriedly packed their haversacks and lay ready to crawl away at the first alarm. But they heard no more shots fired, and they were congratulating them-selves on the fact that the sportsmen must have moved off to another part of the woods, when suddenly they heard a rustling behind them and turned their heads to see a large dog regarding them from the shelter of the undergrowth. Neither moved, and dog and men regarded each other silently. Seconds sped by, but the dog did not trot off as they had hoped it would do. They attempted to crawl away, but at the first movement the dog set up such a barking as to make them hurriedly desist. They threw sticks at the animal; they enticed it with morsels of their precious food; but the brute refused to be either bullied or cajoled. And then they heard a trampling in the undergrowth near by and saw between the trees two men carrying sporting guns. Bretherton whispered to Melford to pretend to be asleep.

The Germans walked slowly to the two tramps lying on the ground, and halted. Bretherton sat up with his hands clasped around his knees and murmured "Good day." The Germans returned the salutation, and one, who by his manner and bearing seemed to be a person of some importance, asked what he was doing here. Bretherton answered that he and his companion were from Cassel on a walking tour. The German listened to the story and then asked somewhat peremptorily to see their pass. Bretherton produced the pass; and while the German was examining it, two more sportsmen arrived with another dog. The German handed back the pass and said, with rather more civility, that it would be necessary for Bretherton and his companion to accompany him to Eitorf to report to the authorities there.

Bretherton saw that he had gained a point by the pass, but he had no wish to go to the village and be questioned by some conscientious German official who might possibly telegraph to Cassel to verify the story. He replied that he had every intention of going down to the village, since that was where he intended to stop the night, but he was very comfortable where he was and intended to remain there for the present.

The German said that he must insist. "Insist!" echoed Bretherton. "I have as much right to be in these woods as you have. I have proved to you who I am, and I have told you that I am spending the night in Eitorf. Am I then to trot backwards and forwards on this hot afternoon just to please every stranger that comes along?" And he lay back and closed his eyes to show that the matter was settled.

The German was obviously uncertain what to do, and he drew aside to confer with his companions. Bretherton strained his ears to catch what they were saying, and he gathered that one of them intended to go down to the village and bring back an official. And presently one of them went off, followed by one of the dogs. The remaining three sat down a few yards away, and the dog lay down beside them.

Bretherton pretended to doze. He lay close beside Melford with his hat tilted over his eyes, and they held a whispered consultation. It would be nearly two hours, they estimated, before the man could return from the village. By then it would be within an hour of dusk, a point of some importance. For an hour they would pretend to sleep, and then they would try the plan they had concocted. Melford was to get up and stroll off as if to fill his water-bottle at the stream which was hidden in the undergrowth some fifty yards away; and to make this appear the more reasonable he was to leave his hat, coat, and haversack behind. These would have to be abandoned. Meanwhile Bretherton was to pretend to doze and so support the pretence that Melford was only going to the stream. The Germans would thus be compelled either to shoot at Melford—which it was very unlikely they would dare to do—or divide their forces. Then Melford and Bretherton were to make a dash for it independently and meet after dark outside Meteren, the next village.

Melford managed to transfer his small stock of food from his haversack to his pockets without being observed by the Germans. His maps and compasses were in an inner pocket. Then they both pretended to doze and lay listening to the murmur of the Germans' conversation and watching the minute-hand creep round towards the hour chosen for the attempt.

At last it was time. Bretherton whispered, "Good luck," and Melford turned over sleepily, yawned, stretched himself, and rubbed his eyes. The Germans watched him silently. He picked up his water-bottle and applied it to his lips. Then he shook it, turned it upside-down, and eyed with disgust the few drops that trickled from it. He mumbled something unintelligible and with a sigh rose to his feet. The Germans, who had been lying back watching, sat up quickly. With one hand in his trouser pocket and the other carelessly swinging the water-bottle he sauntered towards the stream. The Germans called on him to stop, but he took no notice of them. The three men scrambled to their feet and again called on him to stop. One of them raised his gun; but another laid his hand upon the barrel. Melford continued unconcernedly upon his way. Bretherton rolled over sleepily and called testily, "All right: he's only going to fill the water-bottle."

Melford's kit that lay upon the grass and Bretherton's lazy attitude reassured the Germans, for after a hurried consultation one of them picked up his gun and followed

Melford. The remaining two sat down again, and the dog remained with them.

These were big odds against Bretherton, two men armed with sporting guns and a dog. But he feared the dog more than the guns. Fortunately he had cut himself a stout stick in the woods, and as he lay now upon his side with the stick hidden by his body, he found the grip of it comforting. His food, map, and compass were in his pockets. He would have to sacrifice his overcoat and haversack, but with luck he would reach the Rhine that night. He watched the Germans through half closed lids, awaiting an opportunity to bolt and listening for the sounds that would tell him that Melford had got away.

Suddenly a shout broke the stillness of the woods. The two men sat up quickly; the dog barked. The shout was repeated a few minutes later, farther off, and was followed by a shot. The two Germans sprang to their feet and stood looking in the direction from which the shot had sounded. The dog started off into the woods, but was angrily recalled by one of the men and stood behind its masters gazing into the undergrowth with cocked ears.

Bretherton cautiously drew in his legs. He rose swiftly and noiselessly to his feet; he took a stealthy step forward. The men heard nothing, but the dog did and turned its head. Bretherton brought the stick down upon the animal's skull with all his strength, and as it crumbled beneath the blow, he turned and dived into the undergrowth.

CHAPTER XVI

I

BEHIND him the Germans were shouting, and one of them loosed off his gun. Bretherton heard the pellets spattering through the leaves close to him, but he was hidden by the thick undergrowth. He heard the men crashing after him, and he realized thankfully that the dog was not with them.

He ran hard for a hundred yards, and then dropped into a walk and moved with extreme caution. The report of the gun had made him anxious about Melford, though he told himself that in this close country it was unlikely that the German could have had much of a shot, and at the worst a few pellets in the back of a running man were not likely to cause any serious damage.

The sportsmen were shouting to each other, and he could hear them beating the bushes as though they were undecided whether he was hiding in the close undergrowth or had gone on. He set his course westward by the setting sun, the direction of Meteren, near which village he was to meet Melford. Presently he heard the sound of someone moving cautiously through the undergrowth to his right. The noise grew louder, and he hid among the bushes and waited. The rustling of branches and leaves continued intermittently and drew nearer. Beyond the bush where he lay hid was a small glade almost free from undergrowth, and beyond it thick bushes began again. The rustling reached these bushes and ceased.

Bretherton lay on the ground with his stick gripped in his hand and his eyes fixed on the bushes beyond the glade. They swayed slightly, and then a branch was drawn partly aside, and a man's face peered out. It was Melford. Bretherton called to him softly and crawled from his hiding place.

"So you've diddled 'em, G. B.," said Melford. "Stout feller. Let's get a move on. They are still running round in circles back there. I let out a few realistic groans after that chap blazed off at me, and he thinks I'm wounded and lying doggo somewhere."

They went on cautiously at first, and then with greater speed and boldness as no sounds of pursuit reached them. The sun had set, and already dusk was falling in the woods. They forced their way through a thick belt of undergrowth and found themselves unexpectedly in a ride. Bretherton grasped Melford's arm and jerked him backwards. But it was too late, for as he glanced down the long straight woodland lane, he saw coming towards them the German sportsman who had gone to the village. And with him was a soldier carrying a rifle on his shoulder.

The Germans were less than forty yards away. Melford cried, "Run!" and they dashed into the woods across the ride. But here the undergrowth had been recently cut and was not more than a foot or two in height. The Germans shouted to them to stop, but they sped on.

"Better separate," cried Melford, and he swerved to the right. Bretherton swerved to the left. A few seconds later came the sharp crack of a rifle. A cloud of frightened birds rose noisily from the trees. Melford pitched head-first into the low undergrowth.

He was holding his left arm with his right hand and trying to struggle to his feet when Bretherton reached him. "All right, G. B.," he said. "I tripped over something, but that swine got me in the arm—it's all numb. Cut along: I can run all right."

Bretherton hooked his arm round his comrade's body and dragged him to his feet. And then again the crack of a rifle echoed through the woods. Something warm splashed stingingly on Bretherton's face and trickled down his cheek; the strong, sinewy body in his arms jerked convulsively, sagged suddenly, and slid limp and heavy from his grasp.

For a fraction of a second he gazed stupidly at the little hole behind the left ear; and then a great gust of rage swept over him. Melford had been murdered, murdered: Melford, the C.O. of the old divisional company, who had so often sat in the little company office on the banks of the Ancre, who had brought the company out to France and led it across the hills of Picardy and the Somme swamps by Vaux; Melford, the cheery companion of the prison-camp at Ebenthal and the night marches through the silent woods and villages, Melford murdered on the eve of success. He leapt to his feet and started towards the Germans, who were approaching through the trees. With his bare hands he would choke the life out of the murderer.

He had gone only three or four paces before his habitual calm and presence of mind reasserted themselves. Melford was dead, and he himself would be shot down long before he could take vengeance on the slayer. To attempt to do so would be madness, useless suicide. He swerved sharply and ran swiftly between the trees. Thirty yards ahead he saw that the undergrowth rose again to a height of ten or twelve feet. A shout sounded behind him, but he ran on, dodging this way and that among the trunks. He was only a few yards from the shelter of the bushes when again the crack of a rifle echoed through the woods and sent the birds flying with a beating of wings. Something kicked him hard in the thigh, and he sprawled head-first into the shelter of the undergrowth.

II

A dull, insistent pain gnawed at his leg, but he crawled farther in among the sheltering branches and then rose unsteadily to his feet and hobbled on. For five minutes he stumbled painfully onward, and then he tripped and fell. He crawled a few yards to where the undergrowth was very dense, and lay still. The two Germans were calling to each other, and the soldier, it seemed, was prodding among the bushes with his bayonet. But it was now nearly dark in the woods, and the soldier's task was a hopeless one. The men evidently realized this, for the sounds grew fainter and soon ceased altogether.

Bretherton examined the wound as best he could in the gloom. The bullet, he decided, had passed through the fleshy part of the thigh without damaging either bones or arteries. Apart from the danger of tetanus, it was not serious, and though painful, with proper medical attention should heal quickly; but unless he gave up all thoughts of escape he could not hope for medical aid till he had crossed the frontier. Had this happened thirty miles back, he would have had no alternative other than to surrender; but here he was less than fifteen miles from the Rhine, and on that great river he hoped to find a barge that would carry him to safety. But he realized that he would need all his strength to reach the river. Fifteen miles was a long journey for a man with an undressed wound who had lived on very short commons and had suffered considerable hardships.

He tied up the wound as well as he could with a handkerchief, and then he ate the greater part of his meagre rations. It was do or die now; lack of food meant lack of strength, and he would need all his strength before he reached the river. He had dropped his stick, but in that wooded country the loss was not a serious one. He cut himself a stout stick about four feet long with a fork at one end. This he could use as a crutch to ease the weight upon his wounded leg. He had no idea of his exact position—a mile or two within the woods to the north-east of Eitorf, he believed. At all events the road ran east and west, and by going south or south-west he must strike it eventually. But it was still too early in the evening to use the roads, and they were sure to be watched to-night in the neighbourhood of Eitorf.

He set off slowly westwards, steering by compass. The night was dark, which would have made the going slow through the undergrowth, but his leg made his progress very slow indeed, and frequent halts to rest and ease the pain were necessary.

As the time passed, his slow progress became a nightmare to him. It seemed to him that he was in a forest that stretched right round the world. He longed for open spaces, for one glimmer of light, for a glimpse even of a starlit sky; but the night was cloudy, and above the few tiny glades in the woods no stars were visible. To add to his discomfort, rain began to fall. For a time the trees protected him, but soon the rain penetrated the leafy roof, and he was drenched to the skin by the water that ran in rivulets from the branches above him and the dripping undergrowth through which he had to force his way.

The woods were full of sounds, the crackling of a branch, the rustle of some animal among the leaves, the stirring of birds in the branches, and the constant patter of rain and dripping water. He was surrounded by intense darkness; he blundered into unseen trees; wet, clammy leaves brushed his face; thick, clinging branches impeded his body; flexible saplings flew back and cut his hands and face. And before him in the darkness floated the picture of Melford—Melford lying on his face in the darkening forest, with a hole behind the left ear.

At length he could bear the darkness and oppressiveness of the woods no longer. He set a course due south; but it took him an hour to reach the fringes of the woods, an hour of frequent halts and of semi-conscious dragging of one foot after the other with head down, thrusting mechanically through unseen obstacles.

For a time he lay exhausted among the small bushes fringing the wood; till slowly his consciousness began to focus, and he dragged himself into a sitting posture. Twenty yards from him was the railway; a quarter of a mile away a signal lamp glowed through the darkness, a haven of rest to his darkness-weary eyes. Beyond the railway was the stream, and beyond the stream, unseen in the darkness, was the road which he knew crossed the stream and ran south of it just beyond Eitorf. Therefore he was in the neighbourhood of Hennef, less than four miles from the scene of the tragic events of the afternoon. And it was now past midnight. With his failing strength it was doubtful whether he could reach the river before dawn.

He rose to his feet and hobbled painfully beside the railway. The sound of an approaching train drove him from the track to the shelter of the bushes. The train rumbled out of the night, and he saw the figure of the driver peering from the cab and the fireman with shovel lit up by the glare of the open furnace. The engine passed, and behind it came truck after truck in endless succession, rumbling and clanking and moving slowly. Then a sharp distant clank was followed by others, growing nearer as the buffers of the trucks clashed together.

This goods train halting in front of him was heaven-sent, he thought. He doubted whether his strength would carry him the few miles that separated him from the Rhine; but here was a means of covering the distance without fatigue. He had a good memory for maps, and he and Melford had studied the map for many hours; it had been their one diversion during the long hours of lying up in daylight. He knew that the railway ran, converging upon the river, to Cologne. Goods trains travel slowly and with frequent halts. It should not be difficult for him to drop off near the river more or less when he pleased.

The truck nearest to him was a low one, covered with a tarpaulin. He clambered painfully on to one of the wheels, stood upon the grease-box, and slowly dragged himself up. The tarpaulin was wet and slippery with rain, but fortunately was not tied securely. He raised one corner of it and crawled underneath. The tarpaulin was stretched over an iron bar which ran down the centre of the truck, and formed a kind of tent, the roof of which at its highest under the bar was about three feet above the wooden cases with which the truck was laden.

He stretched himself upon the cases. They formed a hard couch, rendered more uncomfortable by the jolting of the train, which now moved slowly on; but he was protected from the drenching rain and the bitter wind, and he could rest his overtaxed wounded leg. His clothes were soaked, and he was shivering with cold, but he was too weary to care about such minor discomforts. The rumble and jolting of the train came as a confused and distant murmur to his ears, and in a few minutes he had fallen into a sleep of utter exhaustion.

III

He realized on awakening that he was very ill. A leaden languor possessed all his limbs, and sharp pains racked his head. His stomach seemed to contain a block of ice. He lay wedged beneath the tarpaulin on one side of the truck, to which he had rolled during his sleep. The train rumbled on its way in the unhurried fashion peculiar to goods traffic.

He roused himself from the lethargy into which he was drifting back. How near the Rhine was he? he wondered. He glanced at his luminous wrist-watch, and then held it to his ear. The hands pointed to twenty minutes to nine. But the watch was still going. He experienced a pang of alarm till he realized that the watch might have stopped, but been set going again by the movement of his hand. And then he remembered that he had looked at it just before boarding the train, between twelve and one, and that it was going then. Now thoroughly alarmed, he turned over and for the first time noticed that it was not absolutely dark in the truck; there was a small slit in the tarpaulin through which shone a bright narrow bar of daylight.

It was day, then, really twenty minutes to nine in the morning. Questions surged through his tired brain. Where was he now? How far had he travelled during those eight hours? While he slept, had he been carried back into the heart of Germany, back through those many miles that he and poor old Melford had travelled so precariously and so laboriously?

He crawled across the truck and applied his eye to the slit in the tarpaulin. A dead-flat, cultivated country stretched away from the railway. No town or village came within the limited range of his vision. He opened his map and studied it by the light from the slit. He had boarded the train near Hennef, he believed, and from that place the railway ran to Cologne, a distance of about fifteen miles. At Cologne the line made two main divergences, one line continuing northwards through the populous Ruhr district, and the other crossing the Rhine and running westwards towards Belgium. He must have passed Cologne hours ago. Had he gone north, he would now be in the industrial area; had he gone west, he would be in the neighbourhood of Aix-la-Chapelle. The absence of villages told him that he was not in the industrial area, and the flatness of the country pointed to the plain that lay across the Rhine westward of Cologne.

In any case, he had left the Rhine, and it mattered little where he was. Five or fifty miles from the river, it was all one. He could not have marched two miles in his present condition.

For an hour and more he lay sunk in a resigned stupor, and the train rumbled on its way. Then with a clanking of buffers running from front to rear of the line of trucks it came to a halt. A sound of music reached his ears. He roused himself and peered through the slit in the tarpaulin. The same flat country met his eye, but now a few cottages and a road cut across the corner of the arc of vision. The sounds of music grew louder, a military march played by a band; and presently he saw a battalion of German infantry headed by a band pass along the segment of road.

He watched them swing past and out of sight. The martial air and rhythmic beat of marching feet stirred his flagging spirit. His will began to grip once more. He was not done yet. His brain began to work clearly, and as the train moved on again, he took out a compass. He was travelling west-north-west. He had crossed the Rhine, then; he was on the plain between Cologne and Aix. Before long he would be across the frontier into Belgium, occupied Belgium, it is true, but out of Germany and in a country in which the inhabitants would be friendly and would help him as much as they dared. Once in Belgium, he must leave the train at the first opportunity and hide till dark. Then he must seek out some German-hating Belgian who would hide and tend him till his wound was healed and his strength restored, and he could make another bid for the Dutch frontier and freedom.

His fear now was that the train would reach its destination before he could leave it. He turned his attention to the cases on which he lay; they might give some clue to the destination of the train. He struck a match and held the flame close to the floor of his travelling tent. One glance was sufficient. He had seen hundreds of such cases during his journey as a prisoner-of-war from the Somme to Ebenthal. They were small-arms ammunition boxes. The train was a munition train, bound, no doubt, for the western front. It was going probably right on into France, to some big dump well back behind the lines. That would be too far for him, however. The war zone would be too dangerous, too strictly watched. France or Belgium for him, preferably France just across the Belgian frontier. The French had no love for the Bosche; they would hide him till he could fend for himself.

But the fear remained that the train might be bound for some nearer destination and the truck be unloaded before he could escape. In his present weak condition he could not leave the train while it was in motion, and although there were frequent halts, they were always amid surroundings which precluded the possibility of leaving the truck unperceived. Therefore he decided that, once across the Belgian frontier, should he get so far, he must take the first opportunity of escaping; and opportunities were likely to be rare, since nothing less than a halt in a wood away from any habitation would serve his purpose.

He fretted at his own weakness. He knew that he would be able to drag himself only a short distance, and that very slowly. Illness, exposure, and hunger had sapped his strength and made a child of him. For a week he had eaten less each day than the average person takes at one meal, and for the last forty-eight hours he had eaten nothing except a bar of chocolate and a few meat lozenges. He ate the last of his store of food, half a bar of chocolate and three meat lozenges, and resigned himself to waiting.

Hour after hour, with frequent halts that were full of suspense for Bretherton, the train rumbled on. Through Aix it rolled, and shortly afterwards crossed the frontier into Belgium. Thereafter it was passing down the valley of the Meuse, and through the slit in the tarpaulin he could see the river flowing green between the grey, verdure-clothed limestone cliffs. Whenever the train halted in lonely stretches of the line he reconnoitred through the slit the possible chances of escape, but always there were people about—military guards on the railway, troops, or the crew of the train itself. And when it halted in busy sidings or crowded goods yards and he heard the engine go puffing off alone, the fear that this was the train's destination and the consequent certainty that he would be discovered was ever present. But the welcome jolt which announced the arrival of a fresh engine revived his hopes, and presently the train would again rumble on its way.

Mons had been left behind, and late in the afternoon, when the train passed the outskirts of a large town and he read the name "Valenciennes" upon a platform, he knew that he was back again in France. He was getting very near the zone of military operations in which he could not hope to remain without discovery. But still no opportunity presented itself of getting away unobserved. Evening came, and with it dusk. The train halted in the half-light in the crowded goods-yard of a small town. Dumps of stores and ammunition lined the railway on either side, and he prayed that darkness might fall before the truck could be unloaded. The light faded slowly, and he had just decided that in another ten minutes it would be dark enough for him to leave his hiding-place, when the truck jerked, stopped, jerked again, and moved slowly on.

He caught a glimpse of the name of the station as he moved through it—Douai. He was perilously close to the line now, and the unloading of the truck could not be long delayed. The train moved slowly on, leaving the outlying houses of the town behind, on through the deepening darkness of the young night.

He made his preparations for leaving the truck. He pulled back the loose edge of the tarpaulin and waited with his head and shoulders through the opening. For a mile or more the train ran on and then slowed, and from the direction of the engine came once more the welcome clash of buffers. It was a lonely spot, very suitable for his purpose. He crawled out on top of the tarpaulin, and as soon as the train came to rest, let himself down to the full extent of his arms and dropped. He toppled over, picked himself up, and stole away.

IV

A hundred yards from the line he halted to rest. The going had been slow and painful. His wounded leg was stiff, and he had no crutch to help him. The train moved on again, and he could hear it faintly in the distance. The silence of the early night surrounded him. A cool wind fanned his cheek. Stars gleamed overhead. The western sky was lit by flashes as of summer lightning. From the distance came the familiar grumble of the guns.

He rose to his feet and struggled on, filled with a new resolution. He was less than eight miles from the line, and he had more than ten hours of darkness before him. His progress was slow and painful, but he could manage to cover a mile per hour at least, and if his strength lasted, he would reach the line before dawn and crawl across the narrow ribbon of no-man's-land to safety. It was a desperate venture, he knew well, but preferable to the only alternative of lying for weeks perhaps, wounded and ill in some hiding-place, relying upon the loyalty and devotion of some stranger for food and safety.

He avoided the roads, but there was no risk of losing his way: that play of summer lightning in the western sky and the restless booming and growling of the guns was a sure guide. Clouds gathered overhead, and rain began to fall heavily. He was in a pitiable condition. His clothes were sodden and in rags, but he struggled on, making a circuit of the farms and lying flat when, as occasionally happened, files of men or formed bodies of troops passed near him.

Hour after hour went by. He reached the zone of the heavies. Individual explosions came at intervals from the darkness that surrounded him. Music and voices singing in German came from cottages and huts that lay unseen around him. Southwards, where a deeper tint of darkness cut the sky and proclaimed a wood, a railway gun, king among weapons, raised its deep voice and was silent.

He rested in a copse surrounding a house from which came sounds of revelry and the clicking of a typewriter; but lying in the inky darkness of the undergrowth, he had no fear of detection. And as he lay weary and shivering upon the sodden ground, a shaft of light cut the darkness surrounding the house and a voice called, "Praegar! Praegar!" Immediately a voice answered near at hand, and less than ten yards from him the door of a hut, that he had not noticed in the darkness, was flung open, and the bareheaded figure of a German soldier was framed in the lighted doorway. The man stood motionless for a second, and then, with a glance upwards at the rain, ran towards the house.

From where he lay Bretherton could see the interior of the hut. A wire-netting sleeping-bunk ran down one side of it. Beside the bunk was a packing-case on which stood an acetylene lamp and half a loaf of bread, and beside the packing-case stood a dainty Louis Seize chair across which lay, neatly folded, the tunic and breeches of a German officer.

Bretherton eyed the bread hungrily. There was no one in the hut, and the man, obviously an officer's servant, had gone to the house. He crawled towards the door, reached it, rose to his feet, and hobbled through. He snatched the bread from the packing-case, and as an after-thought grabbed the uniform from the chair. He limped into the friendly darkness and away through the copse. He gnawed the bread ravenously as he went, and on the edge of the copse exchanged his sodden rags for the dry uniform. And then off again he toiled towards the soaring Verey lights that were visible in the distance.

He was nearing the end of his strength, he realized, and only the will to cross no-man's-land before dawn carried him on. His brain was losing grip. He had fits of coma during which he moved like one in a dream. And he had queer delusions. He fancied he was in Piccadilly and the mutter of the guns was the rumble of traffic. And then it was Berlin, where he had lived before the war. He thought that von Wahnheim, the young Prussian officer with whom he had shared rooms, was beside him, and he found himself talking aloud in German. And then he believed that he himself was von Wahnheim, and he had to go over in his mind the stealing of the uniform from the hut in order to free himself from the delusion.

He was in the field-gun belt now, and had to move warily. Hidden batteries belched unexpectedly from the darkness, and many times he almost stumbled upon a shelter or hut before he discovered it. The borrowed uniform was sodden and soiled with mud and slit by a belt of wire through which he had passed. The country was now bare of cultivation, the forward, civilian-evacuated area over which the rank jungle-grass flourished. Now and then a shell wailed overhead and detonated with a flash of orange flame. British shells, he thought, from British guns. A file of German infantry showed vaguely against the sky, and he dropped flat. He watched them go by, slowly and deliberately in the fatalistic manner peculiar to kit-laden troops entering the line—vague, grotesque silhouettes against the sky. They sank, as it seemed, one by one into the ground, and he realized that they had entered a communicating trench.

He struggled on, fighting against the desire to fling himself down and sleep, sleep—and the hallucinations that clouded his judgment. The Verey lights rose and fell ahead, casting strange running shadows on the scarred ground. He must cross no-man's-land within the next hour or he would never cross it at all.

Away to his right the melancholy voices of gas-gongs sent their warning across the wastes. Voices sounded suddenly from below ground in front of him, and he crawled forward stealthily, and waiting a favourable opportunity, crossed a support trench and the wire beyond. He was very near the limit of his endurance, but very near safety also. One more trench or two at the most, then the wire, no-man's-land, and the British lines. He crawled on, half-consciously, round shell-holes, scraps of wire, chalk hummocks, and other debris that littered the ground. A German machine gun was tap-tap-tapping away to the right.

Suddenly straight ahead, and very close it seemed, there broke out a familiar sound, tut-tut-tut-tut-tut-tut-tut. In joy at recognizing close at hand the sound of a British Lewis gun, he shouted hoarsely and, rising to his feet, broke into a run. He shambled a few yards, tripped over some wire, and came down with a crash. A greenish light soared up from the German fire-trench three yards ahead, wavered for a second, sank, and expired. But Bretherton did not move.

CHAPTER XVII

I

Two German infantrymen stood in the support trench peering across the dreary expanse of shell-pounded, wire-littered ground that stretched between them and the front line. It was an hour after stand-to, and the newly risen sun sparkled on the stagnant water in the brimming shell-holes.

"There, by that stump of tree," said one of them. "Ten metres behind the fire-trench. He was not there yesterday; must have been caught going over the top last night."

The other man, an officer, focussed his glasses on the dirty grey object vaguely suggesting a cast-off ventriloquist's figure that lay in the mud by the shattered tree-stump.

"Looks like an officer," he said as he lowered his glasses. "And dead; but one cannot be sure at this distance. He is in view of the British trench unfortunately, but we will have a look at him to-night."

"It is dead ground some of the way, sir," answered the N.C.O. "And there is an old ditch beyond that. I could get within three or four metres of him under cover."

"All right, get along then," replied the officer.

Before he finished speaking, a sharp smack resounded on the sandbag an inch or two to the right of his head, as though it had been clapped upon its earthen shoulder by a hearty hand. The officer ducked quickly.

"That damned sniper is on the watch," he exclaimed. "We will get down to Potsdam Corner; he cannot see us there."

The two men moved down the trench to where it dipped across a little valley, and at its lowest part, near its junction with a communicating trench labelled Potsdam Corner by a board stuck in the parados, the N.C.O. climbed out and crawled up the valley on hands and knees. Presently he turned off to the left and disappeared up a shallow ditch that bisected the slope.

Some ten minutes later he reappeared. He had got within a yard or two of the man out there, but could get no nearer without exposing himself to British snipers. The man was an officer and alive, though he would not swear to it.

"Well, if he is an officer and alive, we must bring him in," replied the other. "I will send out a couple of men with a stretcher. It is a risk, but I do not think they will shoot."

Above the parapet of the fire-trench near where the wounded man lay a stretcher was slowly hoisted. Immediately came the crack of a rifle, and a tiny hole appeared in the brown canvas of which the stretcher was made. The stretcher was waved slowly from side to side; and then an English-speaking N.C.O. shouted: "Tomee, Tomee! Doan shoot; doan shoot. Ve vetch der vounded." And an answering hail came across the foul ribbon of no-man's-land: "All right, Jerry. Carry on. But I'll knock your bleedin' 'ead off if you try any tricks."

Two men climbed out of the trench in full view of the British lines. They lifted the sagging body in muddy field-grey on to a stretcher and returned with their burden to the trench.

II

Major von Artenveldt, Kommandant of No. 36 Casualty Clearing Station on the outskitrs of Douai, tapped irritably on the table with the butt of his fountain-pen. The afternoon sunlight streaming through the window lit up the sylvan scene painted on the wooden case of the country clock that ticked on the mantelpiece, it glinted from the gaudy china vase that served as a paperweight to some official papers on the table, and revealed the incongruous assortment of office files, papers, and medical appliances with which the little cottage-room was littered. Smoke from the Kommandant's cigar hung in blue wreaths from the ceiling.

With a petulant movement he pushed away the return that lay awaiting his signature and walked to the window. He regarded the dusty, poplar-bordered road and the large white hospital marquee beyond with a frown. Though a medical man and a non-combatant, he was as military in the office sense as any officer of the Imperial General Staff, and he prided himself that no late or inaccurate return had ever been received from No. 36 C.C.S. His enemies said that he thought more of the correctness of his returns than of the welfare of the wounded in his care.

Behind him on the table lay a return awaiting his signature, a return accurate and complete in every detail except in the case of one man whose name and regiment were not stated. This casualty had been brought in during the afternoon. He had been found lying between the fire and the support trenches, but did not belong to any unit holding that sector. It was assumed that he had been on his way up to the fire-trench and, it being dark, had walked over the top to avoid the tedious communicating trench. Unfortunately he wore no identity disc, and beyond the fact, proclaimed by his muddy and tattered uniform, that he was an officer in a Prussian regiment, nothing was known about him. He had been unconscious when picked up and had remained so ever since.

Major von Artenveldt flicked the ash from his cigar, and with a grunt of annoyance reseated himself at the table. He drew the return towards him, ran a fat forefinger down the list till he came to this tiresome casualty, and wrote "Not known" in the columns set apart for name and regiment. Then he threw down his pen and rang the bell at his elbow.

III

In one of the big hospital marquees beyond the poplar-bordered road a fair-haired Saxon nursing sister was bending over one of the beds. The subject of Major von Artenveldt's ill-humour had just recovered consciousness. His eyes travelled slowly down the long line of beds ranged against the opposite side of the marquee, and returned by way of the other rank to his own bed and the face of the girl bending over him.

She spoke to him soothingly in German, caressingly as a mother speaks to her child; and then, remembering the Kommandant's impatience, gently asked his name and regiment.

A puzzled frown appeared on the patient's face, and his eyes roved again over as much of the ward as he could see.

"I—I don't remember," he said at last, speaking slowly and hesitatingly in German. "Where am I?"

The girl smoothed the frown from his forehead. "Safe and sound," she answered. "In Number Thirty-six C.C.S. We knew you were an officer and a Prussian by your uniform; but you had no identity disc. Just whisper your name and regiment, and then don't try to think any more. Just sleep."

"Prussian officer," he repeated thoughtfully as though he were trying to recall where he had heard the words before. "Ah, I remember now." His face lighted up with the animation of a child who remembers its lesson. "Otto von Wahnheim… Captain Otto von Wahnheim, Friedrich Kaserne, Königstrasse."

She shook her head at him kindly. "Poor man, you are not in Berlin now," she said with a smile. "But perhaps you will be soon."

His face resumed the puzzled frown, but she smoothed it away and coaxed him to close his eyes. "Don't try to think," she whispered. "You will remember everything by and by. Just sleep. You must be very tired."

The wounded man sighed, and the lids drooped over the tired eyes.

IV

A few days later a staff officer from Corps Headquarters sat in the little cottage parlour that served the Casualty

Clearing Station as an office. He shook his finger roguishly at the plump little Kommandant.

"Von Artenveldt," he said, "the war is beginning to tell on you—or is it women? Your last return was inaccurate."

The Kommandant flushed to the roots of his close-cropped hair and his eyes glinted angrily behind his glasses.

The staff officer laughed and continued teasingly: "A small slip, it is true; but small beginnings, you know!"

"Perhaps if you would explain," replied the Kommandant stiffly.

"Certainly," agreed the other cheerfully. "It was in connection with that fellow you sent us that chit about—von Wahnheim... Colonel von Wahnheim, Third Prussian Infantry."

"Captain," corrected the Kommandant. "Captain von Wahnheim, Third Prussian Infantry."

"Colonel," repeated the staff officer with a mischievous twinkle in his eye. "That is the inaccuracy to which I am referring."

"He gave his rank as captain," affirmed the Kommandant stubbornly.

"Then he was mistaken," answered the staff officer blandly. "Colonel von Wahnheim commanded his regiment from February '16 up to the Somme. He was reported missing after the first day of the British offensive. Practically the whole of his regiment was wiped out; all the officers were either taken prisoner or killed. He was reported missing, believed killed; but evidently he was a prisoner after all. And now he must have managed to escape. He ought to have some useful information for us. That is really what I came about."

The Kommandant relighted the cigar which in his indignation he had allowed to go out.

"I am not to blame," he said. "He gave his rank as captain, and he believes he is only a captain. I am afraid you will not get much information from him yet awhile. His memory has gone completely. He did not even know that the war had come. He has a blank period dating from about the middle of '14 up to the time that he came round in the ward here. He thought that he was still a captain quartered in Berlin; and his memory even of those days seems to be none too good."

The staff officer scratched his chin. "Poor devil!" he exclaimed. "Then he cannot tell us how he escaped or..."

"No," broke in the Kommandant. "He does not know that he has been a prisoner; and neither did I till you told me. But he has had a bad time. He was half-starved and absolutely worn out. Another hour or two and it would have been all over with him. He had a bullet through the thigh, but it was complete exhaustion rather than the wound that was troubling him."

"Poor devil!" repeated the staff officer. "Any chance of his memory coming back?"

The Kommandant shrugged his shoulders. "It may— and it may not. No one can say. And he is not out of the wood yet by any means. If he recovers his health and strength, he may recover his memory also; on the other hand, these two odd years may remain a blank for the rest of his life. One cannot tell."

The staff officer rose. "Well, if his memory shows signs of improving, let us know. He has had a rough time of it, poor devil! And you, my dear von Artenveldt, are exonerated from all blame." There was a malicious twinkle in his eye. "Your error was due to circumstances over which you had no control."

The Kommandant bowed stiffly. "The accuracy of my returns is a matter about which I am most particular," he said.

The staff officer clapped him on the shoulders. "Bravo! It's fellows like you that are winning the war." And with this gratifying testimonial he left.

V

Colonel von Wahnheim retraced his steps slowly from the valley of the shadow of death. A period of rest in the invigorating air of the Black Forest restored to him something of his health and strength, but effected no improvement in his mental condition. A few names and isolated incidents was all that he remembered of his previous life, and the whole period of the war up to the moment that he recovered consciousness in No. 36 C.C.S. was a blank. From that moment onwards, however, his memory worked exceptionally well. He had employed most of the long hours of his convalescence in making himself familiar with the events of the past two years and in reading military books, so that, in spite of his mental infirmity, he had acquired a thorough knowledge of the military situation.

In due course he was certified for light duty and was attached to a lines-of-communication headquarters at Cologne.

The officers quartered in Cologne belonged to two classes: those called dug-outs, and men whose wounds or ill-health had won them a respite from the firing line. Both old and young vied with one another in their efforts to get the most out of life: the young because the nightmare of the Western Front lay behind and loomed ahead; the old in order to prove that they were not yet too old. Charming female war-workers and even more charming organizers of charity matinées and amusements for the wounded were ever ready to help a young soldier to forget his troubles or an old one spend his pay. Dinners, dances, select supper parties from which neither wine, women, nor song were missing were the usual ending of a day spent among official returns, clicking heels and typewriters, and the other sinews of a paper war.

But Colonel Otto von Wahnheim took part in none of these diversions. A dull fellow, his comrades voted him, caring neither for wine nor women, but a sound man at his job and a glutton for work. His terrible experiences and resulting loss of memory had soured him, no doubt. Often he would clap his hand to his forehead and knit his brows as though desperately trying to recapture some half-remembered thought. Often he would go off into fits of abstraction and answer inquirers only in monosyllables.

A bit potty, old von W., some of the younger members of the staff said.

But von Wahnheim never tried to impose his own austerity upon others. He demanded and saw to it that every man under him knew and did his job; but as long as the job was well done, he did not care how gay his young officers might be. And some of them were very gay indeed. Perhaps the gayest was Lieutenant von Arnberg, a young Austrian of good family, blessed with money, good looks, and a winning personality. No one looked quite as handsome in uniform as young Arnberg, and no one danced quite as well as he. He was the darling of the ladies, but remained surprisingly unspoilt by his popularity, and he entertained a warm admiration and affection for his chief, Colonel von Wahnheim, whose austere, taciturn, and rather repellent personality was in direct contrast to his own charming character.

Young Arnberg had taken a beautiful house overlooking the Rhine at Godesberg, a few miles from Cologne, and his only surviving relation, a twin sister, to whom he was devoted, presided over it. Those qualities of manner, character, and appearance that had made young Lieutenant von Arnberg the most popular and sought-after officer in Germany and yet had preserved him fresh and unspoilt were possessed by his sister also. Her beauty was startling in its perfection; her charm of manner irresistible. Such a woman must the legendary Helen of Troy have been. At the age of eighteen she had obeyed her parents' commands and married the Duke of Wittelsberg-Strelitz. And now at the age of twenty-two Sonia Duchess of Wittelsberg-Strelitz was a widow and the despair of half the officers of the Central Powers. But, like her brother, she retained her charm and simplicity. She was fêted, worshipped, pursued, but cared for nothing but her brother; and to be with him she preferred the comparative dullness of a provincial city to the glitter of Vienna or Berlin.

Young Leo von Arnberg loved his beautiful sister and watched over her with jealous care. She was well able to take care of herself, but none knew better than he the dangers that beset a girl of her exceptional attractions in war-time Cologne. He knew his brother-officers, and he said jestingly that he would not trust even St. John the Baptist where a woman was concerned and particularly such a woman as Sonia. He conducted her home from every dance or dinner she attended, and although this caused much grumbling among the numerous gallant officers who would have given their Iron Crosses for such a tête-à-tête with the beautiful Duchess as the journey in a car from Cologne to Godesberg offered, they agreed that Leo was wise and that Sonia was too wonderful to be entrusted to the care of one man for more than five minutes.

Invitations to dine at the beautiful house in Godesberg were coveted by every officer in Cologne, but they were given sparingly; and the only man who was pressed to come whenever he wished, never used his privilege. Colonel von Wahnheim was too busy for petticoat soldiering, he said. The beautiful Duchess he had never seen, and he could not forgive her the demoralization she had caused among his staff.

VI

Late one evening some documents requiring immediate attention arrived unexpectedly at the Headquarters in Cologne. They concerned matters that came under the control of Lieutenant von Arnberg, and Colonel von Wahnheim informed that young man that he would have to stay probably the greater part of the night. The sudden look of consternation that flitted across his subordinate's face caused von Wahnheim to exclaim sharply, "Well, what is the matter? Cannot be helped, you know. War."

"I know, sir, but…"

"But what?"

"Nothing, sir."

The Colonel looked at his subordinate keenly and then asked more kindly, "What is it Leo? Tell me."

"My sister, sir."

The Colonel frowned. "Look here, Arnberg, I am getting a little tired of your sister. Since the Duchess has been here the efficiency of my staff has deteriorated nearly fifty per cent. There is only one job for a woman in war-time, and that is rearing sons to be soldiers. If she cannot let my officers get on with their jobs, she must go."

Young Arnberg flushed all over his handsome face. The Colonel laid his hand on the younger man's shoulder.

"Sorry, Leo," he said. "I am sure it is not her fault; but we have got to get on with the war, and men are such fools where women are concerned. But what has she to do with this job of yours?"

"I shall not be able to take her home," replied Leo von Arnberg.

The Colonel swung round on him sharply. "From all I hear you will not have any difficulty in finding a substitute," he retorted.

"That's just it, sir."

"Well!"

"Nothing, sir."

Colonel von Wahnheim walked across the room, and then, turning back, saw that von Arnberg had not moved and was still standing rigidly to attention.

"Damn it all!" exclaimed the Colonel. "You don't expect me to take her home!"

"It is very good of you to suggest it, sir," replied young Arnberg imperturbably.

Von Wahnheim stared at his subordinate in amazement. "Suggest it!" he echoed. "Well…!"

"You see, sir," continued von Arnberg, "there is only about one man in a hundred I would trust with a woman—such as Sonia."

Von Wahnheim looked grim, and then suddenly he laughed. "And I am the one in a hundred, eh?"

"Yes, sir."

"You are right, Arnberg. I have no time for women." He rubbed his chin thoughtfully. "All right, I will take her back. You are right to be careful of your sister with these young scoundrels of mine. When and where shall I fetch her?"

Lieutenant von Arnberg overwhelmed his chief with gratitude. He picked up the telephone and gave the number of a fashionable hotel. "Please tell the Duchess of Wittelsberg-Strelitz I wish to speak to her," von Wahnheim heard him say. "Hullo, Sonia! Leo speaking. I cannot get away to take you back to-night; lot of stuff just come in and must be attended to. But Colonel von Wahnheim has kindly offered to do so."

"Offered!" exclaimed von Wahnheim.

"Do not keep him waiting," continued von Arnberg. "He will be there in half an hour. What? Yes, isn't it! Good-bye."

Colonel von Wahnheim's car stopped outside the hotel. He did not enter the building, but sent a message to the Duchess. He was gratified to find that she obeyed her brother's warning not to keep him waiting. In a very short time she appeared, surrounded by a throng of admirers, and von Wahnheim, seeing her for the first time standing in the lighted portico at the top of the hotel steps, decided that report as to her beauty had not lied. He held open the door of the car for her to enter, and then followed and sank on to the seat beside her. The car slid silently across the deserted Dom Platz and down to the Rhine bank.

"It was very good of you to come." Her voice came from beside him in the darkness. He was aware of a faint perfume and a pale shimmer of white. "That is not conventional gratitude," she continued, guessing his thoughts. "I really mean it. Do you hate it very much?"

"I am sure that any of my officers would give three months' pay to change places with me now," he countered.

"Perhaps. But one man's meat is another man's poison."

His grim face relaxed in the darkness. "I am not expected to be polite then?" he asked.

"Heaven forbid! I would much prefer to quarrel with you. Nobody ever quarrels with me. They agree with everything I say and do. They deny their most sacred vows to agree with me. Everything I say or do is right. It is like being God. I think God must get very tired of being omniscient. He must long sometimes for an incorrigible heretic to argue with. Perhaps that is why He created Satan."

Von Wahnheim laughed softly.

"Yes, I should prefer to quarrel with you," she sighed. "But really we have more in common than one might think. I am told that you always say what you think—and so do I. You dislike women, and I dislike men—particularly the Prussian officer type. Will not you quarrel with me over that?"

"Why that type particularly?" he asked amusedly.

"They are so polite and yet so brutal," she answered; "so callous and so sentimental; so fond of heroics, swaggering, and sword-rattling. Ugh! Nasty little boys!"

"And your own countrymen, what of them?"

"All men are insupportable, but some are more so than others. My own countrymen are perhaps a degree better."

"And who are the least insupportable?"

"It is a choice of evils. The English or Americans, I think. Most of them are boors, but a few are nice—as men go."

"But this is treason! They are our deadly foes," exclaimed von Wahnheim with mock horror.

"And the unspeakable Turk is our very dear friend!" she retorted.

Von Wahnheim shrugged his shoulders. "He is a good soldier," he apologized.

"No doubt—he excels in destructiveness. I don't admire his treatment of women."

"*Autres pays, autres mœurs*, you know," misquoted von Wahnheim tolerantly. "You prefer your English and Americans?"

"They treat one as a human being—neither as a chattel nor a Chinese joss. You don't like them?"

He made an expressive gesture with his hands. "The English are our bitter enemies. It is my duty to hate them."

"Man, the master of his fate, the captain of his soul!" she cried mockingly. "But you liked the Englishman who shared your rooms in Berlin."

"Shared my rooms in Berlin!" he echoed in surprise.

The Duchess laughed softly. "This is not the first time we have met, Colonel."

"Ah, this shirking memory of mine! One could hardly forget such an occasion. But tell me, where did we meet before? I go about picking up fragments of my past history like a dog nosing for scraps."

"It was a long time ago, in Berlin. I was staying there with my father during my school holidays. You came to dinner and brought the Englishman with you. What was his name? I have have forgotten it."

"But you have the advantage of me. I do not even remember the man, much less his name," replied von Wahnheim whimsically.

"I am sorry. Forgive me." Her voice betrayed real sympathy for his affliction. "I do not remember his name, and I did not remember your name either. I remember the incident because you and the Englishman were so alike. And yet you were so different. You were the stiff, bowing, polite Prussian officer, and he was the reserved, rather charming English boy. And yet you were so alike facially. It amused me. I liked him much better than you. He seemed like— like your real self surprised on a holiday."

"I sit an interested spectator of my own shortcomings," smiled von Wahnheim. "This wretched memory of mine! What was he, this Englishman, do you know?"

"No. I saw you both that evening only. It was only that incongruous resemblance that caused the incident to remain in my memory. He played the piano very well and had a good voice—delightful little songs he sang, but at that time I did not understand English well enough to follow them. He will be fighting on the other side now!"

"Probably. And if we meet, I shall not know him."

"But he will know you."

"The chances of meeting are small."

"Very."

The car was travelling swiftly over the tree-bordered road between Bonn and Godesberg. A full moon sailed above a silver-edged cloud, shimmering on the broad surface of the Rhine that lay upon the left and silhouetting the black scalloped mass of the Seven Mountains ahead. They were travelling without lights, for Allied aircraft had been reported approaching the river. Von

Wahnheim was staring abstractedly at the broad back of the chauffeur that cut darkly across the front windows of the car.

Suddenly his eye caught a rapidly moving sparkle of moonlight on the road close ahead. Something dark shot past the window, and there came a brief sharp sound of rending metal. The car swerved with a violence that flung the Duchess against his shoulder; it shot precariously between the trees that bordered the road; slithered uncertainly upon the gleaming electric tramrails beyond; slowed; recovered; and bumped gently over the grass back between the trees on to the road again.

Mumbling maledictions against the other car, the driver climbed out into the road. Von Wahnheim opened the door and found him surveying the twisted shred of metal that had been one of the rear wings.

"Narrow shave, that," said Von Wahnheim.

The Duchess had followed him from the car, and as he turned, a sharp cry escaped her lips. The hand that held the cloak shot up towards her throat, revealing the shimmering evening gown beneath, and her head with its helmet of tawny hair tilted backwards till the moonlight fell upon her face. Von Wahnheim saw that it was very pale and that her eyes were closed. He took a quick step forward and caught her as she swayed.

"Lend a hand," he cried to the chauffeur. "She has fainted."

He lowered her gently upon the rug the man spread beneath the trees whose trunks striped the silver river with sombre bars. Slowly the colour crept back to the pale cheeks in response to their efforts. Her eyes opened, and she smiled wryly at the man kneeling beside her.

"You a shirking memory: I a shirking heart," she murmured in a strangled voice.

He helped her to her feet, and she stood a moment holding to his sleeve for support.

"It is nothing," she said presently in her natural voice. "I am all right now."

He helped her into the car, and they rode for some minutes in silence.

"It was unselfish of you to bring me back to-night," she said at last; "and therefore I am the more distressed that this foolish infirmity of mine should have obtruded itself and embarrassed you."

He made a vague motion with his hand. "Dear lady," he said, "I am willing to quarrel with you over anything in reason, but with regard to our infirmities I would like to be friends."

She held out her hand to him impulsively, and he gripped it. "Thank you," she said.

He left her at the doorway of the rose-covered palace overlooking the Rhine, and presently was speeding back towards Cologne.

VII

Contrary to the expectations of many of the younger officers, Colonel von Wahnheim's night ride with the Duchess worked no change, outwardly at least, in his character or habits. His robot-like personality persisted.

As before, he shunned dances, dinners, and the society of women. He lived only for his work. And his work was meeting with recognition. The doctors pronounced him sound in body and in mind, sound as an intelligent animal is sound. Spiritually he was maimed; but with the abstract they were not concerned. He was fit for active service again, and the high command, satisfied with his work at Cologne, appointed him Chief Staff Officer to a division on the Western Front. He said good-bye to his only friend, Lieutenant Leo von Arnberg, promising to do all that was possible to get that young man a post on his staff, and set his face westwards, where eight million fighting men strove in the fields of France and Flanders, and the sullen voices of the guns echoed from the Alps to the sea.

He had no conscious remembrance of his former service on the Western Front, yet it seemed that the tree-girdled château that was Divisional Headquarters, the straight, white, poplar-bordered road, and the colourless jungle grass that flourished over the forward area as stubble upon an unshaven chin, were all familiar. And at the end of a week he was performing his duties with the sureness and confidence of a veteran.

He was a tireless worker, efficient and imperturbable. He was unmoved either by success or failure, uninfluenced by the deflecting magnetics of fear, glory, or sentiment—a machine that worked smoothly in circumstances and amid surroundings that caused less perfect mechanism to function irregularly. From many points of view he was the ideal staff-officer; and the General considered himself very fortunate in having such a subordinate in those days, when, as he affirmed, the army was going to the dogs.

The divisional front faced the Vimy Ridge, that long, low, war-scarred hill that stretched north of Arras to the Lens coalfields. A few weeks previously the British had concentrated troops in the cellars of the city and had launched that great offensive known as the Third Battle of Arras. North of the city the Canadian Corps had swept over the coveted ridge and down the other side. Bad weather, however, and its attendant transport difficulties had slowed this offensive as it had done so many others, and finally brought it to a halt. Both the British and German front lines now lay at the foot of the ridge on the plain that stretched eastward to Douai, and it was the opinion of the Higher Command that no further thrust would be made in this sector.

Von Wahnheim's General, however, did not share the opinion of his superiors. He believed that the comparative quietness of his front was but a lull preceding another great offensive by the British. He was therefore anxious to obtain identification of the units facing him. But attempts to gain prisoners for this purpose had been unsuccessful. The first raid had found the trenches unoccupied, a discovery that increased the General's uneasiness. The second raid had been driven back without reaching the enemy's trench. A third was planned, and, to ensure its success, Colonel von Wahnheim was to direct operations from the German front line.

VIII

Colonel von Wahnheim dined early at Divisional Head-quarters and then drove through the gathering dusk to the trenches. Night was falling when he reached the front line. Before him the dark swell of the Vimy Ridge lay outlined against the fast-falling, pearly-grey, after-sunset light; behind stretched the shadowed plain merging into the purple sky. Overhead two weary planes droned home to roost and left the sky deserted in the after-twilight hour before the black, night-bombing planes set out upon their errands of destruction. From behind the fast-vanishing outline of the ridge a gun banged occasionally, and the fast, high-travelling shell passed overhead with a noise like that of a tube train leaving a tunnel and detonated grumpily and with a smothered flash in the darkness behind. The cool night breeze carried intermittently the sound of distant wheels and hoofs, the ration parties on the roads behind.

The night was dark and quiet. Verey lights rose and fell languidly, casting ghostly running shadows on the rugged ground. The three officers and fifty men of the raiding party stood with blackened faces in the fire-trench awaiting the crash of the box-barrage that would be the signal for them to set out. Colonel von Wahnheim in the close-fitting regulation steel helmet stood in the angle of a traverse, watch in hand. In a few seconds now it would begin.

It began. The darkness behind him was slit by a mul-titude of flashes as of summer lightning; a rolling of big drums broke from the silent plain, and with a noise like that of a covey of birds the first shells tore overhead and detonated in spouts of flame on the British line. The raiding party climbed out, were seen intermittently as dark moving figures against the orange shell-bursts, and disappeared.

Von Wahnheim in the angle of the traverse, straining his eyes across no-man's-land, saw little spits of fire punctuate the shell flashes, and heard the vicious crack of rifles and the hurried stutter of Lewis guns. Bullets smacked into the parapet, twanged vibrantly on the rusty wire, hissed viciously across the trench. Verey lights soared up in endless procession. A rocket traced a dull line of sparks against the blackness of the ridge and broke into a pendant of coloured lights that floated for a few moments and was extinguished jewel by jewel. The moments fled by.

Three figures loomed up above the trench. The raiding party returning—too soon. They had met a pitiless fire; their officers were dead; they had become entangled in wire; they had not reached the British trench. Other figures drifted back, limped back, crawled back. The noise continued: hundreds of blocks of stone rolling down a wooden stairway; and the fireworks—kaleidoscopic flashes, ever shifting and multi-coloured, white, orange, blood-red.

Colonel von Wahnheim collected a score of unwounded survivors of the raid, issued fresh bombs, and led them back over the top. Shells were now bursting in no-man's-land and on the German front line, the artillery support for which the attacked had signalled. A Lewis gun was traversing, and its bullets went hissing and whispering into the darkness. Some of von Wahnheim's men were hit, but the little party moved steadily forward under the eye of their leader. Ten yards from the British trench they were greeted with a burst of rapid fire, and several men fell. Von Wahnheim, pistol in hand, led on the remainder at the double. More men fell; he could not tell how many. One man outstripped him to the enemy's parapet and took a flying leap into the trench. Von Wahnheim saw the narrow gulley open up in front of him and the pale flicker of a Verey light on three or four wet, shining steel helmets and tense white faces. He fired twice at the faces and two of them sank from view. And then he jumped.

Sailing in mid-air, he saw a little flame stab the gloom below him; some huge thing struck him a terrible blow on the shoulder and swung him round. He realised that he was plunging head downwards into a pit. A wall of dark earth rushed up at him, and then all became still and dark.

CHAPTER XVIII

I

CONSCIOUSNESS floated back to Gerard Bretherton, consciousness of dull pains and aches, and above all of extreme lassitude. He lay inert upon his back, possessed, it seemed, of a leaden body that was no longer the servant of his will. It was useless, therefore, to attempt to move, but his eyelids fluttered and lifted. Above him stretched a luminous grey surface—a dull dawn, his sluggishly working brain surmised. But as his eyes travelled slowly downwards towards the expected horizon, they encountered instead a row of iron beds like an armoured car company on parade.

He closed his eyes in order to assimilate this discovery, which filled him with vague surprise. He opened them again a few moments later and made further discoveries. He himself was lying in a bed, one of a line that faced the other martial rank and left an arrow-straight avenue between. They grey dawn sky above resolved itself into the canvas roof of a hospital marquee.

He closed his eyes and pondered. He was puzzled. Laboriously his mind travelled back over the events of the last twenty-four hours. He felt again the hot, dull glow of anger at Melford's death; with wounded leg he stumbled through the darkened woods near Eitorf; he lay long, anxious hours beneath the tarpaulin on the slowly-moving goods train; tramped again the weary night march westward to the trenches; saw again the Verey lights close ahead, and made the final semi-conscious effort to cross the German fire-trench; stumbled and fell into darkness and oblivion.

Slowly his mind grappled with the facts. He had been a few yards behind the German fire-trench when he fell. Therefore he had been retaken; he was a prisoner once more.

His eyes opened again and went questing down the avenue of beds. Outlined in the doorway of the tent a figure in familiar khaki and glossy sam-brown belt stood talking to a girl who wore the plain white coif and red-ribbed cloak of the British Army Nursing Sisters. He was in British hands, then.

The tired eyes closed again, and he pondered on this joyful discovery. He must have gone farther than he had thought. He must have fallen not behind but in front of the German fire-trench—in no-man's-land; and some stout fellow had brought him in to the British lines and safety. He took another gratified look at the neatness of the hospital tent, and then lay with closed eyes still visualizing the ordered ranks of beds, the uniformed doctor, and the army sister in her cool white coif.

And then gradually a change took place in this vivid scene of the mind's eye. The ordered ranks of beds were there, but they were beds of a different pattern. The medical officer in khaki changed to a bespectacled man in field-grey, the white-coifed army sister became a fair-haired Saxon nurse. The change was like a screen transformation wherein one picture fades into another.

This new picture was not strange to him. He recognized it, remembered it—an officer's ward in a C.C.S. near Douai. Captain—no, Colonel—Otto von Wahnheim lay wounded in that ward. Otto von Wahnheim! The fellow he had shared rooms with in Berlin. A good enough fellow, but a Prussian of the Prussians—and an officer. He did not know what had become of him since the war... yes... taken prisoner and escaped. How did he know that? They had told him... the pompous little Kommandant... von Artenveldt had told him. No, not him; it was von Wahnheim he had told. And then he recovered and went to the Black Forest and to a staff job in Cologne. But that was von Wahnheim... not himself. He was thinking as though he were von Wahnheim. Was this delirium?

He opened his eyes, and there again was the hospital ward, the English marquee ward... not the German one near Douai. He closed his eyes again. What queer tricks one's brain played when one was ill. But he remembered it all quite clearly, that time in Cologne... there was young Leo von Arnberg... good-looking chap and a good fellow too... and his sister, the Duchess of Wittelsberg-Strelitz... striking girl... half Cologne was mad about her, and no wonder... that night ride to Godesberg with her that young Leo had let him in for... just as well he had left Cologne... one never knows...

But that was von Wahnheim... all that... the fellow he had not seen since '13 in Berlin... The Duchess liked him better than von Wahnheim... he was the reserved, rather charming English boy, she said... Bretherton, that was the name… she had forgotten the name; and he had not remembered it either… nor the incident…

God! He must be going mad. He *was* Bretherton—not von Wahnheim… but he remembered that pretty school-girl von Wahnheim had taken him to dine with… she had changed, grown into a woman, and a very beautiful woman…

He *was* mad. Curious one could feel so calm and yet be mad.

He had never really believed that the British would attack there again… but the General believed it… rather windy about it… however, it was as well to get as many identifications as one could… Why did they always bungle those raids? … And the British trench unoccupied on one occasion! … But he was to make sure of that last one… That was why he was so mad when they came drifting back from that firework display… He would get into the trench anyway, and they were bound to follow him… Of course it was not for a G.S.O.1 to go trekking across no-man's-land, but the General relied upon him for the success of the raid… It certainly had been unhealthy out there in no-man's-land; that Lewis gun had made a mess of his men… but he had shot two of the English swine before he jumped… he had seen them sag like half-filled sacks of corn… And then he had felt that whack on his shoulder and had come down headfirst…

He broke into a cold sweat. He was mad—mad—mad. And yet he remembered it all as though he really were von Wahnheim… he, Gerard Bretherton. And, good God!

he had been thinking in German... in German. But he was Gerard Bretherton, he *was*; he was English, he was thinking in English. He remembered the old company... A Company, his company—Baron, Pagan, young Gurney, and the rest. He had been captured on the Somme, and that swine of an intelligence officer had made him tramp about all night in order to get information out of him. But the little beast had lost his bounce when they lay in that ditch during that "hate." Beastly noisy affair that was. Lights popping up and down, ear-shattering explosions. Made one dazed. But he had got to the trench and shot two white-faced English swine below there in the darkness...

God! He was thinking in German again.

He would not think. He would keep his mind a blank. He would sleep. He was very tired. Perhaps he would wake up sane—or not wake up at all.

II

He felt better and stronger when he awoke, and although that nightmare memory persisted, he felt better able to grapple with it. He forced himself to think the matter out calmly and coherently, and he collected what appeared to be illuminating facts. Firstly, he seemed to have two distinct memories: that of his ordinary life and that of what appeared to be a portion of the life of Otto von Wahnheim. And with regard to the latter memory his tendency was to think in German. Secondly, his memory of the life of Gerard Bretherton came to an end with that stumble of his a few yards behind the German front line, and began again with his awakening in this hospital marquee. Thirdly, the memory of Otto von Wahnheim began in a German hospital and ended with that headlong plunge into a British trench near Arras.

He pondered long on these points. He remembered that von Wahnheim had suffered from amnesia, complete oblivion of his former life; and the explanation that himself and not Otto von Wahnheim had suffered from loss of memory came like a flash of light to illuminate the darkness in which he groped. He thought it out laboriously. Von Wahnheim was dead, no doubt, as reported, but he himself in his deranged mental state after his collapse behind the German lines had believed himself to be von Wahnheim; and by a coincidence of circumstances he had been accepted as such. That explained most of his difficulties, and especially his presence here in a British hospital with a bandaged shoulder and head.

Another question arose in his brain. Was he in this hospital as Gerard Bretherton or as von Wahnheim, a German officer taken in a trench raid, who had shot two British Tommies with his automatic? Good God! He, Gerard Bretherton, had shot two British Tommies! ...

Now and then sisters had moved about the ward and had approached his bed, and on these occasions he had lain with closed eyes feigning unconsciousness; for at first he had believed himself to be mad and had feared that others would discover it, and now he did not know whether they thought him English or German.

Now again he saw a doctor approaching up the aisle between the beds, and his eyes closed. After some minutes, when he believed that the danger was past, he opened them slowly; but between his half-closed lids he saw not two feet from him a segment of khaki whipcord breeches. The man had halted noiselessly by the bed instead of passing on.

Bretherton did not close his eyes again. He knew that it was too late and that the officer's eyes were upon his. His gaze travelled slowly upwards, up the long frock of the tunic to the first button and the polished buckle of the belt; then up again, past the second and third buttons and the cross-strap of the belt to the khaki tie and R.A.M.C. badges on the lapels of the coat. Here they paused, and then moved swiftly to the man's face.

The eyes beneath the peaked cap smiled into his, and a voice with a faint suggestion of a drawl said, "Well, G. B.! How goes it?"

Bretherton stared giddily. His world was upside-down. He would get the hang of it presently, perhaps. He managed a wry smile. "It's good to see you, Uncle Sam," he said in a stifled voice.

Harding nodded. "Feeling a bit cheap, eh?"

Bretherton murmured, "Very cheap, Uncle Sam— and puzzled."

"So am I," answered the other. "And curious." He eyed Bretherton thoughtfully for a moment or two "I don't know whether you are up to talking. Let's have a look at you."

"Um!" he murmured when he had finished the examination. "Might have been better and might have been worse."

He fetched a folding chair and sat down close beside the bed.

"How did I get here, Uncle Sam?" Bretherton asked.

Harding took off his service cap and ran his fingers through his thin hair. "That is the interesting part," he said. "And I am almighty curious to hear your adventures. After that show on the Somme last year we thought you had gone west. The C.O. was rather peeved about it, you know. Said you ought to have let Baron do the job. Good officer thrown away, was his point of view. Damned professional, these regular soldiers! And Baron also was rather peeved. Thought you were coveting his iron ration of honour and glory. However, he consoled himself with the command of the company and kept it pretty well up to standard, you will be glad to know."

Harding paused and watched his patient with a professional eye. "Not too done up to listen, eh? Well, to continue. The sergeant's report that he had found the bodies of your men but not yours made me hopeful that you were only wounded; for Jerry was not likely to take a corpse for a souvenir. Much against my will, they shifted me to a base hospital last December; but the old battalion and particularly A Company was my first love, and I made inquiries among the brass hats in high places and eventually learned that you were a prisoner in Boscheland. That was in January. In April they gave me this C.C.S., and you can imagine my curiosity when the long-lost skipper of A Company suddenly turns up in one of my wards!"

Bretherton watched him with tired eyes. A man was moaning monotonously at the far end of the ward. From far overhead sounded the bracketed pop-pop, pop-pop of bursting anti-aircraft shells and the pulsating drone of a German plane.

"Tell me how I came here," he repeated.

The not far distant whu-ump of a bomb set the bottles clinking on a table near the tent door.

"I thought we should get some of that," commented Harding. "They moved a battalion into billets here yesterday."

"Tell me how I came here," reiterated Bretherton.

"But it is your story I want to hear," protested Harding.

"I will talk later," murmured Bretherton. "How did I get here, Uncle Sam?"

"Well, that is the intriguing part of it. Jerry made a raid last night near Gavrelle. He put down a box-barrage and came over. And curiously enough it was the old battalion that was holding that sector—at least A Company's Lewis guns were. I got that information from one of them who got a knock on the thigh—a new man since your time and mine."

Harding paused to listen to the faint tap-tapping of machine guns far up in the sky. Bretherton lay with closed eyes, but gave no outward sign of the sudden dread with which Harding's words had filled him.

"One of our planes is after him," commented Harding. "But to resume. They put up a good show. Baron was in command. He stopped a whizz-bang just as it was all over and was brought back here just after dawn—rather a mess, but he will pull through. I passed him on to the stationary hospital."

Bretherton's eyes were closed, but his fingers twisted beneath the bedclothes.

"They put up a good show, as I said," continued Harding. "Baron had kept them up to your pitch. Two men and a boy they were, more or less; but only two Germans got into the trench, and they were laid out. When things had quietened down a bit, Baron's push began to tidy up. One of the Germans was dead; the other, an officer in colonel's uniform, was not. They sent him back here. I was for passing him on; but after I'd a look at him, I decided to keep him."

Bretherton's eyes were fixed on Harding's face, and his brow was lined like that of an old man.

"Von Wahnheim was the name on the identity disc," continued Harding. "The green-hatted intelligence wallahs are like a dog with two tails at having captured a real live staff colonel. They have been ringing up every ten minutes to know when they can question him. And the joke is that not a soul except myself knows that he is old G. B. escaped from his prison camp. But I am agog to know how you got across Germany, commandeered that uniform complete with identity disc, and got across to our lines during that raid."

Bretherton lay silent and motionless for some moments, and then he asked: "If you keep your mouth shut, Uncle Sam, what will happen?"

Harding rubbed his chin thoughtfully, and a grin slowly overspread his face. "Why the intelligence fellers will be buzzing round you like flies round candy, thirsting for information about the German staff that you can't give."

"I can give them a good deal more information than they expect," said Bretherton tonelessly,

"What, pull their legs, eh?" grinned Harding. "But you would be interned as a prisoner of war, and there would be a hell of a row later. Sorry to spoil a good jest, G. B., but their sense of humour wouldn't rise to it."

"And if you don't keep your mouth shut, I stand a good chance of an A.P.M. complete with firing party at dawn—though I'm not sure that is not the best solution."

Bretherton's expression and the sincere ring in his voice caused the amusement to fade from Harding's face. He assumed his professional air. "What are you talking about, G. B.?" he said. "Let me have a look at you." He laid his fingers on Bretherton's wrist.

"I am all right," protested Bretherton wearily. "No fever or delirium. I meant what I said about a firing party. Isn't that the usual end of a soldier who is caught in the enemy's uniform with arms in his hands—after having shot two of his own men, men of his own company? Good God, Uncle Sam, I have killed two men of A Company! Killed them—those fellows I have licked into shape and led like trusting children through this inferno of war. Good God!"

He covered his face with his hands. "But there were reinforcements in A Company, were there not?" he continued in a pleading voice. "You said there were, didn't you, Uncle Sam? Reinforements—many of them? Perhaps they were not men I knew—my men, A Company men. They were not, Uncle Sam, were they? Say you don't think they were."

Harding was bending over the bed. "All right, G. B.," he said soothingly. "It's all right, old lad. Don't you worry. They were new men—worthless fellows," he lied. "Don't worry. Just try to have a good sleep. Old Uncle Sam is here to look after you."

For a few moments Bretherton clung to the hand that held his; then he pressed it and said in a tired but steady voice, "Sorry I have made a fool of myself, Uncle Sam, but I'm rather weak—been through it, you know. I'm all right now. No—no fever, delirium, or anything. Quite sane. And I was speaking the truth. Just let me lie quiet for a moment."

Harding regarded him with a look in which professional deliberation and affection were mixed. "I will get you a little something," he said.

"Thanks—but, Uncle Sam, no dope. A bracer is what I want. I want to talk—really."

III

Harding returned with some potion in a graduated glass, and while Bretherton drank it, an orderly arranged screens round the bed.

"Do fellows ever lose their memories, Uncle Sam?" asked Bretherton when they were alone. "I mean, do they forget their real identity and think they are someone else, and do all sorts of things—damnable things?"

Harding sat with his elbow resting on his knee and his chin clasped in his hand. "Yes," he answered slowly. "Yes, that has often happened."

"It has happened to me," came the tired voice from the bed. "I have been another fellow for the last few months. G. B. has been—God knows where he has been! I have been Colonel von Wahnheim, G.S.O.1 to General Egon von Bulitz—and doing my damnedest to beat the Allies."

A look of understanding and sympathy dawned on Harding's face, and he nodded slowly.

"I planned that raid last night," continued Bretherton. "You said it was last night, didn't you? And I did not come over to escape to our lines, but in dead earnest—to kill… and I did kill… God forgive me!

"I led those fellows over because they had been driven back. But I am glad old Baron stopped my fellows. Both lots were my fellows—English and German. Lord, what a devilish mix-up it is!

"It is not one story, but two: G. B.'s escape from the prison camp at Ebenthal, and von Wahnheim's tour of duty. The two stories do not overlap; when von Wahnheim enters, G. B. exits."

Harding nodded. "Let's have them both—if you feel equal to it," he said.

"I am all right, I think," answered Bretherton.

"That whack on the shoulder will keep you quiet for a bit, but it is a straightforward proposition," said Harding. "And you have had a bump on the head—a touch of con-cussion, nothing more. Shock is your chief trouble, and you ought to keep quiet; but you have got this affair on your mind, and the sooner you get it off, the better. So go ahead, but take it easily."

Bretherton then related his experiences from the time of his capture on the Somme up to the moment that he recovered consciousness in the marquee ward.

"Poor old G. B.!" said Harding, when he had finished. "You have been through it. I have met with one or two cases of dual personality before, and I have heard of several, but I have never heard of such circumstances as yours."

"You see, the firing party was not delirium," smiled Bretherton wanly.

"No-o," replied Harding thoughtfully. "But for the medical evidence there is quite a case against you. Anyway, I guess it was providence that brought you to this C.C.S. Don't you worry. I can get you out of this mess."

"I'm not worrying—not about that. When a fellow has killed two men of his own Company and borne arms against his country, he doesn't worry much about his personal fate."

Harding shook his head. "You must not worry about that, G. B., old man. It was unpleasant, it's true; but war is made up of unpleasantnesses. You couldn't help it. Two hundred thousand men have been killed in the first few days of a big battle; so what are two after all? And as for bearing arms against your country, you couldn't help that either. You didn't do it voluntarily. It was physical and mechanical treason, if you like; but not mental."

"But the devil of it is, Uncle Sam, I can remember everything now. I am G. B., but at the same time I know and feel what von Wahnheim thought and felt. I can feel two ways and think two ways about everything. I am not the fellow I was. I am half German now; I sympathize with both sides. And when I give information to the Staff, as I suppose I shall, I shall feel like a cad giving away my comrades. For they were my comrades."

Harding nodded his head while his keen eyes scanned Bretherton's face. "You must try not to think of it from that point of view," he insisted. "It was a bad dream—vivid and concrete at the time, but none the less a state of things created by your mind and for which you are not responsible. And now you have woken up. You are G. B. of the old battalion and of the old pre-battalion company. That is what you must concentrate upon. Think of it—the old company. We are scattered now since those days round Albert, eh! Groucher went with a Blighty one, you were missing on the Somme, I was pushed off to this C.C.S., Hubbard has gone…"

"What happened to him?" asked Bretherton.

"His cultivation of the A.P.M. bore fruit. He is a full-blown A.P.M. himself now."

"He meant well," commented Bretherton.

"Well, he has gone, anyway," continued Harding. "Now Baron has gone with a good Blighty one—that means Gurney will have the company; you and I are here, and they have killed poor old Melford. Good luck to him! He was a soldier and a white man."

"One of the best," agreed Bretherton.

"So there are not many of the old crowd left with the battalion: Pagan, Gurney, Dodd… and that's all." He rose to his feet. "Will you leave this business to me? Keeping quiet about it is out of the question. I shall have so see the A.D.M.S. and I will ask to see the Corps Commander or the B.G.G.S. Meanwhile, till we know how the land lies, you had better lie doggo. I will leave instructions with the matron and get her to send you a dose."

"You are a dear old heathen, Uncle Sam. I know you will do your best for me—though I don't much care. I'm very tired: I'm going to sleep now."

Harding remained some moments watching the motionless figure that lay with closed eyes upon the bed; and then, with a little smile of affection playing about the corners of his mouth, he left the ward.

IV

Some hours later Harding returned.

"Well, I have fixed up things for you, G. B.," he said. "I have seen the A.D.M.S., and he saw the Corps Commander; and then the General called me in. I caused quite a flutter. They told me to wait. Corps got on to Army, and Army on to G.H.Q. Finally, they made up their minds about you; though what they are up to I don't know.

"They wanted to move you at once; but I would not have that. I am going to keep my eye on you for a day or two at least. Then they wanted your information at once; but I would not have that either. I said not before the day after to-morrow at the earliest. They are going to move you in a day or two. Where, I don't know. A base hospital. Meanwhile—while you are here, that is—you are to remain as Colonel von Wahnheim, and speak German if necessary. That's an order. What the game is, I don't know; but I do know that they have reported through the usual channels that Colonel von Wahnheim was captured in an abortive trench raid, and also—through the usual channels—that Captain Bretherton who escaped from Ebenthal prisoner-of-war camp some months ago, has reached our lines. I fancy that when you leave here you are to be G. B. again. But meanwhile, you are von W., and nobody except myself is to know that you are not."

V

During the next few days Bretherton was visited by a high staff officer from G.H.Q., who questioned and cross-questioned him, and who was obviously very pleased with the several hundred pages of information that were taken down. A mental specialist also visited him. This officer, however, did not communicate the result of his examination to Harding, but sent his report direct to G.H.Q. On the fifth day Colonel Liddel, the staff officer from G.H.Q., appeared again.

"I want to have a chat with you, Bretherton," he said. "We are going to move you to-morrow. We are going to send you to Le Touquet. You have had a bad time and you have been very useful to us. We have notified the O.C. hospital, and you can stay there more or less as long as you like. Get absolutely fit again. There is no hurry. You will arrive there as Captain Bretherton and nobody will know anything about the other business. And you must give me your word that you will not mention it to a soul, nor let anyone know that you have suffered from loss of memory. You may talk about your escape from Germany—not too fully; information gets through to the Hun, and it is not wise to let him know too much about how prisoners escape—and to account for the gap in time, you can say that you were hiding in a wood or were concealed by a civilian, or anything. But not a word about von Wahnheim, you understand? I ask for your word as an officer, but it is an order—and disobedience will be treated accordingly."

"I suppose it is useless to ask questions—reasons?" said Bretherton.

"Quite."

"I give you my word," said Bretherton.

"Good." The Colonel rose and held out his hand. "Good luck, Bretherton. I am going on leave next week, and if there is anything I can do for you—see your people or anything…"

"No, thanks very much," replied Bretherton. "I have only a stray uncle, and he is abroad."

"So much the better," was the Colonel's cryptic remark. "Good-bye. Make the most of the sea-air down there. I will come and have a look at you one of these days."

And Bretherton was left wondering.

CHAPTER XIX

I

WHITE-CAPPED rollers driven before a strong north-westerly wind were breaking upon the coast of northern France. From the clear but distant horizon they came surging in, a never-ceasing succession of green, foam-flecked ridges, mounting higher and higher till one by one they curved glassy green in the sunlight to crash in a cascade of white, and foam far up the broad beach towards the dunes. The dunes, too, ran in parallel ridges like the breakers: the outer ridge bare and dazzling white in the sunshine, the inner ridges clothed with dark pines that converted the bleak bare coast into a green miniature mountain-land.

In one of the wind-sheltered valleys among the sand-hills walked a little group of officers from the Lewis Gun School at Le Touquet. With one exception they were sub-alterns, smooth-faced boys from infantry battalions in the line, to whom the Lewis-gun coarse was a joyous two weeks' holiday. They laughed and chattered as they trudged along, and when three V.A.D.s from one of the many hospitals in the neighbourhood passed, several of them looked back hopefully for some sign of encouragement.

"First English girls I've seen for months," exclaimed one of them. "I shall develop shell-shock and have one of the darlings to mix me a spot when I'm thirsty, another to hold my hand, and the prettiest of the lot to tuck me up in bed and kiss me good night."

"You are delirious, Bunface," chaffed another. "Don't you know that Generals and the gilded staff wallahs bag all the pretty ones and that subalterns in the P.B.I. get only moth-eaten hags from the vicar's needlework guild? Isn't that so, Skipper?"

The man thus appealed to smiled. He wore the ribbon of the Military Cross and was an older man and more care-worn than the others. "Possibly," he said. "I have been in hospital for some months now, and I have never had any such alarming experiences as Bunface suggests. But then I haven't much of an eye for feminine beauty, and in any case I lack Bunface's fascinating manner."

The party separated at the end of the dunes where the seawall and parade of Paris Plage begins. The majority of the subalterns went towards the town, but the man with captain's stars upon his shoulder-straps, Gerard Bretherton, crossed the beach towards the sea.

Four months had passed since he arrived in an ambulance at the hospital among the pines, and he was now fit and strong again.

It was six weeks since he had been passed as convalescent, and a month since that memorable day on which for the first time he had been allowed to wander off alone. How he had enjoyed those walks through the silent pine woods! The canters along the beach on a nag he had borrowed from the staff at Etaples! And the simple amusements of Paris Plage, the civilized shops, the tea-rooms, and the hotels had had the charm of novelty. And there had been the cheery companionship of other patients and of the succession of officers at the Lewis Gun School who flocked into Paris Plage after parades every afternoon, and in the evening hired the local *fiacres* to take them back, and recklessly raced their antiquated vehicles along the road through the pine woods to Le Touquet.

But gradually these amusements had palled. He grew well and strong and restless. Stirring news came from the line. The Messines Ridge had been stormed, and slowly the British were advancing across the almost impassable morass of Passchendaele at the cost of four hundred thousand casualties. He had watched the everchanging personnel of the great camp on the bare hillside of Etaples. He became restless. He was fit again, but he was not pulling his weight. He had applied to go back to his old battalion, but the authorities had replied that there was no hurry; and in these days when a continuous stream of hospital trains ran westward and a like stream of reinforcement trains ran eastward, he was puzzled to account for his special treatment.

That morning, however, he had received an official letter. He was appointed to the staff of G.H.Q. He was to go to Montreuil in two days' time for an interview and to report for duty at the end of the week. He was not enthusiastic about this staff appointment. Many men would have been delighted, he knew. He would have preferred the old battalion and the life and men he knew, but since that could not be, he was resigned.

He turned from the sea and walked back across the beach towards the line of gimcracks, toy-like villas that showed above the digue. He turned down the central street and into the cosy tearoom of *Le Chat Bleu*. It was as usual rather crowded at this hour. There were a number of officers, a few civilians, and a sprinkling of V.A.D.s. He found a vacant table by the window and sat down.

Almost immediately, however, he had a feeling that somebody was staring at him, and his eyes, guided by that mysterious power that operates on such occasions, turned towards a table occupied by two V.A.D.s on the opposite side of the room. One of the girls had half-risen to her feet and was staring at him with eyes that were strangely dark against the pallor of her face. His own heart made a great leap and hung, as it seemed, poised for a second or two in his throat, suffocating him, and then hammered furiously.

He stumbled to his feet and moved towards her. They met in the alleyway between the tables.

"Gerard!" she cried in a hushed voice, and he noticed that her grey eyes were strangely dark.

"Helen!" he stammered, and was dumb.

The colour flowed back to her cheeks, and she turned hastily to the V.A.D. who was seated at the table watching them curiously.

"Marjorie, this is Captain Bretherton," she said. "G. B. they call him in his regiment. He was my brother's company commander. G. B. back from the dead!" she added.

Bretherton laughed awkwardly and accepted the invitation to join them. "Hardly from the dead," he said. "From a prison camp in Germany."

The girl called Marjorie fixed a pair of very large blue eyes upon him, clasped her hands together, and cried excitedly, "An escaped prisoner-of-war! How thrilling!"

"From the dead really," repeated Helen. "You were reported missing—I heard nothing more. And that was nearly a year ago."

A waitress came to take their order, but Bretherton found his brain unequal to the simple task of giving it coherently. He asked the girl called Marjorie what she would like, realized suddenly that he was speaking in French, halted and glanced furtively at Helen. He found her eyes fixed upon him. He looked quickly away and spoke rapidly to the waitress in English, and when she replied in French, he broke wildly into German, stammered, and became dumb.

Marjorie laughed merrily and gave the order herself. He was obviously a hero to her. She plied him with questions about his experiences but he answered her absently with his mind on other things, and it was only later that he realized that she had done all the talking and that he and Helen had said scarcely a word.

And then suddenly Marjorie jumped up. "We must simply fly," she said to Helen. "We have to be back in ten minutes and it is a good twenty minutes' walk."

They were at the door, and Bretherton realized that in a moment she would be gone and that he did not even know in which hospital she was employed.

"I want to talk to you," he began desperately, "about— about your brother…"

"Come on, Helen," cried Marjorie. "We must simply dash."

Helen was standing on the pavement in the dark blue uniform that became her so well. Bretherton, pale-faced, was gazing pleadingly at the little face beneath the close-fitting blue hat. Her eyes strayed from his face, and she played with a button of her coat.

"I have two hours off to-morrow," she said. "From six if you…"

"Yes, yes," he agreed. "Where?"

"You know Gaudin's?"

He nodded. Marjorie had taken her by the arm and was dragging her away.

"Soon after six," she called back.

"Soon after six—Gaudin's," he repeated. And then she was Gone.

II

It was five minutes past six, and he sat in the little upper room of Gaudin's with his eyes fixed on the clock. A sub-altern from the Lewis Gun School was strumming idly upon the piano that stood in one corner, and two Army Nursing Sisters and a Frenchwoman occupied two of the little tables. He was glad that the room was not empty. He had not attained the calmness he had hoped for, and he was afraid to meet her alone. She was free at six. It was twenty minutes' walk from the hospital, the girl Marjorie had said. Twenty past six then, unless she hurried.

At fourteen minutes past six by the ormolu clock on the mantelpiece she walked into the room, a neat figure in her dark blue uniform, and her cheeks were alive with colour. He had carefully rehearsed what he would say to her, but he only grinned foolishly and awkwardly, and said not a word.

They sat down at a table, and she began to talk—rather quickly, he fancied. Uncertain of herself, he thought, and was pleased. She chattered about the hospital, her work, her coming to France. He talked also, about the prison camp at Ebenthal and the humorous side of the life there; and they both laughed rather frequently and rather longer than was necessary at his jokes.

He was aware that another part of him was anxiously watching the other people in the room, and he was conscious of a quickening of his pulses when the subaltern rose from the piano and went out. Another ten minutes passed by, and then the two army sisters rose and went out. There was only the Frenchwoman left. A waitress came in to clear the tables. The Frenchwoman was buttoning her gloves. She rose to her feet and walked out. The waitress had piled the dirty plates on a tray and would be gone in a minute or two. Bretherton experienced the nearest approach to panic he had ever known. He talked rapidly and wildly about Ebenthal, Le Touquet, the Lewis Gun School, anything. From the corner of his eye he saw that the waitress had picked up the tray and was walking towards the door.

She was gone. They were alone. For a few seconds he continued his feverish conversation, and then he caught her eye, stammered, and became dumb. There was silence. He could hear his watch ticking on his wrist. He dared not look at her. The silence was vibrant—like a tuning-fork. Perspiration broke out upon his forehead. He went breathlessly to the piano and dropped upon the stool; and the silence, vibrant with her personality, seemed to follow him like a howling mob.

His fingers wandered over the keys. He struck a note or two softly. The sound seemed like a protective fence flung around him. His fingers moved more quickly and he found that he was playing her song, "Just a song at twilight." He played on, the words and her voice as he had heard it in the little inn parlour ringing in his head. He played the last note and turned slowly on the stool. Silence rushed in again, silence tense and audible, charged with tiny sparks that were all but visible.

She stood facing him. Her hands hung limp and helplessly at her sides, her face passion-pale, and her grey eyes dark with things that are beyond speech. His face was no less pale than hers. His heart seemed too big for his body, and the roots of his hair were a-tingle. He could no longer doubt. He stood stammering and staring.

"Helen…" he whispered hoarsely. "In Germany… a prisoner… always… I thought of you… you… You…"

"And I," she whispered. "Every night… I have dreamed… every day… Oh, Gerard!"

He took her ice-cold hand as though it had been some fragile bloom and raised it to his lips. And at the contact they both shivered.

And then the door was flung noisily open, and Marjorie marched into the room. "Come on, Captain Bretherton," she cried. "Finish anything you have to say to Helen on the way back. If we are late again we shall get a frightful strafing."

They went down the stairs and out into the lighted street and along the road through the sombre forest. Marjorie chattered ceaselessly and contentedly. Helen and Bretherton were silent. At a side door of one of the large villas in the woods they halted.

"Just in time!" exclaimed Marjorie, looking at her watch. "Good night, Captain Bretherton." And she disappeared through the door.

Helen halted on the step, turned back towards him and held up her head. The moonlight striking down through the branches upon her pale, upturned face showed him her eyes, pools of unfathomable darkness. He caught her in his arms and pressed his mouth to hers. Her face, he saw, was strange in its pale intensity.

"God!" she murmured in low, tense tones as he released her.

"I did not know that love could hurt so much."

She disappeared through the doorway, and he was left alone leaning against the wall in the moonlight.

III

He reviewed the situation the following morning as he was driven towards G.H.Q., and he found it good. He no longer desired to return to the old battalion. Helen completely filled his horizon. At Montreuil he would be comparatively near her, and should be able to see her frequently. He did not imagine that staff officers found any great difficulty in obtaining the use of a car occasionally. And she would have a minimum of anxiety on his behalf. Such twinges of conscience as he felt in accepting what was undoubtedly a "cushy" job he stifled with the reflection that he had already taken his part as a fighting soldier in the line and was therefore more entitled to the comfort of the staff than were many men who might have been appointed.

He was received by Colonel Liddel, the staff officer who had visited him during his brief stay in Harding's C.C.S., and whose parting words had so puzzled him. And now again he found the Colonel's attitude perplexing. He was pushed into a chair and offered a cigarette, which he refused in favour of his pipe. The Colonel lighted his own pipe and began to talk.

"I was a foot-slogger, Bretherton," he said, "before I became a staff wallah, and in those days one of the things that struck me about modem war was the comparative impotence of the individual. His contribution to the termination of the war seemed to be negligible. His greatest efforts—though they brought death—rarely brought him the satisfaction of knowing that he personally had advanced the war one millimetre towards a successful termination. Do you know what I mean?"

"Quite," agreed Bretherton, wondering what on earth the Colonel was driving at. "I have had that feeling myself—often."

Colonel Liddel nodded. "Yes. The hardships of this dreary business would be more supportable, I think, if one individually could see, as it were, some return for one's money. Of course it is the united efforts of us individuals that is going to beat Brother Bosche, but precious few of us below the rank of Corps Commander or Chief-of-Staff have the satisfaction of being able to point to some definite step towards success and truthfully say, 'This is the result of my effort.' That must be a great satisfaction. Such a man would be lucky, don't you think?"

"Very lucky indeed," answered Bretherton. "I should think there is hardly an infanteer that would not cheerfully face the music in those circumstances. It is the interminable messing about that never seems to lead anywhere that takes the verve out of a fellow."

The Colonel nodded and took his pipe from his mouth and gazed reflectively at the glowing bowl. And then he went off at a tangent.

"What do you make of this Russian business?" he asked.

"The revolution and the withdrawal of Russia from the war." queried Bretherton.

The Colonel nodded. "Yes. What do you make of it?"

"Well, it is rather a bad business, sir, isn't it?" he answered. He was puzzled by the Colonel's question, for he laboured under no delusion that his opinion on these events could be of any interest to G.H.Q. "It means, does it not, that the German troops on the Russian front will be thrown in here on the west?"

The Colonel nodded. "Yes," he said. "That is what it means. By the collapse of Russia, Germany has something like three-quarters of a million more troops to play with. Thirty-four comparatively fresh divisions to fling against a thin line of tired and war-worn troops. And we have no general reserve worth speaking of to draw upon. Our reserve is the Yanks, but they will not be here in time for the crash. Mr. Jerry will see to that. He will fling his thirty-four fresh divisions in on a carefully prepared scheme, as nearly perfect as his excellent staff can make it—fling them in reckless of casualties, in one great final effort to force a decision." The Colonel paused to apply a match to his pipe. "And," he continued—"and he has every chance of succeeding. As I have said, we have practically no reserve to draw upon, and the people at home don't or won't realize the situation. It will be Germany's final effort, and if it is successful France will be out of the war and so shall we, from a military point of view. But if it is unsuccessful, he will collapse. The war will be over. We have a chance of holding him if we know where and when this big push is coming. The man who could find that out—the man who could tell us that—would be very fortunate indeed. He would have in plenty that satisfaction of achievement of which you and I have just been deploring the absence. *He* would be able to point to this coming great battle an truly say, 'I have decided its result; it was my effort that lost Germany her last throw of the dice.' And that man is——" The Colonel paused and looked solemnly at Bretherton. "That man is—you."

In one vivid flash of illumination Bretherton saw all that the Colonel's words implied. He went very white. "I!" he stammered.

"Yes—you, Bretherton," said the Colonel slowly, and he laid aside his pipe on the table. "You had the misfortune to suffer temporarily from loss of memory and hallucination Through that misfortune you may now render inestimable service to your country."

"You mean——?" queried Bretherton, and his heart was like ice.

"I mean," said the Colonel, "that Colonel von Wahnheim of the Prussian Staff will have unlimited opportunities of learning when and where this great push is to take place."

Bretherton stared at the floor in silence. At length he said, "But Colonel von Wahnheim was taken prisoner."

"True," agreed the Colonel. And then he added slowly, "But he might escape."

Bretherton stared with knit brows at the floor. "You want me to become a spy then," he said bitterly.

The Colonel nodded. "Yes, that is what it comes to. I know the word 'spy' has an unpleasant sound to us soldiers, but one must remember that a spy needs to be a very gallant fellow and he often renders his country more valuable service than even the most successful general or admiral."

"Have you no secret agents with the enemy, that you must ask me to do this?" complained Bretherton.

"Oh, yes, a great number, but none that could get such information as Colonel von Wahnheim could get."

Bretherton flung out his hand helplessly. "Is this an order?" he questioned.

The Colonel took his pipe again and tapped it over an ashtray. "No," he said. "You are a soldier, Bretherton, and this is not a duty for which you are liable. We are not ordering you to do this. But you have it in your power to render your country a great service, and the Commander-in-Chief asks you to do it."

"And if I refuse?" asked Bretherton after a pause.

The Colonel slowly filled his pipe. "Well, it will not count against you theoretically. But—well, you will have refused such an opportunity as few men have had in the war. And there is a black mark against your name already, Bretherton. Some business of a newspaper picture on the Somme early in '16."

"That damned photograph again!" exploded Bretherton.

The Colonel smiled. "Personally I know nothing about it," he said. "And I do not wish to dwell on that Hide of the question. And I would not think about it either, if I were you. What you have to decideis whether at some inconvenience and risk to yourself you will do your country and the Allies a great service. You are perfectly at liberty to refuse—but I don't think you will. And there is no hurry for the moment. Go out and think it over. And tell me to-night, to-morrow, or the day after if you like, what you decide."

It was late in the afternoon when Bretherton returned. He had spent the intervening hours wandering through the country lanes, tormented by the choice he had to make.

He was asked voluntarily to fling away the cup of happiness that was newly raised to his lips and subsitute a poison from which he recoiled with fear and horror.

Colonel Liddel looked up as he entered the room. "Well, Bretherton?" he said.

"I have decided."

The Colonel looked at him for a moment or two in silence, and then said again, "Well?"

"I will do what you ask," answered Bretherton in a low voice.

The Colonel nodded slowly and said, "Good man."

"But I hate the job. I hate it, and—funk it."

The Colonel nodded and pursed up his lips. "I know." His voice was sympathetic. "But you accept?"

Bretherton nodded. "I am superstitious enough to believe that if one avoids a thing simply because it is unpleasant, one will not get away with it. Something else will turn up later, more unpleasant—and unavoidable."

The Colonel nodded in agreement. "That is very true."

"And when do I begin?" asked Bretherton.

"The sooner the better. But we will give you a little holiday first."

Bretherton asked a question that had been worrying him. "How am I to get across the lines?"

The Colonel pushed him into a chair. "Don't worry about that. We have that all cut and dried. There will be no difficulty or danger about that. Your job begins on the other side. And in one way it is easier, since you have no relations to worry about."

"No—no relations," agreed Bretherton bitterly.

The Colonel shot a swift glance at his face and then looked down at his desk. "Is there a—girl?"

Bretherton nodded. "Yes." And he added with a wry smile, "Yesterday I asked her to marry me."

The Colonel nodded his head slowly; he was drawing invisible patterns on the table with his pencil. "War is the very devil!" he muttered.

Then he rose briskly from his chair and laid a hand on Bretherton's shoulder. "Well, if I were you I would try to banish this job from your mind for the time being. Bring your kit along here to-morrow and then go off for a week. Go where you like; do what you like. And—oh—of course, all this must be kept strictly secret. You must tell no one; not even the—little lady. Officially you are at G.H.Q. You might tell her that a special job will prevent you from writing to her for a month or two; it ought to be through by then." He turned in his pacing. "Well, I think that's all. Now come along and have some tea."

Just before they reached the door the Colonel paused, and staring awkwardly at his boots, said: "If you care to give me the little lady's address, I will write to her periodically while you are away—set her mind at rest, you know. And I will go to see her if she gets worried."

"You are very good, sir," said Bretherton gratefully.

"I have a wife and kiddies at home," said the Colonel abstractedly. "I wouldn't be a woman for anything these days, Bretherton." Then he added in a cheery voice, "Now for some tea."

IV

Two figures sat on the dunes to the southward of Paris Plage. On their left the red December sun was no more than a hand's breadth above the pines. Behind them beneath the trees a thin mist was rising, and the air held the half-smoky smell of frost. Below them the cold, foam-edged water ebbed and flowed restlessly on the white, crisp beach.

Helen sat muffled in her blue uniform greatcoat, the collar turned up about her pink, wind-stung ears and cheeks, her gloved hands clasped about her knees. Her shoulders fitted exactly the firm curve of Bretherton's right arm. The peak of his service cap came low down over his left eye by reason of the pressure of Helen's close-fitting blue cap against the other side. His chin was buried within the high warm collar of his British-warm. The northern sea-breeze was bitingly cold, with a tang of salt and sting of sand in it, but warm blood coursed through his veins. The firm pressure of her small shoulders against his side, the soft touch of her head against his, the warm caress of her cheek, held the breathless magic of fairyland. The solitude of the shining sea and beach, the restless murmur of the waves, fitted his mood. Thus they sat, silent, with no need of words. Once he had murmured the magic name "Helen" and pressed more closely the dear diminutive form in the crook of his arm, to be answered by a smooth cheek gently rubbing his and a little whispered "Gerard."

At length she spoke. Her voice was low. "One month, you say—one whole month… perhaps two, without seeing you. It is too long, Gerard. How can I let you go now?"

He pressed the shoulder that snuggled against his coat and murmured inarticulately.

"But you will write... dear letters, Gerard," she half-whispered.

His eyes roved helplessly across the deserted seas; his brows were knit.

"I... it may not be possible." His voice sounded far away.

The cheek that gently rubbed his own ceased its movement, and she was silent for a moment.

"But... but why not?" Consternation was in her low tone.

He laughed unconvincingly. "G.H.Q., you know," he parried. "Special work... red tape... and all that."

"Gerard!" The pressure against his side relaxed; she sat up. "Gerard, what *is* this special work of yours?" Her eyes betrayed fear, the fear of every woman who feels the unknown dragging her man from her.

He held her gloved hand between his own and forced a smile.

"You know I cannot tell you that, little girl... red tape; but there it is."

"Gerard! Will you be in danger?"

He laughed, more convincingly this time, he told himself. "There is always the possibility of danger for a soldier," he countered. "Even at G.H.... or here. Planes and"—he pressed her close—"and little thieves that steal a fellow's soul. Anyway, I am not going to the trenches, if that is what you mean."

"Thank God!" she whispered fervently. "Thank God!"

She snuggled close to him again.

"And in any case," he said with his cheek against hers, "you would not have me shirk my bit."

She nuzzled the hand that caressed her cheek. "No… no," she murmured. "My man must do his bit. But so soon, Gerard!—so soon!"

She clung to him and gazed with unseeing eyes across the darkening waste of water.

CHAPTER XX

I

BRETHERTON sat on his bed in his little room in the prisoner-of-war camp at Ashwick. He stared moodily at the floor as he crumpled in his fingers the tiny scrap of paper that had come to him five minutes before. It contained only two words: "Brixham, S.S. *Dordrecht*"; but he understood.

Three weeks had passed since he crossed the Channel, donned again the battle-stained uniform of Colonel von Wahnheim, and entered the prison-camp at Ashwick. Officially he had been discharged from hospital and been admitted to a prisoner-of-war camp; and east of the Rhine, the German staff that dealt with such matters made one more entry against his name. The dossier was complete. He had been reported a prisoner soon after the abortive trench raid near Arras; he had been reported as wounded and in a British hospital; and now he was reported as discharged from hospital and admitted to the prison-camp at Ashwick. And if corroboration were needed, there were the letters of his fellow-prisoners, who wrote to their relatives in Germany that Colonel von Wahnheim, who had already once escaped from a British prison-camp, was now among them.

Those three weeks had been a time of purgatory to Bretherton. The lot of a prisoner-of-war is never a pleasant one, and in his case it was peculiarly unpleasant. To be a prisoner in one's own country, to be herded day and night with one's enemies, to be exposed to the gaze of one's fellow countrymen and countrywomen as they passed the camp and to read hostility in their eyes, was a bitter ordeal for a returned fighting man. And he had had to keep a strict watch upon himself lest by word or deed he should betray his true nationality to his fellow-prisoners.

The plan of his escape had been most carefully worked out and explained to him by Colonel Liddel. He was to choose a fellow-prisoner to share his escape, and once outside the camp, they were to separate or not as he thought best. Whether the other man reached Germany or was recaptured was a point of minor importance, since his letters to his relations recounting his attempted escape in the company of Colonel von Wahnheim would furnish a convincing proof of the authenticity of that officer's German nationality and patriotism.

Bretherton had chosen the man, a young Major, von Carlenheim by name, and had already discussed with him various plans of escape; and by the prearranged secret signal he had notified the Commandant of his choice and consequent readiness for putting into execution the real plan.

For the last three days he had watched the means of his escape being prepared and knew therefore that the time of its employment was fast approaching. Four workmen had been laying new drain-pipes in the camp. A trench some four feet deep by two feet wide had been cut across the exercise-yard, passing under the wire-entanglement fence of the camp by a short tunnel six feet long and continuing outside the camp to join the main drainage at a distance of fifty yards or more from the fence. The drain-pipes were as yet unlaid, and they reposed in a heap by a rough shelter erected for the use of the workmen at the junction of the trench with the main drainage system. Outside the wire fence at the point where the tunnel passed beneath it, an extra sentry had been posted.

All was ready, and now the time for action had arrived. The twisted ball of paper he held in his hands was the signal. The words "Brixham, S.S. *Dordrecht*," meant that in Brixham harbour, ready to sail the following day, lay the S.S. *Dordrecht*, a Dutch ship commanded by a Dutch skipper, who, the British Secret Service had reason to believe, would not be averse from smuggling an escaped German prisoner-of-war into Holland.

Bretherton tore the paper into tiny fragments and went in search of von Carlenheim. He found him playing tennis on the dust court that had been made in one corner of the exercise-ground, and, the set finished, led him aside out of earshot of the others.

"I am going to have a shot at escaping to-night," he began. "Are you game to come with me?"

Von Carlenheim was game. "But how is it to be managed, Colonel?" he asked.

"That drain-pipe trench," answered Bretherton. "The workmen leave at five o'clock. It is practically dark then, and all we have to do is to drop into the trench when nobody is looking and crawl along it under the wire to the other end where it is practically out of range of the camp lamps."

"But, Colonel, the sentry!" objected von Carlenheim.

"The idea is to get some other fellows to create a disturbance," answered Bretherton. "If they make enough row, the
sentry may walk along to see what is happening and give us
a chance of slipping under the wire."

"But suppose the sentry does not go, Colonel?"

Bretherton shrugged his shoulders. "We shall be lying in
the trench waiting, and if he does not move, we shall have
to crawl back again, that's all. There will be no harm done.
It's a sporting chance. Anyway if you don't like the idea, I
will ask someone else. But I should prefer to have you with
me, since I speak only a word or two of the language, and
your fluent English may be very useful.

"Oh, I am with you, Colonel," answered von Carlenheim.
"A simple plan of this nature often succeeds where a more
complicated one would fail."

II

As Bretherton prowled restlessly about the camp
that afternoon he was reminded of those anxious hours
preceding his escape from Ebenthal with poor Melford.
Then, however, he had been buoyed up by hopes of
freedom and returning to his own people. Now no such
prospect sustained him. And though on this occasion he
was to escape with the connivance of the authorities, the
element of danger would not be entirely absent, for the
Commandant was the only man in the camp who knew
his real identity. The guards would not hesitate to fire at an
escaping prisoner; and death at the hands of his old and

patriotic fellow-countrymen who guarded the camp would be no less final than on the battlefields of France, and far less glorious. And success would be but the prelude to a lonely vigil among the enemy, during which he would carry his life in his hands every moment of the day and night.

At six o'clock the prisoners paraded in one corner of the exercise-ground for roll-call. Daylight had gone, and the electric lamps around the camp threw the wire fence into brilliant relief, but served only to intensify the shadows beyond the range of their rays. A sentry with fixed bayonet stood outside the fence at the point at which the pipe trench left the camp. The trench itself was seen as a black ribbon that emerged from the gloom of the exercise-yard, crossed the belt of light, disappearing for a couple of yards where the tunnel passed the wire, and melted into the darkness beyond.

Bretherton and von Carlenheim stood on the right of the ranks, a position that ensured their names being ticked off among the first few; then they would be free to return to their rooms. Next to them stood the men von Carlenheim had detailed for the task of creating the diversion. As soon as their names were ticked off, Bretherton and von Carlenheim walked slowly away across the deserted yard towards the wash-house from which the pipe began. One glance around showed Bretherton that no one was in sight. He dropped into the trench and was closely followed by von Carlenheim.

He crawled noiselessly forward till he was within some twenty yards of the wire fence; then cautiously he raised his head. On the far side of the fence, with his back towards the camp, stood the sentry, properly at ease beside the trench; and near by on the edge of the pool of light that fell full upon the sentry stood another figure. Bretherton felt a touch upon his heel and turned his head.

"Our luck is out, Colonel," whispered von Carlenheim. "The Commandant himself! The sentry will not move whilst he is there."

Bretherton did not reply. He did not share von Carlenheim's misgivings; for it was part of Colonel Liddel's plan that the Commandant himself should send the sentry to investigate the cause of the disturbance. For two or three minutes they lay motionless in the trench, a period of danger during any moment of which one of the guards might walk across the yard and discover them. And then suddenly angry voices sounded from away to the left; there came a thudding sound as of blows, and a confused shouting that grew in volume to a wild hubbub. Bretherton again raised his head. The sentry's head was turned in the direction of the disturbance, and the Commandant had abandoned his contemplation of the night sky to look towards the same point. He said something to the sentry. The sentry sloped arms, slapped the butt of his rifle, and marched off quickly along the wire. The Commandant followed at a more leisurely pace.

Bretherton crawled forward. He entered the zone of light in which the rays of the electric standard struck directly into the trench, passed into the short, deep shade of the little tunnel, emerged into the light once more and passed on into rapidly increasing shadow. Close behind him crawled von Carlenheim.

At its end by the hut the trench curved so that the hut was between it and the camp, and behind this screen Bretherton rose to his feet. Through a chink in the rough boards he could see the camp, a rampart of light amid the darkness, and at the far corner the needle of light upon the bayonet above the dark figure of the sentry. Angry murmurs still disturbed the evening calm, but the hubbub was dying down.

Von Carlenheim had followed Bretherton into the hut, and he uttered an exclamation of delight as his eyes fell upon some garments that hung from nails on one side of it.

"This is luck indeed, Colonel!" he exclaimed.

"Yes. They could not have been more thoughtful if they had known we were coming," answered Bretherton with a smothered smile.

The garments consisted of an old mackintosh, a much-worn overcoat with a dirty muffler in the pocket, a threadbare Norfolk jacket, and three hats: a check cap, a greasy Homburg, and a broken straw.

"Very thoughtful of the British workman," commented von Carlenheim as he put on the Norfolk jacket and raincoat.

Bretherton dressed himself in the overcoat and Homburg. Von Carlenheim took the cap. Bretherton took a shovel from the corner of the hut and put it over his shoulder; von Carlenheim selected a pick. They turned their backs upon the camp and set out.

Von Carlenheim had a rough map made in the camp and a small compass. Bretherton had studied the country too well to need a map, and his route had been carefully planned beforehand. They were less than twenty-five miles from the coast, and their escape would not be discovered till the morning roll call at eight thirty.

For an hour or more they tramped along without incident, and von Carlenheim gave "good night" to such people as they met. There was no moon; the night was dark, and few people were abroad. Bretherton's route had been planned to avoid military posts and other places where he might be questioned, but as they passed a dark spinney, a figure emerged from a lane and turned into the road they were following.

"Bleedin' dark night, my lucky lads!" called a jocular voice; and the man fell into step beside the two homeward-plodding workmen, as he took them to be. Bretherton saw the stiff outline of a service cap against the sky; he noted the short British-warm with high upturned collar and riding-switch protruding slantwise from the pocket, showing that the man belonged to a mounted unit; and he cursed the man in his heart. He began to wish that he had separated from von Carlenheim; for alone he could have easily carried off the situation, but in his rôle of von Wahnheim he was limited to a few words of English, and those mispronounced. Von Carlenheim must do the talking, and von Carlenheim might make a slip.

The soldier volunteered the information that he was a gunner on leave from Tidworth, special "leaf." "Aunt o' mine just died—special family reasons," he explained with a large wink that was lost in the darkness. Von Carlenheim chuckled in reply, He betrayed no eagerness to get rid of the man. He too was a soldier, he said, an infanteer on leave from France—"only too bloomin' glad to get back into civvies for a day or two." He had been helping his brother—indicating Bretherton—who was dumb, poor chap, and none too strong, to do a job of work.

The soldier nodded and murmured sympathetically, "Poor bleeder!" He appeared to be flattered by the company of a man who had been "out"; he himself was C.3, but hoped to wangle himself across the ditch before it was all over.

Thus they tramped along, Bretherton silent perforce and apprehensive, von Carlenheim good-humouredly communicative, the soldier profanely loquacious; till the man lighted another cigarette and with a "so long, boys" turned up a side road. The tramp of his ammunition boots upon the road and his shrilly whistled version of a popular air were audible long after his squat form had disappeared in the darkness.

Bretherton congratulated von Carlenheim on the way in which he had handled the situation, and his praise was the more sincere since his former experience as a hunted prisoner on the roads of Germany enabled him fully to appreciate his companion's coolness. He decided to keep von Carlenheim with him and if possible enter Germany in his company. The man had proved that his company in England was no added danger, and his testimony to every stage of the escape would lessen any risk of suspicion later on.

It was past midnight when they reached the outskirts of Brixham. They reconnoitred the town and then struck boldly through it to the harbour. The pale gleam of star-light on a bayonet warned them of the presence of a sentry, but by waiting on the mathematical regularity of his pacing they slipped unperceived on to the quay. The slap and plop of water came from the darkness at their feet, and the spars and tackle of shipping showed indistinctly against the stars. Ahead, a dark tubby shape, surmounted by two stumpy sky-stabbing masts, reared itself above the quay; and Bretherton's keen eyes deciphered the words "Dordrecht, Rotterdam," painted in white upon her blunt stern. He twitched von Carlenheim by the sleeve. "A Dutchman," he whispered. "The very thing we are looking for."

Such was Bretherton's confidence in von Carlenheim that he determined to entrust to him the task of negotiating with the Dutch skipper for their passage. He felt that there could be little risk of failure. It was unlikely that the British Secret Service would have chosen the skipper of the *Dordrecht* if they had entertained any serious doubts of his willingness to smuggle prisoners-of-war into Holland. And coming from von Carlenheim, the negotiations would have the very valuable and unmistakable stamp of genuineness.

The deck of the *Dordrecht* was dark and silent; a single plank connected it with the quay. They waited for the turn in the clockwork sentry's beat, and then von Carlenheim glided noiselessly over the gang-plank and disappeared among the shadows on deck. Bretherton crouched in the shelter of a dark awning-covered pile of merchandise and waited.

The time passed slowly. Out at sea the wind whimpered and sighed. Near by, some halliards rattled with machine-gun-like taps against a mast; a smack creaked at her moorings. The tide murmured restlessly against the stones. A clock in the town behind him chimed two. The sentry's heavy tread grew faint and loud in succession as he paced to and fro, and occasionally there came the rattle of his rifle-butt upon the stones as he ordered arms and stood at ease. And then suddenly a dark form flitted once more over the gang-plank, and von Carlenheim's voice called softly, "It's all right, Colonel."

Bretherton followed quietly on to the dark, silent deck of the *Dordrecht*, descended a steep narrow companion-way and found himself in a tiny, warm saloon, brightly lighted by an oil lamp swung on gimbals. A heavy-jowled man wearing a thick blue jersey over his pyjamas sat on a swivel chair at the end of a table. Two dirty glasses and a bottle of spirit stood before him. A bunk with rumpled blankets showed that the skipper had been disturbed from his rest.

The man rose to his feet as Bretherton entered, nodded silently, and taking a clean glass from the rack on the buffet, filled it from the bottle. He pushed the glass towards Bretherton and motioned him to sit down. The question of finance had yet to be discussed.

It was a long and tedious business. The Dutchman insisted at some length upon the risk he was running; but eventually the bargain was struck. A generous sum of money was paid over then and there, with a promise of a further like amount to be paid when the fugitives were landed at Rotterdam.

"Well, gentlemen," said the Dutchman, rising, "I should advise you to turn in for an hour or two. We sail on the morning tide. We shall have the officials aboard early, and I shall have to hide you among the cargo. So be comfortable while you may, is my advice."

III

The grey light of a rainy, wind-orchestrated dawn was filtering through the scuttles when Bretherton slid from his bunk. He and von Carlenheim partook of hot coffee and bacon sitting opposite each other in the enshadowed saloon. The skipper had prepared a hiding-place which he believed would baffle the authorities. The ship's hold was filled with large wooden cases, and two of these had been emptied for the reception of the fugitives. Bretherton disliked the idea, though he admitted the necessity of a hiding-place for the short time that the officials would be on board. He smoked one of the skipper's cheroots and then declared himself ready for entombment. He and von Carlenheim descended to the hold, climbed into the cases, and the lids were screwed on.

The interior of the case was not uncomfortable, Bretherton found. It was large enough to allow of his sitting upright with his legs outstretched; and it was provided with blankets, half a loaf of bread, a hunk of cheese, and a bottle of water, though it was hoped that in less than three hours the ship would be at sea.

He found, however, that the absolute darkness, the silence, and the ever-present sense of confinement were facts that forced themselves upon the attention with increasing persistence as time passed; and at the end of half an hour he had come to the conclusion that a prolonged confinement in these conditions might send a man of nervous disposition off his head. His entombment, however, was likely to be short, and with this thought to comfort him, he curled himself up in the blankets on the floor of the case and coaxed himself to sleep.

He was awakened by movement. For some minutes he was aware of it subconsciously; and then as he opened his eyes to a darkness so intense that only by the slight chill on his eyeballs could he tell that they were not closed, he felt the long, dizzy, downward motion of a ship and the subdued throb of machinery.

It was some ten minutes later that he heard sounds in his immediate neighbourhood, that the lid of the case was taken off, and he staggered out, blinded in the glare of the open hatch, with his forearm pressed across his aching eyes.

All that day the little *Dordrecht* staggered up-Channel before a fresh south-westerly gale. Bretherton, who was a good sailor, watched the masses of green, foam-marbled water racing up astern, but von Carlenheim was frankly miserable.

The night passed uneventfully. Soon after dawn, near the straits, they passed a convoy heading for Folkestone, a black-painted leave-boat and three other ships shepherded by two grey lean destroyers that drove through the smoking seas like dolphins, sliding into great green hillocks to reappear with white cascading decks and reeling mastheads against the low grey clouds. The leave-boat's decks were brown with troops, and snatches of a popular revue tune were borne fitfuly by the gale to the watchers on the *Dordrecht*; and to Bretherton the familiar air heard amid the piping of the wind and the crash of seas was sadder than any dirge. A lonely figure upon a foreign ship, beneath an alien flag, denied even the use of his native tongue, he watched with wistful eyes the convoy bucketing its way towards the reeling dirty white line of the English coast, seen fitfully through the spume and run of seas to port. There were his countrymen and his country, the last he would see of them for many a day.

The convoy faded astern and left only the endless succession of foam-crested, racing seas that flung the little *Dordrecht's* stern and dripping propeller high in the air, whilst her decks ran waist deep in frothy water, till her bows rose with a jerk and she staggered down the reverse glacis. Suddenly in one of her drunken lurches the ship jarred cruelly; she seemed to stop dead for a fraction of a second, and then staggered on with racing propeller. The skipper dragged himself from the corner of the tiny wheel-house to which he had been flung, and in spite of his bulk went nimbly down the swaying ladder to the deck. The throb of the engines had ceased; the ship lost way, and rolled alarmingly as she rose and fell on the chasing seas.

Von Carlenheim, green of face, dragged himself from his bunk and met Bretherton at the foot of the companion-way.

"What is wrong, Colonel?" he asked.

"I don't know," replied Bretherton. "But I fancy we have hit something."

"Any danger?"

Bretherton shrugged his shoulder. "She seems buoyant enough," he grinned, as a sudden lift of the ship caused him to trot a pace or two backwards. "She won't go to the bottom yet awhile anyway."

"I don't care if she does," groaned von Carlenheim. And he staggered back to his bunk.

The skipper, in dripping sea-boots, clumped down the ladder. "We have bumped over something," he said in answer to Bretherton's raised eyebrows. "Submerged hulk most likely. Stripped the propeller, but no other damage apparently. Luckye scape, but bad enough."

For three hours the little ship rode helplessly upon the seas; and then a destroyer came up from the southward and answered her signals of distress. Bretherton and von Carlenheim had to remain out of sight during the colloquy that followed; and after what seemed to them an interminable time, during the latter part of which there was some shouting and much tramping of feet on the deck overhead, they felt the ship once more moving through the water.

Presently the skipper came below and seated himself opposite von Carlenheim and Bretherton in the little saloon. "The little warship is taking us into Dunkirk, gentlemen," he said.

"Dunkirk!" echoed von Carlenheim in dismay.

The skipper nodded. "Yes—a dangerous place for you, gentlemen; and for me too if they find you aboard."

There was silence for a few moments, and then Bretherton asked, "How long will your repairs take, skipper?"

"Two or three days—if we are lucky," answered the Dutchman.

Von Carlenheim groaned. "We shall have to go back to those infernal cases, then, Colonel—whilst the officials are aboard, anyway. Your men will not blab, Skipper?"

The skipper shrugged his shoulders. "There are talkative men in every crew," he answered. "And people will be willing to pay them to speak." He paused, and then continued, looking meaningly at his passengers: "Now if I could assure them, gentlemen, that it will be to their advantage to keep their mouths shut…"

"I sec; it is again a question of finance, then!" put in Bretherton.

Von Carlenheim groaned. "I suppose we shall have to pay up, Colonel—pay up for the privilege of spending a few more hours in those infernal coffins!"

And so the second bargain was struck.

The fugitives retired to their tiny prisons just before the ship entered the harbour of Dunkirk; and although they were to be released at nightfall or as soon as the port authorities had left the ship, it was thought prudent to provision the cases with a supply of tinned food and two stone jars of water.

For the first few hours in his cramped hiding-place Bretherton took refuge in sleep, and he awoke cheerful in the expectation that he would shortly be released. He knew by the absence of movement that the ship was either in harbour or in dock; but no sound reached him and no ray of light. He sat for half an hour, as he judged it, listening in vain for sounds of the skipper's coming, and then, feeling hungry, he opened a tin of corned beef and made a meal. He took a long drink of water, and between yearning for the pipe that was denied him and cursing the skipper, the darkness, and the war, dozed off again.

He dozed off and on for long periods, days, it seemed to him. He ate his little store of food and drank from the stone jar; and as he moved his cramped limbs in the restricted space and longed for a ray of light, he cursed the vigilance of the harbour authorities that was evidently responsible for his long confinement. The darkness began to have terrors for him, and only by the exercise of his thoughts upon other matters could he avoid the direct contemplation of it. And then the fear grew gradually in the subconscious and was ever present, even while the brain was engrossed in other thoughts, like a spectre seen out of the corner of eyes that are fixed resolutely in another direction.

On three or four occasions a series of violent tremors shook the case, and muffled detonations came to his ears in the darkness: bombs, he guessed. Dunkirk with its harbour and docks was a frequent target of the German squadron, he knew; and he prayed that if a bomb struck the *Dordrecht* it might blow him to pieces and not merely sink the ship, leaving him to drown like a kitten in a sack.

The water-jar was empty, and he was suffering from thirst. Thirst began to absorb his thoughts to the exclusion even of the darkness, and he was tempted to shout aloud and thump the case with his heels. That would bring the officials down to him. He would be discovered. But that would mean release, release from his present sufferings and from that hateful task of espionage that lay before him. Oh for a deep, deep drink of water, for a ray of blessed sunlight, to be rid of this uniform and distasteful character of Colonel von Wahnheim. Death in the trenches among his own people had no terrors comparable to this trapped-rat existence.

Time passed. He thirsted and dosed and woke and thirsted. He lost control of himself and shouted and hammered the sides of the case with his boots. He thumped the wood with his fists, tore at it with his nails. But no relief came. He was abandoned, forgotten, left to die.

The frenzy passed and was succeeded by a calmer mood. He knew that he must keep a hold upon himself or his brain would give under the strain. He dozed and woke again. Lights danced before his eyes and mocked him; voices rang in his ears; but there was no sound, no ray of light, only the darkness and silence of a tomb.

Then the frenzy came again. He shouted and hammered upon the walls of his prison with his fists. He must get out. He would be von Wahnheim no longer. Never again would he put on a German uniform; never again speak the German language. Was he to die like this in the darkness? Yet he must keep calm. His scalp tingled violently. His head was burning hot. It seemed that maggots were crawling in his brain. His will was slipping from him down, down into a bottomless pit.

IV

The S.S. *Dordrecht* was already a week overdue when she left Dunkirk. In that port, given over almost exclusively to naval and military needs, delay in work on a neutral ship was inevitable; and the crew of neutrals as such had been suspect and subject to strict surveillance. But at last the repairs were completed. The ship was at sea, and the grassy dunes of the low Flanders coast lay astern.

Von Carlenheim was the first of the fugitives to be released. He was lifted from the case with his eyes tightly shut, calling hoarsely for water. Von Wahnheim followed, and was carried on deck, where he drank with fierce restraint from the pannikin that was held to his lips. He kept his eyes tightly closed against the blinding glare and his arms stretched out in front of him, whilst his body shook with ague. Von Carlenheim recovered slowly; physically he was the worse of the two. He was placed in a bunk where the subdued light enabled him to open his eyes. Von Wahnheim sat at the table and ate a meal; and though still a little shaky on his feet, seemed little the worse for his experience. But when his eyes had first grown accustomed to the world of light, he had expressed surprise at his surroundings. He had recognized neither the skipper, von Carlenheim, nor the ship, and when the skipper offered a brief explanation, had knitted his brows and gone on eating without a word.

Later, when the skipper had gone on deck, he said to von Carlenheim: "I have no idea what that fellow was talking about. Von Carlenheim is your name, is it not? Major von Carlenheim? Tell me, Major, how I came to be here. Begin from the moment that you first met me."

Von Carlenheim, sitting up in his bunk, did as he was requested. Colonel von Wahnheim listened attentively and made no comment till the end. Then he rubbed his chin thoughtfully and said: "So we have escaped from England, have we! I remember nothing about it. I have had these blank patches before. The last thing I remember was jumping into a British trench near Arras. When I came round in that infernal box, it was so dark and silent that I thought"—he laughed mirthlessly—"I thought they had buried me for dead." He rubbed his stubbly chin again and rose from the chair. "Well, when do we reach Rotterdam, Major? It is Rotterdam, isn't it?"

CHAPTER XXI

I

THAT man of iron, Colonel von Wahnheim, twice captured by the enemy and twice escaped out of their hands and now newly appointed Chief-of-Staff of a division of storm troops, found that affairs on the Western Front had moved apace during his enforced absence. The collapse of Russia had set free the troops in the east, and with those transported back across the Rhine, the armies of His Imperial Majesty in the west outnumbered those of Britain, France, and Belgium by some thirty divisions. The low *moral* of the people at home in Germany, the eagerness of the troops in the west to be up and doing, and the expected advent of American reinforcements to the enemy were reasons that called for an offensive.

And preparations were already far advanced. Troops were training in bayonet fighting, in machine-gun co-operation, and in the special tactics to be employed. Officers were attending courses; and the Flying Corps were training not only for co-operation with infantry and artillery but as an independent offensive arm to perform definite tactical missions. Dumps and dummy works were being constructed from end to end of the five hundred miles of front to deceive the enemy as to the actual point of impact. General Headquarters had moved up from Kreusnach to Spa in Belgium.

From Cambrai to La Fère was the sector chosen for the attack, and behind that forty-four miles of front was effected such a concentration of munitions, men, and guns as the world had never seen in all its warlike history: forty-three divisions of specially trained shock troops, some seven hundred thousand men, with seven thousand guns specially trained and reinforced by the pick of the troops from Russia. A gun to every eleven yards of ground, they stood literally wheel to wheel. Opposed to them stood eleven divisions, one hundred and fifty thousand men, and one division in reserve. The Supreme General Staff had prepared their plans with the utmost care and skill for which that body was renowned. Casualties there would be and heavy casualties, but that mattered not since there would be no next year to provide for. In one great thrust they would separate the British from the French, sweep through Amiens to Paris, and win victory in the fifth year of the war.

Advanced General Headquarters moved from Spa to Avesnes, and the five million troops on either side of the trenches gathered themselves for the last and fiercest struggle.

At four-thirty on the morning of March the twenty-first the artillery storm broke; and at seven o'clock the grey flood of infantry burst its banks and flowed westward through the mist. Across the old Somme battlefield surged the grey tide, and hope ran high. Day after day the advance continued. Fresh divisions were flung in with a prodigal hand, leap-frogging the tired divisions. Victory was within their grasp. Before them was but a thin sagging line of tired troops who had fought for several days and nights without rest, without sleep, without reserves, and supported only here and there by artillery. Their cavalry, so long afoot, had taken to their horses, and day and night without rest the squadron rode and fought as gap after gap appeared in the sagging line and the tired men and horses strove to fill them. Victory was near.

The British Commander-in-Chief himself told his troops that with their backs to the wall they must fight to the end. But indeed there was no wall to put their backs to; there was nothing behind that sagging battle-line, neither horse, nor guns, nor foot. Their backs were to the "blue." A handful of recalled "leave" men were lined up on the quays of Havre and Boulogne, told off into platoons irrespective of units, bundled into lorries, and raced towards the oncoming tide. Another handful of cooks, farriers, sanitary men, town-majors' batmen, and labour corps—a scratch collection of the aged and infirm that scarce knew how to use a rifle—was gleaned from the troop-denuded back areas and flung into the widening gaps. Already the towers of Amiens Cathedral were visible to the oncoming host.

But though a hundred divisions had now been flung into the fight, the impetus of the grey tide was spent. The thin opposing line sagged, but did not break. At last supports were moving swiftly to their aid. The blue-clad poilus of France began to trickle across the fields behind them; the Australians deployed from the streets of Amiens; and the grey tide trickled to a halt.

But not for long. Northwards, where the new bulging line swept back around Arras to hinge upon the old trench system, the storm re-broke with undiminished fury. Again wheel to wheel the concentration of guns hurled their hurricane upon the enemy. In six close ranks a hundred thousand men advanced towards the Vimy Ridge. Only two divisions barred the way, and behind them on the ridge some three hundred men, the sole reserve with which to stop the gaps that must appear in the hard-pressed line.

Von Wahnheim bore his part in these great battles. Early in the fiercest fighting, his General had been killed, and he had taken over the command of the division. Later the appointment had been confirmed, and he had been promoted to the rank of General. Stark, hard man though he was, he commanded the confidence if not the devotion of his men. He did not hesitate to use them ruthlessly if the occasion so demanded, but in easier situations he was more solicitous for their welfare than were most Generals. Few men would willingly have transferred to his division, but his veteran troops themselves, who under his leadership were building up a reputation with blood and agony, were proud of their nickname, von Wahnheim's lions, and of their prestige which less hardy troops envied without being willing to pay the price.

No sooner had the Arras tide been dammed than the flood broke forth afresh. North at Armentières it overwhelmed the Portuguese and flowed over the Messines Ridge towards Ypres. Around and over Kemmel Hill it surged, engulfing the blue-clad poilus who fought and died upon it, on towards the Channel Ports. But again the sagging line tautened, and the attack died down.

Again the flood broke forth. Now in the south. Again the tornado of shell fire hammered the enemy, and then four hundred thousand men swept back the opposing hundred thousand to the Marne, and halted only to prepare the crossings of the river. Forty-five miles from Paris they were, and shells fell in the city, and aircraft bombed it by night. The crisis had come.

II

During these weeks of unceasing battle, General von Wahnheim was wounded in the thigh, and whilst his veteran storm troops came out for a hard-earned rest, he was taken far back to a château that had been converted into a hospital for senior officers. It was a large and comfortable old house set in well-kept grounds from which the fury of battle was heard only as a distant muttering. Its clean corridors, neat, cheerful rooms, and general air of mellow dignity and calm made it a fairyland in comparison with the shell-shattered buildings, churned-up earth, and all-pervading atmosphere of blood, filth, and abomination amid which he had lived the past few weeks.

It was not a regular military hospital. It was one of those institutions that were equipped and run by high-born ladies and staffed by ladies of much the same social standing. This particular hospital owed its existence to the generosity and service of Sonia, Duchess of Wittelsberg-Strelitz. And so von Wahnheim met again the beautiful sister of young Leo von Arnberg.

"My crude soldier presence is again forced upon you, Duchess," said von Wahnheim with his slow smile. "But you must forgive me. I thought you disapproved of my profession and all its works, and yet I find you up here working nobly in the cause."

"I disapprove as strongly as ever, General," she answered with a malicious twinkle in her eyes. "My mission is to repair; yours is to destroy. And you soldiers have the advantage of us: your work is so much easier than ours. I know I ought to be proud to have such a national hero as General von Wahnheim in my care, but..."

"But you are not?" he asked with an answering twinkle in his eye.

She shook her head vigorously. "No," she replied with charming candour. "You see, all those exploits of yours that make you a strong, iron hero-man to these poor troops are but so many damnable stains in my eyes. But the wrecked are always welcome here; we will forget that you are a wrecker by trade."

Von Wahnheim laughed softly. "I feel like a naughty boy that has been scratched whilst torturing the cat," he said. "I will be a very good little boy till the scratch is healed."

It was in this spirit of friendly antagonism that they met, and that became a cloak for the growing friendship between them. Von Wahnheim found her beauty and calm, cultured voice soothing to his war-worn spirits. And it amused him to be ordered about and treated like a child by the imperious little ladies who assisted her in the hospital.

All those patients who were not bedridden messed in the great dining-hall of the château, and the Duchess Sonia and several of her staff in evening dress were always present at dinner. As a woman it was her gesture of protest and defiance of the man-made desolation around her. "One must keep some grip on civilization," she said. "Uniforms reduce one to a block of wood, and these soldiers will become like the beasts of the field if we let them." And von Wahnheim was inclined to agree with her.

On one occasion, looking at her neat uniform and thinking of her as he had met her first as the idol of Cologne, he said, "You have not married, Duchess."

"Nor have you, General," she retorted.

"No, I am afraid I am a bachelor for life," he answered with mock sadness. "I could never bring myself to ask any woman; and certainly no woman will ever ask me."

"You poor helpless man!" she jested. "You look so pathetic I am almost tempted to ask you myself!"

Leaning on his stick, he bowed in the stiff Prussian fashion. "As your very dear friend, Duchess, I could not allow you to place yourself in a position of such danger," he answered solemnly.

Von Wahnheim was to look back upon this period as a very pleasant interlude in the serious business of war. The tide had now turned. Attack after attack was delivered by the enemy, and the German armies, exhausted and disheartened by the failure of their supreme effort when victory seemed sure, fell back sullenly before the onslaught. Now in the north, now in the south, now in the centre, the attacks were continued by the enemy whom they had believed to be exhausted and all but beaten. And fresh blood, too, was flowing to their aid. The Unterzee boats had failed before the convoy system, and American troops were pouring into France and taking their part in the great offensive. Men and guns were captured in enormous numbers; the recently won ground was recovered, and in places the old trench line re-crossed. The whole Allied line from the Alps to the sea was advancing.

Already many foresaw the end. And when the great Wotan or Hindenburg Line with its concrete machine-gun emplacements, its dug-outs, and its wire was stormed, the most optimistic knew that victory was impossible. Cases of insubordination and mutiny, such as had been hitherto unheard of in the German Armies, became alarmingly numerous. The rot that turns retreating armies into defenceless rabbles was abroad.

Amid the horde of disheartened, disillusioned, angry humanity von Wahnheim's division of storm troops stood out like an acre of firm ground in a swamp. They had that finely tempered spirit that is possessed by only the best troops. The slackening in the *moral* of the troops around them served only to increase their own military pride. They deployed upon the field of battle with the precision of a parade-ground manœuvre. With perfect rhythm and church-parade swagger they marched disdainfully through retreating troops to check for a moment the oncoming enemy. They knew that the best divisions may be defeated but never disgraced.

Von Wahnheim saw that the end was near. Armistice negotiations were afoot, and he fought only to ward off the threatened *débâcle* till they should be concluded. His one desire was to get the battered remnants of his division across the Rhine in safety. And yet he had offered to make a stand in order to facilitate the retreat of the army corps behind him, an offer which, if accepted, meant annihilation for himself and his men. He cared not for himself, but he did care for his faithful veterans. He himself had little to look forward to. His whole life was in the army; and in the civilian post-war period of national eclipse that loomed ahead there could be no niche for such as he, maimed in mind as he was.

And yet at times his thoughts turned wistfully to that interlude during which he had been a patient of the Duchess Sonia. Her brother, Leo von Arnberg, had written begging to be appointed to his staff, and was with him now. Through him he heard occasionally of the Duchess and even received messages from her. She was more kind to him in defeat than in victory. He thought of her often, now that his world was dissolving around him in blood and smoke.

The situation grew more critical as the days went by. Luden-dorff, Chief of the General Staff, had resigned, and there were rumours of revolution at home. The German armies were streaming back towards the Dutch bottle-neck with serious losses in men and material. The rearguards, of which von Wahnheim's division formed one, were blowing up cross-roads, bridges, and railways to delay the pursuing enemy, and delivering a check upon them whenever possible. But unless an Armistice were agreed to shortly, the retreating armies would dissolve into a rabble, and any peace terms, however shameful, would have to be accepted.

On von Wahnheim's immediate front, however, the situation was for the moment easier. A momentary check inflicted upon the enemy's advanced troops had enabled the retreating main body to get off the heels of their rearguard and given the much needed elbow room for manœuvre. But it was evident that another check would have to be inflicted in a day or two if the main body were to escape.

Von Wahnheim was summoned to Army Headquarters, and as his car sped across the stretch of undevastated and now almost deserted country that separated his rearguard from the retreating army, he saw on every side the jettison of the vast host that had passed this way. The road was littered with abandoned waggons, stores, and equipment; and at one point lay the shattered remnants of a battery that had been caught on the march by enemy aircraft. Horses in the last stage of exhaustion lay where they had fallen and been cut from the traces. Here and there a man lay on the roadside too exhausted to move; and occasionally little parties of stragglers were seen plodding painfully along with faces chalky white and eyes dazed with fatigue.

From doors and windows the French civilians looked on, their faces mask-like from the sufferings they had under-gone, but in their eyes was a fierce light as they noted the signs that told them that this was no pre-arranged strategical retreat. And often they turned their heads towards the west whence must come that deliverance that they knew to be close at hand. One incident showed the change that the last few weeks had wrought. As half a dozen stragglers in tattered uniforms and grimy faces trudged by a cottage, a bent and gnarled old peasant raised his voice and hoarsely croaked: "*Vive la France!*" and "*Vivent les Anglais!*" But the Germans did not even turn their heads; they tottered onward with set faces and staring eyes.

Von Wahnheim found Army Headquaretrs in a state of activity that bordered upon chaos. The conduct of the retreat of such vast numbers of men was becoming increasingly difficult, and already it had almost passed out of the control of Army Headquarters. The situation could not have been more serious. The remnant of von Wahnheim's division was to make a stand. The Armistice terms were very severe, but would be accepted in a day or two, the General thought. Meanwhile a stand had to be made if absolute collapse were to be avoided. The General was very busy; he had to go off somewhere at that moment, but if von Wahnheim would come with him in his car, they could finish their discussion of the projected operations as they went along.

The two Generals were borne along the troop-crowded roads of that wooded Ardenne country; and when the Army Commander had finished giving his instructions, he allowed himself to relax. He spoke enthusiastically of some good stalking he had had in the Tyrol two years previously, and then, glancing out of the window, remarked, "There is a very charming friend of yours near here, von Wahnheim—the Duchess Sonia." He dug his subordinate playfully in the ribs. "You are a sly fellow, von Wahnheim. Most of us old dogs would give a lot for a smile from the fair Sonia, but you with your solemn old face have got the better of us. She has a soft corner in her heart for you; there is no doubt about that. She often speaks of you. She calls you 'that nasty destructive boy!'" And the General laughed.

"I did not know that she was hereabouts," answered von Wahnheim. "I have not seen her for some weeks."

"Then call on her now," replied the General. "She will not be here long; they ought to be packing up now. I will pick you up on the way back."

III

The Duchess was busy when von Wahnheim arrived, and he had to wait in one of those quaint, stuffily furnished little chambers that lie grouped around the principal rooms of many old French châteaux. He had glimpses of her outside in the courtyard where a convoy of ambulances was being loaded with stretcher cases. She came at last, and they exchanged courtesies. He felt unaccountably ill at ease, and there was constraint in her manner also. They talked banalities, and that was a preposterous thing for the Duchess Sonia to do. He was aware of the gloom of the little room and of her sitting stiffly in a high-backed chair. The voices of the orderlies loading the ambulances outside came to him distantly as from another world.

It occurred to him that he was waiting for something to happen, though what he did not know. And Sonia also was abstracted, half listening for something, talking woodenly as though her mind were on other matters.

At last he said, "Your brother—Leo. I have just received orders for an operation to delay the enemy as long as possible, and if we perform that duty satisfactorily, few, if any, of us will be taken prisoners even. I should like to have taken my fellows back in safety, now that it is so nearly all over. They deserve it, Heaven knows. But there..." He finished with a shrug.

The Duchess had risen to her feet, and her face was pale.

Von Wahnheim hastened to reassure her. "But your brother... There really is no reason why he should remain with us during this coming engagement. I will send him back."

"Thank you—thank you, General," she murmured.

And then von Wahnheim understood that fear for the safety of her brother was not the sole cause of her pallor, and he saw also that fear was not the only emotion that glowed in her dark eyes.

He stood tongue-tied in the presence of this sudden revelation. But though very conscious of the feeling of delight that surged through him, he was conscious also that neither this feeling nor the situation was new to him; and even in those moments of exaltation he found himself puzzling to account for the odd feeling of familiarity.

And then the door opened and the Army Commander came in.

"I am sorry to have to take von Wahnheim away, Duchess," he said, bending his plump little body in a stiff bow. "And I am even more sorry to have to deny myself the pleasure of your charming society; but this tiresome fellow Mars will not wait even for Venus herself. You shall have all the transport I can spare, dear lady, for your move—though it will be little enough, I am afraid. If there is any difficulty, let me know. I will attend to it personally." He kissed her hand with another jerky little bow and said, "Come, von Wahnheim."

IV

As von Wahnheim sat beside the Army Commander on the way back to Army Headquarters, he found, oddly enough, that his thoughts were concerned with that unaccountable feeling of familiarity rather than with the great discovery he had just made. Where before had he seen that look in a woman's eyes? A look that no man could see and easily forget. Where before had he felt that tense, vibrant atmosphere in which without words the hearts of two human beings are laid bare to each other? Never before had he seen that look in Sonia's face. In the face of some other woman then? No other woman that he could remember; and he had known so few. And yet he was sure: the dark, liquid expression of the eyes, the breathless, tingling atmosphere were familiar—dearly, poignantly familiar. What woman had looked at him like that before? None that he knew. And yet there were those gaps in his memory—his pulses fluttered at the new vistas opened by the thought—some woman in those chapters of his life of which he remembered nothing had looked at him like that. But if that were so, it meant that she... Bewildering vistas opened before him.

He clung tenaciously to the haunting familiarity of this sensation. With closed eyes he saw quite clearly the unforgettable expression of eyes and face of the Duchess Sonia as she had stood before him in the little room. And then with a startled thrill he saw that Sonia's beautiful face was changing. He felt himself on the brink of a tremendous discovery. The expression remained the same, but the features were changing. Before his mind's eye they changed, and—he *knew* the new face. For a breathless second he hovered on the verge of recognition; and then something seemed to snap in his brain, and in a warm flood remembrance rushed over him. He was back in the little tea-room of Gaudin's with Helen... *Helen* standing mutely before him, with love-dark eyes and pale passion-tautened face... he *Gerard Bretherton... Le Touquet... Colonel Liddel... England...* Everything was whirling round faster and foster, darker and darker. He pressed his hands over his face.

Presently he became aware of a voice at his ear speaking in German: "Run, man, run; give a hand." An arm was round his body supporting him, and someone was breathing heavily in his ear. Hands took his feet, and other hands grasped his shoulders and lifted him. And the voice said again in German: "Steady! Carry him gently."

Mechanically he answered in the same language, "I am all right," and struggled feebly to get his feet to the ground.

"Lord! You gave me a start, going off like that, von Wahnheim. You are as white as a ghost still."

Bretherton realized that it was the Army Commander speaking. He saw that he was outside Army Headquarters, and that he was being helped up the château steps by the driver of the car and a sentry whose rifle and fixed bayonet leant against the door-post at the top. They led him into a large room and placed him on a sofa. A stiff cognac was brought to him.

The raw spirit set his brain working actively, so that although he was still bewildered by the flood of remembrance that continued to crowd upon him, he was in no danger of betraying himself unconsciously as he might have done a few minutes previously. He was aware that he must take heed of what he said and did, but he realized also that any strangeness of his would be imputed to the recent attack of illness. He saw that he was the centre of a little group of respectful staff officers and that the Army Commander was not present. He thanked the officers for their kindness and said that if they would leave him to rest for a short time he would be quite well again.

As soon as he was alone he rose to his feet and paced up and down the room, as was his habit when thinking. With a little tinge of bitterness he realized that he had failed in the all-important mission on which he had been sent—failed, but through no fault of his. He had failed to let British G.H.Q. know the point at which the blow was to be delivered. Yet they had survived the blow; that was the all-important thing. But at what cost, he wondered. He himself had seen the vast preparations for those titanic blows; he himself had taken part in them and knew something of the force that was behind them. And yet the Allies, by a miracle, it seemed, had not only survived those blows but had themselves attacked and broken the German Armies. He was filled with pride in his countrymen and their allies who had wrung victory from defeat.

What a stupendous moment that must have been when the German Armies began to break and the whole Allied line moved eastward! And he had missed that moment— had seen it only from the other side. And what did G.H.Q. think of him? He had sent no message. And Helen…

He must cross the lines as soon as possible; he could no longer benefit the Allies by remaining. He must give them such information as he possessed, though it could be of little real importance now—the war was over bar the shouting. He could give them the position of mines and strong-points. At any rate, he could prevent the useless waste of life of his countrymen and his German division. His division! Odd thought!

He turned at the sound of a door opening behind him, and found the Army Commander crossing the room.

"How are you now, von Wahnheim?" asked the General.

"Much better, sir," answered Bretherton.

The plump little man halted in front of him and waggled a fat finger in his face. "You have been overdoing it, von Wahnheim. You must have a rest."

Bretherton made a movement with his hands.

"Yes." repeated the General, "you must have a rest. It is no good going on. The next breakdown might occur at a more awkward moment than this one has done—might be serious for your men and for you. I have ordered Jagenburg to take over your division for the time being. The men may not fight under him as they do under you; that cannot be helped. But they will fight."

"Yes, they will fight, sir," Bretherton assured him.

"Well, you go off somewhere and rest for a day or two anyway. If an Armistice has not been arranged in the meantime and you feel fit enough to come back, so much the better. If not, well"—he pursed up his lips and waved a fat hand—"no one can accuse you of shirking, anyway. They have sent for your car. Captain Trierforchten will look after you till it arrives." He waved a short arm in the air and hurried from the room.

Bretherton gazed out of the window at the leafless trees and the trickle of uniforms that came and went. This few days' rest would be useful; it would enable him to disappear without inquiries being made. But the problem of how to get through the lines was no easy one; the original arrangements that had been made by G.H.Q. for that purpose were now obsolete. With knit brows he considered the difficulty, and his eyes followed abstractedly the men passing to and fro. He was aware, half-consciously, that the faces of some of them were known to him—German staff officers with whom he had come in contact—and then with a shock that brought his attention back to his surroundings, he realized that one face out there was that of a man he had known on the other side of the battle-line, the face of one who had been with him in the old company in the pre-Somme days and who had later commanded B Company of the old battalion—Hubbard.

At that moment Captain Trierforchten entered the room, and Bretherton seized him and dragged him to the window.

"Who is that fellow, Trierforchten?" he demanded. "See him? The fellow in the nondescript uniform just passing the field pigeon loft."

Captain Trierforchten craned his neck to catch a glimpse of the retreating figure.

"Oh yes, sir. I know him," he answered. "An Englishman. Captured in our push last March, I believe. He had done some small intelligence work for us before that; but he is not to be trusted. You know the breed, sir. Given his own people away and just as likely to give us away if it serves his purpose. We put him in among the prisoners to get what information he can."

Bretherton rubbed his chin thoughtfully. "Do you know anything more about him?" he asked.

"I do not personally, sir. But we have his dossier here somewhere, I believe. If you are interested in him, sir…"

"Yes, I am," answered Bretherton.

"Then I will have it sent to your headquarters, sir."

"Thanks; yes, do. And send the fellow along himself—some time; not now."

"Very good, sir. Your car is ready now. And the General wished me to say that Colonel Jagenburg will be there ready to take over when you arrive."

CHAPTER XXII

I

BRETHERTON sat alone in his room at Divisional Headquarters. He had handed over the division to Colonel Jagenburg, though in the written authority for the change of command, A.H.Q. had emphasized the temporary nature of the appointment and had instructed Colonel Jagenburg to relinquish it in favour of General von Wahnheim whenever and wherever that officer returned. His staff had been visibly depressed by the news, and only the barrier of rank had saved him from too pressing offers of help that would have been embarrassing. He asked them not to bother about him. He did not know yet where he was going even—back somewhere for a day or two. He would go off by himself presently. He preferred it that way. And he would say good-bye to them now.

He felt mean leaving these men who had served him faithfully, and he found difficulty in meeting the appealing look in Leo von Arnberg's eyes as he shook hands with him. But that was over now, and he was alone in his room, free to go.

He rose from his chair and put on his grey overcoat and cap. He parted the heavy curtains covering the window and saw that it was already dark outside. He crossed to a bureau and took therefrom a map and an electric torch, which he put into the pockets of his coat. Then he returned to the centre of the room and stood a few moments rubbing his chin and looking thoughtfully at the familiar possessions of General von Wahnheim that surrounded him—the row of polished military boots by the window, the tunic with the black and white ribbon of the Iron Cross hanging over the back of a chair, the sword in its polished steel scabbard, and the open chest of drawers before which lay a little heap of clothing, left by his servant, who had been interrupted in packing.

His face relaxed in a half-smile as his eyes wandered slowly over these familiar objects, and, catching sight of himself in the long mirror of the wardrobe, he drew himself up and saluted in the German manner. These were his last few moments as a General in the German Imperial Armies, he reflected. Presently—if he were lucky—he would be Captain Gerard Bretherton, M.C., who had rather badly bungled an important mission entrusted to him by G.H.Q. Automatically he felt in his pockets for his pipe, and then realized, with a whimsical smile, that General von Wahnheim smoked only cigars. A pipe and tobacco from the E.F.C. must be his first purchase on the other side. He took a few cigars from a box on the table, turned up the collar of his coat, and with a final glance round the room, passed out through the door.

There was nobody about, and he went down the stairs and reached the courtyard without meeting any of the staff. He walked quickly to the stables and ordered a driver he found reading *Simplicissimus* to get out one of the cars. Five minutes later he had passed down the drive, through the château gates, and was speeding along the dark road westwards. He had told the driver to take him to a unit

Headquarters that lay within a mile of the outposts; but he stopped the car fifty yards from the Headquarters.

When the car had driven off, he followed the road for some two hundred yards, and then, in the shelter of a copse, examined the map by the light of the torch. Then he set off walking westward. He had a very good idea of the positions of the posts, and the occasional round that echoed from the darkness ahead guided him. Presently a cottage loomed indistinctly in the gloom, and figures stirred in the shadows. With his collar well up about his ears and his cap well down over his face, he questioned the men. An N.C.O. answered that their officer was visiting posts; the first was away half-left, some two hundred metres, across that field and on the far side of a copse where two tracks forked.

Bretherton scrambled through the hedge and set off half-left across the field. Presently trees loomed against the night sky. He skirted the copse cautiously, stumbled on to a rutted track, and a moment later was challenged in a low voice. He found the post dug in with a machine gun at the point where the tracks forked. The N.C.O. in charge said that his officer had just passed on to the next post, and he pointed out its direction. Bretherton asked about the enemy. Could he see that slightly darker line against the sky? the man asked; well, that was a largish wood, and the enemy had a post somewhere there. Some of their cavalry had moved out from it just before dark, but had been driven back by machine-gun fire, and there had been a little firing from that direction off and on ever since.

Bretherton said that he hoped to catch the officer at the next post. He moved off to the left into the darkness as though with that intention, but when he had covered about a hundred yards, he turned sharply to the right and moved towards the line of trees the N.C.O. had pointed out.

He went very cautiously. He knew that he was in danger of being fired on by both sides. After a few minutes' very careful going, he reached a fence and a ditch running obliquely to his line of march. He dropped into the ditch and followed it cautiously. Away to his right, a rifle cracked with startling suddenness, and he heard the bullet travelling across the slight depression like a stick drawn swiftly through shingle. Then all was still again, except for his own stealthy movements in the ditch. Then a hedge loomed above his head, and he pulled up short with beating heart as his eye caught a pale flicker of movement at its base. And then, close in his ear, came a hoarse stage whisper in English: "Put your bleedin' 'ands up, Jerry." And a bayonet was pressed against his chest.

He obeyed the command sharply, and said: "All right. I am your prisoner."

"Perfeck little gent; an' speaks the langwidge like a bleedin' native," came again the whisper.

And then another form rose beside Bretherton, and he felt large hands searching him for weapons.

"Edycited at Oxford Collidge, was you, Jerry?" murmured this new figure in a conversational whisper. "Any of yer collidge chums be'ind?"

II

Half an hour later Bretherton was in a tiny cottage room explaining the situation across a coffin-shaped stove to a puzzled infantry colonel. The Colonel stood with his hands thrust deep into his trouser pockets and sucked jerkily at his briar pipe. He stared down at his muddy field-boots and from time to time frowned at his shadow on the aeroplane fabric that did duty for glass in the window.

"I cannot do that," he said at last. "I can't even send you to Corps direct—let alone Army or G.H.Q. For one thing, you would have to walk—and it's a long way. But I will ring up Advance Guard H.Q. and put it to them to get on to Corps; and maybe Corps will get on to Army."

"And Army to G.H.Q.—through the usual channels," put in Bretherton, with a smile.

The Colonel grinned. "Well, I will do my best, young feller. But you may be a Bosche for all I know to the contrary. But, Bosche or no Bosche, have a drink—Scotch, not lager!"

"Tell them," said Bretherton as the Colonel went out to telephone, "to get through to Colonel Liddel at G.H.Q. and to say that Bretherton or von Wahnheim has come back."

Ten minutes later, an order came for him to go to Corps; and he set out escorted by an interested subaltern and a private soldier in fighting kit. A tramp of two or three miles through dark and deserted country brought them to a large farmhouse, guarded by a pacing sentry and distinguished by the familiar coloured lamps of a headquarters.

Here he parted from his escort and made the journey from Advance Guard Headquarters to Corps by car.

Corps, it appeared, had got through to Army, and Army had been in touch with G.H.Q. He was to report at G.H.Q. at once; the Corps Flying Squadron would provide transport. The car passed back through the dark streets of the little town that was Corps Headquarters and climbed to the aerodrome on the flat hilltop beyond. He had to wait a few minutes in the mess while a plane was wheeled from a hangar, and in his German uniform he found himself a centre of interest.

"So you have been playing Brother Bosche in Boscheland!" said Major Impson, the squadron commander, a tall, fair, immaculately dressed youth wearing a monocle and a row of ribbons that gave the lie to any hasty estimate of his character. "Stout feller! Perhaps you can tell us what that gadget is at C.11.b.83." He crossed to a large map on the wall and pointed with the stem of his pipe. "We have taken a couple of photographs from three thousand feet, but we can't make head or tail of it."

"It looks rather like a latrine for elephants," put in a flight commander, "but it seems hardly likely."

Bretherton was able to tell them that the mysterious building was no more than a new pattern delousing station. Then, in a borrowed flying suit, he went out on to the aerodrome, climbed into the observer's cockpit, and a few minutes later the lights of the aerodrome lay far below.

He landed at G.H.Q. in the early hours of the morning, and Colonel Liddel, in pyjamas and British-warm, heard his story. Intelligence, it appeared, had a fairly accurate knowledge of his movements, and had guessed what had occurred.

"We tried to get into touch with you once or twice," said Colonel Liddel. "One of our fellows managed to speak to you, but you did not take the hint, and he was afraid of giving himself away."

"It wasn't Hubbard, was it?" asked Bretherton.

"Hubbard? Hubbard? No. Never heard of him," answered the Colonel. "You have had hard luck, Bretherton. Your information comes too late to be of any great value, but that is not your fault. At any rate, we are glad to have your confirmation of the fact that the Bosche is finished. But most of what you have to tell us is of local value only. You had better get some sleep now, and then we will fit you up with some clothes and send you to the Corps that was your opposite number when you were a Bosche. You will be able to tell them a lot of useful things. And I will give you a chit-to-all-whom-it-may-concern sort of thing—so that you can go wherever you think will be of most use.

"And you had better turn in. I am going to put you in my bed, if you don't object; I shall be busy till morning."

And then, as he left Bretherton at the door of the room, he added, "You will be glad to know that the little lady is all right. I saw her a week or two ago and put her mind at rest as far as possible. Good night!"

III

A few hours later, Bretherton, in a borrowed uniform and accompanied by a junior staff officer, was being driven towards the line. The first part of their journey lay through the pleasant, undevastated country into which the German Armies had failed to penetrate; but soon the appearance of cropless fields and battered farmsteads showed that the battle-area had been reached. Crumbling, deserted trenches in the chalk and tangles of rusty wire among the rank grass marked the position of the old front line, and thence for thirty miles the road ran eastwards across the dreary tundra of the old Somme battlefield to the wire-draped slopes of the Hindenburg Line. Beyond that, life began again. Trees put forth leaves, and villages were more than mere heaps of rubble.

The staff officer had to visit a division on the fringes of the great woods, and it was after midday when he turned back towards the Corps Headquarters that was Bretherton's destination. The car was travelling fast, and at the head of a long straight slope it passed an officer tramping upwards, with a bicycle. Bretherton, noticing the familiar green service cycle with the rifle clips and the company letter and number in white paint on the back mudguard, looked again at the toiling figure beside it and recognized a comrade of the old battalion.

"Gurney! Gurney!" he called.

The driver stopped the car and ran back in reverse.

"Good Lord, it's G. B.!" exclaimed Gurney, leaning across the saddle of his cycle as the car slowed beside him.

"And what are you doing?" asked Bretherton.

"Oh, just finishing off the war," answered Gurney cheerfully. "Vanguard to this old army—doing our pukka job at last."

"Gad! That's interesting," Bretherton exclaimed. "And is it anything like the stunts we used to do on the Plain and in back areas?"

"It is exactly like a scheme," Gurney assured him, "only vastly more entertaining."

"Gad, I wish I were with you!" exclaimed Bretherton, wistfully. "And you have got a company now, I suppose," he added, noticing the three stars on Gurney's shoulder-straps. "Which?"

"A—your old one, G. B. And they are as keen as mustard."

Bretherton opened the map. "What ground are you covering?" he asked.

Gurney pointed out the battalion front, and Bretherton noted that their line of advance, if continued, would bring them to the position that Colonel Jagenburg's division was to hold to the last. But the staff officer, who was becoming anxious about the luncheon he had planned to take at Corps Headquarters and had been fidgeting and looking at his watch, now put an end to the conversation. Bretherton waved good-bye to Gurney, and the car slid on down the slope.

He was glad he had met Gurney, and he was interested in what Gurney had told him. It turned his thoughts back to his days with the old battalion, which he still regarded as his own. He debated whether he could ask Corps to allow him to be with the battalion during these last few days. He longed to be with A Company now that, at last, it was doing the work for which he had taken such pains to train it. Not in any capacity of command, of course—that would be unfair to Gurney and the other officers—but as a supernumerary. They would push along until they ran into Jagenburg's force, and then play about, as he phrased it, till an armistice was signed. For now that the war was on its last legs, so to speak, Corps could not order a serious attack upon a position defended by desperate men—an attack that must cost many lives and could not affect the end that was now within sight.

He passed the afternoon before the large map at Corps Headquarters, pointing out the positions of German troops, of dumps, and of delay-action mines, and giving other information of local importance. Major Impson, of the Corps Flying Squadron, was present, and asked many questions about the country far back behind the German lines.

Bretherton had given the B.G.G.S.—the Brigadier-General-General-Staff—the position of Colonel Jagenburg's division and had ventured to point out the futility of attempting to dislodge it. Then he went to tea.

It was early in the evening, in the course of conversation with the G.S.O.3 that he learnt, to his dismay, that the advance was to be continued as though Colonel Jagenburg's division did not exist. The point of view was that an armistice was the affair of the Higher Command alone, and that till one was actually signed, it was the duty of other commands to attack the enemy as vigorously as possible.

Bretherton went at once to protest against this decision, but both the B.G.G.S. and the G.S.O.2 were out and the Corps Commander was too busy to see him. He protested strongly, however, to the G.S.O.3.

"What good can this do?" he demanded. "That division, I tell you, will fight to the last, and there will be heavy casualties on both sides. Surely there has been enough bloodshed in this wretched business already."

The G.S.O.3 agreed.

"How many men have we lost, do you think?" continued Bretherton.

"Close on a million killed, I believe," answered the G.S.O.3.

"A million dead!" echoed Bretherton. "And more than twice that number wounded, I suppose. And then there are the French—they must have lost well over a million. And the Germans the same. And all the others, the Russians, Austrians, Belgians, Italians, Americans, and the rest. There must have been six millions killed at the very least. Isn't that enough for one war?"

"More than enough, old lad," answered the G.S.O.3. "But I can't do anything; nor can you. I would if I could... but there it is."

IV

Some minutes later, Bretherton was left alone in the office, brooding over the subject. The remains of that veteran division of storm troops that he had led would fight to the last. Against them would come, in the first place, the men of his old battalion, and then others. There would be heavy casualties on both sides. Was ever man in such a position? The men that he had trained and led on both sides would annihilate one another. The old battalion would suffer heavily in what would be its last battle. His old comrades would be killed on the eve of peace—among them perhaps young Gurney, Helen's brother. And he was helpless. A mere captain, he could do nothing to prevent this tragedy. On the other side, he had been a man of some consequence; he could have ordered the division to retire and they would have retired. Here he was nobody.

He rose suddenly to his feet and frowned at the map. Then he turned with sudden resolution and took up the telephone.

"Give me the Corps Flying Squadron," he called. "Is Major Impson there?" he asked presently. And then as he heard Major Impson's voice at the telephone: "This is Bretherton speaking from Corps. Can you drop me behind the German lines to-night? No, it is not your usual line of business, I know, but the circumstances are unusual. I will bring my authority with me—yes. In about an hour. Right-oh! Good-bye."

He put down the telephone and hurried to his room. He took General von Wahnheim's uniform from the pack in which he had brought it from G.H.Q. and put it on. Over it he put the borrowed burberry; and the grey German great-coat he placed inside-out upon his arm. He put his British service cap upon his head and hid the German cap beneath the coat.

"I am a damn fool, I suppose," he muttered to himself. "But there is no other way."

He reached the street without meeting anyone and set off through the darkened town. Major Impson was waiting for him.

"Here is my authority," said Bretherton, producing the paper Colonel Liddel had given him.

The Squadron Commander read it and handed it back.

"Look here, Bretherton," he said, "that is all right as far as it goes, but it hardly covers a job like this. Corps are the people that say 'Come!' and I cometh, and 'Go!' and I goeth; and I have no authority from them.

"And you won't get any from them," cried Bretherton desperately. "This is nothing to do with Corps. G.H.Q. has given me authority to go where I consider I shall be most useful; and that is where I want to go—on the other side of the lines.

"Dug in over there," he went on earnestly, "is a division that I know will fight to the last man; and we are going bald-headed at it. Surely there have been too many poor devils killed in this war already without piling up the number uselessly in the last few days. If you put me over the other side, I can get that division moved back. This chit from G.H.Q. will cover you—I shall leave it behind, needless to say. Will you do it?"

Major Impson polished his monocle with elaborate care on a large silk handkerchief.

"And what about you, old bird—if Jerry catches you moving back troops without orders?"

Bretherton shrugged his shoulders. "That's my funeral," he said.

"Oh, quite!" agreed Major Impson dryly. "Very well put."

"Will you do it?" persisted Bretherton.

Major Impson replaced his eyeglass and held out his hand. "Shake!" he said, with an exaggerated imitation of American accent. "Those staff wallahs always were blood-thirsty babes."

Fifteen minutes later, Bretherton climbed into a machine. Major Impson wished him good luck. A mechanic swung the propeller; the chocks were kicked away; the pilot opened the throttle; and the plane sped swiftly across the aerodrome and up into the night.

V

There was no moon, and from the great height to which they had climbed, nothing was visible below except the occasional flash of a gun and the distant string of greeny-blue "flaming onions" that mounted in the darkness towards some marauding plane. Then the pilot turned eastward and, with engine shut off, planed down through the darkness. Invisible, high up in the night sky, the plane glided silently across the lines, down a long incline that carried it far behind the German outposts. Far below, the dark blur of trees came into view; then the trees gave place to a wide stretch of open country, bordered by dark woods. The plane banked and turned into the wind; down, down it glided.

356

Bretherton released the safety strap and waited with nerves a-tingle. Down glided the plane, bounced gently, and ran on slowly and unevenly. He hoisted himself out and slid to the ground. He waved his hand to the dark ball of the pilot's head that projected above the cockpit, and turned and ran towards the woods that showed dimly against the sky. Behind him, the engine roared suddenly and startingly as the pilot turned, taxied across the field, and took off. He saw for a moment a dark, swiftly moving shape above the trees; heard the receding drone of an aeroplane, and then he was alone.

He peered anxiously to right and left as he moved along the dark margin of the wood; for it seemed incredible that the roar of the aeroplane engine could have escaped notice. Yet no running figures came at him as he feared they might; no swift challenge rang through the night. His tense nerves relaxed a little. The area he had chosen to land in, the area between the German rearguard and their main body, was almost bare of troops, and with the possible exception of a few stragglers and the supply traffic on the main roads, it was unlikely that he would meet anyone in uniform. Indeed, this sparseness of troops that had made possible his landing unobserved now became a difficulty; for he had but a vague idea of his whereabouts and must rely upon passing troops for his direction and conveyance to Divisional Headquarters.

But fortune favoured him. He scrambled through a hedge and found himself in a lane that led him, after ten minutes' walking, to a broad road. Three lorries that passed

He hoisted himself out and slid to the ground.

a few minutes later gave him a lift to the Headquarters of a supply column, and there the senior supply officer placed a car at his disposal.

There was frost in the air, and as he drove through the darkness to Divisional Headquarters, he felt cold, dispirited, and lonely, very lonely. He was one man among many enemies, and it seemed to him impossible that he could succeed in that which he had set himself to do. Some unguarded act must betray him. It was true that he had already successfully sustained the part of General von Wahnheim since the recovery of his true personality, but that had been for a short time only. Now he was to attempt to withdraw troops that had been ordered to stand to the last, and that action in itself must arouse suspicion, even if it were not immediately countermanded by higher authority.

And he was depressed by the knowledge that he was a mental invalid. For he recognized that this second lapse of memory, good cause though there had been for it, admitted the possibility of a further lapse or lapses, one of which might be permanent, and he was chilled by the fear of it. But he realized that, for the time being, he must play his rôle to the best of his ability, and he forced himself to think in German, to forget his thoughts and sensations as Gerard Bretherton, and to concentrate on those that had been his as General von Wahnheim.

His reception at Divisional Headquarters did much to cheer him. The staff were delighted to see their own General return. And he had arrived at an opportune moment. Colonel Jagenburg, though wounded that afternoon, had refused to be evacuated, but now he declared that he was quite ready to hand over the division to its own commander and could go back to hospital with a clear conscience.

The unsuspicious and even joyful way in which he had been received by the men who, after all, as he told himself, had been his comrades for many months, did much to restore his confidence; and as he concentrated upon the many duties which, with the men around him and his surroundings, had once formed his familiar daily life, he found himself unconsciously dropping back into the cool, competent manner of General von Wahnheim. He could even remind himself of who he really was with no such feeling of nervousness as had at first possessed him.

One other fact went far to raise his hopes of success. He learned that the division was now independent of the Higher Command, which had officially wished it good luck and a gallant end and left it to its fate. Little change had taken place in the military situation during the twenty-four hours that Bretherton had been absent, and he quickly mastered such changes in the disposition of troops as had been made.

It was then that he nerved himself for the great effort. It was while following on the map the Chief-of-Staff's summary of the situation that a fairly plausible excuse for retreat occurred to him. He stood now, facing the large map on the wall, and spoke to the Chief-of-Staff without turning his head.

"I have been given a free hand," he said. "And I have a plan for making the division's swan-song livelier than was originally planned. We have enough room for manœuvre now, and my plan in to continue the retreat, but in echelon to the left—here." He dabbed a finger on the map. "Leaving a screen on the original line of retreat to keep the enemy happy. Then, in two or three days when we are clear of him, the screen will stand and we shall come in with all our weight on his flank. A smashing blow of this sort should do him some real damage and will delay him longer than sitting down till we are wiped out; for, after it, he will advance very cautiously for fear of a further dose."

He turned suddenly with his hands thrust in the little side-pockets of his close-fitting tunic and looked at the Chief-of-Staff. The man was smiling, and there was a glint of affection in his keen blue eyes.

"It sounds a very good scheme, General," he said. "I like it far better than the sitting-down-to-be-wiped-out plan. It is sound tactics. And, if I may say so, the division will make its last bow in true von Wahnheim manner."

Bretherton turned back to the map with a sigh of relief.

CHAPTER XXIII

I

FOR several hours, the staff worked hard upon the details of the move and the alteration in orders made necessary by this sudden change of plan. There was much hurried coming and going in the château, much ringing of telephone bells, and purring of dispatch riders' motor-cycles outside in the darkness. Dawn was near before the last order was written and sent off; but already the move-table had come into operation, and the veteran division in fighting kit, like a pefectly adjusted machine, had begun its retreat.

The château was soon almost deserted. The Headquarters staff packed up and went back. Bretherton told them that he would remain with the rear party for a time and rejoin Headquarters later. His intention was to remain in the château till it was captured by the advancing British van-guard. Reports reached him that the rear party were in touch with that vanguard, and he pictured it, Gurney and the men of his old company, in the early-morning light feeling their way forward in the way in which he himself had taught them.

A machine-gun unit of the rearguard arrived and began to fortify the château. Bretherton found a gun team in an ante-room overlooking the courtyard. They had propped mattresses against the window and were mounting the gun. But he sent them away; the château, he said, was not to be turned into a strong-point. And the machine-gun

team departed to take up another position in the surrounding woods.

At last he could relax. He had but to wait for the British
vanguard. He sat alone in the G.O.C.'s room, huddled in an
armchair, worn out from lack of sleep and by the hours of
heavy strain he had undergone. His face was ashen in the
dim light of the guttering candles.

He rose wearily to his feet and threw open the shutters.
The strong morning light flooded through the windows,
dispersing the shadows in the corners of the big room
and disclosing the burnt-out fire in the huge grate, the big
map upon the silk-hung walls, the long low chesterfield,
the dark polished wood of the grand piano, and the two or
three small tables on the thick carpet.

On one of these, a packet addressed to General von
Wahnheim caught his eye. The typewritten sheets it
contained proved to be Hubbard's dossier which Captain
Trierforchten had promised to send him. He dropped back
into a chair and began to read. And as he read, scenes with
the old company and battalion rose vividly in his memory
and took on a new significance: Private Christmas standing
red-faced in the little company orderly room whilst poor
Melford read aloud the letter in answer to the advertisement
of a "lonely soldier"; Hubbard superintending Private
Christmas carrying out his sentence of answering all those
letters; Hubbard with a pile of coins before him playing
nap in the Motor Machine-gun mess; Melford hunting for
the map that disappeared when the aeroplanes bombed
Sericourt; himself under arrest in connection with that

photograph in the newspaper; Hubbard with B Company in the little Somme valley when the missing map was discovered in an envelope bearing the battalion censor stamp. And many things that had formerly puzzled him were clear now.

The document was a brief record of Hubbard's activities from the German point of view. The German secret agent No. 304, a woman, made a practice of answering advertisements by soldiers. One reply she had received, not from a lonely soldier, but from his officer, Hubbard. Correspondence of a harmless nature was carried on between them, in the course of which she learned that Hubbard gambled and was usually very short of money. A photograph he sent her of a British officer outside a café she sold to a paper and sent him the proceeds augmented by German money. He was pleased with this, and other photographs followed, though none of any great military value. All of these she pretended to sell to newspapers and forwarded to him the money she pretended to receive for them.

When on leave, he met her and was introduced to an invalid uncle, who, being unable to move about or read, liked returned soldiers to tell him about the war. Hubbard indulged the old man's weakness, and in return was helped out of his financial difficulties. One or two maps and several photographs were sent to her from time to time and were paid for by the interested uncle. The fiction that this correspondence was harmless was still kept up, though he must have known by this time that she was an enemy agent. The letters were sent to various poste-restante addresses.

Eventually Hubbard was captured in the great German drive of 1918, and in the hope of being set at liberty or of receiving better treatment, he declared himself to be a German agent. This statement was verified, but the German authorities had not sufficient confidence in the man to send him back across the lines, and they used him on odd jobs and occasionally put him in prisoner-of-war camps to report the conversation of prisoners.

Bretherton put down the document with a grimace. A sordid story, he thought. The man had run true to type. He had the guts to be neither a good patriot nor a good traitor. And he had ended up on the losing side; had done more harm to himself than to his country.

Among the papers were several photographic negatives, but that which most interested Bretherton was one of himself outside the café at Ruilly. He held it up to the light, with a wry smile. That negative had caused him much trouble in those old days with the old company—those good old days. He dropped the negative on the table with a sigh and walked to the window.

II

Desultory rifle and machine-gun fire sounded from the distance, and from time to time the woods echoed with the staccato reports of a battery of German field guns that had taken up a position among the trees in rear of the château. The tide of war was moving steadily forward, and Bretherton, by the window, knew that it could not be long before khaki figures broke cover from among the trees.

But the knowledge caused no answering flutter of his pulses. The fatigue and strain of the long sleepless hours weighed heavily upon him. He was oppressed by a sense of the complicated hopelessness of war, of the futility of everything. Painful images flitted through his tired brain: Hubbard's mean treachery; his own desertion of the Duchess Sonia, for whom that part of him that was von Wahnheim still yearned; his killing of two men of A Company; his fighting for the enemy that were yet his friends; his betrayal of those men who trusted him. And he had not even gained the information for which G.H.Q. had sent him; he had accomplished nothing, except perfidy and bloodshed and misery for himself.

The sound of rifle fire had grown perceptibly nearer. The battery in the rear of the château had limbered up and moved back. In the woods, a new sound, like the ripping of calico followed by the bang of a dinner-gong, announced the approach of British field guns.

He had achieved nothing, except this avoidance of further bloodshed by moving the division back... that and... Helen.

The sound of a door closing softly behind him caused him to turn. At the far end of the room, in the shadow of the screen by the door, stood a woman in a long dark cloak. She advanced slowly across the threshold and threw open her cloak, revealing the white evening frock beneath.

Bretherton caught his breath as the light from the long windows fell upon her face. There was no one he less desired to see at that particular moment.

He bowed low, to cover his embarrassment. "My dear Duchess," he stammered, "what brings you here at such a time and in such clothes?"

She came forward, with a slow, shy smile and threw off her cloak. Glancing down at her evening frock, she answered: "As for this—well, you know my valiant effort to maintain some decency in this disgusting war. We dine respectably, though it be off a ration biscuit. But last evening we had sudden orders to move. Your dreadfully wise and grown-up plans had been changed all in a moment, and I had no time to change my frock. I was busy till dawn getting my patients away."

Her face took on a sudden, serious expression, and she came close to him, looking earnestly into his face.

"I heard that you had been ill after you left me—that you had gone back for a rest. No one seemed to know where. And just as I finished packing off my damaged children this morning, I heard that you had returned and were here. At that moment Leo drove up in a car. And so…"—a faint colour tinged her cheeks—"and so after what… well, what did *not* happen because old General Ulrich interrupted us, I… I had to see you."

Grey figures were moving among the trees around the château. From time to time, the crack of a rifle came from the upper part of the building, where a sniper had taken up his position behind a chimney.

Bretherton glanced despairingly around the room. "But you cannot stay here," he cried. "The British are close at hand. Listen! That is one of their Lewis guns." He placed a hand on her arm and tried to lead her to the door. He did not look at her.

She stopped him and, with a hand on either sleeve, gazed up into his face. "You are not angry with me for coming?"

He shook his head despairingly. She let go his sleeve and stood with the tips of her fingers resting on a little table.

"You make it very difficult for me... Otto," she said.

He threw out his hands beseechingly. "I... I am only thinking of... of your safety," he answered miserably.

She dismissed the fear with a little shrug of her bare shoulders.

"Do you remember," she continued, "that you once said that you could never bring yourself to ask any woman; and that certainly no woman would ever ask you?"

He made a little movement of protest with his hands.

"And I answered," she went on bravely, with cheeks aglow, "that I was almost tempted to ask you myself. Well... I..."

"And I," he interrupted quickly, "said that as your friend, I could not allow you to place yourself in a position so dangerous and... and so undignified. Nor can I."

Her head tilted quickly upwards, and a wave of colour swept over her face and neck.

He bowed stiffly before her anger. "I... I have been ill," he said lamely.

The colour faded slowly from her cheeks, and her eyes assumed a more gentle expression. They searched his face.

"Yes, yes; I know," she said. "But you look changed—different. What is it?"

"Nothing... it is nothing. I have been ill; but nothing serious. Let us leave it at that." His eyes met hers appealingly.

She gazed at him for a few moments in silence. "Yes, you are changed," she said at last, slowly. "I understand." Her voice cut like a knife. She laid a hand upon her cloak.

He threw out his hands protestingly. "I have been ill," he repeated desperately. "I... I... you see, I suddenly recovered my memory. It was a shock... all my past life that I had forgotten... before the war... Berlin... everything."

She dropped the cloak and was watching him with serious eyes.

He went on recklessly: "I remembered dining with you in Berlin... when you were a schoolgirl... and that Englishman, my double... Bretherton, he was there..." He laughed mirthlessly on a high-pitched note. "God, I'm becoming hysterical," he thought.

She came round the table and held his arms firmly in her hands and gazed earnestly into his face. "You are different," she murmured in a far-away voice. "Different."

There was a puzzled expression in her eyes. He tried to draw away, but she held him firmly. Suddenly the expression in her eyes changed. The puzzlement disappeared and was replaced by a startled look. Her grip on his arms tightened and then relaxed. she backed slowly from him.

"You... you are not Otto von Wahnheim," she cried in a low voice. Enlightenment was dawning in her face.

"You"—breathlessly—"you… I know who you are… you are that Englishman… Bretherton."

An aeroplane shot low overhead, with a sudden gust of sound.

He made a vague gesture with his hands. "I… I am von Wahnheim," he managed at last.

"No." She shook her head slowly, but with conviction.

"The only von Wahnheim you have ever known," he persisted.

Her eyes did not leave his face. "Where is he… the real von Wahnheim?"

He abandoned the useless struggle. "He… he is dead."

"You… killed him!" The words were scarcely audible.

"No, no. He was missing… killed on the Somme, long ago. You never met him except that once before the war, in Berlin."

"Are you lying to me?" She was watching him intently with narrowed eyes.

"No. I swear it's the truth; I swear." His voice was earnest. "I knew him before the war; shared rooms with him in Berlin. I have not seen him since… nor have you. He was missing on the Somme. I was captured soon after, but escaped. I had a bad time… and… and my memory went. I thought I was von Wahnheim… and all that… Cologne… you know…"

She nodded. She was watching him intently, with ashen face. There was no longer doubt in her eyes.

"Then I was captured by my… the British; knocked on the head… near Arras. I came round in hospital

and… remembered everything—myself, von Wahnheim…"
He stopped.

"But you came back?"

He passed a hand wearily across his forehead. "Yes. On the way back I was shut in a box, in darkness… for days. And my memory went again. I was von Wahnheim. It came back suddenly, in the General's car, after I left you… that look in your eyes. I was trying to remember where…" He stopped suddenly.

"Go on." Her voice was low and commanding.

He remained silent.

"Go on. That look in my eyes," she reminded him. "You were trying to remember where you had seen it… before?"

He nodded miserably.

"And you remembered? You had seen it before, then?" Her eyes compelled him to look at her. "In… some other woman's eyes?"

He remained silent. She stamped her foot with sudden fury. "Tell me—tell me. You had seen it before, in the eyes of some English girl?"

The aeroplane shot back overhead with an echoing roar.

He nodded again, miserably. She was silent for a moment, and then demanded: "What did you do when you disappeared?—when you left the division?"

He did not reply.

"Did you go to… to your own people?"

He nodded.

She toyed with a folded map on the table. "And you came back… but not for me." She looked at him again, and her eyes were hard. "So that is why the division suddenly retreats!"

He made a helpless gesture with his hands. "What was I to do?" he demanded. "It was only to prevent useless waste of life—I swear it. To save the lives of these men I commanded, and of my own countrymen over there." He flung out a hand towards the window. "And you! What could I do? Good God, don't you understand that I am two people? That I have the thoughts and feelings of two men—that even now that I am Bretherton, I know what von Wahnheim felt!" He seized her wrists and went on fiercely. "By God, you shall understand—understand that as von Wahnheim I loved you… and love you; but as Bretherton I…" He let fall her hands and turned away. "As Bretherton…"

She nodded slowly. "I understand."

III

A tap sounded on the door. It opened, and Leo von Arnberg came in. As usual, he was immaculately dressed. He was in the fighting zone, but he wore no shrapnel helmet. The grey service cap, with its shiny black peak and plum-coloured band was set at a jaunty angle. He clicked his heels and saluted.

"I am sorry to intrude, sir," he cried. "But we really ought to leave. Nearly everyone has gone. The British will be here in under half an hour, and they will be turning their guns on us presently. I have that man you wanted to see outside, sir, but there really is not time now. I am responsible for your safety, sir."

The sound of a gigantic whip-lash whistled through the sky and was followed by an ear-splitting crack and a patter of falling stones on the roof. Leo von Arnberg smiled and bowed ironically towards the window.

The Duchess Sonia took up her cloak. "Come, Leo; I am ready," she said. "General von Wahnheim is not coming—yet."

"But really, sir…" began von Arnberg.

Half-way across the room, the Duchess paused and turned to Bretherton. She spoke in English. "Good-bye, Mr. Bretherton. May you be happy with your English Miss. One thing only I ask of you; do not tell her of me."

Bretherton bowed low. She turned and swung the cloak over her shoulders. "I am ready, Leo."

One of the window-panes flew into pieces with a loud report, and almost instantaneously was followed by the dull thud of metal striking a soft substance. Leo von Arnberg spun round like a Russian dancer and collapsed into the chair behind him.

The cloak slid from Sonia's fingers, and she ran forward with a little cry. Von Arnberg's face was drawn and ashen under the tan, but he forced a little smile to his pain-twisted lips. His hand was at his shoulder, and beneath the clutching fingers a damp brown stain was slowly spreading. He struggled into a sitting posture and grimaced.

"We must get him away from here," cried Bretherton, and he ran to the door. At the end of the passage he saw a man in uniform. He called and beckoned to him and returned to von Arnberg. Sonia was trying to open her brother's tunic, and the pain of the movement caused him to grip the arms of the chair till his knuckles showed white.

Bretherton dropped on one knee beside him. "We must slit the tunic," he said, and felt in his pockets for a knife. He could not find one. Beside him he saw the legs and lower part of the body of the man he had called in.

"Give me your bayonet," he cried, and when the man did not answer, he tapped the hanging scabbard without looking up. The man drew his bayonet. Bretherton stood up and put out his hand for it; and then, for the first time, looked at the man.

He stood for a second staring in surprise, with his hand outstretched for the bayonet that was held handle towards him. And then he clenched his fists and strode forward fiercely. "You swine! You dirty swine!" he cried.

Hubbard backed from his accuser. Von Amberg uttered a warning cry as the bayonet point described a semi-circle. But Bretherton, in his wrath, still advanced. The glittering bayonet flickered unsteadily for a second and then swiftly drove forward.

Bretherton staggered back, bent suddenly double. He saw something white slide past him and heard a dull, heavy thud. The Duchess Sonia lay stretched upon the carpet. Von Arnberg rose painfully to his feet. Hubbard was no longer there.

Bretherton was on his knees, swaying, beside the Duchess. "Look to her, Leo… fainted," he gasped.

Bretherton staggered back, bent suddenly double.

Painfully and laboriously, von Arnberg applied all the remedies he knew for syncope. Bretherton had his fingers on her pulse, but he could detect no movement.

"Get—get her to the sofa," came his hoarse voice.

Slowly and painfully, the two wounded men lifted the girl and staggered to the sofa. Bretherton dropped back into a chair. His face was grey and he breathed with difficulty. Von Arnberg worked desperately to restore animation to the silent figure.

Minutes passed. The room was very quiet. Outside, the sounds of war were becoming louder. Painfully and with suppressed groans, Bretherton hoisted himself from the chair and laid a hand on Arnberg's shoulder.

"It is... no good, Leo... no good. Save yourself... in time."

Von Arnberg raised a face that was scarcely recognizable and stared stupidly at Bretherton. Bretherton shook him gently. "Hurry, Leo... hurry."

Von Arnberg rose shakily to his feet. The meaning of the crack of rifles and the zip and plop of bullets outside penetrated his dulled senses. A bullet smacked into the wall opposite the windows.

"Come on, sir," he gasped.

"No, no." Bretherton shook his head. "I'm done, Leo. Leave me... while there is time."

Von Arnberg hooked his arm round Bretherton and tried to raise him, but the pain was too much for his wounded shoulder, and he let go with a groan.

"Good-bye, Leo," said Bretherton, and held out his hand.

Von Arnberg pressed it. "I will get help," he said. "I will get you out of this, General."

He turned and swayed across the room towards the door. And as he went, he fumbled with his pistol holster. "And I'll get that swine!" he cried fiercely.

Half-way along the narrow passage that led to the side of the château, his legs gave way beneath him; the narrow space echoed to the crack of the pistol in his clutching fingers, and the bullet smacked harmlessly into the wall. He swayed and crashed senseless to the floor.

IV

Among the trees that fronted the château, men were shouting. The sound of English voices came through the long, broken windows to Bretherton, sitting huddled and grey-faced in a chair. He opened his eyes and rose slowly to his feet. Painfully and falteringly, he moved towards the window; but on his way, his eyes encountered the piano, and he turned towards it. A twisted smile flickered for a moment across his face. It was months now since he had played. Inch by inch he neared the chair, grasped it, and lowered himself. His hands spread slowly over the keyboard.

The air he played was Helen's little song, "Just a song at twilight." His fingers moved falteringly but more surely as the tune and its associations gripped him. A burst of Lewis-gun fire ripped out in the woods and died away. The end of the war; the last lap. The tune changed to the old war air: "*Après la guerre finie.*" He played on painfully.

Another not-far-distant shout came through the windows. They were coming, the British vanguard, his old battalion… Gurney, Pagan, and the rest… coming. The tune changed to "Tipperary." His strength was ebbing, and he had difficulty in seeing; but his fingers needed no eyes to guide them in that tune. He gathered all his strength and played the last chorus firmly and triumphantly:

> It's a long way to Tipperary,
>   It's a long way to go.
> It's a long way to Tipperary
>   And the sweetest girl I know.
> Good-bye, Piccadilly; farewell, Leicester Square,
> It's a long, long way to Tipperary,
>   But my heart's right there.

The piano ceased. Darkness settled upon him. His leaden arms slid from the keyboard; his head fell forward till it rested upon the rack of the piano.

Somewhere in the silent château, a cautious footstep sounded. Outside, bayonets twinkled among the trees. A sudden rattling roll of Lewis-gun covering fire throbbed through the air. And then, on to the broad stretch of grass fronting the château straggled a line of khaki figures.